DON'T COME BACK A STRANGER

WESTMINSTER PRESS BOOKS
BY JAMES L. SUMMERS

Girl Trouble
Prom Trouble
Trouble on the Run
Ring Around Her Finger
Gift Horse
The Karting Crowd
The Trouble with Being in Love
Tiger Terwilliger
The Cardiff Giants
The Amazing Mr. Tenterhook
Senior Dropout
The Long Ride Home
The Iron Doors Between
You Can't Make It by Bus
Don't Come Back a Stranger

DON'T COME BACK A STRANGER

by James L. Summers

THE WESTMINSTER PRESS • Philadelphia

ISBN 0-664-32482-7

LIBRARY OF CONGRESS CATALOG CARD NO. 72-126129

PUBLISHED BY THE WESTMINSTER PRESS ®
PHILADELPHIA, PENNSYLVANIA

PRINTED IN THE UNITED STATES OF AMERICA

For Rick

1

THERE WERE THOUSANDS of voices that whispered into a life from gone-by times; there were harsh words in the present. There was guilt in the present, something gnawing down deep and never quite away from there. Like dreams.

Dan Miller didn't know. Sometimes he thought he did for a minute when he felt a strike of confidence. Most of the time he was only spinning around, as if he was marooned in the scene.

Mr. Park said, "What are you going to do when the commies come up this hill to Lakefield High School?" He sort of screamed the question, as if the answer had to be a scream.

Mr. Park spun; his words made a heavy spiral that twisted in and out. Dan saw the leaves of the locust tree brush against the classroom window again. It was fall. The upland game birds throbbed their wings outside— away in the river bottom.

What was he going to do?

"What are you going to do, Blundell?" Mr. Park demanded.

"Kill them," said Blundell easily. "Mow 'em down with machine guns."

Dan breathed deeply. He had been terribly afraid that Mr. Park would call on him, because silence would have tongued him out. Stupid. Half the time he mumbled in class because words glued his throat. He envied Blundell for the way he could talk.

"Blundell, Blundell," Dan said in his mind, softly. It was two sounds, starting with prescience and ending with quiet. His father, Paul Miller, was the county tax assessor and used words like "prescience," and his mother knew what it meant; so did Dan by this time.

"Machine guns in the Park, fire fingers in the dark," Dan's mind droned, in spite of commands to stop. Mr. Park taught U. S. history and commies were his history of the world.

Dan Miller felt his skin around him, bubbling like a noise. Pimples strained on his nose. His scalp fulminated with tiny explosions of itch.

Once, long ago, he was with Larry in his boat far off Morro Bay and he had caught a lingcod—gaffed him in. Larry was a big steam fitter, a friend of his father's from long ago—although not so friendly since Mr. Miller had become tax assessor.

"You're all right, Dan," Larry had said.

He had felt good that time. Once. Good all over, proud, and with his skin loose and forgotten. Larry was a man who knew a boat. Janet, he called the boat.

"Janet," Dan Miller said in his mind. Not a real girl, of course, but like her and lovely. The waves slapped the boat in a heartbeat rhythm on wood that was tremulously like the sea and part of it.

Mr. Park was ready to show the Signal Corps film. This was Tuesday; on Tuesdays and Fridays, the films.

8

The shades came down, the locust tree was a ghost, and the projector tickled the ribbons. Color. The color of blood. The barrage from the planes was over and the Marines moved out into the jungle close behind, over-running the shattered enemy. Girls in the class squealed as the Cong cried out in skintight hurt and fear. It was like television.

Dan watched. There were dove and quail in the river bottoms this morning; they tumbled into the thrusts of shot from the hunters and the blood of birds was as thick as a man's. After the fight, the Marines had a beer together—brave men who had lived through danger.

The film ended and Dan winced in the sudden splay of light. When Mr. Park asked questions, he escaped again and felt guilty and anxious. If he had killed a man, he would be terribly frightened and sick and he knew it.

The bell rang and he felt its hacksaw teeth along the backs of his eyes. He gathered his books and made ready to sneak out, still unnoticed, the thief of U. S. history.

His feet blundered along the outer aisle toward the door, aware of themselves and of Mr. Park, staring hard with commies still in his eyes. It was a good class; a lot of the kids liked it because Mr. Park was the real thing, they said.

He was through the door and out; Spanish next. *"Me llamo Dan Miller. ¿Cómo se llama? ¿Verdad?"*

Somebody beside him said, *"¡Me llamo, me llamo, me llamo!"*

Long, golden hair and hazel eyes, a searching of him as he turned, the voice like a note of music remembering a song in which it had once been stranded.

"Wasn't that film awful?" she asked.

"Yes," he said.

She had a faint, wise, terribly solemn and funny smile. "I'm Teresa Bailey," softly.

"I know," he replied, although he didn't know. He never knew at all about real people—who they were. "Teresa Bailey," he called back into his mind and found a harmonic.

"You're Dan Miller," she said, walking with him for an instant of dream.

It was a stranger's name. "Yes," he said.

She smiled again, the same way. "It's—it's nice to have talked with you. Bye. I have to go this way."

"Bye," he said.

She was gone somewhere into the hall, wherever the school goes like a brook. A drop of water in the eddy, into the pool where the trout waits and listens. That day there were clouds cutting across each other, ones from the sea and ones from the valley; they scissored the air and smelled of storm.

Once in a while at school there were real things that happened in the day and found maybe a minute to happen. Dan was stunned by her appearance and when she disappeared he was overwhelmed by a tide of regret. Here had been his one chance and he had been stupid. She had been real. Last night he had dreamed of a world of real things and now reality was lost.

It was too late to think. Here was the room. *Me llamo Dan Miller desde porque la casa y la mesa, por el lápiz* and the bedroom."

Miss Carol Newman smiled. She was young, but not young. Her hips were like too much chocolate and her hands reached everywhere, touching the book and the corner of the desk.

10

"Hello, Dan," she said. *"Buenas tardes."*

"Buenas tardes," he answered, folding under the desk in a square of legs.

"¿Cómo está?" like ice cream. Her lashes were long and full, her eyes heavier than her voice.

"Bien," he managed. *"¿Y usted?"*

"Muy bien," said Miss Newman.

It worried him that he had known the right answer. Answers puzzled Dan because there were so many to everything.

Spanish was the last class of the day before he went out to practice. Yes, he could run, carry the ball, hit the scrimmage line hard. He was big, tall, wide in the shoulders like his father—coordinated, they called it. Football was real; he couldn't dream that carrying the ball didn't really happen. Coach Franks would yell, "Get alive, you knucklehead. Get the lead out of your big butt, Miller."

It was true; he had the lead in his butt and he was scared. Coach Franks knew it even though Dan could run. He was frightened—not of being kicked in the head on the field or even of getting beaten up in the showers. That happened. No, it was more the smell that made him anxious and the taste of blood and sweat in his mouth. Once he had wanted to kill Butch Graber. Graber never gave up riding a person, and killing him had seemed almost logical and too easy. Instead, he had asked, "Butch, please stop now?"

Graber had only laughed and every afternoon in the showers he called Dan chicken. Dan stood still and shook his head into the sharp streams of cold water, saying nothing. It was true: he was chicken.

The gym smelled stale, like old vegetable soup.

11

Coach Franks's voice was a zipper, ripping across the world and splitting it into two parts. Dan was here because his father had played football in high school and he had to uphold the honor.

Of course, his father had never said so exactly. "I'm not at all sure football's so important, Dan. It used to seem that way to me, but now I don't know. It's hard work and it hurts; it keeps you out there on the field until after dark and there's no glory in it most of the time. Why, you couldn't practice, so you'll have to decide for yourself."

He meant the piano. Dan had been born with music floating around in him like dreams, speaking the present like a lingcod. His father said the music was good and his mother just smiled.

The Spanish class took up and went on. People read from the book and then Miss Newman made conversation and corrections. Her voice was soft, somehow pleading.

Once, in the hour, she came and stood beside Dan's desk. She bent over and her thick, full top bulked in his sight under the wool of her dress. She was old—and too young.

"Good, Dan," she said, her words thickening and flowing downward over him. "You're doing very well. You have a nice accent."

That melted him, having a nice accent. He looked upward into her dark eyes that showed one-way windows. Then his glance crept away and the rest of the hour he stared at his book.

Today he needed physical education, and he was glad when the bell rang. Perhaps it was right to go out and get kicked in the head. In scrimmage, he tackled savagely, hitting low the way his father had done in the legends, and not caring if somebody killed him this afternoon. He caught MacCurdy's pass and scored through the first string.

"You had a little fight today," Coach Franks said grimly. "Miller, you could play ball if you weren't so chicken."

He shielded his eyes in regret and humility.

"Why don't you ever say anything?" the coach demanded. "You're the most wooden kid I ever came across."

Dan nodded, but kept silent. There wasn't a thing to answer.

He should have. That night the coach posted the final squad list and last on the second string was Dan Miller. It was pure fantasy. The coach had said in the beginning, "You're big and fast enough to make the team, Miller. I want you out there trying, at least." So he'd gone out, thinking a few days would settle everything.

It hadn't; now he was on the squad. Frantically, he searched for Butch Graber on the roster. God, Graber had been cut off and that was wrong. All wrong. More than anything else in life, Graber had wanted to be on the squad.

Tonight in the showers nobody said a word. He dressed and went home, walking, trying to think of how he could explain. On the way, he remembered Teresa Bailey. "Bye," she had said. Bye. Good-by for never.

The town flowed. It was houses and trees, the oaks with right-angle appointments in their arms, and moss hanging like sleep in their eyes. There were streets and crossovers, stucco in small time, gardens like verses in the Sears, Roebuck catalog. Beyond, the hills of the

Santa Lucias ran down green to the Salinas River, saying a hill again and again.

The creeks cut the town secretly; a boy knew them in his own secret self. They carried the throwaway edges of living and made pools that struggled with water. Under the bridge, brave fish and frogs hid in silence.

Walking home was skytime, a sundown of nothing and everything. Cars were important; they were the real happening of the pavement.

A boy on the streets was inward, alive, but an obstacle to realizations of time. The town had to reject him like an incompatible organ implanted by unrequested surgeons. Dan was nowhere in this town, like any other boy. Except in the river bottoms, there was never even enough air for a boy to breathe without looking around in apology.

Yet there was this simple idea: a guy in his junior year of high school walked home and was young and alive. It made sense to be Dan Miller because without himself nothing else would exist except as a negative being developed by someone in another time.

But being young in this present had a stink to it, and the world could smell the kids. Man, there was a garbage of oil in Dan's face that seemed to flow down into his clothes. Youth held a hand in front of their mouths to smell the vile breath; their sweat crept down to the small of the back. The newspapers said so; everywhere adults could smell the young, and they demanded law and order. Hair was an outright sin. Cut it, kid, shave it all into the Marine Corps.

Walking home, Dan could smell himself even after the shower—as if there was an aura around him ten

14

feet wide and colored purple. He could see it, invisible, and he shivered inside.

The day now had lasted beyond memory, and school still hurt like a nerve. Above him, a small town loomed, showing its teeth. But this was safe, being alone, sutured into a moment when nobody asked questions.

He was coming home in the solemn agony, over the streets with quiet names like Laurel and Grove, Nixon Lane, and Locust Avenue that concealed their character. Home was a place of low-lying furniture and muted music where his father and mother lived. They owned the piano, the books, and the way they spoke in subdued voices.

Ahead, a lawn mower powdered the air with black, one-cylinder dots. The grass here was wide, with forced shrubs that led geometry into service porches. Big flowers celebrated their own life and death.

A woman said, "Hello, Dan."

He turned and smiled mechanically. She was Mrs. Baumann, old and kindly, who had patted his head in church, down low and at various levels.

"Hello, Mrs. Baumann," he said, feeling the smile along his teeth.

"How's your mother?"

"Fine," he said, not stopping. He feared Mrs. Baumann. Her hand on his head had always felt like hatred.

"Tell her hello, Dan," said Mrs. Baumann. "We missed her last Sunday at church." It was an accusation.

"Thank you, Mrs. Baumann," he said, going away as fast as he could without running. "I'll tell her."

For a whole block afterward, he felt Mrs. Baumann

and what she had said of his mother—that she had avoided church. Dan had been an altar boy until pardoned. Always, Mrs. Baumann had been there, leering and winking, her hair tight in a frizz of phony curls. From her he had learned much about his own evil. At the altar, he chose hell.

So at last, this was his parents' house, long in frontage, with a finger wave of ornamental stone low at the knees of the foundation. The lawn here was wide, sloping, carving the flagstone walk into sharp green edges and circling around the wide-bordered flower beds to the spacious garage. Behind was the patio with its glass. On the backyard grass was a place still bare and hard-packed where Dan had shot baskets after his father had put up the board. Long ago, there had been open fields beyond, where the quail netted their young with the morning mist. Now houses sprouted everywhere.

Once there had been a boy who lived here, a kid who had everything, like a shotgun, a dart board, a typewriter, and a room of his own with a bedspread in Navajo colors. A spurious glow had surrounded that boy until he was ten and squatting in security, smug as a silver dime. That boy had gone forever, camping out in recollection.

Somewhere along the edges of a month or a year, Dan had lost himself. One day was safe; the next had turned into a wilderness of blasted landscape and mean animals.

Dan really didn't know what had happened—to him, or to anyone in his life. This house was the same, almost unchanged except for new furniture. His mother and father were older, sure, but they were the identical

16

adults he remembered from long ago. It was the same sky, the familiar town, always a similar sun in the morning. He didn't understand; he was bewildered by the changes in the world and in himself.

Back in the good times his dad had taken him trout fishing in Owens Valley a few times. If anything, Mr. Miller's rules for camping were stricter than those at home. The fire had to be exactly so, dishes washed and dried immediately after use, the tent and sleeping bags kept in scrupulous order. There was even a special way for a boy to clamber along the rocks lining Lone Pine Creek. Because of rattlesnakes, he always looked first before he got a handhold anywhere.

But the rules had reasons; they made sense to Dan. And even now—this long—he could remember when he had caught his first trout, a ten-inch Loch Leven, spotted and utterly beautiful.

"Wonderful," his father had almost yelled, grinning widely, "and the best fish of the day. Dan, this calls for some kind of celebration."

He had gotten out his camera and taken a half dozen shots of Dan and the Loch Leven, and that evening they had driven into Lone Pine for dinner and a movie afterward.

On those trips there had been a kind of magnetic force between Dan and his father, although neither mentioned its presence. It was like a new understanding, the slender beginnings of masculine equality, and within it a boy felt the first awakenings of his own strength.

Now all that seemed lost and it took an effort even to recall it, almost as if the trips had never happened.

Lately, his father had seemed edgy and suspicious.

Ever since Dan had gone to high school they had fought a running battle about his grades. Where he got a B or a C, his father wanted A's.

"How can you expect to get into college if you let things go this way?" his father demanded again and again. "Why not try doing a little work?"

Dan had wanted to tell him the truth—that he had worked, and that perhaps a C was as good as he could do. But his dad always seemed to prefer hearing a lie, with sayings about assignments, getting along with the teacher, and paying better attention in class.

Worse, he had started to ask nagging, persistent questions that couldn't be answered. Did Dan know anyone at school who smoked marijuana? Why had he been so late getting home the night before? Where did he go? What had he done?

Dan had answered as honestly as he could, but even honesty never seemed enough. It was as if the older man wanted him to invent some story that fit a preconception he had of his son and the other kids at school. Now there was an invisible barrier between them that was almost impenetrable, and Dan had no idea how it had got there.

The flagstone walk to the house here curved into the hypocrisy of landscaping, but he didn't cut across. Instead, he kept to its pattern and began to hold himself in the shape the stones wanted. He steadied his mouth and eyes; he hid the weakness of his whole identity and studied the prospect of an afternoon smile from his mother.

He wasn't her fault, of course, and yet why should a mother make evening a sort of nighttime school for her son? Naturally, they had their reasons. At sixteen, a boy should be reaching for their conception of a man. He should practice it. Mothers saw the man in a son before the kid was even born.

But there was no man in Dan Miller, and really no child. There was nothing of either, not even a beginning or an ending. It was only a body on the flagstone walk, a person not even used to his own name yet, a thing heavy with unspeakable secrets.

His mother would hurry to kiss him in a show of womanly grace, a pucker of lips that he accepted but that took in his blood. Beyond her, the house would brood in that insanity of perfection where even the newspapers were folded in waiting. Outside, the lawn would shine; inside, the houseplants would gleam, their broad leaves waxed with infinite care. Somewhere in the background there would be the soul of Muzak, done up in a package of canned Beethoven.

"And how was school today?" she would ask him, recoiling to a sofa where she would sit relaxed and confident, still blond and pretty but as impersonal as a vase.

One day, he had almost told her the real answer to that question—that the gym was a jungle her son had known almost from the first grade. He could have told her that going to school was like going into battle, where the enemy was remorseless and cunning. He could say, "In the showers this afternoon, Mother, I learned what they do in prison to kids. That was the real lesson I learned in school today."

Instead, Dan smiled faintly, thinking about Miss Newman while the expression lasted.

"Fine, Mother," he said.

"You always say that, Dan. What do you mean?"

searching, wanting reality from a son who had only a little more time with a mother—a few years. Men grow so quickly, you know.

He heard an unmistakable yearning in her voice, as if she wanted understanding from him desperately. He loved his mother; when he got home from school—from anywhere—she was always there, always pleasant. She acted as if she was genuinely glad to see him again. And yet—Well, he didn't know what to say to her—as if they spoke different languages.

He looked at her from a great distance—from the back of his mind across miles of nothing. His mother was pretty, small, with a delicacy that photographed a young girl and pasted her in the family album. She could speak like groceries and chat pleasantly with the minister on Sunday morning.

He thought, I met a girl today. Her name is Teresa and we walked a little in the hallway. For a moment beside her, I felt clear; I felt the sun in my head at last.

But nobody talked like that.

"There wasn't anything, really, Mother," he insisted instead. "Just classes—the usual routine, and—" He waited for the rest of the phrase, the forgotten news, sinking with its own weight. "—and I'm on the football team."

"You—Dan!"

"Yes," he said, making his voice seem strong. "Only the second string. I—I guess I made it—somehow."

She swallowed. "Why—why, that's so nice. Your father will be—proud."

"I know," he said. "Well—" It was a question; it was asking permission.

2

AND SO DAN MILLER'S junior year squeezed out its tubes of pain. High school had its American winners, sure, always measuring the dipstick of the town's oily love. Kids who could reflect the dreams of adults always won.

But for most, high school was an untidy time, hurting in the rotten old age of childhood. It was four years when a boy really learned that he was a stupe. The wise planners said it was training for real life.

For Dan, nothing ever actually happened. Miss Newman never progressed beyond chocolate; the commies didn't ever come up the hill. Mr. Park kept leaning on the movie projector, and Butch Graber faded into a gray background. It was as if the legend of Santa Claus had been proved false again.

Chicken Miller had played football, no matter how hard he tried to avoid it. At the end of the torture he had somehow won enough game minutes to rate a letter at the awards assembly. He had stood there paralyzed while the kids applauded politely; they respected the thickness of the chenille. Afterward, the stolen letter burned into his self-respect, and he hid it away in a drawer at home.

"Get the lead out of your fat butt, Miller," the coach had screamed at him all season. "Get in there and make some yardage, you slob!"

Once or twice, Dan had needed to restrain himself from turning back on Coach Franks and telling him. He hated the man for what he was—the symbol and prototype of Establishment adults.

It wasn't all bad; nothing is. There was one part of the junior year that was fantastic and lovely—so much so that at first he'd discounted it as impossible and very likely imaginary. Teresa. Teresa had happened slowly, but all at once, in a sense.

Sure, she didn't run up to him and say, "Dan Miller, I love you," in the style a junior boy would like it to happen so that he didn't have to worry about women anymore.

By now he knew more of her long hair and deep eyes. The hair was too much and too golden and too shiny and disordered in back when the wind blew it or she was excited and tossing around. But it was there to be figured—a lot of hair that could enclose a boy's shoulders if it were spread just right in his dreams. It could fold a guy's whole mind into a full vision and shut him out from the world within a curtain of heaviness and delayed time.

Teresa was only part high school girl; the rest of her was full woman. Her breasts were there, man, and accentuated an inward reserve of narrow waist. She moved like soul; there was a slowness to her swing, something a little harsh in the way she walked.

But that wasn't the real scene about her with Dan Miller. Half the girls in school were trying harder every day with their skirts almost up to their hips and their sheer panty hose down below. Some of the guys still had to keep their eyes on the book, but most of them were simply bored and wondering how long it would be until the final bell rang. It was high school for kids stuck in the times, see?

Kids these days were spending their time hunting up more than girls, they said; high school guys, some of them, were interested in pot, speed, and all manner of contrivances. A hot car sent them farther down the road than the neatest woman in the swimming pool—or so the papers claimed. This, now, was a long, hard day in the present when there was too much of everything and not enough of the lazy bite of nothing. Old men contended they remembered such a nothing-time when it was the American Way for a boy to be interested in a job, or building a kite. Youth today, they said, was nothing but sheer anarchy and revolution.

Maybe so. But Teresa Bailey was of this time and this place even more than Dan Miller. She smiled briefly with her cozening mouth corners. Her lashes swept her wide, terribly hazel eyes.

She said that day, "Do you have the questions for the test Mr. Park wants to give us, Dan? I've lost mine and I wish I could copy yours."

He had them. She lay facedown under the oak tree at noon, copying from his notebook, writing down the stupid questions. He sat dazed, watching her, seeing how lovely she was.

"I'm so glad you had these, Dan," she finally told him, her eyes now shaded with long lashes. "I don't know what I would have done without you."

Without him, you see. She didn't know what she could have done without Dan Miller. He tried to grasp

23

the idea but instead fell into a contemplation of her eyes.

Frankly, for eyes they were out of sight—a mysterious and up-high shade, not brown, not blue or gray. Really over the hill with a rich softness and a bewitching promise. There was no real answer in Teresa's eyes; they held the whole reluctance and disturbance of these times.

So that girl said with the warmth of her hips and her eyes: Are you or aren't you here with me? Or are you Mrs. Miller's little boy still—this late, this late? She asked that kind of unspoken, mocking question. She seemed to say that she was to be taken and used, and loved very sweetly.

Like every other guy, of course, Dan had thought a great deal about the particulars of love, but never quite as a reality that was going to happen to him soon. Despite the new freedom and permissiveness, he was a lot closer to the standards and mores of his parents than they could have believed.

By now, his mother in particular was aware of Teresa and of Dan's feelings toward her.

"She's a lovely girl," Mrs. Miller said with an unexpected warmth. "I'm glad that you know her, Dan."

She meant it sincerely, he realized, as if she thought that a boy and a girl being in love was good, and safe, and right. At the time he was a little surprised at his mother's reassurance, as if he'd thought she would prefer to believe the wild stories about love and youth. Not so.

Sure, she questioned him once or twice, but it was only about the ordinary things that showed interest, rather than suspicion.

His dad said nothing and scarcely seemed to be lis-

24

tening when Teresa was mentioned, but that had to be all right too. Fathers weren't too strong on advice to sons about girls. When they got around to becoming advisers, it was usually about mighty serious matters.

So for a long time his relationship with Teresa progressed in the accepted ways that required no particular effort and no decisions of importance. Dan wasn't prepared at all for what happened.

Once, instead of her real self, Teresa revealed several inches of her inner thigh to him while they were eating lunch together out under the oak tree on the junior lawn. It was done with unconscious impulse, but she might just as well have run naked in the rain in front of an old man's home. He didn't even see her.

But love—the real thing—finally brought Dan Miller down and into Teresa's arms forever. As always, it was ridiculously simple. There was the junior-senior prom. In anguish and regret Dan Miller had asked her to go with him, as if propelled by forces beyond his control.

This she did, and in her new formal and an upswept hair-thing. Throughout the evening, he sweated and strained at tradition, suffering the dance as fully as any junior boy ought to do.

But on the way home in the family car, which happened to be a large and squishy Buick with controls like a motorboat, he stopped by the Templeton Bridge. The fact that this was the road to the Templeton Dump had little to do with the romance of the happening. Anyone can be on the road to the dump without really meaning to dump things.

Somehow, the situation gave him the necessary courage. He clasped his arm around her and drew her close. They kissed, first as a boy and a girl who had been to the prom, and then as Teresa thought they should kiss —which proved to be much different.

Dan Miller found himself deep within Teresa's lips, and there fire caught in his blood. Its molten tendrils surged everywhere within him in a vast and exclusive first knowledge.

"I love you," he said into the kiss, not actually knowing why such an idea should occur to him.

A smile seemed to lick its tongue to the recesses of his brain.

"I love you, too, Dan," she murmured, taking him away from his mother, now and forever afterward.

Love sometimes does its thing unexpectedly. Love is wild, strange as a coyote, tender as a baby's skin. It comes best of all to a very young man in its wildness and strangeness so that a woman's lips can be the formula for all time and space.

Whatever else happened to Dan Miller, Teresa Bailey saved him in his junior year the way a person gets saved from drowning. Suddenly, the stupid kid with the big, overhanging, lead-ladened butt shrunk in the hips in a sort of miracle. One day, he was too much for himself to drag around another minute, and the next he felt light and really slippery. It was the greatest job of shrinking ever accomplished in the history of the American high school. The funny part about it was that he knew what had taken place and who was responsible. The fat didn't simply transpose and go to his head the way it does so often with other guys who happen to meet a genuine girl. It stayed gone.

He started waiting for her every morning at a special place. It was down some distance from the trophy case where various socies waited to get notice every morning. It was neutral territory. And every morning now—

in the waning weeks of May, spreading into June—Teresa met him there. She would come swinging up to him in her loose dress, where the suggestion of everything precious announced itself in fabric rills and fables.

"Hi," she would say.

And, "Hi," he would respond—good enough for a dying boy brought back to life by artificial respiration.

They would stand there for a while, talking, while Dan tried to tell her a little bit about how he felt down in his soul—man, that was where he felt about her. And always, it wasn't enough for him. He wanted poetry, and what came out of his mouth were words through which he jumbled and winced. But Teresa didn't mind.

"I'll see you at noon," she would say, "in the same place by the tree."

And she would.

He'd be sitting in the crotch of this old tree, wondering what he could have possibly done to merit this joy and this freedom. It was blind, stupid luck, of course, like a kid who had hit the jackpot at Tahoe. Sooner or later, Teresa would wake up and come back to her mind. But until that happened, he intended to live while he could.

"You know, Dan," she said once, very calmly, "our family name isn't really Bailey. It's been changed from the Russian or Polish or something. I'm really Jewish. Does that make any difference to you?" She said it in her light, bantering, kidding voice, the way she talked over the telephone when she asked him if he wanted to Indian-wrestle or something.

For an instant, Dan Miller tried to fit being Jewish into his mind, but nothing came one way or another.

27

He had heard some talk among adults, but it had never meant anything to him. Right now, he couldn't even remember what had been said.

"Say that again, will you, Teresa?" he asked. "I wasn't really listening."

"No."

"I mean that," he insisted. "I—I guess I just didn't hear what you meant."

She laughed softly. "Of course not," she said. "You didn't hear what I meant. And I should have known better."

"Better than what?"

"To say that to you. To say anything."

"I don't get it."

"Of course you don't," she answered in a shy, sweet, and somehow scared voice.

He waited.

Silence.

Then, "What've I done? What did—"

She put her small hand on his arm. "Dan," she told him, using the name like a brand of honey, "you haven't done anything. You don't know—anything—about yourself or about the world. You're—you're either in the nineteenth century or the twenty-first."

His eyebrows were up in a puzzle. "Hey, I don't get it," he repeated. "What's going on today? Yesterday we were—"

She took her hand away from his arm and looked off toward the blue Santa Lucias toward the west. "I know what you are," she said in a distant voice. "You're the uncommitted guy. You don't have any positive background or beliefs. But one of these days you'll get some. That's when I'll lose you."

It was preposterous. "Lose—me?" he asked.

"Yes," she said simply.

Right there, the noon bell rang. They went back to class with nothing solved about each other, and that day Dan once again felt the sinking jolt of insecurity. She had probably been trying to tell him to get lost because she was really in love with somebody else.

Afterward, he waited for the ax dumbly, expecting that she'd tell him the truth at any moment. But she didn't.

Not only that, she didn't run out when Barry Wentworth, one of the big arms of the big thing, asked her to a dance being held in the National Guard Armory. Teresa said no. She said she already had a date for that night to the drive-in, where a Swedish bill was playing that no girl in her right mind could miss. And when Barry wanted her to break the date and go to the drive-in with him, she still said no. Dan heard about it from Jack Morris, a freshman who liked to stand around among the wheels and sop up some of the action.

"I couldn't believe it," Morris said. "Any woman in this school would kill herself to go with Wentworth, but she wouldn't. I wonder why?"

"I don't know," Dan had to admit.

"I'll tell you why," Morris concluded. "She's flipped. Teresa must be freaked out on something."

"No, she isn't," Dan replied darkly. "And don't you go around this school saying that, Morris, or I'll—I'll break your arm, maybe."

"Oh, sure you will," Morris said, moving away.

But the disbelief in himself was sharp and deep. Naturally, he summoned what small decency he had and told her the truth.

"You don't love me," he said one day under the oak

tree, feeling the sick shape of the words on his lips. "I don't blame you—only I wish you wouldn't say it anymore—"

Teresa was silent in a sliver of time, looking at him hard with her hazel eyes, hunting through his expression.

Then, "Dan Miller," she said in her firm, smooth voice, "you're—well, I guess vain would be the word. And you're a—a little bit cruel, besides."

That shocked him. He had never considered himself as cruel and the word coiled there like a sunning rattlesnake.

"No—" he began, "I'm—" But he stopped; he couldn't deny anything. If Teresa said so, it was probably true.

"Is that all you're going to offer about this hang-up?"

He nodded.

She looked away and after a while she shrugged. "Love has to be accepted and trusted," she finally said. "It can't be forced. Otherwise—"

He waited. She sounded old, as if lecturing him about a child's lesson he should have learned long ago.

"I don't think I get it," he told her, because he didn't. He hadn't been trying to force anything.

Teresa met his glance. There was a wise and almost tender expression on her full lips. "You don't believe anything about yourself, do you, Dan? That's why you can't believe me."

"I love you, Teresa," he suddenly blurted, knowing at once that the phrase was ice-cold and wrong, but bumbling ahead. "I know that about myself."

She shook her head slowly. "Dan!" was all she would answer.

When he tried to talk with her, to explain how sincere he was and so relieve himself of responsibility, she was silent.

In a junior year, the little loves of a boy and girl hurt sharply for an instant and are quickly forgotten in the broad turbulence of high school life. Or so it usually happens. But not with Dan Miller.

Now and then there is a Teresa Bailey who comes along, a girl with a mind of her own. She knew who she was and where she was going like the way to the corner grocery store. She saw Dan Miller ahead in a sometime of life, the uncommitted junior boy who was destined to succeed himself in a projection of the future.

The Bailey family was like that; they had all worked hard and looked through the future's beckoning windows. They had come far with plenty of distance to go. Teresa was their daughter exactly in the way David was their son. He was a lieutenant in the Army, up from boot camp through officer's school, and so much a soldier now that he sometimes seemed to rattle with the hardware of the role.

So Teresa let Dan shuffle around in the shoes of his indecision for a time, but not really for long. She led him by the hand, a step at a time. Finally, by the end of the year, they were together again.

In the summer he took her to the beach at Avila on the smashing, sun-washed afternoons. Warm, limpid evenings they went to the drive-in or to the artificial lake near town—whatever the moment said to do.

At last there was a sensual purity, a vestal innocence and dedication in the way they explored the margins of each other. First love is like spring embracing the earth, seeking young roots with mysterious tongues of moisture.

Now Dan spoke to Teresa as much with silences as

31

with words to explain the wordless. They ran on the beach hand in hand. They let their tanned, handsome bodies plunge together into the cool, green waves, rolling nowhere for no other reason.

Toward the end of the summer he said again, "I love you!" He did something more. In secret, he composed a song about her, about love, about what she did to turn him on and how much he needed her. He spent hours on the melody, the chords, the beat. But it was never good enough to play for her.

This time, Teresa believed. She laughed; she teased him; her lips were warm, and fireflies of joy lit the evening all over again.

3

To know Dan Miller in his senior year, one needed to know Teresa, as well. She was at the end of the catalog among the shorts and extra talls, an absolute outsider. Not physically, of course; physically, she was a Raquel Welch type. It was her mental attitude that bothered the senior boys.

"That woman sure has a shape," Bud Hathway once said, summing up group opinion for all time.

"Man, how right you are," echoed Bill Wiest. "But she's a—what you call them—a snob. She won't do nothing. I been out with her one time."

"Right," Bud agreed. "Me, too," shrugging Teresa off his fat mouth. "To hell with her. Let's see if we can find Candy Swanson. Now Candy's a real woman."

"You can say that again," Wiest grinned. "You know it."

So that was how it was with Teresa and the brave boys; they knew she belonged somewhere, but they couldn't figure out how that happened to be with Dan Miller.

In senior year, the school began to catch on—that it was Dan and Teresa no matter what. They were there together, everywhere. Finally, they said that Teresa was his girl, but with reluctance because many still suspected that she was the most woman in the whole place. She was a mystery.

That is, everyone but Dan caught on. Even as a senior he couldn't quite grasp the idea that the prettiest woman in school was his chick. In his own mind he was still nowhere, but maybe his sort was really everywhere.

Teresa, of course, had grown up in Cleveland, Ohio, before Mark Bailey had moved his family west. She had gone to a public school in a checkerboard neighborhood and fought her way home all through grammar school. She wore a clean dress every day, and she had her money for lunch and her pigtails and the family honor to defend. Her papa owned a little store bequeathed to him by his father, who had been named David Balinkowsky before he changed it legally. The store was an island in a hostile sea, still viable after fifty years, and there Teresa had lived in quarters on the second floor.

She had been skinny as a pencil in those days, honey-haired, with wild child eyes and the look of an elf out of another portion of the universe. Smart? Teresa knew English and math like a machine gun and protected that knowledge out on the playground and in the secret places. She could fight like a cornered bobcat and did—until at last everyone left her alone on the streets of Cleveland.

From there, her father moved to this town, Lakefield, California, took out his real estate license, and sought a new career. Bailey Realty in Lakefield now competed with the oldest established firms, and Mark

Bailey was known everywhere as a sharp dealer to be watched carefully.

So what did a girl like her possibly see in a confused, scared young stupe like Dan Miller? For one thing, she had heard him play his own compositions on the piano and knew by womanly instinct that he was in a class of his own.

After the business of making money—which came first—the Baileys all had a feeling for music. In fact, Teresa's uncle, Jacob Bailey, might have become a concert violinist if he had not opted for mathematics and gone to work for the Rand Corporation.

When Teresa listened to Dan play "I Couldn't See You There in the Dark," a sort of rock-and-roll fugue he had written, she heard the ghosts of Chopin and Liszt hammering and tendering the keys. Only she didn't give him too much praise. Too much praise hurt an artist, her father always said. A real artist must hunger and yearn first, Mr. Bailey said, so that he learned how to make a living before he did anything else. Thus, the hungering and yearning were never quite forgotten in a man's age, he claimed.

Besides, although Dan was tall, loose, and awkwardly young, he was terribly handsome in a far-out, poetic way—or so Teresa thought. He had dark, brooding, dangerous brown eyes, straight brows, heavy and thick, and his face was lean and solid. That he was really unformed made him all the more attractive to her because he was so unlike most of the too-knowledgeable boys around who had grown so fast. She saw in him the dimensions of tomorrow.

Like her, he really belonged nowhere. At Lakefield there were two groups of kids. One was the socies, who were with the adults and the Establishment. They were the athletes, the cheerleaders, the song girls, and the wheels. On the other, lesser, side were the sub-hippie types, long-haired boys, girls with their phony peace symbols. In between somewhere was Dan Miller, who should have been accepted by both because he was a musician and an athlete. But he rated with neither. And wasn't that where Teresa stood?

It took a girl with a sharp eye and a sharper mind to see where Dan Miller really belonged—at the top somewhere, given a few years to bloom. And she was ready to nurture him there all the way, in her arms. In high school there are girls like Teresa. A few. They wait.

That was ahead of them. Now they were together in their senior year, with Dan not quite knowing why, and Teresa knowing only too well. When the time came, it was she who persuaded him to apply to the University of California for admission—despite deep lapses in his grade record.

"Look," she insisted, "you can try, can't you, Dan? All they can do is turn you down. Your math and English grades are good all through school. They count those—a lot."

"I don't think I can get into college at all," he told her uncertainly.

"How do you know if you don't try?" she demanded.

"I'm almost afraid to, I guess," he admitted. "If I get turned down, it's going to hit my parents hard, especially my dad. Maybe it's because he was out on his own when he was still a kid, so nobody handed him any college." He looked hard at his girl. "You don't know my dad, Teresa," as if asking for understanding. "As long as you do things his way, it's fine. But when you step out of line in his opinion, he can be rough."

"What do you mean? How have you stepped out of line?"

"My grades," Dan said. "Ever since I got to high school, my dad has been on my neck about grades. I've tried to tell him that school is different now, but he won't see it. Where I've gotten C's, he wants A's."

Teresa smiled. "And you probably could have gotten them, Dan—if you'd worked. I'm on your dad's side there."

"I did work."

She sniffed a little. "Work? You've been dreamy, you mean."

"That isn't true," he said, hurt. "Sometimes a teacher can—"

"All right," interrupting. "Let's not argue about that. Just get yourself into college."

He shrugged. "How? Just tell me how. I'd go all right, but—"

"Then try," Teresa said strongly. "And don't ever say you can't. Not to me, Dan."

Dan shrugged. "All right. If you say so."

"I do say so."

Dan applied to Cal and was promptly turned down, as he had expected. He felt no particular surprise or emotion about it. The state university had two applicants for every place in the freshman class. He let it go, thinking he'd get a job, or perhaps go down to the local junior college in Del Obispo.

Not Teresa; her hazel eyes burned with anger at all authority, vested and unvested. "Put in your application at San Jose State," she demanded. "Berkeley will be sorry they rejected you, Dan. Wait and see. I know they will. I don't think much of Berkeley, anyway."

He applied to San Jose State and, for good measure, to Fresno. Then, as a last resort, he sent in an application to Visalia State, the newest of the colleges. After that, he forgot the whole business, because his grades were familiar enough to him. He had had a couple of D's as a freshman and a smattering of C's everywhere else. That meant thumbs down on him.

Meanwhile, the year raced on. One afternoon, Teresa walked downtown and got herself a job at the Baldwin Labs, which ran the medical tests in Lakefield. She had finished most of her required school courses and could work from one until five every afternoon and Saturday morning.

She was an instant success at Baldwin, naturally, filling in for Mrs. Hall, answering the phone, doing the billing, and taking care of the patients who came in while they waited for the technician.

She was delighted with herself—although Dan wasn't so pleased. The job meant that he saw a lot less of her than he wanted.

"It's to be permanent. Full-time after I'm out of school," she told him, with success in her eyes. "It's a wonderful job, Dan, and Mr. Baldwin is cool. I mean, he's nice. I'll be able to work there the whole time—"

"What whole time?"

"When you're in college, of course. And then—"

"Then what?"

"Don't you know?"

Dan Miller gulped hard, feeling about ten years old and scarcely strong enough to cross the street alone.

"Uh—we'll be married," he gasped, frightened silly by the words.

38

"Oh, Dan," Teresa cried, squeezing his arm hard.

He suddenly felt much stronger. Maybe a full twelve years old. Once a man committed himself, he was there, probably. He saw the new Dan Miller out in the great works of the big world, carrying his shovel, with a couple of baloney sandwiches in his pocket for lunch. Right afterward, he shivered inwardly at the crazy audacity of the idea. It was another dream.

But he finally got used to the thing as the year spun away and summer began to dance and burn up ahead, with graduation going and the teachers nervous as hell.

The plans were for sometime, but as real as water. Dan and Teresa spun them together under the night sky. She was in his arms, telling his lips all the silence and wonder.

"I love you," he told her now with conviction.

"I know," softly. "I love you too, Dan."

It was the hard, lovely truth.

Meanwhile, the riots in Berkeley over the People's Park came, endured, and faded. The guy was killed with the police buckshot; the Governor called in the National Guard and sprayed half the town with tear gas. Fifty thousand demonstrators marched in the street, and the papers carried pictures of a couple who took off part of their clothes.

At home, Dan's father talked about the trouble with almost savage loathing.

"Those long-haired, dirty young parasites have gone too far," he said harshly. "Behind every one of them is somebody breaking his neck on the job to keep them in college. And what do they do? They riot, they destroy property, they flaunt authority without any regard for the thousands of other students there to get an education." Dan had the unpleasant sensation that Mr.

Miller was talking directly to him, as if he had long hair and had been out busting windows.

"But, Dad—" he began.

Mr. Miller appeared not to have heard him. "Going to college isn't a privilege for some kind of elite youth corps. It's a responsibility—an obligation both to the state and to the people who pay the freight. Why—why these—hoodlums go in and wreck libraries; they destroy college records that have taken years to accumulate. All of them should be jailed, dismissed from school. Every time a police officer cracks one of them over the head, I'm glad. They've got it coming!"

Mrs. Miller remonstrated. "Dear," she said, "you can't really mean you want them hurt. That's not like you at all."

"Hurt?" Mr. Miller scoffed. "Those toughs? I want them to get what they have coming. What would happen if I went out and tore up the street? I'd get slammed in jail."

Dan's mother said, "You wouldn't do anything like that. Besides—" hesitantly, "dinner is getting cold . . ."

After that the older man calmed down, so Dan didn't say anything.

Dan talked a little about the event with his girl, not knowing exactly what the trouble was about, but favoring the students, naturally. Teresa had a different and more positive view. She said the militants and their Communist organizers were at fault, and that Governor Reagan had no other choice but to call out the Guard. But it really meant nothing to either of them. Not then. The People's Park might as well have been on the other side of the moon.

"While you're at San Jose State," she would say, "I'll

be here working. I'll save my money and buy a car. We'll have something to start with."

"Oh, no, you won't," Dan told her firmly. "If anyone buys a car, I will."

"How?" she demanded. "You'll be there majoring in math and studying hard. You'll need a way to come home on—on vacations and weekends, and—"

"I'll hitchhike," he said stoutly.

"You can't do that."

He grinned. "Sure I can. Watch me."

Suddenly, she laughed and her laughter magically enwrapped them both. "You're funny, Dan," she said.

He huffed a little. "Sure I am. Like comical, and—"

"No. Not that way. Funny, and all right. You're sweet."

"Sweet?" roughly.

"Yes."

Dan had to grin. "Okay," he said, "for you I'll even be sweet."

"I knew you would," she said seriously. "Also funny."

He made a wide gesture. "That's for sure," he admitted.

Not long after that, Visalia State accepted him for admittance and Dan knew that if he went to college anywhere it would be there—even though he had heard nothing from San Jose or Fresno.

The letter of acceptance came on a Saturday morning when Dan was away and when he returned his father hovered around.

Mr. Miller was tall and lean, with a smattering of early gray at his dark temples. People who didn't know him too well as the county tax assessor might call him distinguished-looking. At least he was a self-possessed and precise man, able to carry out the harsh duties of his office without regret or apology. Taxes were just that—to be assessed and then ruthlessly collected because it was the law. The low key of the Miller living room, the records and the stereo, the shelf of colorful book jackets, the waxy shine of wood, had nothing to do with his job.

One of his favorite stories was of how he had broken with his own father, a minister, over a principle of behavior. Paul Miller had left home at eighteen, and had from that day supported himself in the business world.

"It wasn't easy, I can tell you," he was fond of saying, "but what is?"

From the earliest telling, the story had disturbed Dan Miller—as if he was supposed to do the same. But for years they had told him that they wanted him to go to college, as if the idea was a command.

"What's this thing from Visalia State?" his father wanted to know as soon as he entered the door.

Dan opened the envelope and looked it over quickly. "They say they've accepted me for entrance," he said, surprised.

"Visalia State?"

"Yes, Dad."

"Why did you apply there?" his father asked testily. "It's the newest of the state colleges, perhaps not even accredited yet. What's wrong with the state university?"

Dan suddenly remembered that he hadn't bothered to tell his father that he'd applied to Cal and been rejected.

"I did," he said, "but they turned me down."

"Why, why?" Mr. Miller demanded. "What did you do wrong? Did you fill in the form correctly, or—"

42

"It was my grades, I guess, Dad. I've got some—well, weak spots in the record."

Mr. Miller sank into one of the soft chairs. "Yes, of course," he said heavily. "I told you over and over again to keep up your grades. But you wouldn't listen—"

"I know, Dad, but—"

"Don't tell me anything about it," Mr. Miller said. "Don't tell me you 'tried,' whatever you do. You didn't try. And I kept telling you, but you were too smart for me. So now—"

"I'm sorry, Dad," Dan said.

"Sorry! Sorry!" the older man said. "That's how it is with you—you—uh—kids these days. You're all sorry. So sorry—" His voice had risen and Mrs. Miller came to the door from the kitchen, looking alarmed. Raised voices in this house weren't customary.

"I applied at San Jose and Fresno too," Dan said. "Maybe—"

"State colleges, all of them." The man sat up straight. "While you were at it, why didn't you try San Francisco State? After that infernal nonsense that went on up there, they probably need plenty of applicants. Anyone in his right mind would go somewhere else."

"I'm—"

"Don't say another word," Paul Miller declared. "All right. If it's Visalia State you want, that's where we'll go. At least we'll save a little money on you."

And that was how it finally was: Visalia State. Eventually everyone conceded that it was better than nothing.

At last, the senior year came to an ending. Graduation was a blur of the blue gowns and the speeches out in Memorial Stadium—with an almost endless list of scholarships and honors to everyone but Dan Miller.

Teresa won the award from the Business Women's Association, a full two hundred dollars. Then from two podiums, school board members handed out the diplomas. Dan scarcely believed he had graduated until he felt the scroll in his hand and returned to his seat. They all marched out when it was over, two by two up the flight of stairs in the bleachers to the senior lawn to stand in the reception line.

Afterward, everyone took buses to Disneyland—a lately grown tradition to keep the seniors from spinning out down at Morro Bay or elsewhere in the county, full of beer and love, thereby ending promising futures much too early.

Both Dan and Teresa went on the trip and stayed up all night, hand in hand among the plastic artifacts, the rides to Tomorrowland, the Pirates of the Caribbean—which they remembered most—and finally the long ride home.

That night, Disneyland seemed to be the essence of reality, no matter whether the revolution outside boiled. But there was dawn to encounter through their exhausted eyes, and to their credit, they saw the real world through the bus windows—the slums and shoddy posturing of Los Angeles.

"We'll get married," Dan had told her. Now the words burned in his mind like a vow on the way home and in the summer days ahead.

Summer! There is a quality in that season that lulls the senses and confutes the carefully stored wisdom of winter. Dan and Teresa discovered summer like honey in their blood.

It was a sacrament to youth and love—to being alive

and young in the simple ritual of having hope for the future. Teresa's full lips were moist, yielding, and within their encompassing presence, Dan felt both overwhelmed and like a full man. He knew her everywhere, and she him; their young spirits sought each other with a passionate yearning.

But they didn't cross the frontier of love. In a mutual understanding and agreement, they held in reserve the full day of wonder. They consented to wait until the time came that they could wait no longer—that day when everything was right and perhaps a little noble.

While they loved in the hot summer nights, the riots and trouble bloomed in faraway places. Not in the cities this year—in the smaller towns where the cops weren't so skillful with their clubs. The people there, students, blacks, dissidents, all writhed and screamed their meaningless confusion. They said in their way that the country was in a full revolution of sorts and that machine guns were not so far in the background.

Even here in Del Obispo County that summer there had been a bust of real proportions. A bunch of the kids had gone to Montana Diablo State Park for a happening, and in the middle of the music the cops had arrived by the carload, breaking it up in the usual style—with clubs, Mace, and mass arrests.

His father's reaction to Montana Diablo was different. Paul Miller, Dan thought, was genuinely bewildered; that sort of trouble seemed to belong to the cities.

"I can't understand this," he said. "Why, our county is rural. In all the time we've lived here, nothing comparable has ever happened. Do you know anything about it, Dan?"

"No, I don't, Dad," Dan said. "Some of the kids

were from Lakefield, but I don't know them. They say most of the people were around college age—from Cal Poly and that—I think it's called a free university or something."

"Free university," Mr. Miller said. "What nonsense! There has never been any trouble at Cal Poly. This seems unbelievable." He sounded like someone who had always thought the disease was far away and who had awakened to discover it infecting his own neighborhood.

The story Dan had heard was that the happening was peaceful and harmless, and legal because the kids had gotten a permit. They had started to play some acid rock on their sound system, when the cops descended on them without provocation. There had been rough stuff and some arrests. Nobody quite knew what had really happened, but everybody agreed it was the fault of the cops.

Still, he didn't tell his father that; he let it go. In the evening, when the paper came, Mr. Miller sat and read the story in silence. Afterward, Dan looked it over. The reporter favored the kids and some photos showed the police giving a girl a very bad time. It was big news.

But Dan Miller and Teresa scarcely noticed. Certainly, they talked a little about what went on and how it seemed to happen, about the long-haired kids, about pot—all the things. But the scene, even at Montana Diablo, seemed far away and abstract.

The world was their perfect apple, with sorcery in the summer moon. They were a boy and a girl in love, man, for the first time.

Finally the day came when Dan stood at the bus station with his suitcase and Teresa nearby, small, lovely, and subdued.

The men said, "Fresno, Visalia, Modesto," into the air, and the fat bus, reeking of sweat and gasoline, panted at the curb.

"Teresa," Dan choked.

She was clutching his hand, her fingers almost like claws. Now she loosened that grip.

"Yes, Dan?" she asked coolly.

"You're—you're beyond words," he said. "There isn't anything I can say. Nothing adequate." He leaned down with abruptness and kissed her roughly. "All—" he began.

He was equal to the moment, Teresa thought later, after he was gone. Now she said, "Dan! Dan!" murmuring into the kiss. "You'll go now?"

"Yes," he told her. "I suppose I have to."

"You have to," she said.

Then they parted. In the door of the bus, he turned. He didn't exactly wave to her; he had to keep his cool. But he told her somehow that he loved her above all other things.

She understood, because the hot tears came to her eyes when at last Dan Miller went inside and the door closed.

4

THE ROAD TO VISALIA first climbed the round, golden hills of the Temblor Range and then dropped over to the endless flats of the San Joaquin Valley. The smog, creeping this far north from Southern California, blended with the violet haze to obscure the High Sierras on the other side. That made the valley seem limitless. This was a hung-down day.

Dan Miller sat near the front of the bus, scarcely seeing the robot oil-field pumps around Kettleman Hills and, later, the wheeling acres of cotton.

In cadence with the rolling scene, a thread of unheard music took possession of the back of his mind, some tune that at last forced itself into his consciousness. Then he recognized it, and loneliness stabbed him deep. It was the thing he had written about his girl and never played for her because it wasn't good enough.

Leaving Teresa had hurt even worse than the anticipation, and her smarting image now filled his mind. Going away from her—to college or anywhere—today seemed a senseless act, blindly stupid, and painful.

But Dan had gained strength since his confused junior year until now he had become a rational who knew where he was going and maybe why. They had decided he should go to college and he was on his way, no matter how much it hurt. Since he'd known Teresa he had even begun to understand his parents a little better.

Although it was difficult to imagine in his dad, he guessed that they were a little bit scared—the way most parents were these days. There was so much in the papers now, over TV, and everywhere else about the growing drug scene, runaway girls, riots, and violence across the country. Parents had become afraid their own children would go that way too. So they came down hard whenever they could, trying to construct a barrier between themselves, their own, and the world outside. It was unnecessary. But he read the message.

Gradually, his sense of loss and loneliness lessened and he began to see the valley unfolding in its sultry monotony, so unlike the green hills around Lakefield. He thought of his girl as she actually was at this distance, small, delicate, yielding—someone who would wait for him.

"I'll write every day," she had said just before he got on the bus, "and you'll—"

"Naturally, I will," he had told her. "Why not?"

Right now he began to form his first letter in his mind. "I love you," it would say. But he didn't get beyond that first sentence because nothing had happened to him yet. Later on, there would be all the amusing things a guy hit on his first day—mistakes and discoveries. It would be easy to write about them tonight in his silent room.

He had never been near the campus of Visalia State, although it was only a three-hour drive from Lakefield.

Still, he had a vague idea of what it was probably like from reading the brochure. Brand-new buildings, lawns still being seeded—it was that kind of place.

His application for residence in one of the new dormitories had been turned down because they were full, with new student housing still under construction. But his father had taken care of his housing through a political friend who had made necessary arrangements. It was in a co-op called Tindall House that provided rooms and meals for students. All Dan needed was to find the place; his room would be waiting.

He felt himself slip into the shadow of apprehension for the new and unknown; something could have gone wrong. With an effort, he brushed that childish fear aside, imagining how Teresa would react to it. Well, he wasn't a kid; not anymore. He could make his way in any situation.

Visalia was there in the road almost as soon as Dan got around to looking for it after they went through Tulare. Why, he could go home from here in the afternoon and be back before morning if he had to.

They were on the streets of the city now and Dan watched them roll by with a curious disapproval. Most of the houses were frame, of a boxy, high-waisted style that wasn't Victorian, but California in another long-since time. They had been built of redwood siding when it was cut a full inch thick and sold for chewing-gum prices—the plastic of that generation.

He noticed the name of the street—Mineralking. The college was on this one, and the co-op only two blocks north on Plum, walking distance from the town.

They hit the business district, showing a lot of old

brick, although new buildings squatted among the antiques like rich foreigners.

Out on the cement with his suitcase in his hand, he would have preferred to walk to Tindall House and not bother anyone. But he didn't know how far it was or whether buses ran that way. He stood in doubt for a couple of minutes, watching the bleak and angry traffic. Then he went back into the station.

"Is there a local bus out to the college?" he inquired at the ticket window.

"Sure," the man said. "Walk up a block and you'll find it." He stared hard at Dan. "They stop at the benches," he added contemptuously. He had a sharp face and hard eyes.

He found the bus stop and waited there a full twenty minutes. After the ride, he hit the street and the vehicle's door slammed shut behind him. He crossed and headed north.

He recognized Tindall House even from a distance. It was a dreary, utterly rectangular, gray stucco building with a flat roof and rows of windows like teeth in its two stories. The front was set flush with the sidewalk. An area around the front-door latch, up three wide, cement steps, showed the wear of countless urgent hands. A bare bulb was burning above the door even now in late afternoon. Dan tried the latch and the door opened. He went inside.

There was a hallway with streaks at hand height on either side, and beyond that French doors opened off on the right into what appeared to be a dayroom. Nobody was there; the place seemed vacant and dead.

He hesitated, glancing around for some kind of office, but there was nothing, so he turned into the dayroom, which was littered with chairs in disorder. A television set at the far end of the room stared at Dan with its morose, gray eye. Here at this end was a battered upright piano, a Knabe, with an old-fashioned screw-up stool. The room was empty. Dan sat down in the nearest chair, his suitcase beside him, and stared at the piano. Somebody would show up sooner or later.

Tindall House wasn't exactly as he'd pictured it. He'd dreamed up a warm place, pulsing with the action and the guys all over. This was old and grim; a smell of new paint mingled with the mustiness of age. The top of Dan's stomach gnawed with disillusionment.

He waited—how long he didn't know. But nobody showed and he was alone, completely. Because there was nothing else to do, he moved over and sat at the piano stool, running his long fingers over the stained keys soundlessly. The piano was ruined, probably out of tune, although once it had been a fine instrument.

Automatically, Dan hit a couple of chords and ran down the keyboard. He whistled softly to himself. It wasn't out of tune; it was sharp with a sweet tone.

For no reason except that he was lonely and scared, he began to finger the keys with his long, bony reach. He dropped into that far-out thing he'd done for Teresa, rough, and in nobody's manner—no style at all but his own.

Dan closed his eyes while he played; he heard the melody minoring around like a lost kid and the chords running back and forth. It was a lousy tune. Later on, when he had some real music in him, he'd do something decent, maybe.

It was finished. He dropped his hands off the keyboard and let them hang down like a couple of catfish, fresh from the mud. Then he tried it again, making some changes and thinking of Teresa while he played. He celebrated her lips, her shape, her womanliness, and finally her clear and lovely self.

While he played, he became aware that somebody was talking to him. The voice said, "Baby, that's all right. I never heard it. Somebody you know do that?"

He swung around on the piano stool, his face pale from being caught.

Dan's first impression was of the beard held down so close to him that the mass of whiskers almost brushed his clean, shivering skin. The beard was red, and above it was a mass of bushy hair, curly and not too well combed. The beard smelled—not of a smell, but of Dan's fear.

He stared. Somewhere inside the beard was a thin, derisive, and cruel mouth. Above that, above a hawk nose, were blue eyes, too blue to be real. And there was this solemn, high-pitched, soft voice.

"Play that one over again for Sally," the person said. "But hit it a little more once for me." It was a command.

Dan blinked.

"I don't—"

"Charlie," said the Beard, "me—I want to hear you again so I can believe it myself. Yet," adding the last word into the caricature of a smile.

Dan hesitated only briefly. Then he swung around and played. What had he called his tune? "San Anselmo and La Via," maybe. He played until the garbage was over.

"Ah," said the Beard. "Man, it finally happened to Tindall House—"

Dan looked blank.

"It has to happen everywhere in a society," the

53

whiskers moved grotesquely in rhythm to the speech. "I was sitting in that big chair," gesturing to a vinyl job with the tall back turned. "I was thinking, 'Up against the wall, Guru Ranganandi,' and you come along. Some kid just out of high school."

"I don't get you—" Dan held both hands together, wondering.

Suddenly, the Beard laughed. He sent laughter rolling around the empty place.

"Look," he said gently, blue eyes squirting sparks, asking questions and giving some answers. "I'm Sally Conn. I don't live here, but I think you're going to. You're a new freshman at State, right?"

"Yes."

"Sure," Sally said. "And I'll guess you're Dan Miller, from some place called Lakefield. Right?"

"Yes."

"Know how I guessed that?"

"No."

"Naturally, you don't. I've seen Cashew's list, that's how, and except for those from out of state, you're the only one who could be named Dan Miller. You're— man, you're from out in the tules here in California. It shows in your face; I'll bet your old man voted for Reagan."

That was true, but the idea of his father's vote had never seemed important. Dan didn't answer.

"Want to play that thing a little more?" Sally Conn asked. "Where did you pick up that last number?"

He said it with such insulting double meaning that a spark of courage flipped through Dan Miller.

"I wrote it," he declared bluntly. "It's mine."

"I knew it! I knew it!" Sally exploded. "I knew it myself as soon as I woke up. You did this little thing yourself. Now—have you got just one more you did yourself—so I can run a quick check on my judgment? Just one more, please—"

Anger hit Dan. This was a pushing around he was getting—some kind of third degree. It rose up in him and welled around like fire, the way his anger always did—not showing, just boiling.

He spun on the stool and hit out "I Couldn't See You There in the Dark," in a smashing, gunning style, beating the keys like hammers and then gentling them down into a whispering. This Sally Conn had sandpapered him and he hated it. But while he played, his anger cooled, ran away like poured lead and hardened. This was his own fault. He'd come into a place he didn't know and fooled around, probably against house rules for freshmen.

When it was over, he turned slowly and got to his feet. Conn had gone off a little way and filled a chair with his big body, sprawled, feet out. He was staring up at the ceiling and mumbling to himself. Freaked out.

"Sorry," Dan offered. "I didn't know I wasn't supposed to play this piano, but I thought nobody was—"

Sally Conn's peculiar blue eyes narrowed down on him once, focused like peep sights, and they turned upward to the ceiling again. The beard rolled back and forth while the man moaned.

"Sorry! Sorry!" he bleated in a strange, horrifying tone. "Yes! You are probably sorry for playing that useless piano that lies around here getting dusty. That's what they've been doing to us all over America—in the schools and homes with their chicken-little forms. They've made the geniuses sorry to be alive, too hum-

55

ble to lay their fingers where they belong. You mustn't touch anything. You have to be sorry for life, sorry for love, sorry for music—"

Dan stood paralyzed by the disjointed words. He searched his numb brain for what to do, trapped here with a complete maniac.

Then he jumped. The Beard had sprung out of his chair in a sort of leap. He was upon a person faster than a rattlesnake could move, shaking a finger into Dan's face so close that his yellow nail almost touched.

"Was Beethoven sorry?" Sally Conn yelled. "Do you think Mozart trembled about the lousy rules?"

"I—"

"No!" Sally screamed as if seeking out Greek gods on high. "So don't you ever tell me again that you're sorry, Miller. Not in your four years here at State. Not at any time you're with us. If you do, I swear I'll slap you across the mouth or something!"

Dan stood still, his eyes barely able to meet that startling blue.

"Wait here. Don't move an inch!" Conn said abruptly.

He bounded away. Now Dan was aware of how big he was—a full six feet four, maybe, and over two hundred pounds. He was wearing slacks, a faded shirt, and an absolutely beautiful vest of black glove leather.

He was back in the room almost immediately.

"I shouldn't have been so long," he told Dan with a note of genuine apology, "but it still takes me a full thirty seconds to pick the lock on Cashew's office. He's the housemother here. You'll meet him."

"But—"

"I'm getting better," Sally said. "It used to be a full

minute. Well, sure enough, as I suspected, they had you in with Gil Morton and Chris Blaisdell. Morton is business administration, and Blaisdell's ambition is to make a career of breeding sheep. They'd kill you in two weeks. Why, you'd flunk out with Morton and Blaisdell to help you. How they love to flunk out wandering kids like you, Miller."

Something in Dan let go. He felt a resignation, an acceptance of this wild experience. He went over to a chair and sat down.

"Look," he said, "I don't have any idea what you're talking about, you know," meeting Conn's blue blazes full on with real defiance. "I'm new here. I just got in on the bus and I don't get a thing you're saying. So why not give it to me straight?"

Conn clapped a big hand against his forehead. "Naturally, you haven't, and it's my own fault," he said balefully. "I talk too much instead of communicating. I talk first and explain later—"

He paused, gulped deep blasts of air into the beard, and suddenly broke into a broad grin that dropped years from his appearance. Dan saw that he couldn't be more than twenty-two.

"I guess," he said.

"Look," Conn said, "I was sitting in that deep chair —I'm explaining to you now—and thinking about this Ranganandi, this phony. Oh, I suppose he is some sort of Indian philosopher, but pure Establishment and paid for it. He tells us last night to seek the other world and not riot in this one. Pure hoke, you understand, but soothing. So I was in that chair, thinking it out. You came in and played the piano. When I heard your tune, Miller, the whole answer came to me again. They're toads, all of them. This is the time of the toad. We can't believe any of them. We've got to fight our way out of this swamp and protect our minstrels."

"Riots?" Dan asked.

Conn laughed harshly. "Not here at Visalia State, Dan," he said. "Around here they haven't heard of the Free Speech Movement yet. Any riots or demonstrations around here are still locked up with the individuals. But it'll come soon; it's coming to every college in the country—even Texas A & M." He shrugged. "But forget that now. The point is that I changed you from Morton and Blaisdell to Caroway and Gutierrez. It's Room 23. Pick up your suitcase and I'll take you there."

Dan stood, but he didn't move. His father had set this thing up and he was probably supposed to room with Morton and Blaisdell, with plenty of trouble ahead if he didn't.

"Come on," Sally insisted. "Get your suitcase and follow me."

Dan moved at last. He followed Conn into the hallway and up a murky stairway. The bearded guy found a door and shoved it open. Behind him, Dan peered inside.

The room was large, with three single beds. There were three small dressers, closets, blatant posters on the walls, one saying in Spanish, "¡Viva la huelga!" the lettering splashed wide in scarlet.

Dan stared at the poster curiously, vaguely remembering something about it. Suddenly he knew. He had seen it before when pickets had tried to force a couple of stores in Lakefield to stop selling table grapes and instead had gotten themselves run out of town. It was the slogan of the grape strike centering at the town of

58

Delano here in the valley. Some guy named Chavez was trying to organize a union for farm workers. The grape pickers had been on strike for five years now. Some of the aggies around Cal Poly had bumper stickers saying, "Eat grapes, the forbidden fruit."

In a corner was a twelve-string guitar, old and well-used. On one of the beds somebody lay face down.

Sally motioned Dan inside with vigorous gestures. Then he shut the door.

"That's Uvaldo," he said loudly, indicating the sleeping kid. "When Gutierrez sleeps, he dies. That's because he sits up most of the night studying and writing revolutionary tracts about grapes. None of his tracts are worth a damn." The big guy walked close to the bed. "Uvaldo!" he yelled.

The prone figure stirred, shifted, and slept on.

"See," Conn said delightedly. "Isn't it wonderful to be able to sleep that way in the daytime? Gutierrez has a precious talent."

"Why not let him—"

Too late. Sally had advanced upon the bed. He seized Uvaldo by an arm and a leg and literally threw him into an upright posture.

"It's the only way," Sally explained. "Wake up!" he screamed into the Mexican kid's ear. "Gutierrez, the dormitory is on fire."

Even under those circumstances, Dan saw that Uvaldo was handsome, with black, wavy hair, fine features, and an olive skin. He was small—like a bundle in Conn's hands.

"Let it burn," he mumbled. "Who cares?"

He opened his dark-brown eyes and looked at Dan.

"This is one of the survivors?" he asked. "Now that is an example of God's will."

"Shut up, Uvaldo," Conn said good-naturedly. "This is Dan Miller, your new roommate. Wake up and show some hospitality."

The Mexican kid came awake, blinking his eyes. "This is—"

"Dan Miller," Sally repeated. "He composes music. You want him to compose an oratorio for the Di Giorgio ranch next week? He will if you don't do something."

Uvaldo smiled and got off the bed. "Hello, Dan," he said. "Welcome. I hope you like it with us. Bud Caroway is out—maybe with a girl. He plays the guitar. Sit down and I'll make us some instant coffee. You want coffee?"

Dan took a breath. He liked Uvaldo immediately. "Sure," he said. "Thanks."

"Sit down, please," Uvaldo replied. "Take the chair, or perhaps you'd prefer your bed."

"I'll sit on the bed," Dan told him.

"So will I," Conn declared. "It's clean. Now hurry with the coffee, Gutierrez. I'm very dry from the effort of waking you."

"It's—ah—nice to have you, Dan," Uvaldo said. "Don't mind Conn. He's from Texas, which should explain a great deal. He's a Texas Jew, and this is a burden for him."

5

Uvaldo's version of coffee was very strong and primitive, and too hot for the paper cups he served it in. They had barely taken the first experimental sip when the door opened and Bud Caroway stepped inside. He stared at Dan, grinned, and demanded, "Where's mine?"

"Fix it yourself," Uvaldo told him amiably.

Bud nodded. He was tall and loose-jointed, with fine, sandy hair that didn't stay in place. He wore long sideburns and a moustache that curved downward around his mouth corners. His hair bunched heavily around his ears and over his shirt collar, but it wasn't long like Sally's. He spoke with a faint Southwestern accent, all but concealed.

"This is Dan Miller," Conn announced impersonally. "He's your new roomie, Bud."

Caroway shrugged. "Why not?"

He heated the water in his cup with the coil plugged in at the wall, stirred in a heap of coffee, tasted, blew out his cheeks and sat down on his rumpled bed.

"You got troubles?" Sally asked.

"Sure," Bud said. "Economics. Why do I have to

take economics in this college? Any of you ever had a course in economics?"

"Yes," said Sally. "But I'm older and more mature than you are, Caroway. I liked it."

"A guy like you would," Bud replied. "But did you have it from this character, Fulmin?"

"Fulmin?" Uvaldo inquired.

"Right. I just met him," Bud said, making a face like nausea. "Now I have a class with him all next semester. If I didn't have hope and a savage love of life, I'd kill myself."

"You're only a sophomore, Bud," Conn said, using a wise tone, "not a senior like me. Otherwise you'd know that Economics I is good for sophomores. If you get it from Fulmin, all the better."

"Don't give me that," Caroway said.

"I mean it. With Fulmin, Economics I in this college gives you a better picture of the Establishment than you could pay for. A sophomore comes out of Fulmin's class ready to bomb the stock exchange. Good stuff; helps the mind. What do you think college is for, Bud? Guitars?"

Caroway lay back with his legs dangling over the edge of the bed, loose and limp. He drank his coffee that way, turning his head to gulp it. "Sure," he said. "It's for guitars. What else? You think it's for a lot of phony Maoist hoke, Conn. Man—the people are the river and we revolutionaries are the fish. That's what you say. Give me guitars."

Sally turned to Dan. "You see," he said, obviously pleased, "you room with these simple peasants. You'll like it, Miller. Caroway keeps trying to weasel out of his responsibilities in the social revolution, but he's really with us all the way. Why? Because he has to be.

All peasants do." He spoke to the others. "Cashew had him signed up with Morton and Blaisdell, so I—"

Bud sat up abruptly and met Dan's eyes. "What was your crime?" he wanted to know. "Or are you some kind of sheep-management type yourself?"

"He is not," the big guy said. "He composes music."

Bud fell back with a profound sigh. "Oh," he murmured, "another of those."

"Not another. I said, he composes music. Ever heard of music, Bud?"

"How is he on economics?"

"Like you, only worse. You'll have to coach him."

"Okay," Bud said, drinking the last of his coffee. "Hello, Miller. How did you get mixed in with the guerrillas?"

"Hello," Dan said.

"Shut up, Caroway," Sally went on jovially. "I'd take you down to the dayroom right now and have Miller show you. But you're too lazy. You're a discredit to the movement. You can find out later for yourself."

"All right, all right," Bud said. "I believe you. Conn, you talk too much. There's too much of the Thoughts of Chairman Sally Conn around here."

Sally poked Dan in the ribs, grinning through his beard. "See!" he said. "They admire me. I'm their leader. I'm their Marxist guideline."

"Like hell you are," said Bud. "Take not a needle or a piece of thread," sing-song. "How do you like that for a guideline?"

Conn ignored him, still speaking to Dan. "Caroway is just an empty head, like so many students. The great semanticist and college president S. I. Hayakawa calls his kind the 'great middle group.' Hayakawa would enjoy Bud. Now Uvaldo's big thing is grapes. He's the

63

Third World wheel around here, very advanced in his thinking about the grape strike, farm unions, and other trivia. Knows Cesar Chavez and Dolores Huerta personally. Caroway, however, will disappoint you. He's middle class and a tool of the military-industrial complex who imagines he's part of the New Left. I wouldn't be surprised if he went to work for Dow Chemical when he graduates. If he graduates. But he's fairly good on his guitar."

From the bed, Bud made a far-out noise but said nothing. Uvaldo only smiled.

With the cup of hot coffee, Dan's initial shock and embarrassment had faded. Maybe he should have insisted on rooming with Morton and Blaisdell. He resented being forced into rooming with guys he had never seen before. But how could he explain to Mr. Cashew? Better to leave it the way it was.

Conn was watching him closely. Now the guy said to Uvaldo, "I suppose you and Bud have all your stuff piled in Dan's closet?"

"Sure," said Uvaldo. "I'll shove some of it over. He's only got one suitcase."

"Do it, then. Let him hang up his suit. Dan, you brought a suit?"

"Yes."

"Uh-huh. I'm sure you'd have a suit. Well, push over, Gutierrez. Let him hang up; he may have shirts."

"I hope so. I like nice shirts."

"These bums," Sally said. "No manners. A Jew would make you welcome, Dan. A Jew would give you his own closet."

Uvaldo laughed. "Jews!" he exclaimed. "In with The Man. Always writing books, giving speeches, leading revolutions, getting elected, making money."

64

"Trotsky was a Jew," said Sally. "Einstein—"

"Jack Kennedy, Mao, Nixon, Cesar Chavez, Bill Cosby," said Uvaldo, "all Jews. Everybody's a Jew. So don't worry about it, Dan. Conn is some kind of professional."

He had moved to the wardrobe closet and started shifting garments and laying others on Caroway's bed. He picked up a couple of pairs of shoes and tossed them somewhere.

"It's all yours," he finally said. "Cleared."

"I don't need all that room. Put some of the things back."

Gutierrez smiled. "Not now. Later."

Conn lumbered to his feet. "I'd help you unpack your stuff, Miller," he said as if he meant it, "but I've got to split out now. An appointment—" He met Dan's eyes. "And don't worry. You'll get along with these guys. When they tell you the whole student thing is about racism, poverty, and Vietnam war and police harassment, they'll be telling the truth. It's as simple as that, and also very complex."

He took off, closing the door behind him very quietly.

His prediction turned out true, although it took Dan a while to realize that he had been lucky to meet Sally Conn on his first afternoon.

He went to bed early that night without writing the letter he had composed in his mind to Teresa. Even so, sleep was impossible. Bud put in a couple of hours on his guitar with folk rock, good but disturbing, and Uvaldo stayed up half the night reading and hammering out pages of writing on an old portable typewriter.

It wasn't until about two in the morning that Dan fell asleep. He dreamed of Teresa. She was telling Sally

65

Conn to shave and to leave Dan Miller alone, but Sally, in the dream, only laughed and laughed.

He woke up regretting he was here, but he had to change his mind after breakfast in the Tindall House cafeteria. Bud Caroway took him in tow, insisting that he had nothing better to do. They drove to the college in his battered Volkswagen, and the guy shepherded Dan through registration, in the process introducing him to about fifty kids.

Visalia State was as Dan had pictured it, raw and new, with the planted trees along the curving walkways young and small, and new construction going up at the edges of things. The architecture had a no-nonsense functionalism and was all in reinforced concrete.

For a guitar player on about three hours' sleep, Bud had fanciful energy. He dragged Dan everywhere—to his classrooms so he would know where they were, to the little theater, the library, and finally to the administration building.

"We're going to close this one up," he said, "maybe this year."

Dan didn't understand what he meant. Not yet, at least.

They grabbed a sandwich and a Coke at El Vaquero, as it was called, the combined bookstore and snack bar.

"Means cowboy," Bud said, his lips twisting into a grimace. "Us Visalia State kids are *vaqueros*. But if they named us for the local surroundings it ought to be El Grape Picker. Delano isn't too far." He shrugged elaborately. "You feel like a cowboy, Miller?"

"No. I don't."

"Me, neither," Caroway replied seriously, "and not

much like a grape or cotton picker. Uvaldo's the guy who's had experience in that."

Dan shot Bud a quick glance and looked away. For a while this morning he had wondered how he was expected to pay Bud for all the help he was getting. But now he knew. Nothing was expected. For the whole time, Caroway had treated him like a friend.

Impulsively, he said, "Bud, you're all right on the guitar. I play piano a little. Maybe we could get together sometime, and—"

"Why not?" Caroway answered in an offhand style. "Conn seemed to think you had something."

Dan laughed. "You know how it is with nonmusicians. They think the lousiest stuff is good."

Caroway shook his head. "Sally's a kind of musician himself—a—a creative listener. If he says you're good, Dan, that's it. He never told me anything like that. He tells me I have a fairly sharp social sense in music."

That bothered Dan, because Bud was all right. But he decided not to push the thing around anymore. Besides, Caroway said they ought to split. He had to see a girl in about an hour.

Back at Tindall House, Dan went up to the room, which was empty. He wrote a long letter to Teresa, telling her in a dozen ways how much he loved her. He gave her the details of his trip and this first day at the college with regular classes to begin on Monday.

He didn't say much about Bud and Uvaldo except that they were his roommates, and he didn't mention Sally Conn at all. The red-bearded guy couldn't be described to Teresa, because more than once she had expressed deep scorn for hippie types. Besides that, Dan was confused by his new acquaintances. He really hadn't understood them too well, especially the talk about the New Left and "revolution." Half the time they had sounded as if they were joking with each other, and then there was a serious note.

At the administration building, Bud had said, "We're going to close this one up." If that meant what it sounded like, literally, Dan wanted no part of it.

He went out on the street and mailed the letter at a box on the corner. When he returned he went to the dayroom and found Uvaldo there alone, reading. It suddenly occurred to him that Gutierrez was, after all, a Mexican with a dark skin, though yesterday the idea hadn't even entered his mind. There were Mexicans in Lakefield, but they kept to themselves—in school and in the town.

"Hi," he said awkwardly when Uvaldo looked up. "Reading?" It was a stupid thing to say. Naturally, the guy was reading. He had the book open.

"It's about the history of union labor," Uvaldo said seriously. "You know, in the beginning they fought the Establishment to get their rights, and when they had their rights, they fought each other."

"I don't know much about—union labor."

"I guess not. Did you get registered?"

He certainly didn't sound like a Mexican, Dan thought. He talked like anyone else—except that his voice seemed kinder.

"Yes."

"Any trouble? Did you see your adviser? Who's he?"

"Potrero," Dan replied. "John Potrero, I think—"

Uvaldo laughed. "You mean, Juan," he said, "so that tells me you signed up as a major in English with probably a minor in music. I know Dr. Potrero. He's all right if you can forget he's a Mexican."

68

Dan was startled, wondering how to reply. "I—" he began.

Uvaldo had closed his book and walked over beside him.

"That was a stupid thing for me to say to you right now," he offered. "I'm Mexican too, and it confuses you, doesn't it?"

"Yes," Dan admitted.

Uvaldo's eyes seemed to narrow. "Look," he said, "let me put it this way: there's a big fight here in the valley and it can get more bitter between Mexicans. It's like a feud among cousins. Dr. Potrero has position, but he's stayed out of the whole business. Hands off, you see. He's kept himself clean and risked nothing. Know about Chavez?"

"Not really."

"How about the grape strike? Hear of that?"

"Yes," he said.

"Well, it's life and death to plenty of people here in the valley," Uvaldo said, "and Potrero keeps out of it. He's just kidding himself, trying to hang on to a soft touch like so many of these damned Mexican-Americans. You enjoy English literature?"

"I don't know. Not yet."

"Why didn't you sign up for science? Scared of the work?"

Dan's back stiffened. "No, I'm not scared," he said. He felt Gutierrez measuring him down to the final cell, the last corpuscle. He had gotten himself some great roommates.

Uvaldo nodded. "You don't think you're so smart in science. Neither did I. But, Dan, you ought to change your mind soon. I started fooling around with languages, but now I'm going to graduate in math. It's where the money and the power is right now, and I know that the guys want to get as far away from the Establishment as possible. But it's science and math right now if you want to keep ahead in this jungle, believe me—" Gutierrez looked away, off into some distant place in his own mind. "Imagine," he said, a tinge of disgust in his voice, "Potrero lecturing on Chaucer. He's a sellout."

Dan didn't know what to say.

Right then a half dozen Tindall residents clomped in and the dayroom suddenly was full of the telegraphy of mingled voices.

Uvaldo said "Hi" to a blond, stocky kid with a machine-gun haircut that showed pink scalp on top, got his book, and with a gesture of resignation to Dan, got out of there.

Dan stayed and the blond kid came over to him at once.

"Greetings," he said, shoving out a freckled paw. "I'm Waldo Jones. You must be Dan Miller. Heard about you." His voice was a kind of shout. He was grinning and showed a startling row of square, white teeth in a wide mouth.

"That's right," Dan said.

"How'd you get in with that gang of troublemakers so fast?" Jones wanted to know. "Conn, Gutierrez, and Bud Caroway. They'll ruin you, Miller. Get you expelled from dear old Visalia State. And getting expelled from here is like having your visa to Tierra del Fuego canceled."

"I don't know," Dan said honestly.

Waldo grinned. "You're probably a born troublemaker yourself," he shouted. "Next thing, Uvaldo will

70

be having you carry a '*Viva la huelga*' sign down in La-mont or somewhere."

"I don't—"

"Sure you don't. But you will. You'll know," said Jones. "Me—I'm staying out of trouble. Look at my haircut, man. No trouble in me. The Bank of America even lends me money to go to school. I want to get my degree, marry this crazy girl, and make so much money I can't count it. I'm also going to do my hitch in the Army without one bleat of pain. Know why, Miller?"

The impact of Waldo Jones was rough, but Dan felt a compelling warmth in the guy. "Of course not," he said.

"Because I spent a summer in Prince Rupert, Canada. I'm not a bit sure whether I'd rather live there than under fascism and the military-industrial thing. So let Uvaldo talk all he likes about the social struggle. I'll stick around here for mine and see what happens." He looked away. "Well, glad to meet you, Miller. See you around." He paused, reflecting. "Anyone tell you about this thing at Conn's tonight?"

"No."

"They will," said Waldo. "I'll see you there. Oh, they'll hook you. Takes a tough inner character like mine to withstand them. Sirens, they are. Not the women, so much. Maybe a couple of them. But I've got a girl in San Diego who's more beautiful than Elizabeth Taylor ever was, and she doesn't know it. If I hurry, nobody will ever tell her the truth—the stupes."

He started to go and swung back.

"Complete stupes," he said, "vain and arrogant. World's full of them."

Dan hung around the dayroom a while longer, trying to assemble Waldo Jones and everything else in his mind. He was terribly confused. In Lakefield, nobody ever talked about Trotsky and Mao, fascism, or the military-industrial complex. That was stuff you read about in the newspapers—if you wanted to read it. And yet Jones had said he was a born troublemaker. Maybe he was.

He felt a sudden need to go upstairs and write another letter to Teresa. He wanted to tell her everything that had happened and how strange it was. He wanted to say that in all his years at Lakefield High School he had never met anyone like Sally, Bud, and Uvaldo, and that he was drawn to them against better judgment.

He particularly wanted to tell her about Waldo Jones. He sensed that Waldo stood in the dead center of everything, and that he did too. From where he was, he could go in any direction.

6

"HE'S GOT an apartment," Bud Caroway said, "or rather, it's a flat. Four rooms. Otherwise we'd need to get together out in the bushes somewhere."

Uvaldo explained very seriously, "His father manufactures pants in Austin, Texas. This gives him the bread to rent a flat and has influenced his beliefs in some way I don't understand."

Caroway had his guitar; he strummed a couple of chords. "Easy," he said, muting the strings. "Pants, Gutierrez, are a basic. Everybody needs pants—even a Marxist. But if a father makes big money on a basic cultural need, his son is likely to be interested in the class struggle of pants."

Uvaldo sounded annoyed. "Bud," he said, "you always joke. If you'd grown up in Lamont instead of Berkeley and Oklahoma, you wouldn't think it was funny. You know nothing of poverty, beans, hunger, and constant economic anxiety. You don't understand how a whole people can be enslaved by a single agricultural complex. So don't make senseless cracks."

"All right," Bud replied easily. "But I still think there's something in my pants theory about Conn."

73

"So, all right," Uvaldo agreed. "Think it." He turned to Dan. "What we were saying is that Sally—his real name is Sol—is going to have this bunch over to his flat tonight. Nothing important, just some people. Want to go?"

Dan hesitated; he wasn't so sure he wanted to meet a strange crowd tonight. He was tired from the day of registration and the tension of trying to fit into a new place. But Uvaldo's sincerity was impressive.

"All right," he said. "I'd like to. That is, if—"

"Conn told us to be sure to bring you," Bud said from his cot. "You're in, Dan."

"He means you're invited," Gutierrez interpreted, watching Dan with an almost embarrassing understanding, as if he knew what it was to be shy and anxious. "We'll go in Caroway's heap, four cylinders and three 'Hail Marys.' "

"Four 'Hail Marys,' " Bud corrected. "One for each cylinder." He hit it on the guitar with "This Land Is Your Land," and Uvaldo lay down on his own bed as if the matter was settled.

There wasn't any special time to get to Conn's flat. They ate dinner in the Tindall House cafeteria, not too good but substantial in the institutional style. It was nine thirty before they finally set out.

Bud drove in an aimless way through the dark streets of Visalia, up toward the foothills above the college, finally stopping at a two-story stucco building. The street was littered with cars, parked bumper to bumper, and they had to walk a block.

"Conn's opulence," Bud remarked as they reached the building. "A flat. Only the rich can afford to be revolutionaries. The rest of us have to stick with the herd. Who is it that calls them 'Mustang Militants' be-

74

cause they'll drive their sports cars to the barricades?"

"It's Luce, that Young Americans for Freedom guy. YAF is the right wing's answer to the New Left, Dan," Uvaldo said. "And don't mind Bud. He gets carried away."

"Only toward early morning, Uvaldo," Bud replied. "I'm usually all right for a while."

There was a flight of steps in back of the building. The three walked back and mounted the steps.

"It's on the second floor and in back here," Caroway said. "Conn claims that no noise gets out."

"Forget that," Uvaldo reassured Dan. "There's no big noise around Sally's place. It's more like quiet." He hesitated. "Say, some guy up there might just smoke a little pot or something. Maybe drink some wine. Is that going to bother you, Dan?"

"No."

"I don't go for anything myself," Uvaldo said. "Sometimes Bud drinks wine, but not often. He was kidding about being carried out. Bud has maybe one glass of wine."

"Two," laughing. "I'm uninhibited."

"So all right. Two. Conn doesn't touch anything, either. But there might be others, Dan, and—"

"Sure. I understand." It was an old and familiar story, even in Lakefield. Always somebody.

Uvaldo had been right about the noise. At the door no sound reached them. It was unlatched. Bud turned the knob and they went inside, where perhaps twenty people sat around. A low-level stereo of superb quality permeated the room like a fragrance without insisting itself upon the conversation. Dan recognized Berlioz with approval. At the far end of the room was an upright piano, polished darkly.

There were more boys than girls, a few with long hair and beards, but others on the trimmer side. They struck a range of variety that contrasted with the girls, who seemed of a single type, hair long and straight.

The surprise for Dan was Waldo Jones, squatted over by the stereo and in earnest conversation with Sally. He looked as out of place there as a buffalo nickel among Spanish treasure.

Jones glanced up at Dan immediately and waved a greeting, while Conn heaved himself to his sandaled feet and padded over.

"Meet some of these people, Miller," he commanded. "Here's Dirk Hollings."

Hollings said "Hi" and turned back to the girl he was with. He was languid, very black, and handsome. His hair was combed into a tall Afro.

"Hollings is our big BSU cat," Conn said in a proprietary voice. "He's trying to organize something around here, but it's rough going. Black may be beautiful, but not at Visalia State."

"It's like brown being beautiful," Uvaldo put in. "The idea isn't popular."

Quickly, Sally took Dan to others in the room—Joe Phillips, Tom Lawrence, Brooks Nelson, Fran Smith, were the names Dan remembered. They all smiled, coming on cool as if they had known him always.

"And here," Sally finished, "is Jenny Darien. Move over on that pad, Jenny, and let Dan sit down."

"Hello, Dan," Jenny replied, lifting her long brown lashes. She shifted on the cushion and made a place for him.

Dan glanced at her briefly. Her hair was brushed, shining, light brown, and natural. She wore almost no makeup except something faint at her lips, and eye

76

shadow. She had high cheekbones, an oval face with a wide, generous mouth, but beyond that nothing registered. Jenny really was rather plain—a girl like a hundred others he had seen.

He sat beside her while Sally, Uvaldo, and Bud wandered off toward the kitchen.

The girl's hip pressed against him, and he glanced nervously at the edge of the cushion. If he moved over, half of him would be on the floor. He sat still, staring straight ahead while the talk buzzed like a swarm of friendly hornets and Berlioz thrummed violins in an exquisite background. For an instant, Dan almost blamed Berlioz for his discomfort, there being nobody else in the room he really knew.

Not for long. The girl's cool, soft voice enveloped him.

"You're uneasy, aren't you, Dan?"

It was this chick, Jenny.

"Yes," he croaked. "I guess. I'm a—I'm a freshman."

It was a really stupid thing to say—a conversational mudpie. He felt unreasonably awkward; he didn't fit here. For a moment, he thought desperately of Teresa, longing for her.

Jenny laughed gently. "I know what you mean. I came last year at midterm. I'm a freshman and a half, but I'm younger than you."

"What makes you think—"

"You must be at least twenty. I'm only eighteen."

Dan almost said, "Yes, I'm twenty." But he didn't. "I'm eighteen too," he said.

"Do you like it here in Visalia?"

He tried on the lie for size and rejected it. "No," he blurted. "I don't. Not yet, at least."

Again Jenny laughed, her tone low and faintly musical. "I hated it when I first came. I was so lonesome I could have died. But it all came around. It will with you, Dan."

He was silent.

"Where's your home?"

"Lakefield. It's a dumb little town on the coast. You don't—"

"I know," she said. "I've driven through there a lot on the way from San Francisco to Los Angeles. It's really a pretty place—all those hills. You've been lucky to live there. I'm from Oakland."

"Why is it lucky?"

"If you lived in Oakland, you'd know, Dan," Jenny said.

It seemed to him that her hip was even closer. A warm spot burned on his leg; he wished she would move over.

Berlioz stopped and again Jenny turned to him. "Excuse me a minute, will you?" she asked. "I'm going to pour coffee. For those who want coffee. Would you like some?"

"Yes," he said, "please."

She stood with a kind of ballet grace and his eyes followed her as she walked toward the kitchen. The girl was plain, sure, but she had a smashing shape, almost like Teresa's except that the Jenny chick was taller. And she was as nice as anyone he had ever met. It hit him that he had felt an instant friendliness and warmth from her that registered as genuine.

She was back at once with a glass coffee urn, moving around the room with a silence and care that made her almost invisible. Dan noticed that some of the people were drinking wine, but nobody was loud. At least not yet. He had been to a few parties in Lakefield and this wasn't like any of them.

Waldo Jones suddenly materialized, holding a paper cup and standing above him.

"How're you doing?" he shouted, grinning with a flash of those astonishingly white, square teeth. "Having fun?"

"I—"

"You don't know yet," Jones said. "So stick around. You may like us."

He moved away. For a second, Dan wondered about his saying "us" as if he were solidly a part of this bunch where he obviously didn't belong, as if he and Conn were alike in some concealed way. Waldo Jones looked like an assistant manager of something.

Jenny came back as quietly as she had gone, carrying a cup of coffee, which she gave to him. In silence, she folded herself into a lotus, on the cushion beside him. The stereo was mute; nothing but talk punctuated the compound sentence of the room. Into that background she began singing a submerged and unheard tune. It took him a while to pick it up.

He recognized a folk song from the Georgia islands: "Let Your Little Light Shine." Her voice wasn't much, small, fairly pleasant. Music wasn't her thing, that was clear.

In midphrase, she stopped.

"Sally said you're a composer," she ventured.

He laughed. "Not really."

Jenny smiled, wide and bright, and the expression sparkled in her brown eyes. "Oh, one of those," she said. "Modest. No self-image."

"I don't understand you," he said after thinking.

Her smile melted into something serious. "You

79

really don't, do you?" She was searching him, but not sharply. "So you're for real, after all."

"I don't—"

"Of course not," Jenny said. "Sorry for asking. I could have waited and found out for myself. I was rude."

"No," he told her. "It's just that I can't say I'm a composer. Not now, anyway. Maybe sometime in—in a few years, I might do something I—that I liked myself, and—"

She turned away and looked into the endless distances that walls provide. "You're a good head, Dan," she said, coming back to him abruptly. "I so hope we can be friends."

Right there, Hollings lazied by and stopped before them.

"Jenny," he said, "how's everybody's girl friend?"

"Wonderful. And you?"

"Couldn't be better unless I had another glass of wine."

"So—why not?"

"Think I will. I'm already pointed that way."

He didn't even speak to Dan. Hollings acted as if Dan didn't exist. He moved toward the kitchen.

The term "everybody's girl friend" wandered around in Dan's mind in an unpleasant way. It had implications he didn't like, but it was no concern of his. A lot of chicks were "everybody's girl friend" these days.

"Isn't he cool?" Jenny said. "He has potential, but he's still playing games most of the time. I wish he'd get over that."

The girl, Fran Smith, suddenly laughed too sharply so that the tone cut across the room.

"I can't stand this anymore," she said shrilly. "Somebody turn up the music."

Somebody did. Dan watched her. She was tall, pretty, and brunette. Now she was standing and unbuttoning her blouse.

Jenny spoke to him, sounding close. "Fran always has to do her act at every party. It's a compulsion."

Dan forced himself to watch. Now Fran's skirt came off, but beneath she was wearing a black leotard. She began to dance to the music, if that was what she was doing, a free-form undulation that was part sensuous, part bathos—a mixture of the ludicrous and the real.

People looked at her for a while and then grew bored and went on with what they had been doing. Dan felt infinitely sorry for the girl, dancing alone. Obviously she was in a world of her own design and nobody in the room seemed to care.

"Okay, Fran," somebody said quite loudly, but the girl didn't hear. She danced on and on in the center of the room, oblivious to everything else. Her eyes had closed as if by some inward vision. She had drunk too much wine.

Dan riveted his attention on the girl while he tightened his mind around an image of Teresa. The girl was making a fool of herself and by ignoring her, everyone was saying it. But no human being deserved to be ignored that way. He hated it, and everyone there.

Suddenly, Jenny said, "Dan, this isn't what it's all about. It isn't what you're thinking—stupid and cruel. Fran's a great girl who's a straight-A student, but after a glass of wine she always thinks she can dance. It's too bad, but it doesn't take anything away from Fran. She's my friend; everyone here likes her for what she really is."

"Then why do they act as if she wasn't really there?"

"Because it's the kindest thing to do. Dan, it's that leotard that gets you. If she took off all her clothes and was naked, it wouldn't be so self-conscious. It's one silly little aspect of Fran's character, and I'll not have you thinking anything else about my friend, because I like you too much. She's great, and so is nearly everyone else here. You'll find that out after you've been around long enough." She sounded severe, almost maternal.

"All right," he said. And, changing the subject, "What are you doing here? I mean—"

"Not anything, really," she answered at once. "Maybe for the same reasons you're here. Sally's a militant who wants a confrontation at Visalia. But I'm not really an activist. Too scared, I suppose. I like the people here because they're friendly and alive." She smiled at him. "So are you. You can't fool me, Dan Miller, and I like you—a lot. But don't be stupid too long, please."

"Stupid?"

For an instant, it seemed that she almost kissed him with that strange smile still on her lips. But she didn't. Instead she became very serious.

"I'm sorry. It wasn't the right word. I just want to keep you, that's all. I don't want you running off just because Fran happened to do her thing. Maybe next time I'll do mine and then you'll be sorry. Mine is really wild."

He connected that remark at once with what Hollings had said, so he kept silent, and he sensed immediately that she knew what he was thinking.

Well, she didn't mean a thing to him, but she did make him feel uneasy—as if he was missing something important about her. In one way, he was grateful to her. He sensed obscurely that he had reached some sort of turning point in his life. He was in college, registered, and admitted to this scene that was entirely new to him. It was Jenny who had led him into the picture with a surety and warmth that puzzled him. Unless she was everybody's girl, how could she act this way with a total stranger?

Slowly, he began to relax; he lifted his eyes without fear and measured the people in the room, older than he was, most of them, but he had seen their counterparts before.

Sure, Conn and Uvaldo were different; they had something on their minds that shaped every word they said, every action. Dan didn't know what it was, but he intended to find out and to accept or reject them. Visalia State or not, this was his college and he was here, part of a new world.

Oddly, he knew that he belonged and that Jenny Darien had told him so in a subtle way that was kind. He did like her. In a sense, she was his girl too.

He turned to her and grinned. "Thanks," he said.

"For what?"

He almost said, "For being everybody's girl friend," but he held that.

"For explaining—for telling me about Fran, and—and everything. I guess I am stupid."

In an easy gesture, she slipped her hand into his and made of her warm fingers a special greeting.

"Dan," she said earnestly, "I said you were real and now I know you are. Nobody ever sees you anymore.

They even say you don't exist, but you do. Somewhere, someplace, Dan comes along, and he's real," she shook her head, "until day after tomorrow, at least."

"Real?"

"Real," she repeated. Her eyes danced suddenly, as one of those mysterious lulls that happen in crowds made the room almost silent. The stereo had been turned off. "Look," she said in a teasing voice, "if you really like me, you'll do me a favor right now."

He was wary, but still he smiled. "Sure," he told her. "You name it."

"Play the piano," simply.

"No," he replied at once, cold panic in his mind like a mouse in a wall, gnawing.

But she was up on her feet and had bent down to take one of his hands. "Please," coaxing. "Just a little bit—for me."

Dan had seen plenty of people being coy about doing their thing; it was a nauseating sight, because they always got around to it after everyone had begged enough.

"All right," he said abruptly. It would only take a couple of minutes and then he could crawl away somewhere and forget it. "Come on."

He and the girl crossed the room swiftly. The talk had risen again; if he played very softly nobody would even hear him. He stumbled onto the piano bench and began to play Teresa's song again, this time with his touch so feathery as to be almost muted in the sound of voices. He was halfway through before he noticed the silence, and then he was finished. He stood up and began to get out of there.

"Hey!" somebody said. "How about that?"

84

"I told you, didn't I?" another voice responded. "Now maybe you'll believe it."

"That's our Sally," a girl said. "Right again."

Dan didn't look at them. He got back to the pad and sat down, burning. Jenny was beside him. "Sorry," he told her.

"I'm not even going to answer that," she said seriously, "because it's stupid of you to say it. But thank you, Dan, so very much."

"For what?"

"For being so—" She stopped and put her hand on his arm.

"Hush," she said. "Greg Abrams is going to let go of another of his poems about the superstate, or ROTC, or the Establishment's stated principles as opposed to its actions. Listen!"

He glanced hard at her; Jenny's brown eyes were dancing.

"Listen to Greg," she commanded. "He may be the next Allen Ginsberg. But maybe not." Jenny looked away. "No, I don't think you'll catch on day after tomorrow. They'll probably mow you down and it'll hurt. But you'll survive. You've got something inside that can't be touched by anyone, I know. I've seen it once before but I never expected to see it again."

He shook his head. "Now you do have me spinning around."

"Hush," she told him gravely. "Listen to the new Allen Ginsberg."

7

SALLY SAT in one of the straight-backed chairs, reversed so that he straddled it. He leaned over the top like a gargoyle, his beard thrust forward.

"Dan," he said sharply, chewing up each word, "my father had gone to see the sheriff of this town we lived in—Sunnyrim. It's near the Pedernales Valley, not more than twenty miles from Johnson City. Ever hear of it?"

"No."

"Naturally. Texas is full of towns like Sunnyrim that nobody ever heard of. My dad's business is in Austin, but the family lived there."

Dan nodded, trying to understand Conn and Texas.

"Anyway, my father had gone there to see the sheriff about something, maybe a permit of some sort. I was fifteen years old—right at that time they're telling you about how Americans are all born free and equal. If you're fifteen years old in Texas, see, you do a man's work, they say, and you're big enough to know about men's so-called Texas responsibilities. Get it?"

"I think I do."

"No, you don't. But I'm going to tell you. Anyway,

the sheriff had picked up this black girl, around my age. Her daddy was supposed to have shot up one of the deputies real bad—like some birdshot in the groin. But nobody had actually seen him do it. All the local pigs were out looking for him, but he'd escaped. They thought the girl knew where he was."

Dan was silent, getting the picture too sharply in his mind. He believed in law and order, sure. He didn't think that a person should be beaten up or shot on the streets by hoods. It was the job of the police to prevent that. Except for the thing at Montana Diablo, he really had nothing against cops—although he knew that the person most likely to get arrested was a sixteen-year-old kid. But after all, his father was part of the county government and so were the deputies. In a way, that was.

The silence in this room was oppressive. Uvaldo lay on his cot. Bud held his guitar in his hands but made no sound.

"Know what they did?"

"Of course he doesn't," Bud suddenly broke in. "How could he? It—it just isn't in Dan's experience, Sally, so I can't see why you're—"

"Hold it," Conn replied, raising his hand. "Bud, you're always trying to run out on your own feelings. He's got to know, because it happened in Sunnyrim, Texas, which is part of this whole scene. They do it in Lakefield too, only slower, longer, in more chicken ways."

"All right," Caroway answered sulkily. He hit one chord on his guitar and muted it dead. "But this story is so big with you, Sally. I've heard it a dozen times. Maybe since then they've never done it again."

"The hell they haven't," the red-bearded guy declared strongly, his brows pulled tight over his strange blue eyes. "Look, this is the nicest thing I can tell Dan about Sunnyrim. If I got into what that town really is, Bud, you'd claim it was a damn lie. This is the truth because I saw it myself. It has to be told."

Uvaldo stirred on his cot. "Going hungry," he said very softly, "is a lot tougher than getting whipped. I've been slapped around by cops myself. So what happened? I healed."

"Dan," Sally said, ignoring Gutierrez, "they stripped this black girl's skirt up and they whipped her on the bare butt for half an hour. Finally, she broke up and told where her father was. So the sheriff went over there and blew his head off with a shotgun. That's the story. I saw it myself, and I made up my mind that day. It's all got to go. Do you see?"

The black girl, the whipping, the dead father, made a sharp, abstract image in Dan's imagination that revolted him. That had to go, all right. But Sally's conclusion that everything else had to go because of this didn't make sense to Dan. It was the first flatly revolutionary statement he had ever heard from anyone and his impulse was to run from it somehow, rather than to listen. He belonged here, in this order of things, and he couldn't conceive of anything else. If this world went, what would be next? Did Sally have any alternatives, really? Dan felt uncomfortable and trapped. But he didn't offer any argument. Not now.

"Yes," he said, his voice barely audible, "I do see."

"I thought you would," Conn told him.

"You know," Bud said in a peculiar voice, "Sally, a person doesn't always have to be somewhere for sure. He can be in between places a lot of the time, like tak-

88

ing a bus trip. He can be somewhere and nowhere at the same time."

Sally blinked, shifting his stare from Dan. "Not in your case, Bud. Not after you've made a decision the way you have. Like it or not, you're with us, guitar and all. Anyway, the longer you stay in nowhere, the less your chance to get somewhere. I'm not telling Dan where he can be, or what he can think. I'm asking him the question. Is he with the sheriff who whipped that girl, or isn't he? It's fair."

"I'm not with the sheriff," Dan said slowly. "I don't like the idea at all. But it's an isolated case. It happened in a certain town and quite a while ago." His voice gained strength. "Listen, there was never anything like that in Del Obispo County. Nothing I ever heard of—"

Sally chuckled unpleasantly. "Dan," he said, "if it happened anywhere in this country, anytime, it happened to you. Don't give me that Lakefield and Del Obispo County runaround. Reagan territory. It happened to you, baby, and all of us. Don't ever forget that. The grape strike down in Lamont and Delano is happening to you. It's happening all over. That's what I'm trying to say."

Dan Miller looked inside himself and found an inner security, a local pride, a provincial sense of the ordinary people a person met on the street—despite everything awful that had happened to him. There was, for instance, Teresa, and—and life. All the people, his own parents. They didn't whip girls, white or black, or blow off heads. There were the courts, and due process of law—remembering a phrase.

"I don't blame you for feeling the way you do,

89

Sally," he said. "But that isn't the whole picture. You saw it; it happened to you. But one happening doesn't make the whole scene."

"It does," Conn said bluntly. "That's just it. One brutal moment adds up to all the brutal moments, because the established authorities, the real bosses, are able to do it and then justify themselves. Like that People's Park thing in Berkeley—wasn't that a whipping across the butt? Wasn't that nausea gas from the helicopters a whipping for everyone in town?"

"They went about getting the park in the wrong way —by force," Dan said, recalling something he'd read in the paper.

"Sure. The leaders tried secret negotiations for five days before the cops moved in one night. Then forty thousand people marched peacefully in the streets after they'd been shot at repeatedly, gassed, beaten up. And what is the park now? A no-man's-land. Now that the Regents have won with genuine force, nobody will touch the place. The fraternity cats won't use the playing courts they built, the black minority won't handle the parking lot. They can't get an architect to design the planned student housing. Just the local dogs go on the place."

"I—I don't know—"

"Well, how about that guy, Rector, that the pigs killed with buckshot? Isn't that the same whipping? Did he need to be killed, standing there on a roof doing nothing? Why, it could have been any of us here. It could have been you, Dan." Sally's voice was intense, needling.

Uvaldo said, "Take it easy, Sally. Nobody gets it all at once."

Conn got up from the chair. "Right," he agreed. "I

just want you to think a little bit, Dan. About where you are now in the 1970's, and what's going to happen to you, and why. That's all." He took off suddenly, closing the door behind him like a quiet mouth.

Dan followed his departure with his eyes and then turned away. From one angle, Sally had sounded a lot like Mr. Park sawing away on the commies, only in reverse. Conn had a new set of villains. The idea was confusing. He put it out of his mind.

It was now a week into the first semester. He had been all but overwhelmed by new events, finding and fitting into the classes, trying to believe in himself and that he was really here at all.

Monday, a cute girl stopped him in the hallway; she had a book of what appeared to be tickets. "Have you joined VSAS?" she wheedled, smiling pertly.

"No," he said. "I don't even know what it is."

"It's fifteen dollars. It's the Associated Students organization. You're new here, aren't you?"

"Yes."

"Well, membership entitles you to the school newspaper, the *Visalia Vaquero,* full use of the Student Union, and—" She rattled off more things.

Dan had the money. He wanted to be one of the students and to share student life, like everyone else. He fished out a ten and a five and she wrote up the ticket, lending him her ball-point so he could sign the card she tore out and handed to him.

"Thanks," she said. "Bye."

A moment later, he saw her down the hall, talking to another freshman he recognized from English I.

Back in the room that evening, something compelled him to haul out his VSAS receipt and show it to Uvaldo and Bud.

"Is this a good thing to belong to?" he asked.

Bud took the card and turned it over and over in his fingers as if it were something filthy.

"Fifteen dollars," he mused. "That's what they charged you for this?"

"Yes. Is that—"

Uvaldo had gotten up from his cot and come forward. "Let me see it again," he interrupted very softly, taking the card from Caroway. "The Associated Students of Visalia State!" He glanced up at Dan and handed back the card. "I suppose you would buy it," he almost whispered. "You get the school newspaper, and —and what else, Dan?"

"It costs you less to get into games," Dan told him uncertainly. "At least that's what she—"

"Said," Uvaldo finished.

There was a long silence.

"What particular games did you want to go to, Dan?" Bud asked, going back to his cot and folding himself into it. "Football, maybe. I think we play Chico State this year, and Fresno, and—"

Dan's memory flicked back to Lakefield High School, to the locker rooms and showers, to Coach Franks always telling him to get the lead out.

"I don't follow football so much," he said.

"Basketball?" Uvaldo wanted to know. "I used to play that game in Lamont."

"Not really," Dan admitted. He put the card back into his wallet like a dirty thing. In there, it was hidden.

"Last year," Uvaldo said, "when we were trying to picket the Shop-Easy Stores here in Visalia about the grape boycott, the Associated Student football players came and beat us up, Dan. The jocks broke one kid's leg and he had to leave school. They love grapes more than people."

After that there was a heavy sorcery of quiet in the room. Bud went to his locker and rummaged around inaudibly. Uvaldo read in the spot of his bed light, and Dan finally hit his assignment in English I. Something about *Beowulf*.

A moment later, Bud was back at his cot with the guitar in his hands.

"There's a bad moon a-shinin'," he sang very softly.

"There's trouble on the way—"

He broke off suddenly, as if aware that the atmosphere demanded silence, put his guitar down, and lay back and went to sleep. But the snatch of tune held Dan for a long time while *Beowulf* and English were swept away.

The words Bud had sung took him back irresistibly to the long ago when there was nothing for him, too, but a bad moon—until Teresa had come along.

He shivered without knowing that he did. He thought hard of Teresa, drew her picture across his mind like a curtain, remembered her words.

"I love you, Dan," she had said. "We'll work hard, and someday we'll be married."

But the image faded out no matter how hard he tried to hold it in place, and the words became distant and unrecognizable. With some kind of wretched insight, he knew the truth and faced it alone. There was a bad moon a-shinin' and trouble on the way everywhere— here at Visalia State, in Lakefield, in Sunnyrim, Texas, and in himself.

Every kid knew about that bad moon, as the ideals and principles taught by parents and school grew taw-

93

dry and crumbled when the reality of injustice, poverty, and racism became inescapable.

The football players who had broken up Uvaldo's picket line were floating in the bad moon, Gutierrez and Caroway were, and Conn thought he knew some direction out of it.

The war in Vietnam had been carved from its texture and would always be there whether it ended or not. When the Del Obispo cops had busted the happening at Montana Diablo and clubbed and Maced some kids, a bad moon had been festering overhead. When the guys beat each other up in the locker rooms, when whites fought blacks, and blacks fought whites, man, the moon was really bad.

Trouble ahead.

Dan Miller felt trouble in his blood right now, boiling there, not somewhere else, not on the other side of a comfortable little old world. Trouble was here, all around, in the air he breathed and the food he ate. Trouble wasn't a foreigner, the way the adults wanted to teach it. Trouble wasn't commies after dark, in the park. Trouble was a native son, a Californian, a guy from Lakefield who didn't want any part of it, but who had to live with it whether he liked to or not.

For one instant, he saw it all with harsh clarity, as brutal as a mosaic in broken glass. The scene as it really was, and the fatally dangerous way ahead, desolate and lonely.

Gradually, he fought back. He really didn't have any trouble at all. He was here in college studying English lit. He had a comfortable room and good food. He was the son of affluent, middle-class Americans.

In imagination, he saw his mother again in the orderly, perfect house. She was neat, well-groomed, even

94

pretty—and she was smiling at him when he came home from school, as if she was glad he was there. In all the time he could remember, he had always had clean clothes carefully folded in his dresser, and there had always been good food, wonderfully prepared.

A forgotten memory came back to him with a smash. Once, long ago, he had been very sick. His mother had sat up all night a couple of times running. When he awakened, she was there, speaking to him softly until he slept once more. How old had he been? Eight, nine? There had been talk of putting him in the hospital and he hadn't wanted to go.

And his father? Sure, he believed in the rules with a stern conviction that extended even to camping, but he lived by the same rules himself. He didn't get drunk on the pretext of a "social" evening and then lecture his son about the evils of a can of beer. Dan knew that plenty of fathers got smashed every weekend and were half-gone the rest of the time. If their kid stepped out of line experimentally, they blew off the lid as if the guy was up in San Quentin convicted on a murder charge.

No, from this distance and this time and place, he saw the logic of his home at last. It had a decent consistency, a solidarity he hadn't recognized for quite a while. All along, it had been an island in a sea of turmoil and anxiety—even with trouble on the way and the bad moon shining everywhere else.

There was the perfect girl back in Lakefield who said she loved him. Their plans, their future, were as strong as a net of piano wire, protecting them both.

Nothing could change those plans; nothing was more impenetrable than pure, genuine love. Every day, people went to school, got married; they worked at their jobs; they found themselves a secure place. It would be an apartment tucked away somewhere, maybe a house—any little house. The moon could shine however it must; the world could thunder by, muttering and groaning all it liked about war, racism, the destruction of the environment, the bomb. In there, a guy and his girl would be safe.

Sure there was plenty of trouble already, but it was smaller than one thought—a controlled note. All the destruction that had happened on all the college campuses wasn't equal to a single riot in the ghetto. Television, the newspapers, students milling around and demonstrating in a mindless style—they all blew too big and loud.

Now Dan remembered Lakefield in a different way. The rows of well-kept houses and the quiet, treelined streets, the soft hills of the Santa Lucias beyond, all were a new photograph snapped a moment before and just now developed.

Nothing violent ever happened in Lakefield—far too little, really. A riot in Berkeley, a national moratorium, scarcely changed a single beat of its rural rhythm. Nobody even mentioned the bloody trouble in Omaha, Akron, Cairo, Chicago, or Cleveland.

Why? Simply because there wasn't any trouble in Lakefield. There was nothing but the old routine—the government, inflation, high prices, high interest, and the wonderful way the Mets had won the World Series.

He took a hard grip on his strung-out feelings, pushed them together into a tight wedge, and hit *Beowulf* again.

Beowulf was a hero with a hero's super powers; he set things straight the same way it was done in the comic books. Evidently, the story had lasted for hundreds of years. Beowulf was the Vanquisher, Superboy, Mr. Crimebuster.

Dan thought how long the old houses of Visalia had stood, firm through everything. Streets were still named the same, the Bank of America had a branch in every huddle of houses in California. There were plenty of stable things, enduring ideas. They steadied him tonight.

The room was quiet a full hour. Bud got up and went out. Uvaldo read without lifting his eyes from the page or making a sound. Finally, Dan finished the assignment and closed the book.

Then Uvaldo looked up.

"Dan," he said, "some weekend when we're both ahead of the books, maybe you'll go down to Lamont with me for a visit. My parents are both dead, but I've got close relatives all over that town. You can go with me to my uncle's and meet my cousins. How about that?"

"Why, thanks, Uvaldo," Dan came back with natural courtesy. "I think I'd like that. Where's Lamont?"

"Not too far from here. Fifty or sixty miles. You go down Highway 99, then pull a left for a few miles. Just a small town; I grew up there."

"I'd like to go—sometime—" Dan said, putting the time far from him into the year and into something forgotten. Uvaldo wouldn't remember. Neither would he.

"It's a date," Uvaldo said positively. He paused, as if choosing words with care. "Don't let Sally shake you up too much," he finally suggested. "Conn believes that words—dialogue, he likes to call it, although he does most of the talking—accomplish a lot. So he hits you with something like that Sunnyrim story to get your attention, and then walks off. He's got some ideas that he likes to drum on, trying to put them into a person's skull by repetition, I think. Four or five ideas."

"Like what?"

"You'll hear them soon enough. Mainly, he thinks that our whole system, the government and even capitalism, has to go. He believes we have to confront and bring down the people who are really running the country before the colleges can change, or anything else—"

"But why?"

"Because he believes it, that's all. What I'm really saying to you is that Conn means everything he says. He comes on straight."

"I know," Dan nodded.

"Give it all some time, will you?" Uvaldo asked.

"Sure. I have plenty of that. Time."

"Good enough. It's all anyone can have."

Gutierrez went back to his reading. After a while, Dan hit the sack, somehow exhausted. The only time he stirred was when Bud came back in as soundlessly as he had gone.

During the next week, he fell into the routine of his classes easily and did the assignments every day.

College was profoundly different from high school, perhaps in point of numbers as much as anything else. Though Visalia State was small by comparison with other colleges, thousands of students swarmed the buildings and grounds. They formed an impersonal network of individual purposes and responses.

At Lakefield High School, everyone knew you and your weaknesses. Here at Visalia, nobody seemed to care one way or another. Yet there was not the icy cold of social indifference that is one characteristic of random crowds. There was a common purpose that seemed to unite everyone.

Of course, it wasn't all that way. The prof in his English class cut him down painfully in front of forty other people. The prof was fairly young and nasty. He had a way with the girls.

"Mr. Miller," he said with biting acid after Dan muffed a question, "will you *please* not rewrite the morning star of English literature, Geoffrey Chaucer. Later on, if you insist, you can rewrite Hemingway. But not Chaucer, please."

The girls in the front row giggled.

But he survived, as Jenny had said he would, by hitting the books with everything he possessed. The next time he caught a question, he was ready; Dan had the answer down to the last squirm.

The prof raised his brows in an exaggeration of surprise, but then he leveled it. "Very good, Miller," he said honestly. "A complete and thoughtful evaluation."

Nobody giggled, and that night he studied harder than ever. He was putting in six or seven hours on the books every day, so that he scarcely had time to write to Teresa. He did manage to read her letters, which were pages and pages long in her delicate girl-script—all about everything that had happened in Lakefield, and of how much she loved and missed him.

Even his first quizzes were all right. At midterm he picked up an A in a couple of things including English, and B's in everything else. Uvaldo and Bud took an immediate interest.

"Let's see your bluebook," Bud teased. "Don't hide it, Miller. I can see it sticking out of that bunch of papers."

Grabbing the bluebook, Bud whistled a note. Uvaldo came over.

"A," Gutierrez exclaimed. "Now, that's all right. Caroway, we've got a student in this room. You go do some kind of penance."

"Like crawl three hundred yards up the cobblestone street to the cathedral steps, Gutierrez? I saw that happen in Mexico."

Uvaldo grinned pleasantly. "It'd do as a start, Bud, but don't think you can get away with a lousy three hundred yards all your life."

"Okay," Bud said, handing back the bluebook. "Dan, we're proud of you. One of the things we've got to do is get good grades from the Establishment and stay in school."

Uvaldo nodded solemnly. "That's for sure. We stick it out and get a degree. Then we have a little power."

Dan took back the bluebook sheepishly, thinking he was getting a put-on. But later he realized that they had been sincere in their admiration, and that made him feel warm toward his roommates.

They went once more to Sally's apartment, almost the identical group, with Waldo Jones there. Jenny Darien too. Dan had seen her a few times on campus, but only when he was at Conn's did he realize that he had been avoiding her scrupulously.

She spoke to him with the same friendliness, holding him with her for a while. But he avoided her again, even though she was in his mind all the time. He saw her moving around, doing the work as invisibly as ever. Once, she turned and waved at him, flashing a smile.

He half hoped she would come again and sit beside him, and when she didn't he felt a twinge of real disappointment, until a stab of disloyalty to Teresa caught him. Oddly enough, he had had the feeling that Jenny belonged to him in an obscure style. Maybe it was because she had made him look sort of foolish by getting him to play the piano. Maybe something else.

In the light of morning, that faded from his memory. On the next weekend, with three days to spend, he went home to Teresa.

8

DAN HAD BEEN HOME on weekends before, of course, but this trip had special significance because of the quizzes and his good grades. He was frankly proud of them and wanted and expected recognition from both Teresa and his parents.

Yet his sense of anticipation was more than about that. As the highway unfolded through the Kettleman Hills, the insight came to him. He had changed, man, say only a point or two, in a new direction. Not much, but he could feel the difference in himself.

He visualized Teresa catching on. "Dan," she would say gladly, "why, you're different. You're—Why, I just can't believe it."

Well, any change would be an improvement, he figured.

He doubted that his parents would notice; they were old and fixed. He understood them a lot better now; he would probably always be their "little boy."

All they really wanted was that a son go to college, have a good experience, and keep out of trouble. Or, rather, they wanted him to keep them out of trouble. Family trouble. They looked forward to the time when he would get a good degree and a fat job so they could tell themselves that everything was all right and that they had done their best. It was easy to satisfy parents if a person wanted to, and unreal to expect much more from them.

Teresa was another matter. She was young and aware of what went on in the world. Her recognition would be enough for Dan. Thinking about that chick made him smile all the way through the hills.

He thought more than once about Sally and the girl in Texas and that Conn was one of those genuine revolutionaries that you read about in the paper and never meet. Idly, he toyed with the idea of telling Teresa Conn's story and asking her what she thought of confronting the Establishment and bringing it down.

"You know—like getting rid of capitalism and making everything equal so we all had a good job, a decent place to live, and—well, self-respect," he heard himself saying to Teresa. He wouldn't mean it, of course, but he could get his girl's perspective and it would strengthen his resolve.

He stopped himself right there; he knew what Teresa would say to that. She would blow her mind, man, and say he was getting a lot of dangerous ideas she didn't like. No, he wasn't going to tell her anything about Conn. Besides, Sally didn't really count.

Because the bus got into Lakefield so late at night, he hadn't told anyone he was coming. No use to get people out of bed or keep them up to meet a bus. Teresa wouldn't mind, but she would have to borrow the car from her parents, and he didn't like the idea.

The streets were all but empty when he arrived, and he was the only passenger who got out there. He carried his suitcase, small and lightly packed, and set out with it down the silent, solemn little streets.

As he walked he once again felt the sense of small-town security that had come to his support when Sally had talked about the black girl in Sunnyrim. If Lakefield had any crime at all, it was that of too much serenity and too much calm. Dan could recall his father talking about the time when this town was policed by only one man, a constable with a way of talking to the kids. But Lakefield had grown since then, and now there was a sheriff's substation here, with five deputies.

A few cars moved along Main Street, and there were a few more parked around the various bars—as always. Dan saw one man walking alone and unsteadily toward the Lakefield Hotel, and a stray dog skulked into the alley by Jenkin's Men's Store. There wasn't anything else. If Lakefield had trouble, it didn't show.

He was in the residential district now, and as if to answer his thoughts, he heard what was distinctly a series of high-pitched screams. A woman's scream.

Dan stopped dead still on the sidewalk, listening into the night, transfixed by the way a scream knifes through the consciousness.

There was a light on in one of the houses, but the screams hadn't come from there; it had been more to the right and farther back.

He waited—poised—for a moment, but the chilling sounds weren't resumed. Now there was nothing but the ticking of night silences in a small town. So what he had heard was probably the late show on someone's color television set, an individual who didn't go to bed as early as most.

Relaxing slowly, Dan had to grin at himself. He certainly possessed an undisciplined imagination. He set off again down the dark street; it wasn't very far now.

When he had gone a half block farther, he heard the screams again, this time shorter, more distant, and cut off. He slowed his pace, but kept moving. Television, man—it was getting better and better.

He grinned ruefully into the night. Nothing ever happened in Lakefield; it was the center cut of America, the typical place that always went Republican and turned out graduates from the local high school who were winners with short haircuts.

Before long he was at his own house, which he had once thought of as having a finger wave of phony stone. It stood low and neat in the faint light from a sickle of moon.

Well, a kid had to go away first before he knew where home was—the place where they had to let you in when you got there. Only they didn't have to let Dan in. He had his own keys, two of them, to the front and back doors.

He chose the back way, opening the door with care and entering soundlessly. Inside, he moved through total darkness with a comfortable surety of the familiar surroundings. Nothing had been moved.

In a moment, he was in his own room, where he snapped on the light. The place was exactly as he had left it the last time he was there, except that his mother had dusted.

He undressed quickly and fell into the sack, lying

awake and looking up to where the ceiling had to be. No, Sally was wrong. There was a central, unchanging lodestar in the times. It was Lakefield, and all the other Lakefields across the nation—like that small town with the funny name where Neil Armstrong had grown up, holding his destiny to be the first man to step on the moon.

He fell into a solid, dreamless sleep and, since it was going to be Saturday, slept late, until nearly ten. Up at last, he showered, dressed, and went toward the big breakfast his mother would fix for him—anything he wanted.

They were still lingering over coffee when he came out. Both his dad and mother looked up and waved to him across the room. They knew he was here; they had sensed it last night.

"I was just telling your mother," Paul Miller said as he approached, "that if she had listened to the local news she would have heard about this idiot, Horton. He beat up his wife last night—horribly—and threw her out on the street. The deputies found her wandering around dazed and put her in the hospital. Now they don't know if she'll even live—"

"She's only twenty-eight and has two young children," Mrs. Miller added in a distracted voice. "Why would he do something like that? I can't believe it. Why, Mr. Horton was always so nice."

"I can't believe it either," said Mr. Miller, shaking his head. "Why, he's in the Lions Club and the Junior Chamber of Commerce. I guess he does drink a little."

Mrs. Miller was staring at Dan. "What's the matter?" she asked suddenly, sounding alarmed. "You look positively ill, Dan. Simply white. Is there—"

106

Dan couldn't answer at once. Instead, he heard the screams again—shrieking, imploring someone anywhere to help. They pierced him now again and again in their agony and supplication that there would be human help within hearing and it would come. Somehow, the screams blended into the howl of the black girl in Sunnyrim, who finally told where her father was hiding and got his head blasted off with a shotgun.

"If it happened in Sunnyrim, it happened to you," Sally Conn had said.

He recovered himself slowly. It meant that Lakefield wasn't immune after all—at least not for Mrs. Horton.

"I heard her screaming when I came home last night," he said dully, "and I didn't do a thing. I just stood there, deluding myself. Making it easy on me."

"You what?" Paul Miller asked.

"I heard that woman screaming and I didn't do anything," Dan choked.

Mr. Miller put down his napkin. "Now, wait a minute," he said sharply. "What do you think you could have done?"

"Go there," Dan said. "Stopped them—"

"Stopped them!" Mr. Miller exclaimed. "You mean, interfered in a quarrel between a man and his wife? Do you know what could happen to you for trying that kind of heroics?"

"I should have tried," Dan said.

"Nonsense," his father sputtered. "Why—why—if you broke into the house, or went inside at all, Horton could have killed you with justification. At the very least, you could be involved in a lawsuit—"

"I don't care," Dan insisted. "I should have done something."

Mrs. Miller said, "Dan, dear," in the logic of mothers, "of course there was nothing you could have done at all—except perhaps to call the police. Is that what you're learning at college? That you ought to interfere with—"

"By the way," Mr. Miller growled, letting poor, beat-up Mrs. Horton lie where she was, "how is college?" His eyes had narrowed.

"Fine," Dan said in distraction.

"Fine? What do you mean by that? Are you passing your courses? Has something happened over there you haven't told us about?" The voice of the older man was like a finely honed razor, incising.

"No. Nothing like that. I got some good grades on my midterms."

"Good grades? What do you mean by 'good grades,'? C's?"

Dan sighed deeply. "No. An A in English and in math. Some B's."

"That's better," said Mr. Miller. "Now, I'd like to change the subject from this Horton woman. How do we know what her part was in the matter? We don't know a thing." He picked up the morning paper ostentatiously. "Stocks went down again yesterday," he observed heavily. "It cut into Monongahela common. We lost at least a thousand on that just last week. I can't understand the Government's tight-money policy."

Mrs. Miller stirred herself and went over to the stove. "Now, what can I get you for breakfast, Dan? I could scramble you some eggs; you like those. Or would you like some nice pancakes?"

"I'm not very hungry," Dan said. "I think I'll just

have some toast and coffee. That is, for now. I'll—I'll eat a big lunch, Mom."

She looked uncertain for a moment, but she put the slices of bread into the toaster and poured a cup of coffee.

Dan's balance returned to him slowly. Perhaps they were right; perhaps there was nothing he could have done and no reason to be involved.

After that, they talked while he ate the toast—about college and the people he had met, and about what had happened in Lakefield since his last visit.

Jeff Morgan had been killed in Vietnam, a tough little dropout who had volunteered in the Marines. Candy Swanson had married Sonny Wilson, and they were already separated. Sonny was supposed to have told Candy that if she didn't shut up he would cut her heart out, something stupid like that. Candy had run home all the way from Oklahoma and Sonny had followed, pleading that he hadn't meant a word of it but that in his opinion Candy was a mental case.

Three weeks was probably longer than anyone could possibly be married to Candy, and his heart went out to Sonny, trying to talk some sense into that woman.

"Isn't it terrible?" Mrs. Miller said. "I mean, it's a real tragedy. I was talking with Mrs. Swanson, and she simply couldn't hold back the tears. It's awful."

"Candy Swanson is—" Dan was going to give an opinion that favored a saint like Sonny Wilson, but he held it back.

"How do you suppose her parents feel after a huge church wedding only three weeks ago?"

"I wouldn't know," Dan said truthfully. He wanted to tell his mother that Candy was just beautiful enough

109

that she would probably wind up with ten marriages. But he let that go too. If Sonny Wilson couldn't make it, who could?

After breakfast, he did go back to his room and lie down for a little while because his mother insisted. But he didn't sleep. Instead, he resolved for all time that if he ever heard another human being screaming for help, he would go there and fight it out. This would never happen twice to him over toast and milk.

He recalled an incident in the newspapers when a nurse in New York City had been beaten to death while dozens of spectators looked on. They hadn't interfered, and that was what his dad and mother had cautioned him about. Interference. There were risks, they said, the least of which was a lawsuit.

But didn't all human involvement imply risk? Wasn't that part of the trouble today—that nobody wanted to get involved? That was what Sally was really talking about, when you thought about it. Conn wanted to participate in life and to have a hand in shaping the world to come, to make it better according to his principles and beliefs.

Dan couldn't agree with him, but some action was better than none at all—an acceptance of screaming people with a shrug, a feeling that it was none of your business if they screamed.

No, never again.

It was late in the morning when he phoned Teresa.

"When did you get in?" she asked immediately.

He told her and she was angry that he hadn't called her last night, or sooner this morning.

He had the self-possession to laugh. "Oh, sure," he said easily. "I should have called you at two o'clock in

110

the morning and gotten you and your father out of bed. Or before the sun came up today."

She calmed down, especially since she wasn't really ready for him to come and pick her up even now.

"How about going to Avila?" he asked.

"It's too cold," she said. "But we could have a picnic or something at Montana Diablo. It's pretty this time of year."

He remembered the bust at the park at once, and wished she had picked another place. But it didn't really matter.

"I'll be there," he said with love and tenderness.

"Montana Diablo?" his father asked wryly when he was arranging to use the car. "Planning a little hippie action today?"

"Not that I know of," Dan said. "Not with Teresa, anyway."

"Fine girl!" Mr. Miller observed, settling back with his paper. "All business. I was in the labs the other day for some tests and she handled everything like a pro."

Teresa still lived in the huge old frame house Mr. Bailey had bought when he had first come to Lakefield. Despite prosperity, he hadn't moved across the freeway into the hills west of Lakefield along with everyone else who could afford it.

The family was the sort to hang on to what they had with tenacity and purpose, and the only concessions Mr. Bailey had made were new paint and exquisite landscaping. Yet the house was peculiarly appropriate for Teresa, as if she belonged there more than she would in something of fancy plastic.

When Dan arrived and pulled into the circular drive-way, she was waiting for him on the porch with its antique pillars and railing. Instead of flared slacks, she wore a white knit skirt and a bulky sweater.

He walked up the wooden steps toward her. She had risen from the porch chair and was standing to meet him, smiling in her special way.

He had to admit once again that Teresa was lovely, beautiful, wonderful, and utterly beyond him. Her honey hair shone with a dark and smoldering gold in the afternoon sunlight; her lashes were long across her wide, hazel eyes, her lips full and moist.

She waited for him, open, and they came into each other's arms, the young thrust of her body sparkling into his blood as he kissed her, hard.

"I've missed you," she said.

"Not as much as I've missed you," he managed, deep in his throat, almost reverently serious.

He gestured toward the front door.

"Folks home?"

"No," she said. "Mother and Papa had to go to Del Obispo. You can say hello to them when we get back."

A wild thought sneaked across his mind, but he blotted that out.

"Let's go," he said. "Montana Diablo."

She had a thermos of coffee, some sandwiches, and other things in a basket, which he set in the back seat of the car.

They were out on the street when he said, "I got some fairly good grades at the midterm."

"How good?"

He told her.

Teresa literally clapped her hands. "Groovy, Dan," she said. "Oh, I'm so proud of you!" Her arm went around his neck and she hugged him. "Didn't I tell you?"

112

He had to admit that she had. Teresa had been confident all along about how he would do in college.

The way through the canyon to the coast wore a panoply of trees ranging from sycamores to live oak, and afterward to Monterey pines at the summit. The creek that fed the lake flowed along the bottoms beside the road, shallow among the rounded rocks from sparse autumn rains. The way blazed with turning leaf color, winter already in the sap flow, and the winding road presented a scenic snapshot at every curve.

Teresa was silent, and he could feel her eyes on him. She sat close, but she didn't smother a driver the way some chicks did. At last they reached the shore, where the monolith of Morro Rock cut the sea sky, and they circled through Bay City and out along the tidal flats where migrating birds settled to rest. A couple of herons took off as they went by, trailing sticks of legs in their inimitable grace.

She talked now, telling him about everything and nothing, her job, and about the people of the town. Finally, she got around to the awful thing about the Hortons.

So he told her, and how he felt about hearing the screams and doing nothing.

"I'm glad," said Teresa, shivering a little. "Why, Dan, you can't get mixed up in other people's lives. You have to leave them alone with whatever they do. It's like—well, somebody who can't pay the fee at the labs. It's too bad, but we can't help them. They have to find the money somewhere—work for it."

At first, Dan was shocked that her attitude was the same as his parents', but perhaps he was the one who was out of step with reality. He needed to think about it more, so he let the matter drop.

She asked a hundred questions, about the school, his classes, and the people he had met. He answered as best he could, but what he said never seemed to satisfy her.

"Don't say that Uvaldo is 'just a guy,'" she exclaimed. "What does he look like? He's a Mexican, isn't he? How do you like rooming with a Mexican?"

He thought about that; it was part of the way he had changed. To him, Gutierrez wasn't a Mexican anymore. He was a person, a friend, someone to be valued and respected, and to fix him with a racial designation was only the most superficial judgment. Dan wanted to explain that to his girl, but he didn't quite know how to begin.

Instead, "It's all right," he told her.

They were all the way through Surfwood and beyond the dunes before he finished telling her about everything.

When he was done, she said, "I love you so much, Dan. I just can't tell you how much."

It was the way he felt toward her. He stopped the car on the empty road, held her, kissed her.

"I love you," he said into her lips.

After that the way rose into the hills where the sea curled below in thin white lines of surf, and the whole sweep of the coast lay out clean in the bright day.

A little farther beyond, they dropped down and around until they emerged at the scimitar of beach and rocks called Smugglers' Cove. Here were the tables and the public place where the folk-rock happening had been busted by the cops.

Dan regretted immediately afterward that he had brought up the subject at all, because he really knew how Teresa felt. She had already told him.

Still, it had to come out. They had stopped the car at

114

one of the green tables where they could see the whole swing of the cove and could walk on the beach later on.

An unbidden anger rose within him and spilled over.

"I still can't see why they busted that happening here," he said. "The people weren't doing anything that wasn't legal and decent. They even had a park permit. Those gun-happy pigs moved in on them with Mace and clubs, doing an imitation of the big stuff on television. Why, Teresa, we've got a police state right here in Del Obispo County. Do you know that?"

"Dan!" Teresa said sharply.

"Yes."

"You just can't mean what you said right now, can you?"

"I certainly do mean it. The cops were brutal, and those people who were arrested and brought to trial were released. They should have sued for false arrest."

"Dan," she told him, her eyes drawn narrow, "you can't mean that. Why, most of them were hippies—dirty specimens, with long hair, and—"

"So, what's wrong with that?" he asked her. "Suppose a person is a little different. Is that a reason to bust him? Besides, most of them were students, and—"

"Students," she snapped, her lips thinning. "What does that mean? Look at those characters in Berkeley who are supposed to be students! Look at the damage and trouble they've caused!"

"You don't understand," he told her as gently as he could. "Most of the violence up there was caused by the police." Sally Conn had said so.

"That's just a plain lie," Teresa said, blazing. "Dan, you're talking like—like a Communist, or something."

He saw what he had done. She was mad all the way through about something abstract like the Montana Di-

115

ablo bust. This was the last thing he had wanted on this perfect day. He longed to back off, to unsay whatever it was, and a spiny lump was in his throat.

Nevertheless, he plunged on, like someone mired in a swamp and compelled to go deeper toward destruction.

"You're wrong, Teresa," he said in a low voice. "Entirely wrong. I'm not talking like a Communist. I'm talking sense. There's no reason for you and me to go along with injustice."

She looked at him once, and then flung away and went back to the car, where she sat down.

When he got over there, she said, "Take me home."

He knew that he and his girl had reached some kind of turning point that had to be settled one way or another. His first impulse was to meet this crisis head on, to tell her that a person's ideas were valid, and desperately important to his self-image. He could believe one thing, she another, and that didn't mean they needed to quarrel. The world was big enough for a lot of different viewpoints, and now that his was forming definitely, she should keep her cool and accept some disagreement.

But he backed down; he realized that he didn't have the guts to risk losing her over anything, let alone a principle. He felt small, and petty, and a little dirty inside, but nevertheless he gave up.

After that, he sat beside her and talked earnestly for a long, long time. At last, Teresa consented to go on with the picnic, but she let him know he'd ruined the whole afternoon.

That evening, he took her to the drive-in. By then, everything seemed to have been forgotten and it was moonlight all the way home. When he kissed her good-night, the soft glow held infinite secrets in its shadows.

She did say one thing. "You've changed, Dan," Teresa Bailey told him, and instead of feeling proud he felt miserable.

9

For a while afterward, Dan dwelt on that first ominous sign of discord between him and Teresa at Montana Diablo. But his anxiety faded when Teresa's letters were as they had always been—full of love and the pleasant details of life in Lakefield. She was like that; she had forgotten the trivial events of a particular afternoon.

When he went home again, they were as always, two young people terribly in love and planning a future together.

At school, he had begun to enter the current of a deepening stream of college life that at first had only tugged at his ankles and now engulfed him. He belonged. On campus, at least a dozen people always spoke to him, saying, "Hi, Dan, what's the scam?" or something.

It gave him a sense of security and an inner warmth to belong here. He felt like a part of the new world to come, of change, of a vision of the future. In the hours between classes there was talk about the ecology, how pollution and waste must be outlawed in the bright tomorrow when the war was over. In the late-night bull sessions he agreed that poverty, ghettos, and racism were a disgrace and really only the result of mass ignorance and fear. With Conn and the others he began to believe that youth would take over—with him a part of that youth—and solve the problems.

And more than this, his friends took him into their confidence; they trusted him.

So, he knew in advance that there was trouble ahead at Visalia State. Yet he was aware of it only abstractly, like a person who hears of imminent disaster but hopes it will go away. He figured that it was like his own talk, harmless and passive.

Dirk Hollings and a few other blacks of the minuscule BSU at Visalia had been around often, talking with Sally and Uvaldo; they seemed excited. Gradually, Dan was aware that they were discussing some kind of confrontation and that the time for it was now.

"Tried talking with Duell," Hollings said. "Jive. All he gave me was a lot of rap."

"It's just what I've told you," Conn answered. "There's no such thing possible as a reasonable dialogue with them about the issues. You've got to throw a wrench into the machinery before they'll even notice you're alive."

Hollings shrugged his lithe shoulders. "Sure, sure," he said irritably, "but we don't have the strength for that. Not yet, at least."

Conn said, "We have to start somewhere, Hollings. Wait for strength and you'll still be waiting ten years from now."

At first, Dan evaluated it all simply as ideas thrown out in a bull session, the way everything else got kicked around at Tindall House, sex, politics, the government —especially sex.

119

That there had been some sort of sexual revolution was clear even at Visalia. But any other sort? Why, nobody could do anything here that was "revolutionary" in the militant sense of the term. Visalia State was as calm as a clam, with the farm management and engineering students outnumbering the liberal arts contingent at least five to one. Sheep were more important than political confrontation.

Despite the violence at San Francisco State, San Jose, and a couple of other places, most of the state colleges were unlikely scenes for student disorder. Cal Poly had scarcely a ripple in its serene endorsement of the Establishment and was likely to send out a contingent of flag bearers at the appearance of a single new leftist. If they were in step with the adult mores, so much more was Visalia. Conn's mere existence here was an anomaly. He should have been at Berkeley, but Uvaldo explained that Sally had deliberately decided to do his "work" at a new college.

Dan liked Sally—a lot; he listened carefully whenever Conn talked, whether he was denouncing the government, capitalism, and the Bank of America as a representative of corporate evil, or whatever. He didn't agree with the guy at all on those declarations, and a couple of times he opened up a little.

"So what's wrong with capitalism?" he asked. "Obviously, it's not hurting us too much, Conn."

Sally glared at him. "What's wrong with it?"

"Sure."

Sally had jabbed a finger at him. "Thirty million poor people in America," he shouted. "That's the first thing that's wrong."

"But—"

"Really poor," the red-bearded guy plunged on.

120

"Hungry. Hungry in a place where they can burn a million bushels of potatoes to keep the price up. That's what's wrong."

Dan still didn't believe, but that didn't turn him off from Conn. Politics and revolution weren't Sally's whole thing; he would do anything for a friend, and for some who weren't friends. He loved to kid around, go to the movies and laugh at the latest sex film, and as much as he talked, he listened too. Actually, he was a kind person. Dan had seen him run half a block to push somebody's stalled car.

Uvaldo made more sense. There were a good-sized handful of Third World Mexicans on campus, or "Chicanos," as they liked to be called. Of course, their percentage against the whole student body was ridiculous, considering the concentration of Spanish-speaking people in the valley. Money kept them out, and Dan had never been able to figure how Gutierrez managed. His clothes were worn out, and he squeezed a nickel so hard you could hear Thomas Jefferson asking for equal time.

But black militancy? There wasn't a chance for it, although the blacks were the cutting edge of student dissent. They were treated even better by the authorities than white revolutionaries. The cops hated white, middle-class students along social lines. Most of the police had only been to high school and were the sons of blue-collar workers. But here at Visalia there weren't enough black students to be a factor.

Then the impossible happened. The blacks and Chicanos, along with whites—about thirty altogether—took over the Visalia State administration building one night. Bud Caroway went along, protesting every inch of the way that it really was none of his business and that at heart he wasn't an activist at all. Nevertheless, he was there with his guitar. By now, Dan had begun to catch on to Caroway. Most of the time when he talked he was arguing with himself. The biggest surprise was that Waldo Jones was among them. Dan couldn't understand that.

They simply walked in at closing time, chased everybody out, and sat down. A couple of the blacks, like idiots, had brought along shotguns, to build their power image, maybe.

The college president, Dr. J. Palmer Duell, took a leaf from S. I. Hayakawa's book at San Francisco State and called in the cops at once. They tried to reason with the demonstrators by busting a couple of heads, but since Visalia could send only a few, nobody won. Hollings presented a list of nonnegotiable demands, the usual, for black and Mexican ethnic studies, more student participation in college government, and the admission of minority students to Visalia without meeting grade requirements.

As it turned out, the whole thing was an anticlimax. President Duell went down before breakfast the next day and had a talk with the leaders, Hollings, Gutierrez, and Waldo, after which the demonstrators cleared out. They had done no damage at all. Duell issued an amnesty statement but said that he was meeting no demands whatever at this time.

Uvaldo said, "We wanted a show of strength—any strength. We need a beginning. So we achieved our objectives. The reason we didn't ask you to be with us, Dan, is that you aren't ready."

Within a week, the entire matter was all but forgotten on campus—especially since the big game with Fresno State was coming up.

Still, the newspapers didn't forget, nor did the local TV station that had been on the scene of the sit-in. Their televised program had shown Visalia cops confronting student agitators, Communists, Black Panthers, or whatever the viewer wanted to conjure in his imagination.

Even the big-city dailies carried a paragraph or two on their back pages, but the small valley and coast papers treated it like war with China. The *Lakefield Informer* gave the story a banner front-page headline and two full columns of print.

Dan bought a copy at the Visalia newsstand. According to the *Informer*, bearded militants had threatened police and college officials with shotguns while milling around half-naked, women and men together. There was a definite Communist influence, the story said, suggesting that Visalia State be investigated by the FBI.

Dan was so embarrassed by the exaggeration in his hometown newspaper that he said nothing at all about it to Uvaldo and Bud. In time, he reasoned, the whole thing would be forgotten.

Not so. In a couple of days he began to get letters from his parents, instructing him to keep out of the deadly fire of the guns and the destruction of eye tissue by Mace. They said he should mind his own business, the way generations of Millers before him had done.

Teresa's letter was worse. She dredged up the whole quarrel they had had out at Montana Diablo, ascribing it now to the obvious leftist influences of which Dan had become an ignorant dupe.

"I understand now," she wrote. "Dan, Dan, don't spoil everything for us."

His first reaction was to be angry with Uvaldo,

Jones, and Hollings for pulling off something, creating a big production with a gambit that was little more than a joke.

He didn't say anything because deep within himself, he knew that it wasn't so funny, whether there were thirty dissidents or two. If Uvaldo Gutierrez stood alone somewhere in protest about something he believed, it was important. It took real courage here at Visalia where the militants were so few.

Dan knew Uvaldo better now; he was faultlessly decent and thoughtful, desperately sincere and desperately American. Gutierrez actually believed. With him, the day would be not long in coming when justice and equality were done under the law.

He thought that human beings would inevitably become supremely, and perhaps divinely, good. He was a strange mixture of the terribly new and the legendary old ways. Sometimes he could grow cynical and despairing, but he dreamed all the while of the day when the long struggle would be over. He fully believed that the leader of the grape strike, Cesar Chavez, would be recognized by history as one of the great champions of American labor. He foresaw a final accord when there would be a fair shake between the worker and the grower.

Dan thought that Jefferson as a young man must have been like Gutierrez in many ways, dreaming of equality and the rights of man. It was strange that a Mexican should carry that ponderous image here in the San Joaquin Valley.

Bud, of course, was a minstrel. He went to the places and took his guitar along. He sang the sad, wild, visionary songs of youth and skidded through college on the thinnest of ice.

Somehow, Dan saw himself in both his roommates, like Uvaldo in some ways, and like Bud.

Bud said, "This is Caroway, man. This is what I am. I sing of you and myself. I sing about the going away of everything, the somewhere and the nowhere of youth. Youth tells the truth by what it does, what it sings, by the style and the beat."

And himself? Well, by now Dan knew what he was —still an outsider, an observer. He was groping his way. He had been lucky to find Uvaldo, Bud, and Sally, and lucky to know that a Jenny Darien even existed. He stood at a point in life where he at last had a choice to decide for himself about Conn, Lakefield, and Mrs. Horton. Something had happened to make him a person, but he didn't know what.

He had even found the self-assurance to play the piano down in the dayroom with the other guys standing around. He laid it out there and let them think what they liked.

"Hey, not bad, Miller," they said more than once.

He would grin. "You're just tone-deaf, that's all," he would tell them.

"Oh, sure," a couple said. "Tone-deaf. Say, why don't you get up a group, Miller? We need something like that around here."

"Maybe I will," Dan told them, not meaning it, of course.

He had begun to see a lot of Jenny now. A change in her class schedule had provided that she be near the Student Union when he had a break after his math class. He had found her there one morning, sitting on the steps with her arms clasped around her knees. He had avoided her until now, but seeing the girl made him glad.

"Jenny!" he said, surprised. "I didn't expect to see you here."

"I know," she told him. "You didn't expect to see me anywhere."

It wasn't until they had had coffee together three times that he noticed how painfully penetrating her eyes were. She watched him as if she expected something to emerge. It was uncomfortable, because he knew there was nothing within him except a hollowness, a waiting.

Once, she said, "Dan, why do you hold it all in? It's as if you're afraid to find out that you're yourself. Who are you really trying to be? Why?"

"Trying to be?" he asked her, puzzled.

"Yes."

"I'm not trying to be anyone," he told her.

"I know," she replied. "That's what I'm talking about."

In one way it was a kind of quarrel, and he was afraid she wouldn't be there the next day, or glad that she wouldn't. But she was in the same place as if nothing had happened.

"Hi," she said. "You're late."

"I stopped to talk with the prof a couple of minutes."

They had their coffee together as always, and today she talked of nothing in particular. She asked what Uvaldo and Bud were doing, and she spoke about herself a little. She was just an ordinary girl, she claimed, who had gone to high school and then to college. She really didn't know why she was here, Jenny said.

In one way, that was how it had been for him. If you were lucky and your parents had the money, you went on to college and prolonged a sequence of youth.

In that sense, he didn't quite understand Uvaldo and

Conn. They wanted to bring the hard realities of life into a situation that was actually outside life. And yet Dan realized that they were partly right. The scene needed to be debated as much as literature, and the mathematics of a sick society needed to be proved.

A little at a time, he came around to admitting to himself that Jenny had told the truth. He was holding everything inside himself and waiting for life to come along, like a man in a railroad station expecting an overdue train. He was being the person who would marry Teresa later, after he had gotten a degree, after he had pleased his parents. It was all in the future, his real self. But was that so bad, really? Wasn't that what most college students did?

How could Conn and Caroway, for examples, go into the Big E in a Brooks suit, on the make for junior executive, after four years of militancy? He didn't know where Sally, Bud, and Uvaldo could ever fit in the life to come, and the more he thought it over, the more he wondered where he could fit, himself. Maybe there wasn't going to be a place for youth anymore—except the engineering and aggie types.

One thing Jenny said really disturbed him.

They were having coffee again. "Do you remember that first evening at Sally's?" she asked.

How could he forget it. "Sure. Why?"

"You played the piano when I asked you, remember?"

He glanced at her sharply. "Yes, I do," he said, questioning what was coming next. "Why?"

She lifted her lovely brown eyes and met him squarely. "I've never mentioned it to you since then," she said. "Haven't you wondered about that?"

"No," he said honestly. "I haven't."

She smiled, he thought, but maybe it wasn't a smile at all. There was something wistful and tender in the expression.

"The reason is that I've been waiting."

"For what?"

"For you, Dan," she told him gently. "For you to tell me something about music. To invite me in, do you see? To tell me what you feel about yourself and how that relates to spending hours composing something of your own—something good, you know. Uvaldo says that sometimes you play the piano in the dayroom at Tindall. But the rest of the time you keep it all to yourself, like a secret—"

She paused, and now she did smile.

"I was hoping that—" She stopped.

"Hoping what?"

Suddenly, she laughed outright.

"Never mind, Dan. If you don't know now, I'd only ruin the chance forever by telling you."

She wouldn't tell him anything more and left him wondering what she meant. After a while he forgot about it.

One evening Uvaldo said, "We're going to have some time between quarters, Dan." He was paging through an opened letter. "How about going down to Lamont for a couple of days before you go home? I've heard from my cousin," he shook out the letter, "and they expect you. They say there's plenty of room." Uvaldo laughed. "The reason I'm laughing is that they have seven kids in that house and there's always room." He looked up seriously. "One time my uncle from Phoenix came there with nine kids and there was plenty of room that time. Will you go?"

128

"I'm—well, I don't want to put them out."

Uvaldo stared hard at him. "Dan," he said firmly, "I've talked with you more than once about Lamont. You said you'd like to go."

"I know I did. But—"

"But, nothing," Gutierrez came back. "You need to visit my uncle's house. You're a guy who needs to be in a place one night where they always have room." He sounded more Mexican than Dan could ever remember.

He hated it, but he said the words. "Fine, Uvaldo," Dan answered. "I'd—like to go."

"Bull," the other replied, smiling wickedly. "All right, I'll tell my cousin we'll be there in his twenty-room house."

The end of the quarter crawled up, and suddenly it was time for Dan and Uvaldo to go to Lamont. He had written to Teresa and his parents that he would be delayed in getting home. The trip was unavoidable and not to go would be an insult he could never repair.

Uvaldo had borrowed Bud's old Volkswagen.

"Tomorrow's the day," he told Dan. "Are you ready?"

"Sure," Dan said.

Classes finally ended and the day came when he and Gutierrez were in the old car together, heading south along Highway 99 toward Lamont and the uncle's house that Dan had come to dread.

They drove the first twenty miles in near silence, with Gutierrez concerned about the car's performance. It didn't seem to be hitting on all four, and if it was, valves were about to be swallowed, the shaft busted, and rods thrown around.

129

They passed through the grape country. The valley was hazy and interminable, as if it were part of the Midwest, with the horizons too distant to see.

Finally, Uvaldo said, "Dan, I know you don't want to visit my uncle's house and I don't blame you. Maybe I wouldn't want to know your uncle."

"You're wrong."

"No, I'm not. But I lived with you for a lot of months. You need to know my cousins, and I think my cousins need you."

"I don't get it, Uvaldo."

"Naturally not. If you did, I don't think I would have invited you. Maybe you and I wouldn't never have seen each other."

It was the first time Dan had heard Uvaldo make a grammatical error. The thing stuck out like a wound.

He gave up there, settling back in his seat and relaxing. "All right," he said, "I'll take your word for it."

Gutierrez looked over and grinned. "Good," he said. "We're going to have a nice time, after all."

10

LAMONT WAS A LITTLE TOWN about ten miles east of the freeway. Uvaldo made the turn and headed that way through miles of formal vineyards.

At last they came to the place; it had a main street as wide as a parking lot, where dreary, one-story stucco buildings made it seem empty and forlorn.

Uvaldo didn't turn there. He kept going a couple of blocks and killed a right into a narrow street that suddenly became a dirt road. At one of the houses on the right hand, he stopped. There were banana plants growing in the front yard, oleanders, and a profusion of flowers. Dan looked at the house with involuntary revulsion. It was terribly small, frame, and needed paint.

"We're here," said Uvaldo. "This is my uncle's place."

Dan was staring at the faded-brown front door when suddenly it erupted in a wild way. About ten people poured out, big ones and children, like a herd. They headed for the car in a crowd.

"My family," Uvaldo exclaimed. "They're coming to welcome us."

131

Immediately they were overwhelmed with human bodies—kids, adults, girls and boys. There was an absolute hurricane of Spanish, an abundance of kisses, a hugging of everyone. Dan had never been close to anything like it before in his life. It half sickened him—so much hugging and kissing, yelling and calling out small animal sounds. They were only cousins, weren't they?

The demonstrations ended as abruptly as they had begun, but the incomprehensible chattering went on. Dan glanced at Uvaldo imploringly, seeking instructions about how to act.

He got none. Instead, Uvaldo was grinning broadly, as if supremely proud and happy with this reception.

"Come on," he said. "You see, I told you we'd be welcome. They want us to come in right away."

"Me too?" Dan asked stupidly.

"Of course. I explained to them that you're my best friend at college. They love you already. Bring your stuff."

Reluctantly, Dan picked up the small canvas flight bag, in which he had stowed a few things, and followed Uvaldo. Although he fought against it, he felt nervous and embarrassed, especially by the size of the house. "Room for everybody," Uvaldo had said, and he imagined how that would be, all of them stacked somewhere like cordwood, with him on the edge. Such a crush of humanity repelled him with his Yankee impulse to stand off from strangers.

Inside, Uvaldo gestured. *"Ponga sus cosas aquí,"* he said. "Put your stuff here. Then I'll introduce you."

Dan put his bag down in a corner of the living room. Catching his eye first was a niche in the wall with a crucifix and a small, brightly painted statue within it. Opposite, on the far wall, was a color photograph of

John F. Kennedy in an elaborate brass frame resembling a shadow box. It featured a small lamp for illumination, with a twist of faded flowers behind it.

The room was larger than Dan thought possible. It ran the full length of the house, and except for the niche and framed portrait, was quite recognizable and ordinary—except that the furniture was heavily worn. An old black-and-white television set stared over the scene.

Dan became aware that all those people were watching him, the children with huge, timid brown eyes and serious faces. The adults were smiling at him expectantly, as if he meant something important. He squirmed within himself, not knowing what to do next, and feeling as conspicuous as a garbage pail.

Uvaldo solved the problem. He took him by the elbow and steered first to the oldest man in the room, who smiled more broadly as they approached. He had a scraggly moustache, graying and stained, that dropped around his mouth and his yellowing teeth. Gray possessed his temples. His face was lined with the trouble of his years.

"Uncle Pablo," Uvaldo said deferentially, "I want to present to you my excellent friend, Dan Miller."

The old man extended his hand at once, and Dan knew what had marked his face as he took the gnarled and knobby fingers. It was hard labor—something Dan had never experienced—labor out in the punishing sun and driving wind, in the fields somewhere.

He expected to hear unintelligible Spanish, but he got a surprise.

"Welcome to our house," Uncle Pablo said in English without an accent. "It's good to have a friend of our nephew's visit us."

Dan found his voice. "Thank you, sir," he replied courteously. "It's a pleasure to be here."

Uvaldo was delighted with the exchange. "Now, my beautiful aunt," he said, tugging Dan along to a woman with whitening hair. "Sit down, sit down, Auntie. We don't expect you to stand for a couple of kids. This is Dan Miller." He followed that with a string of Spanish.

The woman smiled, still standing. Her whole face lighted with the inexplicable charm the old sometimes possess.

"Gracias por haber venido," she said.

Dan met her eyes; they were deep and kind. "Thank you," he said.

They moved around the room quickly after that, but with the same scrupulous formality.

It wasn't until Roberto, the smallest of the children, had piped, "Pleased to meet you," that Dan realized everyone had spoken to him in English except the old woman.

Later on, he perceived that although the girls and women working in the kitchen spoke Spanish to each other like small machine guns, and the children squabbled good-naturedly in that language, every scrap of conversation voiced in his presence was English.

He found himself sitting on one of two threadbare couches, talking with Jenoveva, a very pretty girl with laughter in lovely brown eyes as saucy as sparrows. The questioning and stiff formality had melted from the room.

The children went outside to resume their play, and their shouts reached inside. The women faded into the kitchen, and two of the older young men excused them-

134

selves and took off somewhere down the street in an ancient Chevrolet, badly in need of a muffler.

Uncle Pablo appeared and offered Dan a small glass of wine. Dan glanced a query toward Uvaldo, who had all the other girls in tow. Gutierrez gave a quick, unseen affirmative nod, and Dan drank the thimbleful of liquid, red and dry but not bitter. Obviously there was little enough of it in Uncle Pablo's meager store, and when that was gone, there probably would be no more. But Dan understood, it was a high honor to be accepted.

Uvaldo had a full week of conversation with his cousins that he was trying to compress into a couple of afternoon hours. Dan had never seen him so animated and happy. Nevertheless, Gutierrez found time to tell him that big things were due in Lamont tomorrow. There was going to be a traditional parade down the main street.

That wasn't considered the important event in this house. The followers of La Causa (the grape strike), farm workers Chavez had finally organized, had applied for a permit to march in the parade. Despite every obstacle the officials raised, the permit was in order and nothing in the parade rules could prevent it. True, the committee had relegated the marchers to the end of the line, but it was a great victory just the same.

Afterward, there was to be a big rally of the Chicanos and their friends in Lamont's public park, with speeches, music, and much free food furnished by the women of the church. Chavez couldn't be there because he was desperately ill in the hospital, near death, some said. With merely a broken leg, Chavez would have crawled to such a rally—a man who took only

135

five dollars a week from union funds as his pay. That was all Dolores Huerta, or any of the officials earned, Uvaldo said. The rest came from gifts, if it came at all —food, perhaps a place to sleep.

There were plenty of others besides Chavez to take up leadership, good men from the Filipino Hall in Delano, and a black who had worked with Chicanos on the Di Giorgio ranch until he had gone on strike with them.

A little later, Dan went out in the yard with Jenoveva to watch the children play, argue, and fight amiably over the nothings of childhood.

"You like college?" she finally asked, the wistfulness in her tone scarcely concealed, her eyes big and her full mouth soft.

"Yes, I do," Dan told her honestly. "It's—all right."

"Tell me about it," Jenoveva begged. "Uvaldo never tells us nothing that's true. It's always about big ideas and never about real things. Are there many pretty girls there at Visalia?"

Dan thought about the girls, first of Jenny, and then those who sat next to him in class. "Sure," he told her jokingly, "lots of them. They're all over the place."

"Oh—" Jenoveva breathed, a note of envy.

"But none of them are prettier than you," Dan said, because it wasn't far from the truth.

A wonderfully shy smile lit the girl's olive-skinned face. It made her cheekbones high and her eyes lambent and exotic. She laughed self-consciously.

"You're fooling me," she said, pleased. "Uvaldo says I'm ugly. Only once in a while do I look like a real girl, he says."

"It's Uvaldo who's fooling you," Dan insisted. "He lies all the time."

136

Jenoveva shook her head. "He doesn't lie. He tells the truth and he's smart. A—a real genius. That's why—"

"Why what?"

"Why he was selected."

"For what?"

"To go to college for us," she replied.

Dan understood at once; she had answered a question that had bugged him for a long time. How did the guy manage to pay his way if his cousins had to live like this?

Now he saw the whole story. It was a family, or maybe a community effort, with many giving a little. It explained why Uvaldo was on the books so much, why he stayed in his room studying when Dan and Bud went to a movie or something, and why his grades were always at the top.

Gutierrez was in college for a purpose—many purposes, really. He carried a load of obligations and responsibilities unlike anything Dan could imagine. Perhaps from all over this town, the bright Mexican was getting five dollars here and five there as the preselected emissary into the ranks of the educated. In that case, why had he risked getting expelled by helping to organize the sit-in at the administration building? That took some understanding.

The day passed, and it was time for dinner. Dan was ushered into the kitchen, huge as kitchens go, with the stove and fixtures old but gleaming. There was a long table spread tonight, with two snowy cloths and chairs for everyone.

The dinner was very Mexican and delicious. Dan was hungry and loved the food. Only in retrospect did

137

it occur to him that he had eaten mostly beans and flour tortillas, laced with sharp sauces.

That evening, the younger children were sent to bed early somewhere at the rear of the house, which Dan learned later was a screened porch. The talk turned once more to the parade. Everyone was to assemble at the park and wait for instructions.

"There will be many from far away to march with us," Uncle Pablo predicted.

Finally, Dan learned the answer to a question that had nagged him since his arrival. There had been many yawns by now; even Uvaldo's eyes were heavy. Still, nobody had left the room.

He finally got the message; they were waiting for him. He realized that Gutierrez had said a couple of times, "Getting tired, Miller?"

They wanted him to take the lead.

He said, "I—uh—wonder if there's a chance to hit the sack fairly soon, Uvaldo."

The guy grinned like a sleepy cat. "Sure," he replied mischievously. "Man, I thought you wanted to stay up all night."

He spoke to his uncle in rapid Spanish, the first time the language had been used. Uncle Pablo jumped to his feet.

"I had to translate," Gutierrez explained. "I don't think my uncle knows 'hitting the sack' yet."

"Come this way," the old man said graciously.

Dan followed him into a dark, narrow hallway, illuminated with a bare 25-watt bulb in the high ceiling.

"Here is the toilet," Uncle Pablo remarked, gesturing to an old-fashioned paneled door. "The light is made by pulling a string."

He pushed the door open, reached inside to a dangling cord. Another 25-watt bulb showed the washstand and toilet. Nothing else.

"And here is your place to sleep," pushing open a similar door adjacent. He stepped back with what had to be a flourish.

Dan saw that it was a large closet or storage space. Within, crammed narrowly, was a single cot. An opening was cut into the wall and screened.

"Thank you," he said.

"De nada," the old man returned. "Good night. Sleep well."

Dan did sleep well; he was exhausted from the trip and the strain of meeting Uvaldo's relatives. But after he had stripped out of his clothes and lain down in the blackness of the hole, for that was what it was, he had lain awake listening and thinking.

One thing was clear: here in this house he had been treated like visiting royalty and this cot was part of that reception. He wondered how many children he had displaced tonight, or whether Uncle Pablo slept here himself, as the patriarch deserving the best. But it didn't worry him.

"There's always room in that house for everyone," Gutierrez had said.

It was true; there was room even for an honored guest, and Dan was pleased with the family and himself. Somehow, he had carried off the most difficult social situation he had ever been in. But it had been easy, too.

The next day, he and Uvaldo went to the park early, although the parade didn't begin for an hour. The place was already crowded with Chicanos dressed in their best clothes. They milled around in small groups, talking and gesticulating. Uvaldo introduced Dan to a few of the younger men.

"They've been on strike for five years," he explained, "ever since Chavez began organizing. Then they won a decent contract with the company and they thought the starving was over. Not now."

"What happened?"

Uvaldo laughed harshly. "A neat trick. The company sold out to a dummy buyer, which declared the contract void. Really, the fight is about agricultural workers daring to have a union at all. Now the contract has to be renegotiated with the fakes, and that doesn't seem possible. Not for years, maybe."

"How does the grower operate without workers?" Dan asked.

"A half million Mexican nationals are imported by the growers to break strike," Uvaldo answered.

"The boycott isn't really working then?"

Like most Californians, Dan had some vague knowledge of the table-grape boycott that Chavez had finally been able to invoke. Plenty of retail stores around the state had been picketed by sympathizers. The independents and small chains had gone along fairly easily, perhaps because grapes were so perishable that they were difficult to handle at best. But the response of the huge food combines had been spotty. They were too big to be really hurt, and local managers had to make their own decisions. In rural areas where the Farm Bureau was strong, the boycott hadn't worked at all.

"Whole countries have supported us," Uvaldo said, "although the Pentagon has shipped huge quantities of table grapes to Vietnam. Sweden used to buy plenty of California table grapes, but not now. That's only one place and there are plenty of others. The boycott isn't completely successful, but it's working. Chavez says it's a great victory."

Dan remembered something he had read. "What about the claim that the growers use so much DDT and other pesticides that it damages the workers' health?"

"Dirty and true," Gutierrez said strongly. "You eat some grapes, you'd better wash them real good, Miller. You know DDT piles up in a person. In ocean and freshwater fish, birds, everything. Pretty quick we'll all be full of DDT."

"I thought the agriculture department said—"

"The agriculture department—" Uvaldo spat on the ground. "The Government—what does it mean with the lobbies they've got? How about that guy who was appointed to the commission that supervises drugs? He wanted drugs sold by generic instead of brand names. So the drug companies got him kicked out. That's the Government."

Dan didn't have too many opinions about politics. He glanced up the street. People were gathering on the sidewalks.

"I guess the parade is beginning," he observed.

Uvaldo shrugged. "Some parade," he said. "Let's get up there and watch it. It'll be a couple of hours before we march."

They walked past the dinky courthouse where the first units had formed and awaited the starting signal. There was the inevitable contingent from the armed services, with a drum and bugle corps. The Lions Club had a funny car that bucked and did gyrations because of off-center axles. Next was a high school band in woolly pants and gold braid.

The spectators were more interesting. There were

girls with peace medals and long hair and sandals, accompanied by solemn, bearded young men, some with expensive cameras. Other groups were squares, men and women with a priest or clergyman leading them, and still others in ordinary business suits and street dresses.

"People are here from all over the state," Uvaldo said, "sympathizers, I guess you'd call them. They may not know exactly what it's like to pick grapes, but they've helped us a lot. Many a family around here has been kept alive by donations from different groups—churches, the Federation of Teachers, California Democratic clubs, and so on."

The parade began, and it was the saddest caricature that Dan had ever seen. To make it appear bigger, the committee had insisted on an interval of a couple of city blocks between each unit. The flag bearers and bugle corps started up the vast, wide street and were lost in the expanse of pavement. An unenthusiastic photographer shot pictures with his long lens.

"Why do they spread it out this way?" Dan asked when a group of poorly trained children tried to be a sort of drill team. They wore pathetic costumes their mothers had sewn hastily.

Uvaldo smiled. "It's Lamont's festival spirit, I guess," he said. "They've been doing it for years. I think it reflects the attitude of the growers more than anything else."

A man in a phony *paisano* costume approached with a sheaf of papers, which he was giving out to the spectators.

"Here comes their scab," Gutierrez whispered. "He's got the growers' propaganda. Take one when he comes by us. I can't."

142

Dan took one of the sheets. It was mimeographed. He glanced through the script, which featured a line drawing of a happy grape picker. The strikers, it said, were led by godless Communists. They refused good wages and excellent working conditions. Most of them were troublemaking, lazy toughs who didn't want an honest day's work. He handed the paper to Gutierrez, who read through it quickly.

"Not bad," Uvaldo said. "They're getting better at this every year. Notice that they leave out any mention of what we really want—union recognition and the right of collective bargaining. That sellout Mexican passing them around comes from Orange County. He never picked a grape in his life. He's a public relations man."

The parade dragged on interminably until it neared the end.

"Let's go now," Uvaldo said. "The marchers are forming in the park."

They hurried back and found the line already in place. At its head, four men held a huge banner across which the slogan had been painted in red: ¡VIVA LA HUELGA!

Behind in ranks were two thousand Chicanos and their sympathizers of every description, from hippies to those in stiff business suits. Dan and Uvaldo had to move back toward the end of the procession to find a place. In their rank was a woman about thirty, her eyes bright with excitement. She wore a button reading: "Women's Liberation Front."

"Hello," she said to them.

Suddenly, a tall black man gave the signal and the marchers moved forward. Then the thousands began singing in Spanish, a strange, wild thing Dan had never heard. They moved out briskly, ragged, but marching in closely bunched formation.

And suddenly the parade in Lamont, California—that sad parody of all parades—caught fire and lived.

The people on the sidewalk felt it. They were shouting *"¡Viva la huelga!"* from individual voices, and the deep-throated crowd roar came back from the marchers: *"¡Viva la huelga!"*

They moved up the long, cold street, filling it at last, lighting it with their living presence. The workers, the strikers, those who had gone hungry but kept the faith with La Causa for five long years.

Dan felt it go through him; he was caught up in the surging strength of this march and he knew that the strike could not, must not, fail. If it did, the soul of America would go down with it.

They marched two miles; at the end of the wide street they turned right and continued down the dirt road past Uncle Pablo's house. Every yard was thronged with cheering people—the gaunt women, the trusting children, the old men.

Finally, they were back at the park, and the line broke up into groups and individuals, became abruptly a picnic.

And Dan Miller? He didn't know it. Not yet. But his life had changed forever. He had moved forward to a place from which he could never return again.

11

ALL THE WAY BACK to Visalia, Dan thought about Lamont, the grape strike, and Uvaldo's cousins. "We want
a chance to live," one of the park speakers had said
from the back of a sound truck. "We want our children
to have a fair share of the future. As Chavez says: 'We
know America can construct a humane society for all
of its citizens—and that if it does not, there will
be chaos.' "

Dan thought of the little house, the gnarled, ruined
hands of Uncle Pablo, and of Jenoveva's wistful voice
when she asked about college.

"You're quiet, Miller," Gutierrez said. "Didn't you
have a good time?"

Dan thought a second. It hadn't been exactly a good
time for him. Part of the time it had hurt, and he had
felt embarrassed and sick at heart. In a way, he was the
representative of the middle-class American who
helped keep the Chicano in poverty and despair. In all
his life, he had never missed a single meal because
there wasn't enough food. He had had all the advantages, goods, and services of affluence. And why
couldn't they have as much?

145

"I enjoyed myself," he replied. "Your relatives are nice people."

"They're for real," Uvaldo admitted. "They've got to be."

There was a silence.

"Some time soon," Dan finally said, "maybe you'll come over and visit me in Lakefield."

Uvaldo smiled. "Sure I will," sincerely, "but you've got to invite me first, Dan."

Dan thought that over. Of course Gutierrez would need a firm invitation, but that would be the smallest part of the matter. Dan wasn't at all sure how his parents would react to a Mexican houseguest, although they had talked endlessly about equality, in the easy style of middle-class Americans.

Now that he thought about it, though, Dan couldn't recall a single minority person who had ever been to his house as a guest. Sure, when his father was running for reelection he had campaigned in the Mexican areas, shaking hands. Once, a picture had been in the paper showing him conferring with members of the Mexican-American Cultural Association. But he had never brought any of these people home.

They got back to Visalia late on Sunday. Bud met them.

"Got back with my VW, did you?" he said. Then, "Say, you know Waldo Jones—"

"Sure. He was in the demonstration."

"Maybe that's it," Caroway said grimly. "Anyway, he lost his student deferment. Reclassified 1-A. He'll be drafted."

"You're kidding!" Uvaldo exclaimed.

"Not so. Say, maybe you'll be next, Gutierrez. Of

course Waldo comes from San Diego County. A lot of flag-wavers down there."

Later, Dan packed his suitcase, and Bud drove him down to the bus depot.

A black, moonless night obscured the countryside beyond the bus window and turned his thoughts inward. He dwelt upon the discrepancy of his father's statements about equality and what he practiced. He measured that against his reception at Uncle Pablo's house.

It occurred to him that the idea of "integration" was all upside down. The term really meant that white Americans were trying to force blacks and browns to conform. Yet the black or brown man's skin inevitably kept him apart, no matter how skilfully he aped white ways. Unlike European immigrants, who were white, he would always be an imitation in the eyes of the complacent whites.

Sure, there were glittering exceptions, like the highly respected black doctor who practiced in Del Obispo County. All he did was make the falsehood respectable; if an individual had the education and was good enough he would get there despite everything. The blacks and Mexicans—the majority of them—were still the janitors, the laborers, and domestic workers.

It helped explain one of the demands that blacks made of the universities—that a certain number be admitted without meeting entrance requirements. The ghetto areas had schools with lower standards. He'd read somewhere that of forty thousand graduates from the New York City schools who qualified for academic diplomas, only seven hundred were black or Puerto Rican.

No. Dan began to visualize a parallelism as the solution. Uvaldo's family didn't need to become phony whites. Instead, Mexican culture, especially in California, needed to be regarded as an enrichment of the whole society.

Only in the areas of mutual necessity ought the black and brown cultures to coincide: education, jobs, the duties and privileges of common citizenship.

There would be problems, of course. To receive a really equal education, for example, a Mexican kid raised in a bilingual home ought to be taught in a bilingual school. But that was a dream that couldn't happen.

Dan shrugged so elaborately that his seat partner gave him a questioning stare, thinking, possibly, that another youth was about to freak out in public.

Sure, it would be expensive, but a society that could spend eighty billion dollars a year on a useless war ought to be able to solve some of its problems at home. Parallelism wouldn't be easy, but it was simple and cheap compared with the alternatives—the wild violence of frustrated peoples.

In Lakefield, people thought that street fighting could never come their way. But Dan recalled reading in *The Wall Street Journal* of racial violence that had hit the small cities, some no bigger than his own hometown.

Well, it was all wrong, Dan decided. It was wrong and wasteful. The white middle class had a calculated illogic and shortsightedness that completely denied everything they taught the kids in school. All that stuff about equal protection under the laws, equal rights, and equal opportunities was just so much crap. He

148

didn't have to take part in the enormous hoax any longer.

Or did he? The whole sticky glue of the established order swept back upon him. It was impossible to change. Nothing would really happen; Conn's "revolution" couldn't happen. So what could one guy do, or a handful of militant students? It wouldn't work.

Dreaming, he suddenly visualized an entire opera with the grape strike of the Central Valley Chicanos as its theme, bound together by a love story. Jenoveva, and an Anglo boy from Visalia State—Romeo and Juliet all over again, as it had been in *West Side Story*.

The overture would be that smashing march the grape pickers had sung in the parade, expanded and dwelt upon, with a forest of brass, especially trumpets, and the ominous roll of kettle drums. Against this would be set a flute solo, as pure as truth.

It would open upon Uncle Pablo, alone in his house, a bass singing in despair of five years of want and rejection in a world where women sought gifts for men who had everything. Then the family would come home, the little children first, the women, and the strong young men. Finally, Jenoveva herself. The mood would change—to the joy of life, to teasing family love. The lyrics, in English and Spanish, would swell from the sopranos of children to Uncle Pablo's bass, all bursting with the passion of living. In a trio, the older brothers would tell Jenoveva that she was too eager for love too soon and really only an ugly child that no true Chicano would even look at twice. Then, in a voice like the angels, she would sing alone, confessing to herself that she loved no Chicano at all. She loved an Anglo boy who had come to Lamont in an expensive sports car and was as distant from her as the stars.

149

For an instant, he saw it all, even heard some of the music in his mind—not much, yet something an individual could do, given the talent and the will. But—

Dan sighed deeply and put the whole thing out of his mind. He began thinking about Teresa. In another hour he would be home, and tomorrow they would be together again. It was pleasant and comfortable to think about.

He relaxed and so did his seat partner. Apparently, the riot wasn't going to begin just yet in these close quarters, although the violent young could be ready to hijack buses by now.

Once again, Dan walked home through the deserted streets of Lakefield, and this time not even a dog barked. This could as well be a central biopsy of a perfect America, a place where people lived in calm security. The houses were darkened; they scarcely breathed in their exhalations of day into night. A low moon had arisen over the brooding live oaks. The hills around rocked the Salinas Valley in a cup of silence, and the feverish alleys of Oakland, Watts, or Detroit, with their uncollected garbage and their rats, were far away.

He entered his own house, hit the sack, and fell asleep instantly.

Morning bore in upon him like the second act in a play, the curtain rung up by a high sun. He had slept longer than he intended and it was nearly ten o'clock. The bedroom door was slightly ajar, so he knew that his mother had looked in to see if he had come home; they were expecting him.

He dressed quickly and went out for breakfast, where his mother greeted him gladly, love for an only son in her eyes.

150

"Hi," he told her, seeing how small she really was—not even as tall as Teresa. "It's nice to be home."

She nodded, thinking it nice too.

His father came in and sat down at the table to pour himself another cup of coffee. His expression was very serious.

"I want to talk with you, Dan," he said.

"Sure, Dad. Why not? What about?"

"College," said Paul Miller in a somber tone. "Specifically, about this riot you had."

Dan recoiled. He knew perfectly well what his father was going to say, and he didn't want to hear it. There was a gulf between the generations all right, but it wasn't one of misunderstanding. Maybe too much understanding contributed to it.

"Riot?" he asked. "What riot?"

"The one at Visalia State," Mr. Miller said. "The one where those young hoodlums took over the administration building, fought the police, and destroyed public property. What else?"

Dan summoned all his cool. He put down his fork and met his father's stare straight on. "It wasn't a riot, Dad," he said honestly, "and there wasn't any damage to public property."

"Don't say that."

"I have to, Dad. I read the story in the *Lakefield Informer* and it wasn't like that at all. Nothing really happened. A few students sat-in all night in the building. But that was all."

"I don't believe you," flatly, "but even if what you say is true, it was destructive in principle. I want to talk with you now about these punk stunts, so you never get involved."

151

"Why?"

Dan asked the question, even though he knew why. Parents of college students all over the state were reacting in the same style—lecturing, threatening, cajoling the sons and daughters about the whole business of dissent. The reason was clear. They were scared silly of their own children. They were frightened that the hokum they'd taught had backfired and that a son would be deluded by professors into getting in the line, facing the riot clubs, and be jailed. Or a daughter could become one of those nuts who stripped and danced in an orgy of excitement. There was logic in their hysteria, of course. The hard-core militants were few, but *Fortune* magazine had polled the uncommitted center of college population and found that 40 percent favored the rioters. Anyone could be sucked into the whirlpool by circumstances and chance.

" 'Why?' you ask me!" Mr. Miller said harshly. "Because I think it's my duty as a father, that's why. It's a good reason, as good as any."

That was true enough. "All right," Dan said.

He listened. It could have been Reagan doing his thing about campus violence, almost word for word. The essence was of the high privilege in getting a free college education, and of the constitutional sacredness of private or public property. College prepared a student for something Paul Miller called life, which really came down to a good, high-income job with a home in the suburbs. He decried the influence of bearded, pseudo-intellectuals who were, as Vice-President Agnew had put it, nothing but "impudent snobs." Students were bad enough, but professors who sympathized were infinitely worse.

It came to Dan that his father was supporting the

very qualities that were wrong with Visalia State and all other colleges. He had no grasp at all of the motivations for dissent—the poverty of people like those in Lamont, the war, the suppression of minorities, or the whole alienation of youth by a senseless technology that ignored human values.

He felt he must interrupt and counter his father's dogma and lack of information, but he kept silent. After all, what good would it do? He couldn't educate the man or correct his absurdities. Instead, he wanted to escape and find Teresa. She was young and he loved her. She would understand.

He gave a stock response. "I'll think about what you've said very seriously, Dad."

Mr. Miller's energy faded after that, but not before he had talked of the tough job the police had to do, keeping law and order. The police were a student's best friend.

He finished. "Your job," he said, "is to stay in school and get an education."

Dan winced. That was exactly what the militants wanted most—an education of the right kind, one that treated the actual scene realistically. But he didn't say so.

A few minutes later he left the house, walking. Reluctantly, he put his father out of his mind stain by stain. And yet he wished fervently that his parents could understand that in today's college, involvement was inevitable. They needed to know that the pressures were on every young person in America—to choose—to decide something. It wasn't possible anymore to do the job and simply be apathetic or in limbo about everything else, postponing life to a later time. At every hand, on every turning, the young were asked: "What do you believe?" "What are you going to do about it?" Even the Young Americans for Freedom, the right-wing student society, had made a decision and knew where they were in time. Like it or not, Dan thought, the world had changed since the '40s or '50s, and now, up ahead was the inevitable war, the bomb, the destruction of society. Why, the earth screamed for decision the way Mrs. Horton had screamed that night.

Teresa was radiant and a surprise. Dan had forgotten she was so utterly great. She kissed him there in front of her mother with a sort of natural gesture of possession.

Mrs. Bailey just smiled in her plump, maternal way, and offered spiced cookies and chocolate. Then she disappeared on a pretext of work. With her, it was settled. In time, Dan would be her son-in-law.

"Give the boy more chocolate," she told Teresa severely, as if the girl could forget the implacable needs of a stomach.

"Yes, Mama," Teresa said. "I'll take care of Dan."

When her mother had gone, she turned to him with a desperately passionate kiss and, searching him, "You weren't near that awful trouble over there, were you?"

He set down the cup and met her hazel eyes, seeing how the light tangled evocatively in her shining hair. This was his girl; he needed her.

"Of course not," he said.

"I was worried."

"Please don't," he said. "There's no reason."

That was the truth, he thought wryly. He had kept himself remote from any of the action. But there was no use in trying to explain to his girl; she wouldn't agree with him.

154

She was disappointed that he hadn't brought the car, but was good-natured about his suggestion that they walk to the lake.

Out on the sidewalk, she fell into the mood with childlike enthusiasm. She skipped along, swung his hand in hers, and teased him relentlessly. She was so womanly it hurt, a poem without words.

Man, this was the way the world should be—like this, walking along together, enmeshed in all the fragrances of love, in delight to be young and alive together. Dan wished that all the trouble and violence could vanish into love like this.

They reached the lake and sat down on the grassy bank. She lay back with her face turned to the sky and with one arm drawn across her breast. He stretched out beside her, closing his eyes.

"I hate them," said Teresa suddenly.

"Hate them?" he asked in surprise. "Who?"

She sat up rigidly. "Those dirty, foulmouthed Communists. Those blacks and stupid white militants. What ego they have. I know about them. I read it in—well, never mind. Why—"

"Hey," Dan said in alarm, sitting up beside her. "Hold it a second. Do you mean—"

Teresa made a derisive noise. "Do you know what they really think? They believe they're in some kind of struggle to 'liberate us from the system.' They think we're—well, peasants, and they need to show us the way. They talk about revolution. I despise them. I wouldn't spit on them."

Her ferocity stunned him.

"I wish they'd die," she said. "I wish the cops would kill all of them and end it, the dirty niggers."

"Niggers?" Dan asked in a shocked voice.

155

"Niggers!" Teresa spat out with venom. "That's what they are. I know. I lived with them in Cleveland. Dirty niggers! And they're going to liberate me. They want to go to college for nothing and sleep with the white girls—"

"No, Teresa," Dan said firmly, "you're wrong. Completely wrong. You don't know what you're talking about. You ought to quit that job of yours and go to college and find out for yourself."

"What did you say?" she demanded.

"I said you were wrong. They're not Communists. They think Communists are squares. At least the ones I know do, and—"

"You know them?"

"They're my—well, friends," honestly. "And they aren't—niggers. I know one black militant, Teresa. He's—he's all right. Please don't be stupid when you talk about—"

"Stupid!" she said in a low voice, getting to her feet, with the hot color mounting in her face. "So you think I'm stupid—"

As a fight between a boy and a girl, it had classic proportions. All afternoon, Dan tried to reconcile the argument, but she wouldn't let him. They walked home in silence, and she left him at her door without saying a word.

He suffered the rest of the afternoon in a torrent of regret. What did any of it matter—dissent, Lamont, anything at all—if it meant he was going to lose his girl?

At last he telephoned Teresa and told her how abjectly sorry he was. He begged for forgiveness and for her to make up and go somewhere with him that night. She refused, told him she never wanted to see

156

him again and that she hadn't realized what a fool he was. But finally she relented; he could come for her at eight.

That night, on a hillside overlooking the silver thread of the Salinas, brought to life by recent rains, he held her close. He felt her warmth, and she responded in a wild way he had never before experienced. Her lips opened to receive his, and she lay in his arms with her head thrown back and her hair a net around them both.

So finally they reached the barrier—the one they had agreed must surely be kept until marriage.

Now Dan stopped thinking; he moved forward automatically into that ultimate expression, the final moment. She was a yielding flower, now carried into the sea and the rhythm of the waves of emotion.

Then. "We mustn't," she cried. "Oh, darling, we mustn't. We can't. Not now."

She was crying; the hot tears moistened Dan's cheeks with fire.

"We can't," she managed through her sobs. "We can't; we can't!"

Finally, he drew away from her and sat trembling and alone.

12

DAN HAD BEEN BACK at Visalia only one day when, as he might have expected, Isla Vista happened!

He knew the place. It was a student housing community just off the campus from the state university in Santa Barbara—or, rather, in Goleta nearby. There the grounds ran down to a lovely sweep of the beach, and some people said it was the most beautiful university campus in the world. Parents sent their kids to Santa Barbara because in all the turmoil, it seemed serene and safe. The city was a planned haven for businessmen who had retired wealthy, real estate prices were out of sight, and only an oil spill from an offshore well had upset the solid conservatism that permeated the community soul. Seabirds had died by the thousands, the white beaches had become a sink of oil slime, and five hundred yachts in the blue marina were up to their gunwales in crude oil. Worse, tourism fell to nothing.

But that had gradually gone away, Dan remembered. The oil company had cleaned the beaches with the help of county prisoners. The dead birds were picked up and insurance claims paid. Santa Barbara slept on.

Still, trouble was on the way.

It had begun slowly, when the contract of a favorite professor was not renewed and had gradually thickened with the familiar student complaints. Finally, a mob had taken over the administration building, provoking a confrontation with campus police.

Isla Vista was another matter entirely. It was actually a kind of student ghetto, and for years the kids had complained about gouging rents and police harassment. Squad cars patrolled the place incessantly, broke up gatherings of people, and pushed them around. Plainclothesmen and narcs were everywhere, smelling out pot and ransacking apartments.

Then somebody in the student government invited William Kunstler, the defense attorney for the Chicago Seven, to speak. Kunstler was out on bail from a massive contempt-of-court charge levied by Judge Julius Hoffman. The Seven, of course, were militants—Abbie Hoffman and Jerry Rubin, Hayden, Dellinger, and the others—charged with crossing state lines to incite a riot at the 1968 Democratic National Convention.

Kunstler talked to five thousand kids at the University, decrying violence, but at the same time telling his audience to "take to the streets." "All power to the people!" Kunstler said.

That night, Isla Vista blew up. A thousand rioting kids tore the place apart. They burned down the Bank of America, destroyed the real estate offices and other small businesses, broke all the windows in the tiny business district, and held off the cops and firemen while the bank burned. The local police, reinforced by cops

159

from surrounding counties, were still unable to penetrate the barrage of rocks and bottles. They dropped back while patrol cars were upset and burned, powerless to do much more than carry away their buddies to first-aid stations. A couple of the cops were seriously injured.

Inevitably, there was the aftermath. The Governor flew in to Santa Barbara, called the rioters "cowardly bums," and ordered out the National Guard. The Bank of America offered a $25,000 reward to turn in the riot's leaders, with no takers, so it contented itself with full-page ads in the newspapers. The riot subsided, and quiet was restored.

At last the police promised to reduce the number of prowl cars at Isla Vista and replace them with "friendly" officers on foot. Glowingly, the papers described two cops sitting at an outdoor café and having coffee with five smiling hippies.

Visalia State, like every other college campus, rocked with heated discussion over the riot, with most of the students against it—especially the destruction of property. But that died down in only a few days.

Dan knew that everything was back to normal one morning when Caroway grabbed him.

Bud said, "Stop! Stay right where you are, Miller."

Puzzled, Dan stood still near the doorway. He was on his way to the dayroom to pick up a book he had left there. Now Bud came toward him with an expression of bemused astonishment.

"What's up?" he asked.

Caroway didn't answer. Instead, he peered closely into Dan's face and then walked all around with an air of scientific scrutiny.

"It's true," he announced. "Gutierrez, get up and witness."

Uvaldo sighed and came over.

"Say, you guys," Dan protested, "what's all this crap?"

"Hear that, Gutierrez?" Bud exclaimed. "I tell you, the switch has flipped."

Uvaldo eyed Dan. "I don't see anything different," he said.

"Look again," Bud insisted. "Think. What's different about Miller?"

"Nothing. Well, maybe he hasn't shaved today. That's all."

Caroway put back his head and laughed. "Wrong. He has shaved. Notice the clean places coming down to a line."

Dan flushed. "Lay off," he snapped, finally understanding what went on. "I just—"

"Miller's growing a beard," Bud said to Uvaldo.

"What's so big about a beard?" Dan demanded.

"It's big with you, Dan," Bud said. "It means something. I think it's a good sign."

"Sure it is," Uvaldo agreed. "Dan, pay no attention to Caroway. For brains he's got guitar strings."

"That's true," Dan said. With sarcasm in his voice like cyclamate, he added, "Can I go now?"

"You can go," Bud told him, still grinning.

As he walked downstairs, Dan rubbed his fingers across the stubble on his chin. He had begun the beard the day he got back from Lakefield, and he was surprised that nobody had noticed until now.

The book he had left was still in the dayroom, so he went back upstairs expecting more needling, but there was none. Both Uvaldo and Bud were studying.

The last trip home had been especially disturbing. He couldn't understand Teresa's attitude, nor the wild reconciliation afterward. His parents were something else. They were old, with a certainty in the rightness of their beliefs.

But Teresa? The vitriolic force of her attack on dissent had shocked him profoundly, because it meant there were irreconcilable differences between them.

In the past, he had been able to dispel the feeling, but not this time. He had come back feeling uneasy, and the pervasive mood simply wouldn't go away.

The night on the hill when they had reached the barrier and Teresa had stopped them, first inviting, then rejecting? He hadn't thought about that, because it was too painful and complex. But somewhere, far back in his mind, his emotions told him that there had been a finality in that episode—either a beginning or an ending, and he couldn't face either one.

Not knowing where you were in these times could be fatal in the long pull. If a guy planned to take his college degree right to the center of American society and accept the rewards, he simply had to believe in the philosophy and principle of the Establishment, the way Teresa believed. And there wasn't any mystery or doubt about what those principles were; they bleated their message from every television set and the pronouncements of most of the leaders. It boiled down to something Dan remembered from being an altar boy: If you were asked to choose between God and Mammon, you chose Mammon.

One thing, Dan finally knew what his father did on the opposite side. There wasn't any middle ground left to stand on securely. Every young person alive needed to make a total decision about how he related to this scene, and to the future.

With him now was a growing sense of the urgency of the present, perhaps a need to be somewhere, that was almost like hunger. Like it or not, Teresa's tirade had crystallized that need instead of persuading him to accept her view.

But a beard? Straights everywhere wore beards and longer hair, thick sideburns, mod clothes. It meant nothing. It was the old who grew excited about such personal matters. Long hair and beards were a terrible affront to a lot of aging adults.

He planned to cut it off before he went home again; no use in stirring up the animals. All he wanted now was to see how he looked. Merely a whim.

On Monday afternoon, Gutierrez came on to Dan with something that might fit a guy with a dark stubble.

"Next Saturday," Uvaldo declared to nobody in particular, although Dan, Bud, and Conn were standing around, "some of us are going to picket the Shop-Easy again. They're selling grapes, naturally."

For a couple of seconds, there was no answer.

"You asking for recruits?" Sally inquired. "I mean, you come on in such an inconclusive style, Gutierrez. I'd hate to have you leading my revolution."

The Mexican smiled. "Maybe so. All right, Sally, will you be there at nine o'clock Saturday and carry one of our inflammatory signs? Like *'Viva la huelga'*?"

"Saturday?" Conn mused, as if flipping through a filing cabinet for previous appointments. "For how long?"

"From nine until we get busted."

"Oh," Conn said easily, "for about half an hour. Sure, I'll be there. Only find me a better sign. Let it say,

163

'Down with the capitalistic class and their grape guzzling.' "

"You don't guzzle a table grape, Conn," Bud offered. "You munch it."

"How about you, Caroway?" Gutierrez asked.

"Not me," instantly. "Uvaldo, you've got a real talent for trouble. This Isla Vista thing comes on and right-thinking citizens are ready to machine-gun demonstrators. So that's the time you decide to picket the chain stores. Count me out, Gutierrez. I've got a guitar lesson Saturday morning. Think I want four or five of those jocks jumping up and down on my spine?"

"See you there. Bring your guitar." Gutierrez turned to Dan, hesitating. Finally, "Miller?" he asked.

Dan was aware of their questioning glances. "I don't know," he replied honestly. "I really don't. I'll have to think it over for—a while."

"Sure. You need to think it over," Uvaldo said. "Even I did at first. And don't let it burn you. It's no great thing. We won't change Shop-Easy's mind and we've got plenty of others to help this time. Even Jenny."

Bud had sat down on his bed, grumbling. "Gluttons for punishment," he muttered to himself. "Always looking for trouble. Why can't everyone ease off?"

Nobody said anything, but Dan thought it was a good question.

Actually, he decided immediately. He would be there and carry a picket sign, and, like his friends, he would stand up to the jocks and the cops as best he could. If Jenny could do it, so could he.

Hell, the National Council of Churches endorsed the grape boycott, although a lot of fascists claimed the Council was a pack of commies. But they said that about nearly everyone else. If you didn't wave the flag and fight sex education as a Moscow plot, you were a dupe.

That didn't keep him from sifting around for plausible reasons to stay out of the line. A real confrontation could mean anything from injury to getting expelled, and Caroway was right about the timing. Finally, though, he had to admit that his indecision was chicken, psychologically and physically. The jocks couldn't break everyone's legs.

The compelling factor was Jenny. She was frail, and had no more business in a picket line than a heron standing up to bulldozers. Her presence, somehow, meant that he had to be there.

He knew what had kept him from saying yes immediately. Fear. He was frightened of what would happen to him in an unknown situation. He didn't want to get hurt or go to jail, but more than that, he didn't want the embarrassment he knew he would feel if he marched around with a sign in front of people. And right there it occurred to him that he had been afraid all his life—afraid, maybe, of living at all. Who was it that said America had a death-oriented society? The scientist who invented vitamin C, Dan recalled. So he decided.

On Wednesday, he said to Uvaldo, "Count me in on that Shop-Easy thing."

Gutierrez nodded. "I knew you'd decide that way, Dan," he said. "Uncle Pablo will be proud of you."

Until now, he hadn't said anything to Jenny about the boycott, because he had been waiting for her to tell him. But she hadn't.

On Wednesday at the coffee break, she suddenly giggled. "It's a beard, isn't it, Dan?" she asked, her brown eyes sparkling.

He didn't take offense; Jenny didn't create anger or embarrassment.

"Sure," he told her grandly. "Want to feel it?"

By now the stubble was a full quarter of an inch long, giving him the appearance of being a long way from soap and water.

She lifted her hand and touched her fingers against the beard.

"Magnificent," she said. "May I ask why? With you it's quite a change. Did anything happen?"

"No," he lied. "I just decided to see how I looked behind a hedge. Everybody's doing it."

"I know."

"Well?"

She stood back a step, eyeing him in a mock-critical pose.

"I can't say it's much of an improvement, Dan," she ventured. "I liked you the way you were."

"Naked that way?"

"No. Just being yourself. You looked like what you really are: a musician, a poet, and—well—a nice guy. You didn't need anything else."

"I'll think that over," he told her. He grinned. "Jenny, the truth is that it itches unbearably. It takes real sacrifice to grow a beard."

"I shouldn't wonder," she answered. "You look as if you'd suffered."

They sipped their coffee. The time to move on was only a couple of minutes away.

"Are you really going to be in that picket line at Shop-Easy?" he asked suddenly.

She glanced up at him.

"How did you know?"

166

"Uvaldo told me."

She looked away. "Yes," softly. "I feel obligated to be there. Those people have had a terrible time, and Uvaldo has always been so kind to me. That's why."

"I'll be there too."

She seemed surprised.

"Are you sure you want to, Dan? There could be trouble. There was last year."

"What about you?" he demanded. "You can handle trouble better than I can?"

Strangely, she nodded. "Yes, I think so," leveling, "because I've had experience. A person has to keep nonviolent and nonaggressive all the time. If you get mad and resist, they hurt you."

"You think I'd be like that—lose my temper."

"Yes. I think there is violence in you, Dan."

"I'll risk it," he said.

It was time to go.

"Bye," she told him.

He nodded. "See you Saturday."

She shook her head. "Maybe you shouldn't," she replied. "Anyway, take care."

They headed for class in opposite directions.

On Saturday, Dan awoke with the grape boycott heavy in his mind. He was scared, both of being there in public carrying a sign, and of the trouble that was sure to come.

But he couldn't chicken out. Not now. Gutierrez was already up, moving around. He shook Bud out of the sack. Caroway sat around, mumbling unprintable comments on the occasion. But after a while he came to life.

The three of them were at the Shop-Easy lot by nine

o'clock. Bud parked the ancient VW a full block away, claiming he didn't want the cops or jocks to damage the delicate mechanism in their insane zeal.

A few people were already there, standing around, mostly Chicanos, and Conn, of course. Jenny hadn't arrived, and Dan hoped she had decided to stay home.

But just as he was thinking about her, she appeared.

"Hi," she said to him briefly, and then went over and helped with the picket signs.

Uvaldo was the organizer.

"Want a sign, Dan?" he asked speculatively.

"Sure, why not?"

His sign said, "Grapes Keep Children Hungry."

By now the parking lot was beginning to stack up with cars. The doors were open and customers had begun to enter and leave. Gutierrez gave his instructions. The pickets were to walk at a certain distance from the entrances in a circle that didn't block the driveways into the lot. There was to be no violence. Cesar Chavez had repeatedly insisted that no grape striker would resort to that. The pickets were to talk quietly and persuasively, but only if spoken to.

In half an hour, the store manager came out. He went directly to Conn, who was taller and bigger than anyone else in the line. The man was of medium build, pale, with a heavy beard shaved close, and thin-lipped.

"What are you doing?" he asked Conn loudly.

"We're picketing your store because you're selling table grapes," Sally said in his ominous monotone, his brand of nonviolence.

"This is private property," the manager said. "I can call the police and have you evicted."

"If you do," Conn said, "it'll ruin your business for

168

the whole day. We won't make trouble. We're only protesting your sale of table grapes."

"Well, damn it," the manager said, his voice rising,
"what do you expect me to do? I get the grapes on consignment. This is grape country. What am I supposed
to do?"

"Get rid of your table grapes," Sally intoned. "Table
grapes mean hunger for kids in this valley. They mean
despair, and men out of work for years and years."

"I can't help that," the manager yelled. "I get the
damned grapes on consignment. Now get off this lot."

"Not until you get rid of the grapes," Sally Conn told
him in the same funereal tones.

The picketing went on after the manager had
slammed back into the store. In the first hour, nothing
happened. A few people spoke to the pickets, especially
to Jenny. A couple of older people grew very loud and
angry. But most of the customers simply pretended
there was nobody there. They walked around the line
the way pedestrians walk around something dirty that
has been deposited on the sidewalk during the night.

After two hours of walking, it began to look like a
long day and Dan was ready to sit down and rest. He
thought of the thousands of items a store like this had
to sell, and how futile it was to insist that grapes be
part of the stock. Why not hang up grapes and forget
it? he reasoned. The customers really didn't care that
much; all they wanted was suitable food at a decent
price.

About then, the monotony split apart.

The jocks of Visalia State got there. They pulled
their Mustangs into the lot and went to work. The manager had probably called them.

169

The picket line stopped, frozen as the jocks appeared in close order. Dan recognized Bill Pritchett, a fullback who was in one of his classes. Pritchett was short, terribly wide, with a butch haircut and close-set eyes. In class he was a fairly nice guy.

The signs went first, torn to shreds. Next the beatings began. Dan faced a tall guy who threw a punch at him. He saw it coming, ducked, and stepped away. But his memory later was of the face, twisted into real hatred.

Somebody was screaming. He moved backward, turned, and saw that it was Jenny. One of the jocks had her by the arms from behind, pulling them around cruelly. He ran that way, got there, with the blood in his mind, boiling. He came up sideways and kicked the jock viciously in the groin. The guy let go, babbling in pain, doubling over with the agony.

In a red haze, Dan had Jenny by the arm, impelling her forward.

"Run," he said, "get out of here."

They were through the gate and out on the sidewalk, still running. After a while, they subsided into a walk.

"Dan," Jenny sobbed. "Dan!"

He didn't answer. When they reached Caroway's car, he opened the door and pushed her inside.

"We should have stayed," Jenny panted. "The others—"

"They can take care of themselves. Anyway, I'll go back."

"You hurt that person terribly," Jenny said.

"I hope so," Dan Miller replied.

By now, police sirens were threading the air with their cacophony of disaster. A moment later, Uvaldo and Bud reached the car.

170

"Get going," Gutierrez said.

"What happened?" Jenny asked when they were out on the street.

"Not much," Uvaldo said. "Sally took a couple of pokes in the face, and a couple of others were roughed up. But nothing serious. Everyone got out."

"We should have stayed and waited for the cops," Jenny said.

"Not this time. We made our point. We picketed and stood up to the jocks—after all, we only had fifteen people. Next time, Jenny, when we have more, we'll wait."

"Uvaldo," Jenny moaned. "When will this end?"

Bud Caroway laughed.

"Never," he said.

13

THE CONFRONTATION in the Shop-Easy parking lot hardened Dan's attitude. In the locker rooms at high school he had faced the jocks, just as every kid had to do. For a while, they had terrified him.

But not now; on Saturday he had felt no fear. His only concern had been to get Jenny out of there before she got hurt. In a way, he felt sorry for the jocks, as if they were victims too.

The grape boycott made sense. If people refused to buy table grapes, eventually the growers would have to yield. They would have to pay fair wages and recognize collective bargaining with the people who worked their fields. Sure, the growers had rights too. It was their land, their plantings, their water, their money. But somewhere in the center of such a dispute lay justice to both. It was wrong to deny that this center existed.

Of course, the boycott was Uvaldo's special thing. Dan had bigger conflicts to solve for himself. He wanted to graduate, marry Teresa, and live happily ever after. The formula was simple and quite American.

But after Saturday, Dan knew what he had suspected all along—ever since those terrible days in high school. He didn't have a place to be anywhere. He didn't even exist. Not yet.

Perhaps once there had been a time in life—his dad's, maybe—when a person could decide to wait and see. He could follow the right crowd, do what it was doing, fit in somewhere, and succeed.

Maybe, Dan thought. But maybe not, too. Perhaps history had always demanded that the young decide. The difference now was the bomb, poverty in an affluent society, the war in Vietnam, and the terrible scurvy of racism. Had their counterparts been around in other generations?

Fundamentally, Dan felt sorry for everyone: his father and mother, the grape strikers, the store manager, the jocks, and the cops. They all had jobs or roles to play that superseded their human judgment. Most of them were paid to act the way they did. But that didn't explain the jocks who were students, like himself. As for the cops, they were just that, cops. Like all police everywhere. A gun and authority did something to human beings.

The issue to Dan was clear enough: whether a guy was with the Establishment, or against it.

The Establishment! That was a big, amorphous term invented by the young. It could mean everything that was classified as straight, from a haircut to money in the bank, stocks, interest, the corner grocery store, a Detroit car, or church.

Dan put these easy definitions away. Too many good things had happened to allow him to condemn or reject the simple forms of living. He wasn't ready to accept Sally's explanations about capitalism.

173

But he hadn't been ready for the jocks of the Establishment, either, charging down on a few quiet people carrying signs. He wasn't ready for the cops and their riot sticks and Mace.

Slowly and painfully in his freshman year at Visalia State, Dan Miller began to make up his mind. In this he was like thousands of other uncommitted college students all across the land. He faced decision, like them all, not because he wanted to, but because the jocks and the cops and the militants forced him. It was a time in history—just before the massacre at Kent State.

The adults were naturally confused. Pantie raids on girls' dormitories, goldfish-eating, Volkswagen-packing, and even the smashing of old pianos had seemed normal kid behavior.

But this? Questioning authority, the Government, parents, even the structure of society? Why, this was anarchy that had to be crushed.

All the factions overlooked the Dan Millers, quiet young men and women who made up their minds one way or another. Because they did, they were a unique generation of American youth.

When Dan went home to Lakefield again it was with his mind almost made up. Not about everything, of course. For example, he stood a long time in front of his mirror examining the beard.

It looked terrible, giving him less the appearance of a young intellectual than of an adolescent bum.

Holding the razor, he fingered the stubble for a long time, speculating on its effect at home—as if he didn't know. At last he put the razor away and kept the beard, perhaps out of vanity. If a guy decided to grow a beard, that was his business.

He got home late at night, went to bed, and met his

parents in the morning at the breakfast table. They stared at him. He had expected laughter, but that wasn't their reaction.

"Dan!" his mother exclaimed. "Why—why, I don't know what to say."

Dan smiled, half amused at himself and still hoping to turn the matter of his so-called beard into the joke it was.

"It's a beard, Mother," he said, "although you may not recognize it. Everybody's got one. I'm just going along with the crowd."

His father's reaction was more explicit. "Shave it off," he commanded, his expression dark. "You look like an idiot. Get that thing off your face today."

Dan took a deep breath. "Why, Dad?" he asked.

"Why?" The man stood up and waved his arms dramatically. "Because you look like a hippie. No son of mine is going to look like a hippie."

Dan thought that over for a second because Paul Miller was so positive. Plenty of parents had needed to accept sons who grew shoulder-length hair, beards, and the works. The matter of appearance or individual differences was no big thing. Perhaps if he talked it over quietly, kept his cool, his dad would understand.

"I don't think I look like a hippie," he said, "but if I did, would that be so bad?"

"Bad?" Paul Miller thundered. "Now, look here, you know very well I'm in a county administrative position. An elective position. What does it say of me if my son is running around with a beard? How do you think that'll strike the voters next year?"

"I don't know," Dan said truthfully. How a beard could change votes was beyond him.

"Of course you know!"

"I don't."

"Then think now!"

"But, Dad," choosing words carefully, "how could something I do about my appearance have any bearing on your job? Who would care?"

"Shave it off!" Paul Miller said harshly, his voice shaking with emotion.

"Now, Paul," Dan's mother said, "he's only a boy. He probably wanted to see what Teresa would say, and—"

"No, Mother," he told her. "That isn't it. I know what she'll say, and I'm not just a boy at all. I'm—"

"You're a fool like all the rest," Mr. Miller declared. "Now, I've told you I want that—whatever it is—off your face today. Do you understand?"

Something died there in Dan Miller—the hope of ever recapturing an accord with his dad. The recollection of the trips to Lone Pine Creek flashed across his mind. Those ancient days were gone forever. From here on, his way and Paul Miller's way had to diverge toward unknown destinations.

"I understand."

His father left the room. A moment later, he stamped out of the house, shutting the front door loudly.

After he had gone, the silence in the room was heavy. Mrs. Miller sat down at the table looking anxious.

"More hotcakes?" she inquired.

"No, Mother," Dan said. "Breakfast was great."

"You will shave it off, won't you?" the woman asked timorously. "I haven't seen your father so angry for—well, a long time. It's terribly important to him, Dan.

176

He's been having a lot of trouble lately, and anything can upset him."

Dan felt a surge of resistance within him and he measured that against his mother's plea. His father had been terribly serious, as if a beard was something to fear.

"It really doesn't mean anything to me, Mother," he said, "and it does to you. I'll probably get rid of it."

He did. Before he went over to Teresa's he shaved himself clean, the razor grating over the stubble. Then he called his girl. She was at home.

He didn't stop to get his mother's reaction; he knew that she would be grateful that he had avoided trouble and obeyed his father. But he wasn't at Teresa's five minutes until he wished he had kept the beard.

"Dan," she told him almost at once, "you've changed."

That was probably true. After a beard is shaved, the skin hangs limp and white for a day or two.

"Sure," he said, "but I'll be all right by tomorrow."

"Tomorrow won't be soon enough," Teresa said.

He blinked. "I don't understand."

"You've changed," she repeated. "You're not the same at all, ever since that day at the lake."

"What are you talking about?"

"You know very well."

He didn't know. "Give it to me straight," he said.

"All right. You've changed about everything. Everything we've planned and believed in. Everything that meant we could be married and love each other. You've said you don't want any of that. You don't want me!"

A numbness swept over him as he tried to comprehend what she was telling him. If he had done anything to cause this, he would call it back. Change? Why, change was the rule of life. Teresa had changed, but that didn't make his love for her any less.

"I haven't said that at all," he replied. "You know I haven't."

Abruptly, her hazel eyes bloomed with tears that broke and spilled down her cheeks.

"That's the awful part," she said, controlling herself. "You don't really seem to know. Since you went to college, Dan, you've become somebody else, somebody I —I don't even know—"

"Somebody else?"

"Yes," meeting him in challenge. "Oh, I know you've pretended to agree with me—about Montana Diablo, about—well, all those far-out, wild things. But I know. Once we were together and now we're miles apart."

"How? How can that be in a few months?"

Her eyes narrowed. "How should I understand that? You've been on a trip—away from me, away from everything I am." She laughed in a phony style. "Now you're trying to weasel out of it."

"Weasel?" It was an ugly word.

"Weasel," she said. "You've been exposed to all this crazy New Left stuff, and you haven't the guts to stand up against them."

"Guts?" he began. "I—"

She spoke poisonously. "Of course you don't get it, because you want to be everywhere at once. You can't make up your mind; you don't have the courage to love me, and believe in me."

"That isn't true," he said.

178

"Stop it, Dan!" Teresa almost yelled. "I can't stand you anymore. I can't. I can't!"

She began to cry in the way of women, like a leak in a gas line that can't be stopped.

"Teresa," he said, coming forward, "I'm sorry—"

"Sorry! Sorry!" she sobbed.

"Yes," he told her dully, "and if you'll let me, I'll—"

"Fix it all up!" she snapped mockingly, the tears gone as miraculously as they had appeared. "Oh, I know you will. You'll do anything I want."

"Of course."

Her lip curled in scorn. "Well, I don't want you to fix this up. I don't want you in any way. Now go home to your mommy, you little kid."

Eventually, that was what Dan did; he went home. But not before he stood there and dissembled, talking desperately in an attempt to salvage something from this wreckage.

He hated himself for his cowardice even while he talked, but he remembered Teresa as she had been last year and the year before. Change? Why, she had changed him more than any other factor in his whole life. She had made that time endurable and full of hope. More than that, she had structured self-confidence within him and was really responsible for his being in college at all. Somehow, some way, perhaps they could work out their differences.

And Teresa cooled down. They kissed perfunctorily and made up—if a person wanted to call an armed truce the settlement of a quarrel. He was supposed to take her to the drive-in tonight, and it would all be the same again. The same!

At home, he lay down on his bed and thought of

179

Teresa Bailey—of their years together. She was a certain type of girl and she was true to herself, to her family and its traditions. She couldn't be any other way. She saw her life running parallel to all the established ways, and the person she loved had to go that direction too.

It would all be easy enough. He could forget everything, move away from Uvaldo and Bud, and adopt the philosophy of the jocks. Perhaps he could even transfer from Visalia to another college, or better yet, drop out, get a job, and marry Teresa now.

For a moment or two, he indulged himself in that fantasy. Then he rolled over and groaned. It wouldn't work. In a month or two, they would be fighting like mad. There wasn't any solution.

Day wore down and became evening, when his mother called him for dinner. They were waiting for him, Mrs. Miller nervous and his father solemn and stern.

The table gleamed with snowy linen and polished silver. Candlesticks in the center lit the pretty display. Dan pulled back his chair, aware that his father's eyes were on him with something like triumph for his victory over the beard.

Suddenly, the whole issue for Dan Miller was settled, then and in the future. There on a silver tray between the candlesticks, their perfect beauty laced with jewels of moisture, were bunches of table grapes, two varieties—purple and green. Dan stared at them as if they were coiled rattlesnakes.

"Mother," he said evenly, gesturing toward the fruit, "those are grapes."

Mrs. Miller smiled ‑modestly. "Yes. Aren't they

lovely? I found them down at Smathers'. You know it's been so hard to get—"

"I can't eat dinner with those grapes on the table," Dan said quietly. "You'll have to take them away."

"Why—"

Mr. Miller came in. "What now?" he demanded. "What's this drivel about grapes?"

So it was that Dan faced his father at last on equal terms.

"It isn't drivel," he said earnestly. "It's a matter of life and death for people. Real people, Father—men, women, and children who are going hungry tonight. That's the meaning of table grapes."

"Nonsense. Talk sense this minute, young man, or I'll—"

Dan did talk sense. He began at the beginning while the dinner cooled. He said it all, about the grape strike, about Uncle Pablo, about the picketing at Visalia and the attacking jocks. He told them what college militancy was about—the injustices of the Establishment, the discrepancies between what was said and what was done.

"I don't want to be obnoxious," he finished, "but I simply can't eat while we have grapes in the house."

A silence ticked ominously, like a bomb.

"Well, don't eat," Paul Miller shouted at last. "Get up from this table and go back to your room, you impudent slob."

Dan did, but not before his father had said a lot more. A son was entitled to his own way of thinking, Mr. Miller said. He could promote the grape boycott; he could identify himself with the student "revolution" and the militants. Nothing could prevent that.

But parents didn't need to go along; they didn't have to pay their hard-earned money to have their son indoctrinated in beliefs totally foreign to them—not one thin dime. Either he went back to college, got down to its real business so he could eventually be prepared for a job, or he could make it entirely on his own. He had that choice.

Finally, Dan Miller was on the bus again and heading back to Visalia. At the drive-in the night before, Teresa had melted into his arms. "Please, Dan," she had begged, "don't ever leave me. Don't become a stranger."

That was how he felt now, like a stranger, even to himself.

He pictured his parents, both of them hard-working, honorable, good people. Loyal Americans. They wanted their son to be exactly like them and to go to college to learn how to do it. And what did it mean to be exactly like them?

He didn't know. Right now it seemed to mean that he must be indifferent to the real world and be forever "thinking it over." It meant that he must shut his eyes and hide everything that was happening under the covers of an affluent death.

And Teresa? A changing world frightened her, even though she knew it was there all along with its ominous implications. She wanted to tell herself it was all a schoolgirl's dream that would somehow go away.

Dan shut his eyes hard. He had gone to Visalia a confused and indifferent high school kid. Out of his confusion he had forged a couple of ideas—that was all. But just a couple of ideas had altered him so profoundly that he was totally unacceptable to them now—to the people he loved, Teresa, his parents. They wanted to tell him that he didn't exist.

He couldn't have a self—not one of his own. Yet wasn't that the reason a person went to college, to find a self? to learn what he believed and what went on?

Sure, they had been fair. His father had the right to tell him he must conform as long as he was being supported; Teresa had the right to withhold her love.

But what were his rights? Dan asked himself that.

He shook his head from side to side in the agony of decision. Slowly, there on a bus in the middle of the Central Valley of California, he made up his mind at last. He had to be his own man; he had to do it or die within himself. Whatever the price, it must be paid.

Life itself was about that, he guessed—finding the way to self-determination—knowing what you held true.

He had to go there.

Dan didn't do anything big or dramatic. His fees were paid until the end of the quarter, and he had a little money left. He would take it as it came.

That evening, he went over to Conn's with Bud and Uvaldo. Jenny was there. He sat down beside her.

"Jenny," he said after a while, "when I first met you here you sang a little folk song."

"I remember," she said. "It's called 'Let Your Little Light Shine.'" Her eyes searched him. "What's the trouble, Dan?" she asked.

"Nothing," he said.

She looked away an instant but then turned back, her face very serious. She slipped her warm hand into his.

"Nothing?" she said. "All right. But sometime you

183

may want to tell me. Anyway, the song went like this."

She began to sing the words almost inaudibly—just for them alone.

"Maybe I will want to tell you," said Dan Miller. "Someday."

Biography of
JAMES L. SUMMERS

JAMES L. SUMMERS was born in Oshkosh, Wisconsin. When he was a child, his family traveled a great deal, so that he went to school in Wisconsin, Indiana, Illinois, England, Germany, Connecticut, Cuba, Hawaii, Oregon, and finally Arizona, where he graduated from elementary school. After graduating from high school in Milwaukee, Wisconsin, he spent a year in footloose travel in Canada and the United States, and went to sea from Brooklyn as an engine wiper. He visited the West Indies and other ports and finally returned to school at Chaffey Junior College in California. After a year there he matriculated at the University of Wisconsin, but his college days were cut short by illness.

The following year he attended summer session at the University of Southern California, where he met the girl who was to become his wife. They were married the next winter, while Mr. Summers was a student at the University of California at Los Angeles. During the depression Mr. Summers had to leave school, and he worked at many jobs. He was a vacuum-cleaner

185

salesman, a neon-light repairman, a truck driver, and eventually owner of a small electrical business.

Still wanting to finish college, Mr. Summers got a night job, and after two years received his A.B. degree at U.C.L.A. He then started teaching. Writing also interested him, but it was a few years before he sold any stories to the national magazines. One day an editor sold a story for him to *Seventeen* magazine, and from then on he wrote almost exclusively for young people. Now Mr. Summers is writing novels for teen-agers and young adults. His story *Girl Trouble* was selected as an Honor Book by the *New York Herald Tribune*'s Spring Book Festival Committee. *Prom Trouble, Gift Horse, The Karting Crowd, Tiger Terwilliger, The Amazing Mr. Tenterhook, Senior Dropout,* and *The Iron Doors Between* were Junior Literary Guild selections, and *Ring Around Her Finger* was a selection of the Young People's Division of the Literary Guild. Mr. Summers lives in Atascadero, California, and has retired from teaching to make writing a full-time career.

THE SWISS
HOW THEY LIVE AND WORK

The Swiss

HOW THEY LIVE AND WORK

NEIL ALEXANDER

DAVID & CHARLES   Newton Abbot

PRAEGER PUBLISHERS   New York

ISBN (Great Britain) 0 7153 7190 8
ISBN (United States) 0-275-56340-5
Library of Congress Catalog Card Number 75-42591

Set in 11 on 13pt Baskerville
and printed in Great Britain
by Latimer Trend & Company Ltd Plymouth
for David & Charles (Publishers) Limited
Brunel House Newton Abbot Devon
and Praeger Publishers, Inc.
111 Fourth Avenue, New York, N.Y. 10003

Contents

Contents

List of Illustrations

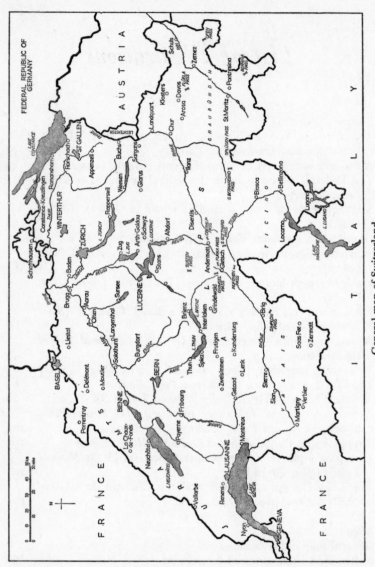

General map of Switzerland

Introduction

SWITZERLAND is a land of contrasts—its geography, its climate, its history, and the language, religion and racial background of its people are far more varied than one might expect in such a small country. It is a land of misconceptions too. For some, Switzerland is a land of perpetual snow, a land of chalets, of cuckoo clocks and edelweiss where the inhabitants spend their time eating milk chocolate and yodelling to each other across the valleys; for others, it is a land peopled by bankers and financiers, men who manipulate the western world's currency systems for their own ends; for others again, it is the epitome of stability, the neutral state *par excellence*, above the squabbles of other nations, the home of the Red Cross and the Geneva Convention.

Of course, there is an element of truth in all these exaggerations and generalisations. Switzerland *is* a tourist country, with enough picturesque traditions to satisfy even the most demanding holiday-maker, enough breath-taking landscapes to satisfy his deepest need for communion with nature. It *is* one of the world's major financial centres, and a home of world government. But Switzerland in the twentieth century is more than all this. It is a highly industrialised state, exporting to all parts of the world the high-quality goods it is able to make so well, from the gigantic engineering equipment to the watches and clocks which have become a byword for accuracy, precision and reliability. This is where Switzerland's wealth lies nowadays.

What does the future hold for Switzerland? For the past quarter of a century the country has known prosperity on a scale never dreamt of before. It is virtually certain however that in the years to come its economic growth will not be as rapid as hitherto, irrespective of the international economic situation, for the size of the foreign labour force on which that prosperity is based has now reached its limit and any future economic growth must be based on greater productivity alone. During the next two or three decades the depopulation of the countryside will continue, as more and more people move to the towns, and it is foreseen that four urban centres will expand to over 200,000 inhabitants by the end of the century. At the same time, new issues such as the protection of the environment will become of key importance.

Over the past century Switzerland has given the world a great deal to admire, and despite its increasing involvement with the crisis-torn world of the present day, it still justifies its reputation as an oasis of calm, good sense and reliability. Those who love Switzerland hope that it will long continue to do so.

Note: the names of many of the cantons and the larger towns exist in two, and sometimes three, language versions. Throughout this book the spelling preferred is that which is used in the canton or town itself, eg Vaud, not Waadt; Graubünden, not Grisons; Basel, not Bâle or Basle, except where a commonly used English equivalent exists, eg Geneva, not Genève or Genf.

I

The Country and the People

SWITZERLAND, or the Swiss Confederation to give the country its official title, is a federal state of central Europe. It is a small country—smaller, indeed, than is often imagined. Half the size of Scotland or the state of South Carolina, twice as big as Wales or New Jersey, it covers an area of 15,944 square miles, about half of which is forested or rocky, or covered by water, glaciers or perpetual snow. A landlocked country, it shares common frontiers with France to the west, the Federal Republic of Germany to the north, Liechtenstein and Austria to the east and Italy to the south. By far the longest of these frontiers is that with Italy, which twists along the southern side of the Alps for 460 miles, thrusting out into one great salient after another. The Franco-Swiss border runs from Lake Geneva to Basel, a distance of 350 miles, that with Germany curves eastwards from Basel to Lake Constance over some 225 miles, whilst the frontiers with Liechtenstein and Austria add 125 miles to give a total of 1,160 miles for the full perimeter.

For the most part these frontiers follow the great natural barriers—the Alps, the Jura mountains and the Rhine—except for that between Italy and the canton of Ticino, which spills over into the upper Italian plain almost as far south as Como. This is the southernmost tip of Switzerland and from here to the most northerly point in the canton of Schaffhausen is approximately 145 miles as the crow flies. At its widest, Switzerland stretches almost 220 miles between the commune of Chancy in the west and the most easterly point of the Engadine. The present border was determined in 1815 following the Congress of Vienna and apart from a few minor adjustments

and exchanges for administrative purposes it has remained unchanged ever since.

PHYSICAL CHARACTERISTICS

To many people 'Switzerland' and 'the Alps' are synonym-
ous. The tourist brochures and the chocolate box pictures
conjure up visions of endless ranges of snowy mountains, fierce
rocky peaks, giddy journeys in cable-cars, dazzlingly white ski-
slopes dotted with happy, colourfully dressed holidaymakers. In
fact, the Alps cover only about a half of the country's surface
area, and Switzerland itself has a comparatively small share—a
fifth—of the Alpine massif as a whole. But it is true to say that
Switzerland offers some of the most spectacular Alpine scenery,
with over twenty of its peaks topping 12,000ft, culminating in
the 15,217ft Dufourspitze in the Monte Rosa chain, the highest
peak in Switzerland. (Mont Blanc, the highest mountain in
Europe, is of course not in the Swiss Alps.) The tangled network
of mountain ranges, rounded summits and dramatic peaks,
valleys, passes and high pastures which make the Alps such a
delightful haven for skiers, mountaineers, walkers and nature
lovers in general reflects the highly complicated geological
structure of the western Alps. This is itself a result of the violent
compression and folding that this part of central Europe under-
went during the tertiary era. These ancient fold mountains,
dislocated by subsequent intense pressures, were gradually
worn down by climatic action. New sedimentary rocks were
then laid down over them and contorted and eroded in their
turn.

The fulcrum of the Swiss Alps, and a crossroads of great
strategic value, is the St Gotthard massif, the source of two of
the most important rivers of western Europe, the Rhine and the
Rhône. The catchment areas of these two waterways cover
almost nine-tenths of the surface area of Switzerland. The
Rhine first flows eastwards to Chur and then turns north to
form the border first with Liechtenstein and then with Austria.
It empties into Lake Constance near Rorschach, and flows out
of the lake in a westerly direction, through Schaffhausen, over

the spectacular Rhine Falls, and then, dividing Switzerland from the Federal Republic of Germany, on to Basel, where it leaves Switzerland and makes its way northwards to Strasbourg, the Ruhr and the North Sea. The Rhône Glacier gives birth to the Rhône only a few miles from the source of the Rhine, but nowhere else are the two rivers as near to each other as they are here. The Rhône makes its way westwards down to the broad alluvial plain of the Valais; at Martigny it turns sharply north to empty itself into Lake Geneva between the Dents du Midi and the Diablerets. After leaving the lake at Geneva, the Rhône very soon enters France, passing through Lyon and Avignon on its warm journey to the Mediterranean.

The St Gotthard massif is the mother of a third river-child, with different ambitions again. The Ticino flows south to Locarno and into Italy through Lake Maggiore, joining the Po south of Pavia and bringing Swiss Alpine water to the Adriatic. Fifty miles to the east, the river Inn (or En) begins its own long journey in the Engadine, near St Moritz, to flow through Austria into the Danube and thence into the Black Sea. This part of Switzerland has been called the 'watershed of Europe', a description that is clearly justified, for the rivers of which it is the source flow north, south, east and west into four different seas. The St Gotthard massif is also at the crossroads of the major east-west and north-south rail and road links through the St Gotthard, Furka and Oberalp passes, a geographical situation that has had a considerable influence on Swiss foreign policy over the years.

The peculiar hedonistic appeal of the Alps is, in the opinion of some forward-looking thinkers in the Alpine countries, a source of possible danger in the future. They see, in the proliferation of ski resorts in hitherto virtually unpopulated mountain valleys, a threat to the precarious ecological balance of the Alps. There is a risk that man, and particularly those who are busy developing the newer and bigger resorts, may upset the environmental pattern by introducing into the high Alps those aspects of modern life which incite people to flee to the mountains in the first place: the noise, the crowds, the raw concrete apartment blocks, the crowded roads, the pollution.

By slashing new ski runs through forest barriers the developers may create avalanche corridors and, indeed, some new ski resorts have been established in areas that are notoriously avalanche-prone. On the other hand, the tourist industry brings in a great deal of revenue for the Alpine nations. In Switzerland, for instance, tourism is the third most important source of income. The need, therefore, is to strike a balance between economic needs and the community's right to enjoy its leisure time on the one hand and the preservation of the environment on the other.

The Alps are not the only mountains in Switzerland. The Jura mountains, partly in Switzerland and partly in France, take up about a tenth of the surface area of the country. They bear little resemblance to the Alps, however. Stretching in a gentle curve from the Rhône to the Rhine and forming Switzerland's north-western frontier, they are heavily wooded and much lower in average height. In fact, with their most lofty peak standing not much more than 5,000 feet high, they hardly count as mountains by Swiss standards—no glaciers, no eternal snow, no permanently white peaks. Yet these comparatively simple fold mountains have their own charm and offer more than merely the splendid view they give of the Alps (on a day without haze, mountains 80 miles away and more are clearly visible). Rising eastwards in a series of gradual escarpments from the river Saône, in France, the Jura mountains fall suddenly and steeply away towards Lake Geneva and the Lake of Neuchâtel, the western banks of which are thus dominated by an impressive mountain rampart. North-west of the Chasseral, the highest peak of the central Jura, the ridged parallel valleys behind the rampart give way to the great upland pastures of the Franches-Montagnes, some 3,000 feet high. This is a landscape to be enjoyed between spring and autumn, on foot or on horseback, a region where cattle and horses graze in freedom over the broad, wooded, almost park-like meadows and where the squat stone houses prepare to sit out the long winter, hunching themselves against the fierce, blasting north winds. Further north and east again, the Jura break up into a group of flat table mountains, stretching across the cantons of

Baselland, Aargau and Schaffhausen and into southern Germany. Here the woods and meadows have a melancholy fascination that recalls Scandinavia.

It would be wrong, however, to imagine that Switzerland is a land of mountains alone. To do so would be to disregard the broad plain, the 'plateau' as the Swiss call it, which sweeps from Geneva through Lausanne, Fribourg, Bern and Lucerne to Zürich and Lake Constance and on into Germany. These towns are not Alpine towns, and their inhabitants are much the same as any other city-dwellers, even though many of them may be imbued with a love of the mountains. Significantly, the population density of the plateau is near to 650 per square mile, whereas that of the country as a whole is about 390 to the square mile. In fact, some two-thirds of the Swiss population live and work on the plateau, where the milder climate provides an added incentive.

The plateau, however, is not a true plain but rather a succession of wide, shallow river valleys and lakes, separated by undulating higher land. Although the soil here is particularly fertile, the major economic importance of the plateau resides not in its agriculture but in the industry of the cantons of Zürich, Aargau, St Gallen and Geneva.

CLIMATE

Switzerland's climate is as varied as its geography. When the grape harvest begins in the Valais, the warmest and driest region of Switzerland, and on the slopes overlooking Lake Geneva and the Lake of Neuchâtel, the first autumn snows have already fallen on the Alps. Fig trees too flourish in the Valais, and palm trees grow on the banks of Lake Maggiore; yet the Jura uplands are swept by winds that have earned the area near La Brévine the name of 'Switzerland's little Siberia'. There is indeed a remarkable range of climatic activity within this pocket-sized country which has affinities with all the European climatic regions. The country's weather is further affected by differences in altitude, by orientation and by the protection of the mountains so that at certain times of the year three seasons can be found at the same time, depending on the altitude. Faced with such a profusion of micro-climates, one is hard put to it to make comparisons. In general terms, we may say that summers in Switzerland tend to be warmer than those in the United Kingdom, and can be scorchingly hot, whereas winters are usually colder, although less humid. One does not en- counter those bitterly cold and damp English days when an east wind chills the very marrow—the Swiss *bise*, the north wind that blows from central Europe across the plateau, is in winter a cold but dry wind, and the humidity level in Geneva in January often falls below 40 per cent. The *bise* is actually a fine-weather wind, although in spring and early summer it can play havoc with the young green shoots on the vines and fruit trees.

Winter is often marked by long anticyclonic periods, which are the cause of one disagreeable aspect of the Swiss climate as far as the inhabitants of most of the plateau towns are con- cerned. Those who have visited Geneva, Lausanne or Bern in the summer only, when a pseudo-tropical sun blazes in an ultramarine sky, would be disillusioned if they were to return in January or February, the bleak months when the sky can be almost permanently covered by layers of low stratus cloud, and all is quiet and drained of any colour but grey. These are the days, too, when the *bise* can blow for days on end, keeping midday temperatures well below freezing, so that the roads are covered with black ice and the hours drag endlessly.

Fortunately for the spirits of the plateau-dwellers, the upper limit of the stratus is rarely above 3,000ft, and therefore, every Saturday and Sunday in winter, streams of cars from the plateau cities can be seen making their way up the twisty roads to the nearest ski-slopes, which, although well above the banks of stratus, are usually within an hour's drive of the town. To drive from the grey and misty streets, through the cloud layers, to the snowy slopes scintillating under a cloudless anticyclonic sky is an unforgettable experience. Small wonder then, that many tens of thousands of Swiss people own a 'secondary residence'—a chalet or a flat—in one or other of the mountain villages of the Alps or the Jura. An idea of the frequency of the grey days may be gained from an examination of the annual meteorological statistics. For instance, in 1971, Zürich, Neuchâtel, Lausanne and Geneva each averaged about 60 days of fog—and fog is virtually unknown outside winter.

The *bise* has a southerly counterpart, the *föhn*, a strong, warm wind that can completely upset the weather conditions of the Alps in a matter of hours. It springs up following the development of a climatic situation characterised by a low pressure area north of the Alps, with higher pressure over Italy. Moist air from the Mediterranean is drawn rapidly towards the low pressure system, sweeps up the southern face of the Alps and is thereby cooled, bringing torrential rain to the windward slopes. Having shed all its moisture, it blows over the Alpine ridge and descends the leeward valleys, becoming warmer and drier as it progresses. During the winter and spring, *föhn* conditions are accompanied by a serious risk of avalanches, trickling mountain streams become angry torrents, the hazard of fire in the mountain forests becomes suddenly more immediate and indeed smoking can be forbidden in some areas that are particularly at risk. Moreover, for some people the *föhn* can be a cause of psychological malaise, although why this should be so is imperfectly understood. On the other hand, the *föhn* does melt the snow early and thus opens up the high pastureland for sheep grazing.

Mention may be made here of the many sanatoria that have been established in the Swiss mountains—proof that the climate is sufficiently health-giving and the air still sufficiently pure to be beneficial to sick people.

HISTORICAL SUMMARY

After the fall of the Roman Empire in the fifth century AD the territory of present-day Switzerland was infiltrated successively by tribes of Burgundians, Alemans, Franks and Goths. Vestiges of the cultures of these peoples are frequently uncovered by archaeologists. It is interesting to notice that the ethnic characteristics and differing temperaments of the present French- and German-speaking populations of Switzerland can

B

be traced directly back to Burgundian and Alemannic influences respectively, and that the dividing line between the two groups—the river Sarine, or Saane in German, flowing north through the canton of Fribourg—has marked the approximate limits of these influences since early mediaeval times.

The area next fell under the control of the Holy Roman Empire, and the history of Switzerland over the following centuries is closely linked to that of the Empire. The centralised administration of the Hapsburg emperors, however, was at complete variance with the traditional Swiss system of self-government and mutual co-operation, and the rising discontent on the part of the proud and independently minded mountain people came to a head at the death of the Emperor Rudolf I, in July 1291. On 1 August 1291 the men of the future cantons of Schwyz, Uri and Nidwalden concluded a perpetual defensive alliance. This date, still celebrated as Switzerland's national day, marks the true foundation of the Swiss Confederation. The opening of the original Latin text of the pact, preserved in the Archives of the Covenant of Confederation, reads in translation:

Let every man know that, in view of the troubles of the day, and in order better to protect their lives and their worldly possessions, the men of the valley of Uri, of the Landesgemeinde *of the valley of Schwyz and of that of the lower valley of Unterwalden have faithfully sworn to succour each other with mutual help and advice and with all their might . . . within the valleys and beyond, against all and any men that dare to molest them, all or any one of them, by any hostile act done to or intended against their life and belongings. And each community has vowed to rally speedily to any other, if the need arise, as soon as such help be called for, if necessary at their own cost, to resist any onslaught by men of ill will and to seek revenge for any injustice done . . .*

These noble words, read aloud at patriotic gatherings on 1 August each year, have served as guidelines to the Swiss people for nearly seven centuries. (It was significant for the future development of the country that the three cantons concerned were German-speaking. Indeed, it was to be over five centuries before the first French- and Italian-speaking cantons were affiliated to the Confederation, and the consequences of the Alemannic predominance persist to this day.)

The history of the young Confederation during the centuries following the signature of the Perpetual Alliance gives little sign of the reputation that modern Switzerland enjoys as a peace-loving nation. The fourteenth century was marked by an almost uninterrupted struggle between the Hapsburgs and the Confederation, to which five more cantons—Lucerne, Zürich, Glarus, Zug and Bern—became affiliated during that period. The Swiss rapidly made their name as a nation of fierce fighters and, because of the country's serious lack of natural resources and therefore of employment, many young men emigrated and took up arms as mercenaries in foreign armies. The fifteenth century was equally turbulent, with external troubles compounded by serious internal wrangling and disputes that were tantamount to open civil war. In 1481 two city-states, Fribourg and Solothurn, were admitted to the Confederation, followed by Basel and Schaffhausen in 1501 and Appenzell in 1513. Here it should be mentioned that, although all the newly affiliated cantons had alliances with the three original or 'primitive' cantons, they were not necessarily allied to each other, a fact which later was the cause of considerable complications.

If a date can be ascribed to the first glimmerings of the future Swiss tenet of neutrality, it is probably that of the battle of Marignano in northern Italy in 1515. Here the Confederation's forces suffered such a serious defeat at the hands of the French king, François I, that, fearful of seeing the Confederation disintegrate, the Swiss withdrew from the international stage and succeeded in standing apart from the major European wars for almost three centuries. The country nevertheless continued to supply fighting men to other European countries—it could be said, in fact, that warriors became the principal export of this small, impetuous mountain state. A great diplomatic victory was gained with the recognition, at the Treaty of Westphalia in 1648, of the Confederation's independence from the Empire. During this period, however, the country was torn internally by fierce religious strife for many decades, as we shall see in the section 'Religion' below.

Thus the Swiss Confederation enjoyed comparative peace with its neighbours between the sixteenth and eighteenth centuries. The Napoleonic Wars, however, marked the beginning of more troubled times. In 1798 French forces crossed the Swiss frontier. After a series of defeats the federal armies collapsed and the Confederation was dissolved, after over five centuries of independence. In its place Napoleon set up the 'Helvetic Republic' and initiated a policy of strict authoritarian rule. The Republic, the nature of which was ill suited to the Swiss temperament, survived for only five years, during which the territory was ravaged by battles between the opposing forces of Napoleon and the Austrian, Russian and Prussian armies, and by numerous local insurrections. In 1803, by the Act of Mediation, Napoleon recognised the peculiar federal tradition of Swiss government and the Helvetic Republic ceased to exist. A further six cantons—Aargau, Graubünden, St Gallen, Thurgau, Ticino and Vaud—now joined the revived Confederation, which immediately reintroduced the policy of neutrality and contrived to keep Switzerland free of entanglement in the main wars of the imperial Napoleonic era. At the Congress of Vienna in 1815, after the fall of Napoleon, the great powers recognised the principle of perpetual Swiss neutrality, and the cantons of Geneva, Neuchâtel and the Valais joined the Confederation, while certain territories in the Jura, Savoy, the southern Valais and the southern Graubünden which had previously formed part of Switzerland were relinquished. As we have seen, it was at this time that Switzerland's frontiers took on their present aspect.

At this period the cantons were in fact stronger in political power than the Federal Government. It was unfortunate therefore that during the 1840s religious problems came to the fore once more, culminating in a breakaway movement by seven Catholic cantons which became known as the 'Sonderbund'. This dangerous situation, which could easily have led to the collapse of the Confederation, was resolved by a short civil war which ended in victory for the federal troops of General Dufour (who became an authentic national hero to match the legendary William Tell) and brought about the general reconciliation of the opposing factions. The most important result of the Sonderbund war was the introduction of a new Federal Constitution in 1848 which, with the incorporation of major revisions in 1874 and sundry smaller modifications since, is still in force today.

Since 1848 Swiss energies have been mainly devoted to building up the nation's economy and its industrial resources, to improving the communications network and to preserving Switzerland's neutrality. A sign of the new determination for non-involvement was the end of the mercenary tradition in 1859 when Swiss citizens were henceforward forbidden to serve in foreign armies. Another important new step was taken in 1864 with the foundation, on the initiative of Henri Dunant, of the International Red Cross Committee which is a purely Swiss body, as opposed to the League of Red Cross Societies. Swiss neutrality was maintained and respected during World War I, after which Geneva was chosen as the seat of the League of Nations. During World War II too, Switzerland managed to remain neutral and, following the end of hostilities in 1945, numerous international organisations of the United Nations family and others were established in Geneva. Switzerland has held on to the tradition of neutrality by declining to become a member state of the United Nations itself, although there is a possibility that this state of affairs may not be long-lasting. Despite her neutrality Switzerland can no longer be looked upon as a small, peaceful country set apart from a war-torn world. For better or for worse, the nation is being drawn back into the international arena, as an integral part of a wider community of nations—in effect, a global application of the Covenant of 1 August 1291.

POPULATION

The results of the December 1970 census put the total population of Switzerland at 6,269,783 persons. This figure may be compared with the United Kingdom's total of 56 million (of which London takes 7·38 million) and the 209 million of the

United States (New York, 7·90 million). As might be expected given the physical structure of Switzerland, these 6,269,783 people are very unevenly distributed over the land area, the population density of the plateau being 60 per cent higher than that of the country as a whole. The urban population in 1970 totalled 3·66 million, whereas 2·61 million persons lived in rural areas, yet by the standards of the United States and the major European countries the cities of Switzerland, whose names are so familiar, are small. Indeed, at present only five have over 100,000 inhabitants within the city limits: Zürich (423,000), Basel (213,000), Geneva (174,000), Bern, the capital (162,000), and Lausanne (137,000). In other words, Geneva, for instance, is approximately the size of West Bromwich or Gary, Indiana. However, the worldwide twentieth-century phenomenon of rural-urban migration, which results from increased industrial-isation and from the lack of facilities in rural areas, is evident in Switzerland too and in this connexion it is significant that the population of Baselland, the dormitory area for Basel itself, in-creased by 38 per cent in the decade between 1960 and 1970. Population projections for 1985 indicate that the 1970 urban population of 3·66 million is likely to increase to just over 5 mil-lion by that year, while a fall of 270,000 in the number of country-dwellers is predicted over the same fifteen-year period. Thus the percentage of the total population represented by the inhabitants of urban areas will inevitably be considerably higher by 1985, for all authorities agree that the rural-urban drift may be slowed but not stopped. Indeed, the towns of St Gallen, Lucerne, Aarau/Olten and Bienne/Neuchâtel are expected to have more than 200,000 inhabitants each by the end of the century.

The 1970 population statistics reveal an annual growth rate of 1·2 per cent since 1963. The *natural* increase in the population, however, as represented by the difference between the crude birth rate (15·2 per 1,000 in 1971) and the crude death rate (9·2 per 1,000 in 1971) was only 0·6 per cent. The difference be-tween the natural increase and the over-all annual increase is explained by the steady influx of non-Swiss persons, many seek-ing work or a place to retire, into the Confederation's territory.

At the present time no less than 17 per cent of the total population—over 1 million souls—is of non-Swiss origin (the figure in 1950 was 285,000). The proportion varies from 7 per cent in the 'primitive', rather conservative canton of Uri to 27 per cent in Ticino and as much as 36 per cent in Geneva, where the percentage is boosted by some 10,000 foreign-born officials of the United Nations and its specialised agencies and by the staffs of various international, governmental and other bodies. Many United States enterprises too have offices in Geneva and there is a sizeable population of resident Spanish and Italian workers. As we shall see later, the large number of foreign workers in various parts of Switzerland has become a major political and economic issue and has led to severe restrictions on foreign settlement in the country.

We have already noticed how Switzerland's lack of natural resources led Swiss men to enlist in foreign armies. Another cause of this population movement out of the Confederation was that the steadily increasing population inevitably meant that more people were looking for work. This demographic expansion gathered pace over the years; whereas it took nearly two-and-a-half centuries for the population to double from 1·1 million (in 1600) to 2·2 million (in 1837), only one more century was required for the figure to double again (2·5 million in 1855 to 5 million in 1955). In the fifteen years between 1955 and 1970 another million people were born in or moved into this small state. Although in normal times there is a shortage rather than a surplus of labour in Switzerland, there is genuine alarm in some quarters at the increasing number of non-Swiss persons in the country. Of course, this demographic flow is a two-way movement, for there is a steady exodus of Swiss citizens who leave their country to take up employment in a foreign land, thus maintaining the centuries-old tradition. The number of those living abroad is now over 300,000 and together they constitute what is known as the 'Fifth Switzerland'—that is to say, the fifth group of Swiss-born people after the four linguistic groups of Switzerland itself.

LANGUAGES

Switzerland is a paradise for linguists. Four national tongues —German, French, Italian and Romansch, the first three of which are also official languages—exist side by side, a voluble testimony to the success of the federal system in the Swiss Confederation.

Of the four languages, German is by far the most widespread. It is the first language of 64·9 per cent of the population (over 4 million persons) in sixteen of the twenty-two cantons. In written and formal contexts Standard High German is utilised, and this varies little from the form of the language spoken in the Federal Republic of Germany. However, the spoken German of Switzerland is a different matter altogether. This is Schwyzerdütsch, an almost purely conversational language spoken by all social classes and deriving from the old High Alemannic dialect. Schwyzerdütsch has been aptly described as 'not a language but an affliction of the throat'. Moreover, each city and canton in the German-speaking area has its own dialectal version of Schwyzerdütsch—thus we have Barndütsch (from Bern), Zürcherdütsch, Baslerdütsch and so on. The variations are such that a Schwyzerdütsch speaker a score of miles away from his home town or village immediately stands out as a 'foreigner'. The speaker of Schwyzerdütsch is a figure of fun to his northern neighbours in the Federal Republic—how else could they react, indeed, on hearing for the first time the peculiar hybrid phrase *merci vielmals?* (For a hilarious account of Schwyzerdütsch, see George Mikes' *Switzerland for Beginners*, published by André Deutsch.)

French is the first language of 18·1 per cent of the population (about 1,135,000 people). Spoken with a characteristic lilt, it differs only in small details from standard French—for instance by its employment of *septante* and *nonante* for the numbers 70 and 90, and by its strange use of the adverb *seulement* in phrases such as *allez-y seulement* and *faites seulement*. The influence of the German *nur* in similar phrases is discernible here. There are no longer any strong dialectal forms of the language to counter-

balance the thriving, vigorous and omnipresent Schwyzerdütsch across the Sarine. The local patois of Vaud, the Jura
and the Valais, which are all that remain of the old dialects, are
in fact slowly dying out.

South of the Alps, in Ticino and parts of the Graubünden,
Italian is the main language now spoken by just under 750,000
people. Its share has risen from 6 per cent in 1950 to 11·9 per
cent at present, mainly because of the number of Italian workers
now living in most of the large cities.

The fourth national (but non-official) tongue is Romansch.
This linguistic relic from the old Roman province of Raetia was
once spoken over a much wider area. It survives now only in
mountain communities of Ticino and the Graubünden although it does have its own radio and television programmes.
Some 50,000 people, or 0·8 per cent of the total population,
speak it as their first language. In fact, Romansch is not a single
idiom but a collection of some half-a-dozen dialectal forms, in
which the German or Latin influence is stronger or weaker
according to the geographical situation of the dialect. Whether
it is Sursilvan, Ladin, Engadinish, each has its own peculiarities.
To take an example, in the semi-official form of the language
the days of the week are *dumengia, lindasdi, mardi, mesemda,
gievgia, venderdi, sonda,* but 'Wednesday' in Ladin is not *mesemda*
but *marculdi*. Inevitably, the future of Romansch is uncertain
despite the attempts of preservationists to save it, for the language is up against the same problems as confront all minority
languages—lack of facilities, need to speak a second language
(in this case German) for all but local activities, and so on. The
rapid development of St Moritz as a major ski resort, for instance, led to the supremacy of German in the village in less
than a generation. Evidently, the profusion of subdialects makes
preservation more difficult still.

Non-native languages, with Spanish and Portuguese pre-
dominating, are spoken by 270,000 persons, representing 4·3
per cent of the total population.

The dividing line between the French-speaking and German-
speaking regions is very clearly marked over much of its length
by the river Sarine (Saane). The towns that bestride this river

are truly bilingual, perhaps the most well-known example
being Fribourg, or Freiburg, where the two languages are
strictly equal in importance. Indeed, it is quite common in
Fribourg/Freiburg to hear conversations between two persons
one of whom is speaking French and the other Schwyzerdütsch. Morat (Murten) and Bienne (Biel) are other bilingual
towns.

Clearly, Switzerland is an ideal place for learning languages,
and the task is made much easier by the fact that a great many
commodities are packed in trilingual containers. Indeed, in
some cases the translated name of these commodities seems to
reflect the reputed national characteristics of native speakers of
the language in question—not so much for comparatively
straightforward items such as *Milch/Lait/Latte* but rather for the
more esoteric purchases such as disposable nappies. The
French, as might be expected, is clear, logical, brooking no
contradiction or opposition: *langes à jeter*. In Italian it's much
more emotional: *pannolini da gettar via dopo l'uso. Dopo l'uso . . .*
one can almost see the excited explanatory gestures. But it's
when one reaches the German that the real, faintly sinister
nature of the product is revealed, ominous, redolent of dwarfs,
the Black Forest and Wagner: *Wegwerfwindeln*.

RELIGION

Until the mid-nineteenth century the religious history of
Switzerland was as turbulent as its political history. Christian-
ity was introduced in Roman times, and early bishoprics were
established at Geneva, Martigny and Chur. This first flowering
of the Christian faith was shortlived and yielded before the in-
vading Burgundians and Alemans. Late in the sixth and early
in the seventh centuries Irish missionaries, among them Gallus,
a follower of Columba, converted the Alemannic tribes to
Catholicism. Gallus settled on the banks of the river Steinach
and there founded the great Abbey of St Gallen, whence there
radiated a tremendous spiritual and intellectual influence that
ultimately affected virtually the whole of Europe. At its apogee
in the tenth century this abbey possessed some 4,000 domains

and fifty-four churches, from which it derived a considerable income.

In the sixteenth century the religious reform movement known as the Reformation split the Confederation into Catholic and anti-Catholic camps. Ulric Zwingli, in Zürich, violently condemned the sale of papal indulgences and preached a religion that was akin to Lutheranism, converting Zürich, Bern, Basel, Glarus and Schaffhausen, together with several territories that were later to join the Confederation, to Protestantism, while the 'primitive' cantons, Solothurn and Fribourg, remained true to the older faith. Outside the Confederation's boundaries, in Geneva, Jean Calvin preached a much severer, more austere form of Protestantism than Zwingli, a doctrine which tended to take root abroad rather than in Switzerland (John Knox, in Scotland, was one of Calvin's followers). The legacy of the Reformation and the Counter-Reformation, as far as Switzerland was concerned, was a nation torn for many centuries by politico-religious feuds and skirmishes culminating, as we have seen, in the Sonderbund and its accompanying civil strife.

The new Constitution of 1848, drawn up immediately after the Sonderbund war, introduced complete religious freedom throughout the Confederation. This move gradually brought about a considerable intermingling of the denominations, although in the majority of the cantons the predominant religion today is still that which prevailed in the sixteenth century. There is no state religion; under the Constitution religious belief is a private matter in which the state has no right to interfere: 'no person may be compelled to become a member of any religious body, submit to any religious instruction, perform any religious act or incur any penalties, of whatsoever kind, by reason of religious opinions' and 'no person may be compelled to pay taxes the proceeds of which are specifically appropriated in payment of the purely religious expenses of any religious community of which he is not a member.' (A. J. Peaslee: *Constitutions of Nations* (The Hague, Martinus Nijhoff, rev. ed. 1968), Vol III.) Relations between the various Churches, of which the major ones receive financial support from the state, and the state itself are conducted at cantonal, not federal, level. It is possible that at some future date the church and the state may be completely separated.

At present Catholics and Protestants are almost equal in numbers (49·4 and 47·8 per cent respectively). There are about 65,000 non-Christians and a growing number of persons who profess no religious belief. Broadly speaking, French-speaking Switzerland is predominantly Protestant, apart from the cantons of Fribourg and the Valais; central Switzerland, except the canton of Bern, is Catholic, and north and east Switzerland are Protestant. It is a curious fact that the inhabitants of Geneva—the city of Calvin—now divide their allegiance in the proportion of 53·4 per cent to Catholicism and only 38 per cent to Protestantism. This seemingly paradoxical situation is explained by the presence in Geneva of numerous resident Italian and Spanish workers. The statistics for Swiss-born citizens alone reveal that the majority remain Protestant.

NATIONAL CHARACTERISTICS

If it is difficult to characterise a country that has but a single national ancestry and a uniform racial, linguistic and religious background, it would seem virtually impossible to do so for a nation composed of men and women of different racial stock, with different religious beliefs, different and often opposed historical traditions, speaking different languages and living in widely differing geographical regions. It would not be at all surprising if the Swiss failed to exhibit any particular national trait and if the members of each linguistic group had far more in common with their counterparts across the frontier than with their fellow Swiss. Yet certain characteristics are typically Swiss, the fruit of several centuries of co-existence. Perhaps the most striking of these is the intense patriotism of the Swiss people, which seems simple and unsophisticated to those from countries where it is the fashion to belittle one's nationality. Swiss patriotism expresses itself in many ways: in the flying above private houses of the Swiss national flag—the white cross on the red background—and the often colourful cantonal flag, both of which are also reproduced on the rear number-plate of all motor vehicles; in the constant references in the press and on radio and television to 'our country'; in an insularity and a reserved attitude towards foreigners, born of the long tradition of neutrality (what might be called the 'nous sommes beaux, nous sommes neutres, nous sommes Suisses' syndrome); and above all in the preservation of the past and the love of tradition. One of the current handbooks to Switzerland devotes no fewer than eighteen pages to a list of dozens of 'popular customs and festivals', from the January *Schlittedas* in the Engadine, via the great city carnivals and fairs to the New Year's Eve ceremonies in Lenzburg. Scenes from these ritualistic gatherings and processions frequently form part of the daily television news programmes and at times the sight of middle-aged men prancing through the streets in mediaeval costume, following on a news item of catastrophe or war elsewhere in the world, can seem incongruous to say the least. The survival of yodelling and the deep-braying alphorn, the traditional wrestling and flag-throwing contests, are other reminders of the past.

By nature the Swiss tend to be rather serious, particularly those in the German-speaking area. They have a respect for thrift, cleanliness, honesty, private initiative, and for public and private property. They are a sober and disciplined race on the whole, with a dislike of fanaticism and a respect for authority. In a comparatively simple matter such as crossing the road, many a Swiss pedestrian will wait for a pedestrian-crossing light to turn green, even if there is no wheeled vehicle anywhere in sight. As befits 'a nation of clockmakers' and manufacturers of precision goods, they are themselves precise. Open table wine is served in exact measures of 1, 2, 3 or 5 decilitres—there is none of the gay abandon of the French *quart de rouge* here—and it comes as something of a shock to an Englishman to see signs stating, 'Tea: 3 decilitres, 1·50 francs' in a café or bar. Traditionally producers of quality goods, the Swiss in turn look for quality and value in the things they buy, paying a good deal of attention to matters such as good design and finish. They expect, and usually get, prompt deliveries and first-class after-sales service for their purchases. Yet this is not the whole picture.

The younger generation, the 'teens and twenties, kick against what many of them see as outdated attitudes and it must be admitted that there is a certain lack of realism in, for instance, the Swiss-German tendency to look upon Geneva, which despite its international vocation is possibly the most bourgeois town in Europe, as the 'Sin City of the West'.

On the whole these characteristics, that seem to apply to a sizeable proportion of Swiss men and women today, are praiseworthy if unexciting. One could of course point to idiosyncrasies that make the citizen of Locarno different from the citizen of Lucerne or Lausanne. The basic characteristics, however, are the traits that have helped the country to draw the greatest benefit from its scant natural resources and to develop from a collection of independently minded mountain clans into a prosperous and economically powerful state.

2

How the Country Is Run

CONSTITUTION

THE fundamental legislation of the Swiss Confederation is embodied in the Federal Constitution, adopted on 12 September 1848 after the Sonderbund war, considerably revised in 1874, and modified in minor respects on numerous occasions since then. The Constitution transformed Switzerland from a motley collection of more or less independent cantons, each with its own local policies, customs regulations, coinage, postal service, and so on, into a modern federal state. It lays down that the people of the twenty-two cantons, which are sovereign to the extent that their sovereignty is not limited by the Constitution, together form the Swiss Confederation. (At the time of writing, the Constitution of the Jura, which when adopted will make the Jura the twenty-third canton, has not yet been drawn up.) Their rights and duties as Swiss citizens, and the rights and duties of the federal authorities, are laid down in 123 articles which cover a wide range of moral and material issues. Under the Constitution, all Swiss citizens are equal before the law and enjoy complete personal freedom of conscience and belief, association and domicile; they may marry without impediment of religion or 'considerations of a police nature'; and they may not be expelled from the Confederation or their canton of origin.

The basic tenets of the Constitution, as they affect the citizen, thus echo that desire for complete freedom and equality before the law that inspired the men who drafted its provisions during the troubled decade of the 1840s. In recent years, however, it has become increasingly apparent that developments during the twentieth century have overtaken certain articles of the

Constitution which are no longer adequate to meet current needs and are ill adapted to present-day conditions. In the mid-1960s a vast nationwide investigation was initiated to determine whether any revision of the Constitution was in fact called for, and if so to what extent. From the thousands of replies submitted by cantonal authorities, political parties and other interested bodies, it emerged that considerable modification would be necessary if the Constitution were genuinely to reflect Swiss needs and aspirations in the second half of the twentieth century—needs that are quite different from those that characterised the Switzerland of the 1840s and the 1870s. In particular, it was clear that a nascent tendency towards mistrust between the state, the citizen and society had to be countered. It thus seems more than probable that the Constitution will be thoroughly overhauled within the next decade, resulting in obsolete articles being deleted, incomplete articles completed and new articles added, in order to put a stronger emphasis on social rights and social justice and to introduce recent notions such as the protection of the environment.

DEMOCRACY IN ACTION

It has been said with some truth that 'Swiss government works upwards, not downwards'. In other words, the highest authority is vested not in the Federal Assembly (the Swiss Parliament) but in the electorate. Of course, it might be said that in all states with democratically elected governments the individual has a say in government through his elected representative. A particular characteristic of Swiss democracy is that the Swiss citizen has the possibility of affecting the administrative and legislative process *directly*. First, all projected amendments to the Constitution (which frequently concern relatively minor matters) must be submitted by the government to the people in the form of a compulsory referendum, for approval or rejection. For such amendments to be approved they must obtain not only the majority of individual votes throughout the country but also the majority of the cantonal votes (the majority vote within a canton is taken to express the vote of that canton).

Second, all federal legislation (except emergency regulations) and certain long-term international treaties are subject to the so-called 'optional' referendum, which is held when 30,000 signatures opposing such measures are collected within ninety days after their acceptance by the Federal Assembly. Third, the people have the important right to launch their own popular 'initiative' to propose an amendment to the Federal Constitution. In this case 50,000 signatures are necessary. It is likely that, if and when the Federal Constitution is revised, the number of signatures required will be doubled in each case—a sensible proposal when one considers that the size of the electorate is now six times larger than when these figures were decided upon.

This principle of the ratification of Switzerland's national and international policies by popular vote, although extremely expensive to put into practice, is cherished by Swiss men and women. Their approval of the issues put to them is by no means automatic and there have been numerous instances where the people have rejected legislation which, in retrospect, seems to have been well founded. Perhaps the most recent instance of this was the defeat, in 1973, of a proposed constitutional amendment to overhaul the Swiss educational system.

It would be wrong to suppose that all but a few citizens turn up at the polling stations on the day or days of a referendum or initiative. Some of the issues on which they are called upon to pronounce—particularly economic matters—are well beyond the comprehension of the ordinary man and woman, and yet as long as the ratification of such issues would involve an amendment to the Constitution they must be submitted to the people for approval. In most cases the political parties indicate whether their adherents should vote for or against a proposal. Nevertheless it is not unusual for measures which will affect the life of every citizen but which, because of their complexity, arouse no great emotional involvement one way or the other, to be adopted on a turn-out of no more than 20 or 30 per cent. There has also been a disquieting tendency in recent years for the popular initiative to be used as a purely political weapon rather than as a means of safeguarding the interests of the people as a whole.

The referendum and initiative procedure applies not only at

C

the federal level but also at the levels of the commune and the canton, where the issues are more often local matters within the grasp of the man in the street—for instance, whether hunting should be forbidden on the territory of a particular canton, or whether funds should be allocated for the construction of a new school, or whether apprentices should have three or four weeks holiday a year.

The *commune* is the smallest administrative unit in the Swiss Confederation, and has complete freedom within the limits of its autonomy. The communes form the backbone of Swiss democracy and typify the sovereignty of the citizen. Their responsibilities cover the administration of communal lands, the granting of primary citizenship to those who wish to take up Swiss nationality (the essential first step), public services and social matters at the communal level and many other local affairs. They vary widely both in population—from a score of inhabitants in certain communes in the cantons of Vaud and the Graubünden to 422,640 in the commune of Zürich—and in area—from tiny villages in the Ticino covering less than a sixth of a square mile to Bagnes, Davos and Zermatt, each of which is nearly a thousand times larger.

The 3,053 communes are grouped in twenty-two *cantons*, of which three (Unterwalden, Appenzell and Basel) are each made up of two demi-cantons. Most of the larger cantons are divided into districts (*Bezirke* in German), which bring together a number of communes and in which the cantonal administration is represented by a prefect. The cantons which, as will be recalled, were originally independent political states, retain their political sovereignty to this day, except in matters that fall under federal responsibility. Each has its own written constitution and legislation. Executive authority is vested in the State Council and legislative authority in the Grand Council of each canton. Elections to these bodies are by majority vote or proportional representation, according to the canton. There is in fact considerable variation between the electoral systems of the different cantons, as regards number of members elected, method of election, age of suffrage, right of women to vote, and so forth.

Here we should turn aside to look at a genuine survival of Swiss direct democracy in its most primitive form. Instead of registering their votes at polling stations, the citizens of the cantons of Glarus and of the demi-cantons of Obwalden, Nidwalden and Appenzell (Inner and Outer Rhodes) gather in the open air in the spring of each year to elect their cantonal representatives and to take decisions on cantonal matters by a show of hands. These *Landesgemeinde* are accompanied by religious processions, appeals to patriotism, the Swiss television cameras and hordes of sightseers. Yet despite the present-day tendency to look upon these gatherings as quaint survivals of a picturesque chocolate-boxy past, it must be remembered that during an earlier period of Swiss history they represented the only occasion when the people had the chance to express their views on political matters and to influence the course of events. Indeed, before the promulgation of the 1848 Federal Constitution there were over eighty *Landesgemeinde* in various parts of the country.

The seat of the Federal authorities is in Bern. The legislative authority is vested in the Federal Assembly, which is composed of two bodies: the National Council, and the Council of States. The National Council is made up of 200 members from the various cantons, elected for four years. The number of seats to which each canton is entitled is calculated on a proportional basis in relation to the population of each canton (roughly in the ratio of one member per 24,000 people): the canton of Zürich, for example, has thirty-five seats, Vaud has sixteen, Solothurn seven, Zug two; the five smallest cantons and demi-cantons have one seat each. The Council of States has forty-four members, with two members representing each of the twenty-two cantons. The fact that each canton is thus equally represented in the Council of States, no matter what its size, importance or population, helps to prevent the smaller cantons from being totally overwhelmed by the larger and more powerful ones. On the other hand, the Council of States reflects not so much the strength of the parties in the country as a whole (witness the low Socialist representation—see the table on p 42) as the predominant political hue of the individual cantons.

Executive authority at the federal level is held by the Federal Council, the seven members of which are elected by the Federal Assembly. Each member is elected for a period of four years (and usually re-elected for subsequent periods) and is responsible for a particular government department—in other countries they would be known as ministers. The tradition, which is not always respected, is that four Federal Councillors are chosen from the German-speaking cantons, two from the French-speaking area, and one from Ticino (the Italian-speaking canton), with no more than one member from the same canton. Other factors are taken into account also, in order to preserve some sort of balance between Catholic and Protestant councillors and between the most important political parties. The President of the Confederation is elected annually from among the seven members of the Federal Council; in fact, this is a pure formality, as each member occupies the presidential chair in turn, according to a rota. Inevitably, some capable men are unable to sit in the Federal Council under this system of balanced representation of canton, language, religion and party; yet it does mean that there is a certain continuity in federal policy and that governmental crises are rare. It also means that the personality cult is less apparent than elsewhere: the Federal Councillors tend to be devoted civil servants rather than limelight seekers. Most British people or Americans would be hard put to it to name a Swiss politician—any Swiss politician; in return, not a few Swiss people would first pause for thought before giving the name of the President of the Confederation for the current year.

The administration of justice in federal affairs is a matter for the Federal Tribunal, whose members are appointed by the Federal Assembly and whose responsibilities will be examined in the section on the Swiss legal system below.

The responsibilities of the Federal Government are clearly defined, and any attempt by the central authority to encroach on the functions of the cantons usually meets with strong resistance. At the time of writing, the Federal Government exercises supreme authority in matters of war and peace and as regards the conclusion of treaties with other states; it controls the army and the air force; it is responsible for all public works and services at the national level (railways, roads, rivers, oil and gas pipelines, and atomic energy); and it strikes the coinage.

In 1972 the Swiss Confederation employed 127,310 persons. Of these, 31,876 worked in the various government departments, 5,289 for state monopolies (for instance, alcohol and army workshops), 49,772 for the postal, telephone and telegraph services and 40,373 for the Swiss Federal Railways. There is a considerable amount of decentralisation, in that each canton and all but the smallest communes have their own public servants, who are responsible for the administration of those activities that fall within their competence.

ELECTORAL SYSTEM

The electorate comprises all Swiss citizens over the age of twenty. It is a significant example of the persistence of the old traditions in Switzerland that it was one of the last of the developed nations to give women the vote. Indeed, universal suffrage at the federal level was not achieved until February 1971 and even today there are cantons and communes where local matters are still decided by the male inhabitants alone. This is particularly true of the *Landesgemeinde* cantons.

Since 1919, elections to the National Council have been held under the proportional representation system. Candidates for the Council of States are chosen by the parties and elected, usually by simple majority vote and for a period of four years, by the people, Grand Council or *Landesgemeinde* of each canton. At the cantonal level there is no uniform system throughout the country: in some cantons the people vote according to the simple majority system, in others proportional representation is preferred; and the life of the elected assembly is not necessarily four years. The same pattern is repeated at the communal level. There is no doubt that proportional representation is a more democratic electoral procedure than the simple majority system in that it gives at least some representation to minority groups; but in Switzerland it has often led to coalition, compromise and a general weakening of effective administration.

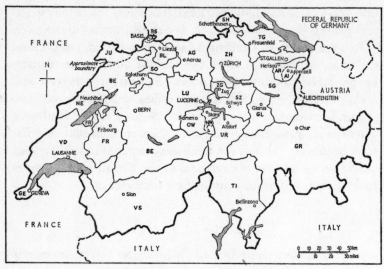

Switzerland—the cantonal boundaries

The Swiss Cantons		Official abbreviation	The Swiss Cantons	Official abbreviation
Uri		UR	Schaffhausen	SH
Schwyz		SZ	Appenzell (Inner Rhodes)	AI
Nidwalden	Unterwalden	NW	Appenzell (Outer Rhodes)	AR
Obwalden		OW	St Gallen	SG
Lucerne		LU	Graubünden	GR
Zürich		ZH	Aargau	AG
Glarus		GL	Thurgau	TG
Zug		ZG	Ticino	TI
Bern		BE	Vaud	VD
Fribourg		FR	Valais	VS
Solothurn		SO	Neuchâtel	NE
Baselstadt	Basel	BS	Geneva	GE
Baselland		BL	Jura	JU

Moves to lower the voting age to eighteen years have so far been unsuccessful (except in the canton of Schwyz, where eighteen-year-olds may vote on cantonal matters). Nor has it yet been possible to extend the right to vote to the many foreigners who live in Switzerland despite a persistent campaign for such a move. Here it is possibly significant that two cantons, Neuchâtel and Aargau, now allow foreign residents to vote on cantonal affairs.

POLITICAL PARTIES

As a consequence of the peculiar structure of Swiss government (in that the seven members of the Federal Council, the supreme executive authority, are chosen from the most important political parties), there are no official 'government' and 'opposition' parties in the sense in which these terms are used in other countries. Moreover, because the name under which a political party is known and the doctrine it professes may vary from canton to canton, or because a cantonal party may or may not be officially affiliated to the corresponding national party, or again because the aims and priorities of cantonal and national parties may not be exactly the same, it is virtually impossible to give a detailed account of the policy pursued by each party. This is all the more true because policies may temporarily be modified to facilitate *ad hoc* alliances between two or more parties. These constant shifts of emphasis are compounded by the appearance of splinter groups which break away from the parent party in order to press for a limited objective of purely local appeal. In the 1972 elections to the Grand Council of Baselstadt, for instance, no fewer than four such ephemeral fringe parties sprang up. Between them they won rather less than 1·5 per cent of the total vote.

Bearing these reservations in mind, we may briefly examine the general guidelines of the main parties which may be divided into two groups: those which support the private ownership of the means of production and advocate a market economy, and those which call for public ownership of the means of production in a planned economy.

As might be expected, in view of the high esteem in which private initiative is held in Switzerland, the majority of Swiss parties fall into the first group. If we leave aside for the moment the extreme right-wing National Action and Republican parties, the right wing is represented by the Liberal or Liberal Democratic party (the name varies according to the canton). This is the party of the professional, industrial, commercial and banking establishment, supporting private enterprise and social welfare of purely limited scope and opposed to any increase in the authority of the Federal Government.

The Radical Democratic party, the history of which goes back well over a century, claims to be a party of the centre. It supports the strengthening of the federal authority while still respecting the legitimate rights of the cantons. Its adherents maintain that radicalism is not a political doctrine but a method of government, and this is in effect the strength and weakness of radicalism—its strength in that it is not obliged to solve political problems within the straitjacket of a political doctrine, and its weakness in that it lays itself open to charges of political opportunism, of sacrificing its principles for immediate political results. This is essentially a party of the middle class. Historically it also had links with freemasonry, although the connection nowadays is perhaps less close than was the case fifty years ago. The Radical Democratic party is represented in all parts of the Confederation and although it no longer enjoys the same great popularity as in the early years of the twentieth century when it held the absolute majority, it is still a potent force in Swiss political life.

The Christian Democratic People's party, like the Radical party, presents itself as a party of the centre. It derives its policies from the social doctrines of the Roman Catholic church and the Christian trade unions. Consequently, in certain matters on which the Catholic church holds strongly conservative views—the role of the family, the emancipation of women, the evolution of morals, for instance—the party tends to tread warily, notwithstanding attempts by the party leadership to consider these questions objectively. Despite its efforts to attract Protestants, its membership is still drawn predominantly from Catholic rural, industrial and clerical workers of the middle class; it is particularly strong in the three 'primitive' cantons.

The Socialist or Social Democrat party, since 1975 the largest single party in the National Council, has developed from the first truly socialist Swiss party, founded in 1892; but the main influence of the present party dates from the introduction of proportional representation in 1919. During the first half of the twentieth century its policies oscillated between democratic and revolutionary socialism, and even today its members are split into two camps: those who incline towards the type of social democracy practised in, for instance, Scandinavia or the Federal Republic of Germany, advocating wider participation by the State in industry and strong social legislation; and the left-wing militants who on occasion have allied themselves with the Communists and do not necessarily follow the official party line. Most of the Socialist party's supporters are industrial workers; the party relies heavily on the moderate trade unions, and there is a vigorous Young Socialist movement.

Between them the three main parties—Radical Democratic, Christian Democratic and Socialist—hold almost 75 per cent of the 200 seats in the National Council. Of the remaining groups, the Swiss People's party is the most important, particularly in central Switzerland. It presses for agrarian reform, protective tariffs for agriculture and liberal social policies. The Independent party has had a chequered career since its foundation, in the years before the Second World War, as what was in effect the political wing of the large Migros commercial undertaking, itself founded in Zürich in 1925. This party can be said to represent the middle-class consumer, as well as disillusioned refugees from other parties; however, despite the proliferation of Migros stores in the French-speaking cantons the Independents are still looked on as being predominantly Swiss-German in outlook.

All these parties support the Government to a greater or lesser extent. The only party which can legitimately claim to be in opposition is the Labour or Communist party, whose aim it is to bring about a fundamental change in the existing order through the abolition of capitalism and its replacement by the communist system of public ownership of the means of production. Despite its low representation in the National Council it has a certain influence in some industrialised cantons (for example, Zürich, Baselstadt and Geneva).

The Communist party is counterbalanced on the extreme right by two newly created groups, the Republican and the National Action parties, the aims of which can be summarised as national independence, the internal maintenance of order, and hostility to foreign immigration and to the international organisations established in Switzerland. The successes of these vociferous parties have to date been modest.

The representation of the various parties in the Council of States and the National Council after the 1975 elections, and their share (if any) of the seven seats on the Federal Council, was as follows:

Party	Council of States	National Council	Federal Council
Christian Democratic People's	17	46	2
Radical Democratic	15	47	2
Socialist	5	55	2
Swiss People's	5	21	1
Liberal Democratic	1	9	–
Independent	1	11	–
Republican and National Action	–	6	–
Communist	–	5	–
Total	44	200	7

The 'permanent coalition' type of government that is so characteristic of the Swiss political system tends to prevent the appearance of violent political conflict of the kind seen in other countries. Nevertheless, the lack of an effective large opposition party does mean that the smaller parties outside the coalition are often forced to adopt corrosive, even violent tactics if they are to win any hearing at all. Generally speaking, however, Swiss government is basically undramatic in nature, particularly at the federal level.

PROBLEMS OF FEDERALISM

Inevitably, federalism as practised in Switzerland is beset by a number of delicate problems. Perhaps the most serious of these concerns the relationship between the federal and the cantonal administrations, and more particularly the impact of federal legislation on the cantonal finances. A steady stream of federal decisions pours forth from the Federal Palace in Bern and it becomes increasingly difficult for the cantons, particularly the smaller ones, to put them into effect and to enact supporting measures at the cantonal levels. The implementation of these measures may call for human and financial resources beyond the means of the authority concerned. Indeed, there is a serious risk that the smooth-running wheels of the federal system may grind to a halt unless measures are taken in the near future to combat the danger. The matter is further complicated by an intricate network of intercantonal agreements and by differing attitudes among the twenty-two cantons towards regional co-operation and the degree of independence that is desirable. Thus the French-speaking cantons in the west strive for the greatest possible independence as a means of strengthening their political influence, whereas the German-speaking cantons, with a majority of the population, tend to favour closer links with Bern.

We have already seen that the first French-speaking cantons did not become members of the Confederation until over five centuries after the signature of the Covenant of Confederation in the year 1291, and the German-speaking cantons still look upon their neighbours west of the Sarine as comparative newcomers. In this connection the position of Geneva is significant: its great prestige in its pre-Confederation days, its long-standing tradition of frankness and outspokenness, its position as a centre of world government have not passed unnoticed in the older-established cantons. It is perhaps revealing that well over fifty years have passed since Geneva, notwithstanding its importance and prestige, last held one of the seven seats in the Federal Council.

During recent years the Confederation, and more particularly the canton of Bern, has had to face up to another thorny problem, potentially even more dangerous than the cantons' financial difficulties. This concerned the status of the districts of the Jura mountains which formed a French-speaking minority in the canton of Bern—a huge, predominantly German-speaking canton occupying almost one-sixth of the land surface of Switzerland. It is over a quarter of a century since the first call for the creation of a new, independent canton of the Jura was heard but not until the 1960s did the matter take a more serious turn, in the form of manifestations and minor acts of violence by members of the separatist movements in various parts of the canton. The geographical and linguistic isolation of the Jura districts, and the dual role of Bern as the capital city of the Confederation and the principal town of the canton, were at the root of the problem. In 1974, following a plebiscite throughout the Jura, the French-speaking districts broke away and formed a new Swiss canton, the first since 1815.

Some problems of federalism are peculiar to Switzerland. Others are shared with most federal states—the difficulties deriving from an educational system run at the cantonal rather than at the federal level, the differing social security systems, the differing levels of taxation, the differing local legislation—it is in matters such as these that the drawbacks of federalism become apparent.

NEUTRALITY

Since the recognition of perpetual Swiss neutrality at the Congress of Vienna in 1815, Switzerland has succeeded in avoiding international military involvement. After World War I, when Switzerland became a member of the League of Nations, the principle of Swiss neutrality was recognised by the other powers in the League, and Switzerland was excused all military obligations. During World War II Switzerland's frontiers were at times exposed to the danger of attack, but a combination of armed neutrality and threats to sabotage the main lines of communication—such as the St Gotthard and Simplon rail tunnels—in the event of invasion seem to have contributed towards diverting the threat of invasion.

Since 1945 the Swiss Confederation has continued to stand aside from military alliances—the country is not a member of the North Atlantic Treaty Organisation, for instance. Furthermore, Switzerland is at present one of the few countries in the world not to be a member of the United Nations, although the possibility of Swiss adhesion, on condition that her traditional neutrality is maintained, is now being examined by the Federal Council. Opinions on that question are very much divided: the protagonists point to the need for close and constant international co-operation in order to preserve world peace; the antagonists, in particular the extreme right-wing groups, allege that the United Nations is an ineffective body and maintain that to reconcile traditional neutrality with the United Nations principle of collective security would be an impossible task. In any event, the question will certainly be put to the people sooner or later under the referendum procedure.

Despite the country's absence from the list of member states of the United Nations, Switzerland does belong to many of the United Nations specialised agencies. These include among others the International Labour Organisation, the World Health Organisation, the International Telecommunications Union and the World Meteorological Organisation (all of which have their headquarters in Geneva), the United Nations Educational, Scientific and Cultural Organisation, the Food and Agriculture Organisation and the United Nations Development Programme. It is a member also of numerous other intergovernmental bodies including the Organisation for Economic Co-operation and Development, the International Energy Agency and the European Free Trade Area. Indeed, Switzerland's membership of the last three organisations emphasises the European trend in her foreign policy, a trend that was emphasised in 1972, when agreement was reached between Switzerland and the European Economic Community for the gradual elimination of customs duties on industrial goods.

It is probably true to say that the philosophy of neutrality is less appreciated by the great powers nowadays than was the case a quarter of a century and more ago. Nevertheless, Switzerland continues to fulfil her traditional neutralist roles of humanitarian action, hospitality and mediation. The Confederation represents the interests of numerous states in countries with which these states have no diplomatic relations—for instance, in 1974 Swiss diplomats were representing the Philippines in Bulgaria; the United Kingdom in Guatemala; Israel in Madagascar and Hungary; Poland and the German Democratic Republic in Chile; and ten countries in Cuba.

Some Swiss people interpret the philosophy of neutrality as implying total isolation from the world and its problems. It is certainly true that Switzerland's financial assistance to the needy developing countries of the Third World falls rather lower than one might expect from what is the richest country in the world, in terms of gross national product per head. In 1974 Switzerland devoted only 0·74 per cent of its gross national product to this purpose, and even so three-quarters of this contribution was raised not from public funds but from private sources (industry, charitable organisations, and so on).

CURRENCY AND FINANCE

The monetary unit of Switzerland is the Swiss franc, which is divided into 100 Rappen or centimes. It has the reputation of being one of the strongest currencies in the world, the stable currency *par excellence*. Yet the franc itself was once devalued, when the maintenance of the gold standard before the Second World War seriously curtailed the Swiss export trade and led to a considerable amount of unemployment, so that eventually, in September 1936, the Swiss franc had to be devalued by about 30 per cent.

On 25 March 1976 the exchange rate stood at approximately 4·90 francs to the pound sterling and 2·60 francs to the US dollar. The Swiss National Bank, with its main offices in Zürich and Bern, has the exclusive right to issue bank notes and coins. These notes are attractive to look at as well as to have in one's pocket. They are issued in denominations of 10, 20, 50, 100, 500 and 1,000 francs. Cupro-nickel coins are minted for 5, 10 and 20 centimes and for $\frac{1}{2}$, 1, 2 and 5 francs.

Switzerland is of course one of the world's major banking nations, and the financial services the country provides make a significant contribution to its balance-of-payments position; accordingly it seems preferable to discuss Swiss banking and insurance activities in Chapter 4, 'How They Work'.

TAXATION

Taxes, both direct and indirect, are levied by the federal, cantonal and communal authorities. Direct taxes raised by the

Confederation are the exception, one example being the federal 'defence tax' which is levied on income, profits and the capital value of corporations. The Confederation's main source of income stems from indirect taxes (which include a turnover tax), profits from state undertakings and customs duties. The total federal income in 1973 was 10,846 million francs. Total expenditure amounted to 11,625 million francs and thus produced a deficit of 779 million francs. The size of this deficit and of the equally large shortfalls expected when the 1974 and 1975 accounts are finalised is a source of serious concern to the Government, since it indicates a too-rapid growth of public spending. In 1973 the federal authorities spent 2,556 million francs on national defence (representing 22 per cent of the total), 2,457 million (21·1 per cent) on social welfare, 1,742 million (15 per cent) on transportation and public utilities, 1,195 million on education and research (10·3 per cent) and 1,105 million (9·5 per cent) on agriculture; the remainder went on disbursements to the cantons and other sundry items.

At the cantonal and communal levels, income in 1974 from direct taxes, fees, shares of federal income (the exact amount for each canton being determined according to a carefully worked out assessment of its financial situation) and various subsidies amounted to approximately 16,890 million francs, and expenditure to 17,660 million. The level of the taxes levied varies from canton to canton. Thus, in 1973 a married man without children, residing in the chief town of a canton, paid the following percentage of his gross income in federal, cantonal and communal taxes:

Percentage of Income Paid in Tax, by Canton of Residence

Annual Income (*francs*)	Baselland	Baselstadt	Bern	Fribourg	Geneva	Lucerne	Uri	Vaud	Zürich
30,000	7·3	9·4	12·6	12·4	10·8	12·4	9·6	12·3	10·8
50,000	11·6	16·4	17·7	17·4	16·8	17·2	12·8	17·2	16·6
100,000	19·6	26·4	26·0	25·0	24·9	24·1	17·9	26·2	25·0
200,000	34·8	31·2	32·8	30·3	31·4	29·1	21·9	33·3	33·2

(Source: Union Bank of Switzerland: *Switzerland in Figures, 1974*)

In addition, the same man would pay a graduated tax, the amount of which again varies according to the canton, on his net assets.

The cantons and communes spend their share of income from these taxes on the tasks and services for which they are responsible under their individual constitutions. In all the cantons the departments of public education, public works, social welfare and public health are the most favoured; in the communes, the maintenance of public utilities (water, gas, electricity, roads, police, fire brigade, etc) takes the lion's share. All decisions on cantonal and communal budgets may of course be put to the populace under the optional referendum procedure, provided that sufficient signatures are obtained.

Recently a specially appointed federal commission began work on a draft proposal for a value added tax system to replace the present federal turnover tax. This value added tax is seen as the cornerstone of a complete overhaul of public finances, the main purpose of which would be to redistribute responsibilities among the Federal Government, the cantons and the communes, to bring about an equalisation of taxes among the cantons, and generally to lead to a more harmonious and uniform tax structure. The important question of how much authority the Federal Government should have to levy such taxes remains unanswered; and yet it does seem illogical that a

---

The annual *Landesgemeinde* gatherings are held in all weathers. Here the citizens of Appenzell (Outer Rhodes), assembled at Trogen on the last Sunday in April, vote on cantonal matters by a show of hands

For the votes on a referendum or popular initiative, local halls or schools serve as temporary polling stations

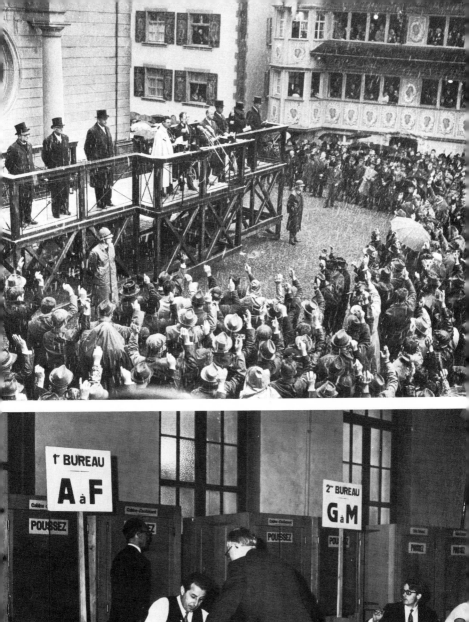

nation of only six million people should have over a score of different direct tax systems and that the taxes levied should vary so much from canton to canton.

ARMED SERVICES

Under Article 18 of the Federal Constitution, military service is compulsory and universal for all Swiss men, and few exemptions are allowed other than on medical grounds. Thus national defence is in the hands of a citizens' militia rather than a professional army, with continuity being assured by a small nucleus of full-time commissioned and non-commissioned officers. The administration of the army is shared between the cantons and the Confederation, with the main burden falling on the latter, which holds the supreme authority. The cantons have certain limited powers—for example, they may promote officers up to the rank of captain, whereas appointments to the higher posts are the responsibility of the Confederation. It is significant that in peacetime the Swiss army has no general; this post is filled only when the army is put on a war footing and the two chambers of the Federal Assembly meet together to make the appointment. The general so appointed is responsible to the Federal Council, a civilian body.

The Federal Assembly meets in the Federal Palace, overlooking the river Aare at Bern

The architectural style of this contemporary secondary school in Geneva contrasts starkly with that of the Federal Palace

D

A Swiss man is liable for military service between the ages of 20 and 50 (55 for officers). Servicemen are divided into three groups according to age. Those between the ages of 20 and 32 serve in the *Auszug* or élite formations, following a basic training course of 118 days at the age of 20 and then giving twenty days of service each year until they are 32 years old. From 33 to 42 they serve in the *Landwehr* or first reserve, for thirteen days every two years. Finally, between 43 and 50, they are members of the *Landsturm*, the second reserve, and complete two refresher courses, each of one week's duration. In all, a man serves in the forces for just under a year, and some 300,000 men are called up for national service annually. The Swiss system is unusual in that between his periods of training the Swiss serviceman keeps all his personal equipment—uniform, weapons and ammunition—at his home.

The army is composed of armoured, infantry, frontier and mountain units, together with a few mounted troops, but the days when the cavalry was an integral part of the Swiss army are over. Since World War II the number of horse soldiers has steadily decreased—from thirty squads in 1948 to eighteen in 1961—until in 1972 the Federal Council decreed that the mounted units were to be replaced by armoured divisions, notwithstanding vigorous opposition from the French-speaking cantons in particular.

The air force, which operates as part of the army, has its own training procedure for aircrew personnel. The initial training period lasts for one year, during which 200 hours of flying time are clocked up; subsequently the airman spends six weeks per year with his squadron until at the age of 36 he is assigned to ground staff duties.

Much of the army's weaponry is made in Switzerland, as might be expected, since armaments manufacture is an important sector of the Swiss engineering industry. Some of the tanks and other armoured vehicles are bought from other Western European countries and from the United States. At present the air force is equipped with jet fighters of British or French design, but these are to be replaced by 72 American-designed *Tigers*—note that, as befits Switzerland's essentially defensive military strategy, the air force has no bombers. It is the Federal Council's wish to keep the Swiss armed forces equipped with material that is as up-to-date as the Confederation's finances allow. Traditionally one of the largest items in the national budget, national defence is expected to swallow up no less than 15,000 million francs during the period 1974–79.

The mountainous nature of the Swiss terrain dictates that to a very large extent the country's military strategy is defensive. Strong fortifications overlook all the road and rail entrances to the Alps and the more important Alpine and Jura passes and plans exist for the large-scale destruction of the communications network in the event of an attack. Switzerland's state of military preparedness is designed to deter a potential aggressor by making it clear that an attack is simply not worthwhile. This policy seems to have paid off in World War II, when the Swiss Government threatened to blow up the St Gotthard and other trans-Alpine tunnels in the event of attack from Italy (although it is possible that in any case Italy preferred to have a neutral Switzerland as its northern neighbour rather than an aggressive Nazi Germany).

This tradition of defensive security, linked with the principle of compulsory military service (which goes back to the earliest days of the Confederation), has met with strong opposition during the past decade. Many Swiss find it hard to justify the existence of their army and air force. Either they optimistically believe that the threat of military confrontation in Europe is becoming less and less serious, or they pessimistically maintain that a small nation such as Switzerland would inevitably be at the mercy of the super-powers in any European conflict, for it would be too much to hope that Swiss neutrality would be respected a third time. The contrasting views of the young and the older generations on this matter are very evident and objections to military service on conscientious grounds are becoming increasingly common. The creation of some form of social service unit for conscientious objectors is currently under consideration. Acts of indiscipline by servicemen undergoing their military training have served only to heighten the con-

troversy. It is true to say, however, that even those who support
the principle of national defence believe that some revision of
its basic conception is long overdue. On a less philosophical
plane, some cantonal authorities, newly imbued with the ideals
of environmental protection, have begun to voice their opposition to the presence of army shooting-ranges on their territory.
Clearly the conflicting interests involved make this a problem
that is unlikely to be solved for a good many years to come.

LEGAL SYSTEM

Supreme judicial authority is vested in the Federal Tribunal.
This body sits at Lausanne, in accordance with the wish of the
drafters of the Constitution that one of the supreme federal
authorities should have its seat in French-speaking Switzerland
(and here the attitude of the French-speaking cantons towards
the possible concentration of all federal power in Bern can
readily be imagined). The Tribunal is composed of twenty-six
to twenty-eight members, who are nominated by the Federal
Assembly with an eye to the maintenance of linguistic and
political balance within the Tribunal. They serve for a period
of six years and are eligible for re-election. It is in fact extremely
rare for a judge, once elected, not to be re-elected.

The Tribunal has a dual function. First, as the constitutional
court, it pronounces judgement in suits between the Confederation and the cantons, in intercantonal suits, in suits between the
state (either the Confederation or the cantons) and a corporation or individual citizen and in certain other clearly defined
cases. Second, it is the supreme court of appeal in both civil and
criminal cases.

The principles of civil law are contained in the Swiss Civil
Code and the Code of Obligations; those of public law (ie those
bearing on the relationship between the citizen and the state)
are laid down in a number of documents, amongst them the
federal and cantonal constitutions and the Swiss Penal Code.
Until just over thirty years ago each of the Swiss cantons had
its own penal code, a state of affairs which hardly made for
uniformity in legal decisions. In the common interest, a pro-

posed federal code was accepted by the people in 1938 under
the referendum procedure and this came into effect in 1942.
Under one of its provisions capital punishment was abolished
except for treasonable offences in wartime.

The great majority of offences against Swiss law, whether it
be federal or cantonal, are dealt with in the first instance in
cantonal courts which although they apply the federal codes
nevertheless retain their own individual procedures. Many of
those who serve in these lower courts are non-jurists—that is to
say, they usually follow another profession or occupation in
addition to carrying out their legal duties. In this they are not
unlike the English justices of the peace. In nearly all the cantons
these officers are elected by popular vote. In a good number of
the cantons the jury system has been adopted for criminal cases,
but not for civil cases. State aid is available for those who
cannot afford to pay legal fees and in general the cost of going
to court is lower than in other countries.

POST OFFICE

Of all the Swiss administrative entities it is perhaps the Post
Office and its associated sections that provide the greatest
social services for the nation. It is in fact more than a 'post
office' in the British or North American sense of the term. Besides undertaking its accepted task of providing postal, tele-
phonic, telegraphic and telex services it offers an efficient
method of transferring money which is much more popular than
the banker's cheque system (so much so that only 26 per cent
of all households have a bank account) and an intricate network of post bus routes used by well over 50 million travellers
every year and over which some 46,000 tons of freight are carried
annually (see Chapter 6, 'How They Get About'). In addition,
the Post Office is responsible for the building and maintenance
of radio and television studios, transmitters and relay stations
(but not for the programme content); each television set and
radio receiver sold in Switzerland must bear an official Post
Office stamp of approval.

Postal services are very reliable and letter delivery within

Switzerland usually takes less than two days. There are some 4,000 post offices handling about 1,500 million inland letters, 220 million items for foreign destinations and 130 million parcels each year. Delivery services within the country are accelerated through the use of a simple four-figure postal code number which immediately precedes the name of the locality— for instance, 7500 St Moritz, 3920 Zermatt. This makes for much easier sorting of postal items.

The telephone service too is excellent. Subscriber trunk dialling is in operation throughout the country, and many foreign countries (including virtually the whole of Western Europe and some states in Eastern Europe, as well as the United States, Israel and Japan) can be dialled direct through the International STD system. In 1974 there were 2,390,852 telephone subscribers—rather more than one subscriber to every three members of the population—and 3,790,351 telephones. Public telex facilities are available from the main post offices in the larger towns and from the many hotels where the telex equipment has been installed. In 1974 there were 20,806 telex subscribers, and as their numbers increase so the popularity of the telegram declines.

3

How They Live

PIERRE LAVEDAN, the distinguished French authority on architecture, once wrote: 'A house is not only a historical record, it is the expression of a geographical and social background.' It is hardly surprising therefore that, within its European context, the traditional Swiss dwelling place, be it rich or poor, simple or luxurious, varies so much in style and appearance, from the elegant townhouses in the older districts of the cities to the rambling farmhouses of the rural areas, each with its own characteristic design developed over the centuries. Of these, one particular style, the *Schali*, or 'chalet', of the Bernese Oberland, has been reproduced in miniature in tens of thousands during the twentieth century and has come to typify Switzerland in the eyes of the average foreign tourist. More typical of late twentieth-century Switzerland, however, are the outcrops of small suburban villas and above all the monolithic glass-and-concrete apartment blocks, unfriendly and impersonal sleeping-places gathered together in brooding groups on the fringes of the larger towns and cities, defying Lavedan's dictum, devoid of any true individuality.

At the end of 1970 there were some two million houses and flats in Switzerland and of these, just over one-quarter were owner-occupied. As the table shows, this is a much lower proportion than in England and Wales and the United States; it is also somewhat lower than the average for the whole of Western Europe. This unexpected state of affairs is explained in part by the large number of foreigners living in rented accommodation in Switzerland, by the high cost of land and property in urban areas when set against the hitherto comparatively low rentals, and by the simple fact that until recently the urge to possess one's own dwelling-place was dormant rather than active. A change in this attitude seems to be heralded by a new Article of the Federal Constitution, approved by popular vote in 1972, which commissions the Federal Government to promote residential construction and the acquisition of privately owned flats and houses.

Type of Accommodation	*Switzerland* (1970) (%)	*England and Wales* (1971) (%)	*USA* (1970) (%)
Owner-occupied	27·9	50·1	62·9
Rented	72·1	49·7	37·1

(Source: United Nations: *Statistical Yearbook, 1973*)

Funds for the purchase of property are normally available from a variety of sources. In 1973, 58 per cent of all mortgage loans were advanced by the Swiss banks. Other sources were private insurance companies (8 per cent), private and public welfare and pension funds (9 per cent) and private individuals, companies and the Government (25 per cent). 'Building societies' as such do not exist in Switzerland, their role being filled by the banks. At present mortgage rates are low, less than 6 per cent (the lowest rate in the world) for a long-term first mortgage covering half the assessed value of a property and approximately 8 per cent for a second mortgage covering up to a fifth of the assessed value and repayable over a much shorter period. Curiously enough at first sight, in view of its relatively low percentage of owner-occupiers, Switzerland is the country with the largest mortgage debt per head (see the table below). This apparent paradox is explained by the fact that the amortisation of mortgages, particularly first mortgages, was virtually unknown until the end of the Second World War, although the practice is now becoming increasingly common.

Country	Mortgage Indebtedness in 1972 Per head (Swiss francs*)	Percentage of GNP
Canada	2,740	15·0
Great Britain	2,725	25·9
United States	10,340	48·9
Sweden	12,900	64·9
Switzerland	16,915	93·0

*At average exchange rate for 1972
(Source: Union Bank of Switzerland: *Business Facts and Figures*, March 1974.)

As a consequence of the international trend towards uniformity and standardisation in design, postwar apartment blocks in Switzerland differ little in appearance from those in other developed countries. The standard of construction, however, is generally high and the flats or apartments themselves are usually provided with built-in refrigerators, constant hot water, fitted cupboards, communal washing machines and driers, and so on, and the roofs of the more luxurious blocks often sport a swimming pool. These buildings are commonly situated in their own small parks, or they may be grouped together in virtual satellite towns such as those at Meyrin on the outskirts of Geneva. Here it is worth mentioning that if at first sight Geneva seems to be ringed by a white girdle of modern apartment blocks the reason is that between January 1953 and June 1975 Geneva's housing accommodation more than doubled—from 72,917 units to 160,493 units—and the great majority of these units were in modern eight-to ten-storey blocks.

The central areas of Swiss towns still retain a great deal of their individuality, and many have carefully preserved 'Old Towns' which have not been allowed to degenerate into slums as so often happens elsewhere. On the contrary, those who live in such surroundings often believe that their apartments are far superior to the hygienic boxes in the modern luxury blocks. In the German-speaking region the façades in these older districts are in many cases covered with vast biblical, allegorical or historical paintings and those of Stein-am-Rhein, St Gallen, Aarau, Lucerne and Schaffhausen are particularly attractive.

It is in the rural areas that traditional Swiss architecture is seen at its most varied, and if it can be said that there exists a true Swiss architecture then this is to be found in the astonishing stylistic diversity of the big farmhouses rather than in the urban houses, the design of which tended to follow the European style of the moment. These farmhouses are so characteristic of, and suited to, their particular region that it would be un-thinkable to attempt to construct them in other parts of the country. In those of Vaud, Neuchâtel and the other French-speaking cantons the barn and the living quarters shelter under the same roof. In the Engadine and the Graubünden the houses have a heavy, massive appearance, big enough for two or three families to live in, irregular, ornate and higgledy-piggledy both inside and out. The houses on the plateau, east of the Sarine, are characterised by their huge, sloping roofs, sweeping down to the first-floor level and outwards though often cut back on the leeward side to give light to the upper storeys. Ticino too has its own style; here the houses are built with thick stone walls and roofed with stone slabs, with staircases outside rather than inside. The dwelling place that is considered by visitors to be the most typically Swiss is the rectangular chalet of the mountain regions, built of thick wooden planks with a stone-covered roof capable of standing up to the great weight of snow it must support for weeks on end. The chalet farms of the Bernese Oberland are particularly ornate, those of the other mountain areas less so.

Everywhere, the design of the traditional Swiss rural house is admirably suited to local conditions and needs, and sensible use is made of local materials. Let us hope that these traditions will be maintained for many years to come, notwithstanding the growing tendency to use reinforced concrete where, formerly, wood and stone were considered adequate.

Until very recently the most serious housing problem con-fronting those living in Switzerland was undoubtedly the lack of accommodation either for rent or for sale, especially in the cities. As the new apartment blocks go up the demand for accommodation is gradually being met—but at a price. Whereas the monthly rent of a comfortable three-bedroomed flat in a block built in 1968 might be 850 francs, the cost for a similar flat in a block completed in 1976 could be almost double that amount. In an attempt to restrain rents the Federal Government was authorised, in an amendment to the Constitution accepted in 1972, to take steps to protect tenants from being charged excessive and abusive rents in communities suffering from a shortage of housing accommodation. Rent control was, in fact, already being exercised with regard to publicly financed or subsidised flats but this control, which was originally introduced for social reasons, has given rise to an unintended, and unsocial, side-effect—flats with controlled rents are hardly ever offered on the market. Tenants rarely vacate them and if they do the flats change hands without being advertised. The unfortunate result is that young families and newcomers are obliged either to take flats in the expensive modern blocks or, if these rents are too high, to live well away from their place of work, perhaps in a neighbouring canton or indeed in a neighbouring country when their workplace is not too far from the frontier.

Of course, high rents are not exclusive to Switzerland. Indeed, figures put out by the Union Bank of Switzerland for mid-1973 revealed that, if rents in Zürich were taken as a base (=100), those in New York reached 152 for pre-1960 and 167 for post-1960 buildings, while the relative cost in Chicago was 143 and 166 respectively. In London, on the other hand, the figures stood at 57 and 66. The significance of these figures is naturally affected by the level of the average earnings of those living in these cities, and the Union Bank therefore calculated that to pay the monthly rent of his post-1960 flat the 'average' citizen would have to work for 51 hours in Geneva, 61 in Zürich, 75 in London, 79 in New York and 93 in Chicago.

A possible alternative for those who wish to own property but cannot afford the high urban prices is to continue to rent their accommodation in the town and to buy, at a rather lower price, a chalet or chalet apartment in the mountains for weekends and holidays. The 1970 census revealed the existence of 131,000 'secondary residences' of this kind (ie 6 per cent of the total number of dwelling places), and this percentage is almost sure to rise with the increase in leisure time expected during the years to come.

STANDARD OF LIVING

The vagaries of currency exchange rates over the past few years, coupled with the basic strength of the Swiss franc, led to a situation in which, in US dollar terms, Switzerland became in 1973 the richest country in the world on the basis of gross national product per head. (In 1974 Switzerland was pushed into second place by Kuwait.) In that year GNP amounted to $6,200 (the figures for the next two countries, Sweden and the United States, were $5,850 and $5,500 respectively, for Canada $4,700 and for the United Kingdom $2,800). It is therefore not surprising that the Swiss standard of living is one of the highest in the world. Approximately 33 per cent of the total consumption expenditure per household goes on food and drink, 13 per cent on rent, 12 per cent on education and leisure activities and 10 per cent on clothing. At first sight the comparatively low rate of expenditure on transport (including the cost of private cars), which stands at 5 per cent, may seem surprising; but this is due in large part to the fact that distances in Switzerland are short. The ratio of one car to 4·3 people in 1972 is in fact about the average for European countries.

Of the money spent on food and drink, one-fifth goes on meat and one-fifth on milk, milk products and eggs; vegetables and fruit take up one-sixth and bread and cereals one-eighth. One-tenth of the expenditure in this category is for meals taken outside the home (in restaurants, for example). The expenditure on alcoholic drinks has risen sharply over the past decade— from 582 francs per year in the mid 1960s, for every person over the age of eighteen, to rather more than 700 francs in 1973— and Switzerland is now among the countries with the highest annual consumption of alcohol per head.

The average daily consumption, in grams per person, of certain items of food and drink at the beginning of the 1970s was as follows:

Country	Meat	Cereals (flour)	Potatoes	Sugar and sugar products	Tea	Coffee	Milk	Daily intake of calories
Switzerland	199	218	158	126	0·6	27·1	618	3,190
United Kingdom	209	200	279	136	10·6	5·3	592	3,170
United States	310	176	151	140	0·9	17·2	689	3,300

(Source: United Nations: *Statistical Yearbook, 1972*)

There is not a great deal of difference between the average daily intake of calories in the three countries considered, but it is revealing to compare these figures with those for certain less developed countries—for instance, Ecuador, 1,970; India, 1,990; Tanzania, 1,700.

Clothing is expensive. A man's two-piece, off-the-peg business suit, of reasonable quality and bought in a tailors' shop, is likely to cost at least 400 francs; made-to-measure suits are much more costly. A woman's ready-to-wear medium-weight dress costs in the region of 250 francs. In neither men's nor women's fashions does Switzerland lead the way; a good many purchases are made with more than half an eye on the coming winter, and fur coats for men are not uncommon. Most men have some form of warm headgear too, with earflaps that can be pulled down, to brave the *bise* on an overcast January morning.

The great majority of Swiss homes are well equipped with domestic aids: 95 per cent of all households have a washing machine, 80 per cent a refrigerator and 20 per cent a dishwasher. It is characteristic of the Swiss concern for cleanliness that the modern apartment blocks make use of hygienic refuse disposal containers of standard design which are automatically hoisted and tipped into the refuse lorries with the minimum of human intervention.

Domestic help is provided for the most part by Spanish or Italian 'charladies' who are usually the wives of immigrant workers. The rate per hour varies between 8 and 9 francs.

Switzerland is a popular country for *au pair* girls, particularly from the United Kingdom, Germany and Scandinavia. Their conditions of employment are carefully regulated and they are entitled to devote part of the day to private study or to attend courses at an educational establishment.

FOOD AND DRINK

The dry statistics of the preceding section reveal nothing of the gastronomic pleasures that await the visitor in every Swiss canton. For if the main tradition of Swiss cooking has been strongly influenced by the culinary practices of its neighbours, particularly France and Germany, Switzerland has nevertheless a variety of regional dishes of its own to offer. They may not reach the topmost levels of *la haute cuisine* but they are none the less tasty and nourishing. The cheese *fondue* is a case in point. This speciality of the French-speaking region is childishly simple to prepare. First, boil up some Swiss white wine in an earthenware pot, and then add varying proportions of Gruyère, Emmentaler or Vacherin cheese, depending on the region, and stir until melted, keeping on the boil. Add a touch of garlic, spices, kirsch, etc, and the *fondue* is ready to serve. To eat it, one dips small cubes of bread, stuck on a special long fork, into the seething yellow magma. The idea is that anyone who drops his bread into the pot pays a forfeit—having to buy more white wine for the assembled company is a common penalty. Another cheese-based speciality is the *râclette* of the Valais, a centuries-old dish which was first mentioned in a book published in Zürich in 1574. Here the local cheese is heated before an open fire or a grill, scraped on to a plate and eaten with potatoes boiled in their jackets.

Pork and beef are by far the most popular meat foods: each inhabitant consumed 81lb and 41·2lb, respectively, in 1973. Poultry and veal make a poor third and fourth (16·5lb and 13·7lb), whilst lamb and mutton are virtually unknown (4·1lb per head per year). The most original of the Swiss meat dishes is the dried and smoked beef of the Graubünden, served in paper-thin slices. There is a wide variety of both smoked and unsmoked pork sausages, with picturesque Schwyzerdütsch names—*Gnägi, Klöpfer, Schüblig*—and a copious dish, piled high with bacon, sausage, ham, sauerkraut, potatoes and French beans, known as the *Berner Platte*. But of all these delicacies perhaps the simple *Rösti*, the grated boiled and fried potatoes of the German-speaking area, is the most appealing. The waters of the larger lakes abound in fish, and lakeside restaurants offer great quantities of perch fillets with chips.

To wash down this solid, wholesome fare the Swiss are fortunate in having their own well-stocked wine cellar (Swiss wine production in 1974 was estimated at 80 million litres). Four-fifths of Switzerland's vineyards are located in the valleys and on the lakeside slopes of the French-speaking cantons; the remainder are in eastern Switzerland and Ticino. White wine accounts for some 60 per cent of the total production, the best known being the light, dry Fendant and the medium-dry Johannisberg, both of which come from the Valais. Of the red wines, Dôle again originates in the Valais. It is produced from the Pinot Noir grape of Burgundy, sometimes with the addition of some Gamay, the Beaujolais grape.

If these wines are not often seen outside Switzerland this is not because their quality is poor—on the contrary—but because they do not travel well, are rather uncompetitive in price, and of course because the Swiss themselves like these wines. In fact, the local production does not satisfy the local demand (the annual consumption of wine is about 50 litres per head), and the wine industry appears to be losing ground to imported French and Italian wines which are often less expensive despite the duty payable; about two-thirds of the red wine drunk in Switzerland is imported.

The beer consumed in Switzerland (about 75 litres per year per head) is almost all brewed within the country. It is of good quality and is of the light lager type. Swiss breweries produced 457 million litres of beer during the 1974–75 brewing year, all but 0·8 per cent being for local Swiss consumption. The two main mineral water sources are Henniez and Aproz.

SOCIAL SECURITY

By 'social security' we mean all those legal provisions which protect the population against the effects of want in old age, invalidity, sickness, family needs, occupational injury and unemployment. In this chapter we shall look at all but the last two of these contingencies, to which we shall return in Chapter 4, 'How They Work'.

Social security in Switzerland is administered both at the federal and at the cantonal level. An additional complication is that developments within each branch of social security have not been uniform and as a result we have once again an over-all pattern that is remarkable for its diversity rather than for its uniformity. A third consideration is that the social security system of the Confederation and the cantons is backed up by numerous private social institutions. This accounts in part for the fact that the benefits received under the public social security schemes are somewhat low in comparison with those received in countries where social security is entirely, or almost entirely, a concern of the state. In fact, state expenditure on social security benefits, as a percentage of gross national product, stands currently at about 8 per cent, as compared with 12 per cent in the United Kingdom.

The gigantic retaining wall of the Grande-Dixence dam in the Valais is almost as high as the Eiffel Tower

Seasonal workers are often housed in prefabricated buildings near their workplace. Separated from their families, these men enjoy a Sunday afternoon game of cards

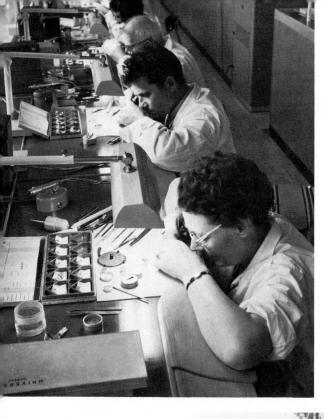

The most important branch of Swiss social security is the old-age and survivors' insurance scheme. The underlying concept of this scheme, which was incorporated in the Federal Constitution following a popular vote on 3 December 1972, is the so-called 'three-pillar' system: governmental social insurance; collective benefit schemes for employees; and personal provision for the future through savings, personally contracted insurance policies and so on. The compulsory Federal Old-Age and Survivors' Insurance Plan—the 'first pillar', dating from 1948—assumes the responsibility for meeting the basic living requirements of the old, and of survivors following the death of the breadwinner. The minimum full benefit payable to single beneficiaries is 500 francs per month and the maximum 1,000 francs. For married couples the minimum benefit is 750 francs, the maximum 1,500 francs. These rates, which were those in force on 1 January 1975, are increased more or less automatically to compensate partly for rises in the cost of living.

This basic provision is supplemented by the 'second pillar', which is the compulsory insurance that an employer takes out on behalf of his employees to protect them against the effects of old age and disability and for which he has to assume at least half the premium. Such policies are offered through several thousands of private insurance schemes, the growth of which is

––––––

Inside a watch factory in Geneva. The painstaking and delicate nature of this work is well suited to the Swiss temperament

During the Basel Carnival, or 'Fasnacht', isolated groups of masked fifers roam through the city streets. These players express, far better than the procession of floats and *fanfares*, the the true spirit of carnival

E

all the more remarkable in view of the fact that the benefits provided are supplementary to those of the federal scheme. Private life insurance and savings schemes also make up a large part of the 'third pillar' and here the fact that the 'third pillar' is recognised as an integral part of the social security system bears witness once more to the high regard in which the Swiss hold private enterprise and personal initiative.

Closely related to the old-age and survivors' insurance scheme is that for invalidity, which came into force in 1960 and protects the persons insured against the economic consequences of disablement. Wherever possible, vocational rehabilitation is preferred to the payment of a pension. Financial assistance to the disabled is in large measure furnished by a number of old-established private philanthropic organisations and by various cantonal and communal schemes.

In Switzerland, as in many other countries, sickness and medical care insurance is one of the oldest branches of social security. To date, sickness insurance has not been made compulsory throughout the country, and instead the Confederation has empowered the cantons to declare the insurance compulsory for some or all classes of their populations if they so wish. The administration of sickness insurance (including maternity benefits) is at present carried out by some 750 recognised non-profit-making sickness insurance funds, both large and small, private and public. All these funds are subject to federal supervision, but they vary greatly as regards both the level of contributions and the level of benefits, a situation which is seemingly accepted as inevitable in this federal state. A major revision of this form of insurance is currently under way, however, and a comprehensive medical care insurance plan, financed by the Federal Government, the cantons and the insured person and supplemented by a daily indemnity plan financed by the insured person alone, should enter into effect before the end of the decade. Both these types of insurance may be declared compulsory by the Federal Government or by the cantons, or they may be stipulated to be obligatory for certain segments of the population only (at present some 90 per cent of the population are covered under the existing health insurance schemes, 23 per cent compulsorily and 67 per cent voluntarily).

Family allowance schemes, like those for sickness insurance, vary considerably. This is because, here too, matters have long been in the hands of the employers and employees concerned, with the cantons entering the field more recently, while federal participation has been confined to a scheme for agricultural workers only. So far the various efforts made to combine these various systems in an over-all federal scheme have not been successful. At present the amount of the allowance ranges from 15–35 francs per child under the cantonal programmes to 30–45 francs per child under the federal agricultural programme.

MEDICAL SERVICES

In the middle of 1972 there were just over 10,000 doctors in practice in Switzerland, giving a ratio for the whole of the country of one doctor to about 615 inhabitants. (These figures should be compared with the ratios of, for instance, one to 4,795 in India, one to 13,056 in the Sudan and one to 25,847 in Indonesia. Considering western countries other than Switzerland, the figures for England and Wales were one to 787 and for the US, one to 634.) It seems likely that the Council of Europe's recommended ratio of one doctor to 500 inhabitants will be attained by about 1980, and indeed there is some talk of restricting the number of medical students over the coming years. Of these 10,000 doctors some 5,700 are in general practice (with the proviso that well over half of these specialise in a particular area of medicine and thus cannot be likened to the familiar British 'GP' or family doctor) and nearly 3,900 worked as junior hospital doctors; the remainder held official positions in administration or in industry. About 15 per cent of these doctors are women.

Doctors are free to practise where they wish and to engage in private practice with a certain degree of liberty regarding their fees; however, as about 90 per cent of their patients are likely to be participants in a health insurance scheme, few doctors accept private patients to the exclusion of all others. Chief hospital doctors are also permitted to engage in private practice and to place their patients in private wards. In return for this privilege, a percentage of their fee is made over to the hospital.

The administration and financing of hospitals falls for the most part to the canton or commune concerned, although some hospitals are privately owned. In 1971 there were about 71,000 hospital beds or rather more than eleven beds per 1,000 inhabitants. A quarter of these were private beds. The daily cost of a bed in a public ward ranges from 40 francs in Geneva to 168 francs in Sion (Valais). However, under the comprehensive medical care insurance plan discussed above, free hospitalisation in a public ward (and both treatment and maintenance) should eventually be made available to all residents.

CARE OF OLD PEOPLE

Switzerland is an old country which is steadily becoming a country of old people. This trend is due not so much to the fact that people are living longer as to the falling birthrate (only 15·2 per 1,000 in 1971), so that whereas in 1900 six people out of every 100 were over 65 years of age the ratio in 1970 was eleven to every 100. This phenomenon is encountered to a greater or lesser degree in most developed countries, and it is a burden which will become increasingly onerous since the percentage of economically active people—that is, those on whom the main weight of taxation falls—will decline while the social expenditure on old-age pensions and sickness benefits will inevitably rise as the percentage of old people increases. Indeed, it is estimated that by 1980 social security requirements in Switzerland will absorb 20 per cent of the gross national product.

As we have seen, the 'three pillar' system, which is now firmly anchored in the Federal Constitution, is intended to allow old people to continue in their accustomed way of life. It remains to be seen to what extent the planned cost-of-living increases will enable pensioners and retired people to cope with the high degree of inflation from which Switzerland, together with the rest of the western world, is at present suffering.

4

How They Work

OF the 6,269,783 people living in Switzerland at the time of the
1970 census, 1,973,288 men and 1,022,489 women were in
paid employment. The working population of 2,995,777 souls
thus represented 47·8 per cent of the total population. In 1974
the average length of the working week in industry was 44·1
hours, as compared with 44 hours in the United Kingdom
and 40 in the United States.

There is a deep-rooted belief that Switzerland is a tourist
country producing nothing but cheese, milk chocolate, watches
and cuckoo clocks, with not a factory in sight. This is far from
being the truth. Less than 8 per cent of the working population,
or some 230,000 people only, are engaged in agriculture, as
against 44 per cent (1·3 million) in commerce and services
(that is to say, banking, insurance, transport, the hotel industry
and so on) and 48 per cent—well over 1·4 million people—in
heavy and light industry. At first sight Switzerland seems to be
a country that is ill suited to such a high degree of industrial-
isation: it is woefully short of natural resources—only salt, lime,
water and wood are found in any quantity within its frontiers—
and it is therefore obliged to import virtually all its supplies of
raw materials; the home market is small and industry is thus
heavily dependent on the export market for the bulk of its sales;
and the mountainous nature of the terrain made communications difficult before the construction of the modern road and
rail network. On the other hand, the country is fortunate in
that until very recently it has always had ample energy resources to meet its needs and has known neither prolonged
unemployment nor industrial unrest.

The United States has shown considerable interest in the

Swiss economy, and almost $2,000 million of American money were invested in Switzerland in 1972. Some 600 American companies are now in operation in the country, staffed by 54,100 people of whom 4,000 are United States citizens; 140 of these companies have their main offices in Zürich, 81 in Geneva, and 34 in Zug.

MAIN MANUFACTURING INDUSTRIES

By far the most important Swiss industry, in terms of the number of employees, is the manufacture of machinery, including electrical machinery and scientific and optical instruments (252,000 workers in 1974). The next most important industries are the manufacture of metal products (111,000) and chemicals (67,000), with watch and clockmaking (65,000) in fourth place. The garments and textile industries each employ just over 50,000 persons.

Heavy industry is concentrated in the northern part of the country, in the Zürich-Baden-Schaffhausen-Winterthur region. Here are produced the highly specialised machine tools and equipment, textile machinery, turbines, locomotives and so forth which are to be found in the four corners of the globe— indeed, one in every three ocean-going diesel-powered ships is said to be equipped with an engine designed in Switzerland, and the reliability of Swiss machinery is a byword in industry the world over. The iron and steel industry too is mainly located in northern Switzerland, and in 1973 the foundries of Gerlafingen (canton of Solothurn), Schaffhausen and Winterthur produced some 598,000 tons of crude steel from imported iron ore. The aluminium industry operates in the Valais, where the three mills at Chippis and Martigny produced approximately 86,400 tons of aluminium in 1973.

The heart of the important chemical and pharmaceutical industry is in Basel where the first dyestuffs works was opened in 1859 in answer to the needs of the then-famous Basel silk ribbon industry. Changing fashions and the commercial decline of silk obliged the dyestuffs industry to seek other outlets, and during the following century considerable diversification took place into drugs, perfumes, cosmetics, bulk chemicals and finally into insecticides and plastics. Other centres of lesser importance are located in the cantons of St Gallen and Aargau, at Bex, Monthey and Visp (Valais), at Vallorbe (Vaud) and at Bodio (Ticino). Like the metals industry, the chemical industry is heavily dependent on imported raw materials. Its rapid and successful development over the years owes much to the considerable sums spent each year on research, estimated at well over 500 million francs—a figure which greatly exceeds the sum allocated for academic research in universities.

The watch and clockmaking industry was born in Geneva in the sixteenth century but soon moved northwards to the townships of the Jura mountains where it has made its home ever since. The main watchmaking centres in the Jura are La-Chaux-de-Fonds, Le Locle, Neuchâtel, Bienne—unfamiliar names, perhaps, but the goods they produce are known to all, for Switzerland is the world's major watchmaking country, with no less than 97 per cent of the industry's production being exported. In recent years, however, competition from other countries, especially Japan, the USSR and the United States, has been increasing (and this at a time when shifting exchange rates have hampered international trade and when more rapid technical advance has made considerable new expenditure necessary), and Switzerland's share in the world market fell from 68 per cent in 1970 to 63 per cent in 1974.

Since its earliest days the watch industry has been characterised by its fragmentation into hundreds of small and medium-sized enterprises (the national average number of employees is 58·7 per enterprise), each of which concentrates on the manufacture of a specific component—the movement (balance-wheel, spring, pivots and so on), or the housing (case, glass, hands, dial), or the assembly of the hundred or so parts which go to make up a watch. For instance, in 1974, in the canton of Neuchâtel alone, there were 68 enterprises making parts for movements, 106 making housings and 72 engaged on assembly work, with a total of some 15,600 employees. Each of these craftsmen has his own field of specialisation and concentrates on the production of a particular part which may be so small as to be almost invisible. Yet the degree of standardisation and inter-changeability is such that components made by many different manufacturers can be brought together in a single watch without difficulty. Some degree of concentration seems likely to occur in the future, however, and this has been the cause of some concern both to employers and to employees. The centuries-old traditions of what is virtually a cottage industry, despite its technological development, cannot be swept away overnight; yet the demands for costly technical innovation will make their ultimate disappearance inevitable.

The watch industry offers a fine example of the type of activity which is ideally suited to Switzerland's industrial needs and abilities. It calls for a high degree of skill and small-scale precision work but is sparing in its use of precious imported raw materials; moreover, the finished product is light in weight, relatively expensive to buy, and easily transported at low cost.

AGRICULTURE

The basic aim of Swiss agricultural policy is to make certain that Switzerland's farms are efficient enough to ensure that the population's food requirements can be adequately met if, for any reason, the country's food imports were reduced or cur-tailed altogether. This principle is in fact embodied in the Federal Constitution.

A hundred years ago agriculture was the most important economic sector in Switzerland, and even fifty years ago well over 600,000 persons, or three times as many as today, gained their livelihood in the fields, the vineyards, the orchards or the forests. As we saw in Chapter 1, Switzerland has not been un-affected by the worldwide 'drift to the towns'. The increased demands of industry and commerce, the wide range of jobs available in the town in comparison with the limited oppor-tunities in the village, and the additional facilities for entertain-ment offered by the town have continued to entice the farm worker away from the rural areas.

Yet although agricultural workers drift away into other jobs, although the number of farm holdings and the area under cultivation are steadily diminishing and although the total population continues to increase, agriculture still meets about the same percentage of the country's food needs as was the case twenty years ago. The tremendous gain in efficiency that this implies stems mainly from an increase in mechanisation and technical 'know-how' and from a general tendency towards large-scale (and hence more economic) farms which in due course should make possible an even greater use of sophisticated farm equipment. The statistics are eloquent enough: whereas the number of farms of less than 15 hectares fell from 187,617 in 1955 to 124,381 in 1969, those extending over more than 15 hectares increased from 18,380 in 1955 to 24,925 in 1969.

The type of farming carried out in Switzerland is strongly affected by the climate and the nature of the terrain. The relatively high annual rainfall and the generally rugged character of the land (25 per cent of which is unproductive) are more favourable to stockbreeding, feed crops and pasture than to arable farming, and only on the plateau is arable farming developed to any great extent. Elsewhere the emphasis is on animal farming and dairy production, and many mountain farms are based entirely on grassland exploitation. In 1972 there were 1·84 million cattle, 873,000 of which were milch cows; and indeed there are regions of Switzerland where the car-driver seems to come upon a herd of the light-brown Schwyz or reddish-brown Simmental cattle at every turn in the road. There is in fact substantial over-production of milk and milk products and the federal authorities are now endeavouring to encourage farmers to concentrate on meat rather than on milk. For some years too there has been a steady tapering-off in consumer milk sales; as a result the quantity of milk consumed in the home now represents only about 25 per cent of the total production. The cheese industry, which has steadily increased its sales despite stiffer international competition, accounts for about 40 per cent and the rest is absorbed by the butter, milk products and chocolate industries.

Switzerland is an important fruit-growing country. As well as the battalions of vines arrayed with military precision in the vineyards of the valleys and lakeside slopes there are numerous apple and pear orchards; cherries, plums, apricots and damsons are also produced in significant quantities. These fruits are highly vulnerable to sudden temperature changes and the hail-storms and high winds that not infrequently beset Switzerland in the late spring can decimate the year's crop in a matter of hours.

The forests which cover one-third of the productive land area, predominantly in the cantons of Bern and the Graubünden, are particularly important since they represent one of the few natural resources occurring within Switzerland's frontiers and indeed the great part of the country's need for wood is met by its own forests. The area of these is gradually increasing as new plantations replace the felled trees, for 125 acres are planted annually as against only 90 acres felled. The value of the forests is not only economic: the silent ranks of fir and pine protect mountain villages from avalanches, floods and soil erosion; they serve as windbreaks for the smallholdings on the plateau; they purify and filter the air; and they offer a source of relaxation for the flat-dwellers of the towns and cities. Trees are a form of raw material in a state of constant renewal, and the value and beauty of wood should not be overlooked by those who seem to foresee for us a prefabricated and plastic future.

One of the outstanding and most intractable problems of Swiss agriculture, indeed of agriculture in most countries, is that of the low incomes of the farming population in relation to those enjoyed by workers in industry and the services sector. These sink to a minimum of 845 francs a month for an un-married agricultural labourer in the canton of Bern, as against the national average (1974) of 1,019 francs for this category of worker. Women farm workers earn on average 20–25 per cent less than the men. Even though board and lodging is provided free, these wages are unduly low. There is no doubt that they would have been lower still without the protectionist policies initiated by the Confederation.

BANKING AND INSURANCE

On winter evenings the garish neon signs shine out over the misty waterfronts of Zürich, Basel and Geneva, publicising airlines, watches, insurance companies—and banks. In 1971 there were no fewer than 1,629 banking institutions in Switzerland, with total assets of 196,874 million francs, ranging from the big names such as the Union Bank of Switzerland, the Swiss Bank Corporation and the Swiss Credit Bank with their immense reserves, to the small private banks staffed by half a dozen people. Switzerland is one of the world's major banking centres and the success of the Swiss in banking can largely be attributed to the country's economic prosperity and political and financial stability, backed up by the thrifty disposition of the Swiss themselves.

Both the Confederation and the cantons exert a strong influence in the realm of banking. Not only are the activities of the private commercial banks regulated by numerous federal decrees but the government-supervised Swiss National Bank, the twenty-four state-owned cantonal banks and the state mortgage banks are all active banking institutions in their own right. The Swiss National Bank is a semi-private institution owned by the cantons, the former issuing banks and the public; it acts as a central clearing-house and participates in many home and foreign banking operations. In 1972 the cantonal banks accounted for 23 per cent of the combined balance sheet totals of all banks covered by the statistics; they managed 43 per cent of the total savings deposits and handled 50 per cent of all mortgages taken out in Switzerland. The state institutions are privileged from the fiscal viewpoint, whereas the big private banks are not only among the biggest taxpayers in the country but also make a sizeable contribution, through the income from their service facilities, towards offsetting the Swiss balance-of-payments deficit.

Swiss banks have often been accused of creating, or at least contributing to, currency instability by transferring huge amounts of money from one country to another. Who has not heard of the 'gnomes of Zürich'? But the banks themselves do not cause currency crises. They do, however, provide the facilities for others, such as the oil-producing nations and the sprawling multinational firms, to do so by making possible the transfer of vast sums of money across national frontiers.

The morality underlying the activities of Switzerland's banks has often been called into question, both as regards the mechanism of currency transfer and perhaps more so as regards the coveted 'numbered bank account'. It is in fact quite easy to open such an account. All one needs is the money and a sufficiently plausible reason for wanting to do so. Although many countries do not allow their nationals to open a private bank account abroad, Swiss law makes no discrimination against foreign account-holders and the banks' attitude in such cases may be summed up as 'I am not my brother's keeper'. The result is that, besides money that has been honestly come by, a good deal of wealth derived from tax evasion, crime, political terrorism and dictatorship finds its way into Swiss vaults.

It would be wrong to suppose that the banks are unperturbed by the reputation they have acquired as a safe haven for this kind of money and indeed they resent their ambiguous, slightly sinister image. On the other hand, banking secrecy also protects the victims of political repression and tyranny—after all, the system was first introduced to protect the investments of persecuted German Jews in the 1930s.

By and large, no government, either Swiss or foreign, is given information about or access to accounts, and under Swiss law the lifting of banking secrecy may be ordered only by examining magistrates in the investigation of formal criminal (not civil) complaints. A chink in the banks' armour was nevertheless opened in 1974, when the Swiss Government ratified a treaty of mutual legal aid with the United States under which banking secrecy may be lifted to enable enquiries to be made regarding the proceeds of American organised crime deposited with Swiss banks.

Insurance is another field in which Swiss activity is intense. The state participates directly in the insurance business, for instance through the Swiss Accident Insurance Institution,

which was founded by federal law and is the only body authorised to operate employee accident insurance. At the end of 1973,
79,435 companies belonged to it; its income from premiums
amounted to 410·7 million francs, as against the private firms'
income, from domestic business, of 640 million francs.

The expansion of the Government's social security programme
has contributed to a decline in the sale of individual life insurance policies but the imminent federal law requiring companies to sponsor pension schemes for their staff—the so-called
'second pillar'—will inevitably bring much new business to the
insurance companies.

The eight professional reinsurance companies licensed to
operate in Switzerland earned a premium income of roughly
3,410 million francs in 1972 or roughly one-quarter of the
entire domestic and foreign business carried on by private
Swiss insurers. The foreign share of this premium income was
over 90 per cent and this indicates the traditionally international nature of Swiss insurance activities. Indeed, it is rare
for a major disaster to strike—tornadoes, floods, shipwrecks,
conflagrations, air or rail crashes—without Swiss insurers being
involved in one way or another. As with the banks, the income
from the country's insurance and reinsurance activities makes
a considerable contribution towards the improvement of its
balance-of-payments position.

TOURISM

Tourism is the third most important source of income for the
Swiss Confederation, with net receipts amounting to almost
2,530 million francs in 1974. Travellers from abroad account in
a normal year for no less than 60 per cent of all overnight stays
in Switzerland. The Swiss hotel and restaurant industry is thus
highly dependent on foreign visitors. In recent years, however,
inflation and the remarkable appreciation of the Swiss franc
against the currency of virtually all other countries have made
Switzerland a relatively expensive country for holidaymakers
from abroad—for instance, the fall in the exchange rate for the
pound sterling from 10·25 francs in 1972 to 4·90 francs (March

1975), and for the US dollar from 4·32 to 2·60 francs over the same period, has hit tourists from these countries hard. In 1973 and 1974 the number of overnight stays in hotels by foreign visitors actually fell, these being the first such setbacks for a number of years (the growing practice of renting holiday flats or houses is also partly responsible). Few people will be surprised to learn that visitors from the Federal Republic of Germany are by far the most numerous (29 per cent of the total in 1973); they were followed in that year by France in second place (13 per cent), with the United States (11·5 per cent) and the United Kingdom (9·6 per cent) in third and fourth places respectively.

The majority of Swiss hotels are surprisingly small. Only 5 per cent offer more than a hundred beds, whereas 82·5 per cent provide fewer than fifty. The national average is in fact thirty-four beds per hotel, giving a total of 270,000 beds in the country's 8,000 or so hotels. The 1960s and 1970s have been marked by an increasing tendency towards centralisation, and United States hotel chains have now gained a firm foothold in the Swiss hotel industry.

The tourist industry, particularly as regards winter sports, can be strongly affected by adverse climatic conditions. A winter without snow or where early snow fails to settle, can turn a potentially delightful holiday for tens of thousands of skiers into a dismal experience and a potentially good season for Switzerland's hotel-keepers and restaurateurs into a financial setback.

A more serious problem affecting the hotel and restaurant industry is its chronic shortage of labour. A survey conducted in 1972 showed that the industry was about 30,000 workers under strength and in an attempt to recruit new staff a training hotel was opened in Ascona in 1973 to encourage Swiss nationals to enter the hotel industry. Two years later the old hotel school at Lausanne moved to much larger and more modern premises at Chalet-à-Gobet, just outside the city. But there is a limit to the relief that can be obtained by measures to recruit new staff and to rationalise hotel and restaurant operation, and at the heart of the matter lies the seemingly insoluble problem of the foreign worker in Switzerland. We shall now examine this problem as it affects the Swiss economy as a whole.

IMMIGRANT LABOUR

The fundamental cause of international economic migration in Europe lies in the unequal economic development of the countries involved. Switzerland, the United Kingdom, Sweden and other Western European 'host countries' are all highly industrialised; Spain, Italy, Portugal, Yugoslavia and the other countries from which migrant workers come are still 'developing countries', at least by Western European standards.

The migration of workers from Southern to Western Europe is, at least in its present form, a comparatively recent phenomenon and owes its origin to virtually full employment and severe labour shortages in certain sectors of the economies of the highly industrialised nations in the 1950s. This, set against a political background of increasing international co-operation and combined with rising education standards, led to a growing dislike by native-born workers in the industrialised countries for certain types of unskilled, heavy, dirty or otherwise unpleasant, low-status jobs and for jobs involving awkward hours of work. In the prevailing situation of labour shortage, foreign workers were engaged to fill these vacancies.

The result is that what seemed in the 1950s to be a purely temporary phenomenon has become an integral part of the economic structure of the Western European countries in that over the years they have come to rely on a steady supply of labour from abroad in order to fill these socially undesirable jobs, which nevertheless are crucial to the continued smooth running of their economies and to the maintenance of their living standards.

Switzerland offers no exception. Foreign workers have played an essential role in the development of the Swiss economy, to such an extent that in August 1974 there were almost 600,000 foreign workers in Switzerland, the majority of whom were Italians or Spaniards. In Europe, only Luxembourg has a higher proportion of foreign workers per head of population.

The figure of 600,000 includes workers in all economic sectors but excludes the 150,000 or so seasonal workers, international civil servants and diplomatic staff and the 110,000 people who work in Switzerland but live across the frontier in a neighbouring state. It represents 57 per cent of the total non-Swiss resident population of 1·05 million persons, who themselves make up about one-sixth of the total population of Switzerland.

It is not surprising that reactions to white foreign immigrants have been more hostile in Switzerland than in any other Western European country. At first, immigration was accepted as a necessary but not intrinsically desirable phenomenon. However in 1962 the number of foreign workers abruptly increased by no less than one-third, and 1963 saw the first of a series of restrictive federal measures designed to cut down the inflow to manageable proportions and eventually to bring about a degree of stability by the end of the 1970s. These measures were not enough to quieten the small but noisy parties of the far right, which launched a series of popular initiatives designed to reduce drastically the number of foreign workers in the country; to date, none of these has been accepted.

Other political parties take the view that the most urgent needs are, first, to stabilise the foreign population at or near its present level and then to deepen the human and social relation-

---

Flag-throwing is one of Switzerland's traditional sports. Here a flag-thrower from Uri tosses up his canton's flag

Swiss-style wrestling, or *Schwingen*, is an essential element of Alpine sports gatherings and attracts large crowds

ship between Swiss and non-Swiss by extending to the latter the same rights as are enjoyed by Swiss citizens. The conditions of work and life of the migrant workers do, it is true, leave much to be desired, although the Italians in Zürich are said to be better off than, say, the Algerian workers in France or the Turks and Yugoslavs in the Federal Republic of Germany. Minimum accommodation standards are laid down in various Swiss cantons but in practice the standards are not always met. Seasonal workers in particular are reported to be often inadequately housed in spite of the efforts made on their behalf by a number of industrial firms. The situation is not eased by the shortage of low-rent accommodation. As for political rights, no foreigner is allowed to vote in federal matters and only in two cantons, Neuchâtel and Aargau, are non-Swiss residents permitted to vote in cantonal affairs. Little attention is paid to the importance of uniting families on humanitarian grounds: Italian and Spanish workers may bring their families only after they have worked in Switzerland for eighteen months; in the case of Yugoslav workers the delay is three years; and seasonal workers, who are admitted to the country for periods of up to nine months, may never bring their families with them, although their work permits can be extended over several years.

What, in fact, would be the result of a severe reduction in the

---

The 'Old Town' of Bern has retained all its charm and its seventeenth- and eighteenth-century houses have been carefully preserved. But this is no museum quarter—it is a thriving and animated district, the centre of intense activity

A house in Mendrisiotto, in Ticino. Its characteristic porches and balconies show a strong Italian influence even though Ticino has been part of Switzerland since 1803 number of foreign residents in Switzerland? No canton would be unaffected, and some of the highly industrialised cantons (Zürich, the city of Basel and Schaffhausen among them) would lose over half their resident foreign labour force, with predictable results on their economy. The survival of the clothing industry, where two out of every three workers are foreign, would be seriously endangered; the effect on industry in Ticino, which is already in some difficulty, would be catastrophic. Services in hospitals, where about half the staff is foreign, would be imperilled. The hotel and restaurant industry is, as we have seen, already suffering from a serious shortage of staff which would be aggravated if its foreign waiters and chambermaids had to leave. In the longer term there would be considerable repercussions on the Swiss social security system, particularly as regards old-age and survivors' benefits, as over the past few years about 20 per cent of total social security contributions have been derived from foreign workers' earnings. The expulsion of a sizeable proportion of these workers would mean that, even in order to retain benefits at their present level, the contributions of both Swiss and the remaining foreign workers would increase proportionally, the more so since the number of retired persons in receipt of old-age pensions is steadily rising.

The Swiss people are therefore in a dilemma. Their present high standard of living and their thriving economy are based to a considerable extent on foreign labour; and yet their intense nationalism makes them hostile to the presence of over a million foreigners in their small country. Should they accept a lower standard of living as the price they have to pay for the presence within their frontiers of fewer foreigners; or should they accept that presence in order to maintain their living standards?

TRADE UNIONS AND EMPLOYERS' ORGANISATIONS

About one-third of Switzerland's wage and salary earners are members of trade unions, the majority of which are grouped together in the Swiss Federation of Trade Unions. In 1973 the

Federation, which is associated with the International Confederation of Free Trade Unions, had some 450,000 individual members. It represents the most important unions: the Swiss Federation of Metalworkers and Watchmakers, the Union of Workers in the Woodworking and Building Trades, the Union of Commerce, Transport and Food Workers, the Swiss Union of Public Services Personnel and the Association of Swiss Railway Workers, among others.

A second group is represented by the Swiss Confederation of Christian Trade Unions, about 100,000 strong and associated with the World Confederation of Labour. Talk of fusion between these two groups, possibly including other unions such as the Swiss Federation of Independent Unions, has as yet come to nothing, ostensibly because the programmes and ideologies of the various federations are still too dissimilar to permit their integration. In addition to these bodies, a federation of white-collar workers, the Federation of Swiss Employees' Societies, has some 120,000 members. In recent years the attitude of the Swiss unions has become more militant but they are still far less powerful than those in other Western European countries.

Employers are organised in industrial and commercial groups or cantonal associations. The three largest employers' organisations are the Central Federation of Swiss Employers' Associations, the Swiss Association for Commerce and Industry and the Swiss Federation of Arts and Crafts. All employers' organisations are inevitably attacked by the unions as being right-wing and reactionary and this is so in Switzerland too; there are nevertheless signs that these organisations are showing increased awareness of their responsibilities both towards their employees and towards the state itself.

The situation in the agricultural sector is peculiar in that the powerful Swiss Peasants' Union covers the entire range of activities which in other countries are usually divided between employers' and workers' organisations. It groups together the principal agricultural societies and chambers of agriculture, the federations of agricultural co-operative societies, milk producers and stockbreeders and other federations representing the highly varied interests of Swiss agriculture. The Union's domination of agricultural activities in Switzerland has not gone unchallenged, however. The Union of Swiss Producers, a militant splinter group with some 6,000 members mainly from the French-speaking area, claims that in the past the Swiss Peasants' Union has been far too accommodating in its relations with the Federal Government and that as a result Swiss farmers have been less well treated than workers in industry and the services sector, particularly as regards average incomes.

LABOUR RELATIONS

Over the years Switzerland has acquired an enviable reputation in the field of labour relations. Industrial disputes are commonly settled peacefully, by arbitration and collective bargaining and the success of this approach is clearly evident from the statistics in the table below. Even bearing in mind the relative size of the Swiss, United Kingdom and United States labour forces, these figures tell their own story.

Country	Year	No. of Industrial Disputes	No. of Workers Affected	No. of Working Days Lost
Switzerland	1971	11	2,267	7,491
	1972	5	526	2,002
	1973	—	—	—
United Kingdom	1971	2,228	1,178,200	13,551,000
	1972	2,497	1,734,000	23,909,000
	1973	2,873	1,527,600	7,197,000
United States	1971	5,138	3,279,600	47,589,100
	1972	5,010	1,713,600	27,066,400
	1973	5,353	2,251,000	27,000,918

(Source: ILO: *Year Book of Labour Statistics, 1974*)

Most collective agreements are negotiated bilaterally between the local union and the employer, but occasionally the Federal Government may extend the application of an agreement to an entire industry. A typical example is that of the metalworking and watchmaking industries, where the union concerned and the employers pledged themselves as long ago as 1937 to shun work stoppages completely and to settle all disputes through an agreed conciliation and arbitration procedure. To this end each party deposited 250,000 francs with the Swiss National Bank as a guarantee. The agreement has been renewed regularly ever since (although the terms of renewal have frequently given rise to some hard bargaining), and its success is a testimony to the good faith of both employers and workers. Similar contracts exist in other industries, the most recent being that drawn up for the hotel and restaurant industry in 1974.

Perhaps the most controversial issue affecting labour relations at present time is that of the participation of workers and of their organisations in the management of an undertaking. There seems little doubt that the principle of participation will eventually be written into the Constitution; the question is, however, to what extent the principle will be developed. The workers feel that they have a right to have a say in any decisions taken concerning the factory or undertaking to which they supply their labour; the employers, and to some extent the Federal Council, feel that this has become a political rather than a social matter and are in favour of moving cautiously rather than with precipitate haste. The idea that trade union militants may one day be represented on a board of directors is one for which, frankly, many employers feel little enthusiasm.

WOMEN AT WORK

Women play an important role in the economic life of Switzerland. Approximately one in every three women is in employment, and women account for slightly less than one-third of the total labour force. About three-fifths of the women in wage-earning employment are found in the services sector, as against just under two-fifths in industry. Women's participation in economic activity is thus concentrated almost exclusively in the non-agricultural sectors.

Only about a fifth of the women at work are married and to some extent this reflects traditional Swiss attitudes. The Federal Government has declared that, although for married women whose children no longer need constant attention their participation in economic activity is not only a personal right but also, in certain circumstances, a social duty, it would nevertheless be contrary to the ideas and way of life of the Swiss people for the state to encourage women with family responsibilities, particularly those with young children, to take a job. Be that as it may, a study carried out in Solothurn a few years ago revealed that the youngest child of two out of every five working mothers was less than six years old.

WAGES AND PURCHASING POWER

The average earnings (in francs per hour) of male skilled and unskilled workers and women workers in 1973 in various key industries are shown in the following table. Perhaps more interesting than these general figures, however, are those which compare the wages paid in specific, well defined occupations in Switzerland, the United Kingdom and the United States respectively. Let us take five people in identical job situations: first, a 35-year-old male, married, primary-school teacher with no children, with ten years' teaching experience in state schools; second, a 35-year-old married bus driver with two children; third, a 25-year-old car mechanic with five years' experience after completing his apprenticeship; fourth, a 35-year-old bank

| | | Men | |
| | | Semi-skilled, | |
Industry	Skilled	Unskilled	Women
Printing, publishing	13·29	10·18	7·24
Chemicals	12·86	11·43	7·98
Paper, paper products	11·79	10·20	6·71
Metal and machinery	11·35	9·73	7·00
Building	11·02[1]	9·28[2]	—
Textiles	10·96	9·61	6·69
Watchmaking	10·60	8·90	6·64
Clothing	10·26	9·44	6·62
Average all Industry	11·31	9·75	6·80

[1]Skilled and semi-skilled   [2]Unskilled

(Source: ILO: *Year Book of Labour Statistics, 1974*)

clerk, married with two children and about ten years' experience in his job; finally, a secretary with five years' experience working for a department head in an industrial organisation and knowing one foreign language. The net earnings (after deduction of tax and social security contributions) of these five people in June/July 1973 are shown in the table below.

Of course, any information on average net earnings must be complemented by data on the purchasing power of these incomes. What can the average worker afford to buy with his money, as compared with his counterpart in other cities? And more revealing still, how many hours would he have to work in order to meet certain basic items of expenditure?

Occupation and Locality	Annual Net Earnings (dollars)	Percentage of Gross Income	Hours Worked per Week
Teacher			
Zürich	8,943	75·3	28
London	4,270	74·1	35
New York	13,098	72·8	30
San Francisco	9,804	80·4	37·5
Bus driver			
Zürich	7,760	79·6	44
London	4,398	77·9	40
New York	9,168	79·5	40
Car mechanic			
Zürich	6,631	77·4	45
London	3,418	73·3	40
New York	9,598	77·4	40
Chicago	7,543	80·7	40
Bank clerk			
Zürich	9,242	76·9	44
London	4,331	80·2	35
New York	8,339	84·2	35
Secretary			
Zürich	6,281	78·1	44
London	3,788	70·2	35
New York	6,790	72·2	35

(Source: Union Bank of Switzerland: *Prices and Earnings Round the Globe*)

A person earning the 'average' Swiss wage—for our purposes here, the average of the net earnings of our primary-school teacher, bus driver, car mechanic, bank clerk and secretary—would have to work for 16·8 hours to pay for a 'shopping basket' of 25 basic items of food and drink, whereas the 'average' Londoner would need to work for 18·8 hours, the New Yorker for 10 hours and the Chicagoan for 11 hours to buy the same commodities. As for men's clothing, Mr Honegger in Zürich needs to work for 35·7 hours for his basic outfit; Mr Smith in London for 47 hours; Mr Doe in New York or Chicago for 29·8 and 32 hours. Mrs Honegger's basic mini-wardrobe would cost her 18 hours of work, as against Mrs Smith's 16 hours and 12·3 and 19 hours for the Mesdames Doe. It is worth pausing here to reflect that the 'shopping basket' in Istanbul calls for 40·75 hours of work by the average Turk and 94·7 hours by the worker in Bombay; and that in Bombay our average worker would have to work 200 hours for those new clothes.

(The Union Bank of Switzerland's booklet *Prices and Earnings Round the Globe* (Zürich, 1974) was particularly useful during the preparation of this section.)

UNEMPLOYMENT

In normal circumstances, unemployment is virtually unknown in Switzerland. Between 1965 and 1974 the average number of unemployed workers registered at employment offices topped 300 only once, in 1968, and the official figure for 1973 was eighty. (By 1975–76, however, the number of unemployed increased steeply to over 32,000 as a result of the effects in Switzerland of the international recession; in addition, some 136,000 workers were estimated to be on short time.) These statistics must be taken with a pinch of salt, however, and another way of looking at the situation is to say that Switzerland 'exports' its unemployment problem in that when industry's labour requirements fall the authorities merely reduce the number of permits delivered to foreign workers, who thereby become unemployed in their own homelands rather than in Switzerland.

Unemployment insurance is based on the Federal Law of 22 June 1951 and is administered by a large number of private and public (cantonal or communal) insurance funds: in 1971 there were no fewer than 153 such organisations. In the majority of the cantons some form of contributory unemployment insurance is compulsory throughout the canton; in most cantons, however, agricultural workers are excluded, while some also exempt hotel and restaurant employees. Foreign workers with an establishment permit are treated on the same footing as Swiss citizens. A law to make unemployment insurance compulsory throughout the Confederation, with the Federal Constitution being amended accordingly, seems likely to be adopted in 1976.

OCCUPATIONAL ACCIDENTS AND DISEASES

One of the oldest types of social security in Switzerland is the scheme providing compensation for occupational injuries and illnesses, which was inaugurated in 1918 with the foundation of the Swiss Accident Insurance Institution. Coverage is compulsory for all employees of industrial, construction and transportation firms and for those in other specified jobs with high accident rates. Special schemes run by private insurance companies exist for agricultural workers and seamen.

The cost of occupational accident insurance is borne entirely by the employer, at contribution rates that vary with the degree of risk of his undertaking. Benefits include free medical care and a daily allowance of 80 per cent of earnings payable until the worker has recovered or has been certified as permanently disabled; in the case of total disability he receives a pension of 70 per cent of earnings up to a maximum of 875 francs per month, rising to 100 per cent where special care is necessary. For partial disability the pension is proportionately less. Broadly speaking, insured foreign workers receive the same benefits as Swiss nationals on condition that reciprocal arrangements exist between Switzerland and the worker's mother country. In the case of death, the survivor's pension amounts to 30 per cent of the deceased's earnings for widows (or invalid widowers), plus 15 per cent for each orphan up to the age of 18 (21 if a student), or 25 per cent for full orphans, up to a maximum of 60 per cent.

The protection against accidents is of course a very important feature of the compulsory accident insurance scheme and employers are required to take all relevant accident prevention measures, both technical and psychological, in an attempt to reduce their number. Despite these measures the rate of fatal accidents in manufacturing industry has scarcely declined over the past ten years, although the figures in building have dropped slightly.

POWER

Switzerland's abundant water resources have earned the country the nickname of 'the reservoir of Europe', and in the almost complete absence of coal deposits it was inevitable that its turbulent mountain streams, swollen by the melting snows, would become the nation's main source of home-produced energy. Today well over 400 hydro-electric power plants generate four-fifths of the electricity consumed in Switzerland; vast dams have changed the landscape of the high mountain valleys, and in the gigantic Grande-Dixence plant the Swiss have the tallest gravity dam in the world, a huge wall 880 feet high (on a level with the top landing of the Eiffel Tower) situated in the Valaisan Alps at an altitude of over 7,000 feet.

The story of the construction of some of these massive dams recalls the great civil engineering epics of Telford and Brunel in the nineteenth century. Emosson, the great Franco-Swiss power station, is a case in point. For six years, in all weathers, hundreds of workmen had toiled to build this huge wall in a forgotten valley high above the Chamonix-Martigny road, until at last, on 31 August 1973, the job was finished. The morning mist still hung over the valley as the workers gathered together to celebrate the end of their task; the dam was bedecked with pine and fir branches and draped with the Swiss, French, Italian and Spanish flags, and a burst of cheering broke out as a cement mixer moved slowly forward to tip out its last load.

Glasses were filled with champagne, red Italian wine or white wine from the Valais; speeches were delivered; the mass was celebrated; and in true Swiss style, a local folklore group struck up a rousing chorus to commemorate the event.

The completion of the giant Emosson dam in all probability marks the end of an era. Other, smaller dams will still be built in Switzerland; but hydro-electric power alone is no longer able to meet the country's need for electricity. The demand is still increasing: by 4·4 per cent in 1971–72, by 5·8 per cent in 1972–73. Indeed, in 1971–72 the Federal Energy Authority was obliged to import electrical power from abroad for the first time ever. Admittedly, this was partly due to a prolonged drought which curbed the output of the hydro-electric plants, but nevertheless the Authority's projections show that by the end of the 1970s Switzerland will no longer be able to produce enough electricity to meet its needs unless urgent action is taken now. The hydro-electric plants can produce no more; the country's few conventional thermal generating stations are sources of considerable pollution; Switzerland's neighbours are themselves short of energy and cannot be relied on as a source of imported power. The federal authorities have therefore decided that nuclear power stations alone can provide the answer.

Switzerland already has two nuclear power plants in operation, at Beznau-Döttingen on the lower reaches of the river Aare and at Mühleberg in the canton of Bern, some 12 miles from the capital. It is true that on economic grounds nuclear plants have much to commend them (high output, low fuel consumption, negligible pollution, radioactive emanations well below those found in nature) and that in Switzerland they have blunted the edge of a potentially serious electricity crisis. On the other hand, no safe way has yet been found to dispose of or neutralise radioactive waste and understandably enough there has been fierce opposition within the country to the construction of new nuclear plants. The opponents of such plants have campaigned actively, evoking the dangers of atomic power and the risk of catastrophe, questioning the need for the construction of nuclear power stations and claiming that they would destroy the ecology and natural beauty of Switzerland's

Alpine valleys. In such circumstances the procedure for obtaining approval for nuclear power projects has made slow progress. Successful delaying tactics have held up the start of work on the Kaiseraugst (Aargau) plant; similar trouble is brewing around the proposed Verbois plant, some 7 miles from the centre of Geneva, and the projects at Gösgen (canton of Solothurn), Leibstadt (Aargau) and elsewhere have also given rise to strong, organised protest on the part of the local communes.

The total amount of electric power produced in Switzerland in 1973–74 reached 37,248 GWH, a figure which represents about 17 per cent of the country's total consumption of energy. By far the most important energy source, accounting for about 78 per cent of total consumption, is imported oil, all but a small proportion of which is used in the form of heating oils of all kinds (9·7 million tons in 1973) and motor vehicle and aircraft fuel (4·0 million tons). The refineries at Collombey-Muraz (Valais) and Cressier (Neuchâtel) handle over 6 million tons of crude oil annually.

The remaining sources of energy are negligible: coal, 1·9 per cent of total consumption in 1974 and falling steadily; wood, 1·3 per cent; and gas, 2·2 per cent. With the introduction of natural gas into Switzerland, however, the future for gas seems brighter. The inauguration in 1974 of the natural gas pipeline between Holland and Italy, which enters Switzerland near Rheinfelden (Aargau) and crosses into Italy over the Gries Pass 100 miles to the south, marked the first step towards linking Switzerland to three of the main international gas transport networks, which in turn are connected to the large European and Russian natural gas systems. On the completion of this project, probably in 1977–78, Switzerland will have access to ample supplies of natural gas per year, and it is estimated that by the end of the century gas will meet over 6 per cent of the country's total energy needs.

IMPORTS AND EXPORTS

As a result of the country's lack of minerals and other raw materials and its limited agricultural production, Switzerland relies heavily on imports of industrial raw materials, food and fodder, which it finances with its exports of manufactured and semi-manufactured goods. In 1973 goods to the value of 36,590 million francs were imported, of which raw materials and semi-manufactured goods accounted for 15,070 million francs and consumer goods 12,470 million francs. The value of exports was 29,950 million francs, of which just over one-half (15,900 million francs) was derived from the exports of the metal and machinery industries and just under one-fifth (6,340 million francs) emanated from the chemical and pharmaceutical industry, which in fact exports 90 per cent of its production. It is interesting to notice here that exports of watches and clocks, for which Switzerland is traditionally known, amounted to 3,240 million francs in 1973, or slightly less than 11 per cent of total exports.

The bulk of the country's trade is with the nine countries of the European Common Market, which supplies seven-tenths of its imports and takes about half its exports. In each case, trade with the Federal Republic of Germany is the most important (29 and 14 per cent respectively). In 1974 also imports from the United Kingdom and the United States were almost equal in value at just under 6 per cent of the total, as against exports to these countries worth respectively 7·2 per cent and 7·1 per cent of the total. In 1972 Switzerland negotiated a Special Relations Agreement with the Common Market, under which virtually all the existing free trade arrangements between Switzerland and the United Kingdom which had been made when both countries were members of the European Free Trade Association were maintained, and the existing customs duties between Switzerland and the other eight Common Market countries were to be phased out by mid-1977.

With the value of its exports regularly amounting to only some five-sixths of that of its imports, the country has a regular foreign trade deficit; however, its income from banking and other services, investments abroad, insurance and the tourist industry normally compensates for this shortfall. Switzerland's customs tariff is the largest single revenue-raising item on the federal budget but as a result of the phasing-out of customs

duties between Switzerland and the Common Market referred
to above, this source of income will soon become less vital.

'THE FIFTH SWITZERLAND'

In former times over-population obliged many Swiss citizens
to emigrate in order to earn a living, either in mercenary
service or as skilled workers and tradesmen. It has been estimated that between the late Middle Ages and the year 1859,
when Swiss citizens were forbidden to serve in foreign armies,
2 million Swiss soldiers enlisted under alien flags. Furthermore,
the colonisation of the New World brought about a real mass
emigration spread over the eighteenth and nineteenth centuries.

In 1973 some 320,000 Swiss citizens were registered at Swiss
embassies and consulates abroad—this formality is compulsory
for any Swiss national who has lived in a foreign country for
more than three months. These people make up what is known
as the 'Fifth Switzerland', the existence of which was officially
recognised in 1966 in an amendment to the Constitution (the
first four 'Switzerlands' are of course the four national linguistic
groups). Swiss expatriates with dual nationality totalled 157,290
in 1973, compared with 161,985 who held Swiss nationality
alone. Both groups are found in virtually every country in the
world. Emigrants to France are the most numerous (28·7 per
cent), followed by those residing in the United States (11·1 per
cent) and the Federal Republic of Germany (7·5 per cent).
Italy, Canada and Argentina are other countries that are
currently finding favour with Swiss emigrants, whose numbers
are regularly greater than those returning to their home
country after a spell abroad.

Whereas during the past 100 years most of those who went
abroad were drawn from the industrial and services sectors,
nowadays a surprisingly large proportion of those who join the
exodus are scientists and university personnel. Between 1964
and 1973, 11,991 such 'intellectual workers' left Switzerland,
chiefly for the Federal Republic of Germany, the United States
and certain African countries. However, most migrations of
this kind prove to be only temporary, and the net loss to

Switzerland through the 'brain drain' during the ten years in question was only 300 persons.

The recognition of the 'Fifth Switzerland' in the Constitution is significant, since it reinforces the impression of devout patriotism that marks this small heterogeneous country. There is a long-standing tradition that at regular intervals the Swiss abroad take advantage of their holidays to forge new links with the homeland, and for over fifty years an annual congress has been convened in the mother country each August to enable those resident abroad to come home to discuss their situation and problems. For instance, the education of Swiss children abroad often poses problems for those whose emigration is purely temporary and in a number of countries the expatriates have established their own schools—for instance, in Italy, Spain, Peru, Brazil, Thailand and elsewhere—which receive financial assistance from the Confederation (8·3 million francs in 1972). The popularity of these schools in the host countries is such that nowadays only two out of every three pupils are Swiss. The curricula followed are basically the same as those in Switzerland itself, to which we shall turn in the next chapter.

5

How They Learn

UNDER Article 27 of the Federal Constitution, primary education must be provided for all children of school age in Switzerland. This education, which notwithstanding the use of the word 'primary' covers the whole period of compulsory schooling, is placed under the exclusive control of the civil authorities. In the public schools, which are open to children of all religions, it is free.

Article 27 also states that 'the cantons shall provide for primary education'—that is, education is a cantonal and not a federal matter. In laying down this requirement those who drew up the Constitution over a century ago tacitly recognised a *fait accompli*, since by that time most of the cantons had in any

––––––

A Swiss Air-Rescue helicopter hovers over a snow-bound mountain hut near the Matterhorn

A group of youngsters in a ski class at Gstaad. Most Swiss children are quite at home on skis by the time they reach their seventh birthday

case already set up their own school systems, each in line with its own historical development and based on its own customs and traditions. The effect of the requirement, however, is that as there are twenty-five cantons and demi-cantons, Switzerland now has no fewer than twenty-five school systems for a total school population of a million children. Despite what has been called their 'spiritual unity', which in large part derives from their common inspiration in the teachings of the renowned Swiss educationalist Heinrich Pestalozzi (1746–1827), these twenty-five systems show wide outward differences owing to the many historical, cultural, religious and linguistic traditions involved. The table below gives some idea of the lack of harmony between the various cantonal laws on education; the most significant difference perhaps lies in the duration of compulsory education, which may be seven, eight or nine years depending on the canton.

The cost of maintaining such a fragmented pattern of schooling is high, and education is a domain for which the Swiss system of federalism with cantonal sovereignty seems ill suited. At the human level, too, there are disadvantages: a child who is obliged to change from one cantonal educational system to another—if his parents move house, for example—may find that he is re-learning what he has already learnt, or alternatively

---

An alphorn player in the Bernese Oberland, near the Jungfrau. The lugubrious sound of the alphorn may carry for several miles across the mountain valleys

The graceful and elegant lines of the Lake Geneva motorway curve round the hillside above the Château de Chillon, Switzerland's most popular tourist haunt. The technical difficulties facing Swiss motorway engineers can be immense. In the far background the motorway can just be seen crossing a lofty viaduct, high above the town of Montreux

G

that his level of attainment is lower than that of the children of his age in his new school.

Canton	Beginning of School Year	Age at Entrance	Duration of Compulsory Education (years)	Length of School Year (weeks)
Aargau	Spring	7	8	40
Bern	Spring	6	9	39
Geneva	Autumn	6	9	39½
Glaris	Spring	6	8	40–42
Lucerne	Autumn	7	8	39
Nidwalden	Autumn	7	7	40
Schaffhausen	Spring	6	8	40
Vaud	Spring	7	9	39
Zürich	Spring	6	8	39–40

(Source: from Hans Tschäni: *Profil de la Suisse*, 1968)

Swiss educationalists are naturally well aware of the anomalies of the present system, and several attempts have been made to bring about a greater degree of co-ordination on a voluntary basis. One of the most recent and most important of these measures was the so-called 'Concordat on Educational Co-ordination' adopted in 1970 at the annual Conference of the Heads of Cantonal Departments of Education. This agreement, which has now been accepted in principle by the majority of the cantons, covers a wide range of topics relating to the administration and curriculum of a standardised educational system under which most of the outstanding inconsistencies would be eliminated. Simultaneously the French-speaking cantons are devising a common system, based on the concordat, which is to be progressively introduced in all schools under their control. A major problem here is that of harmonising the system in, for instance, the traditional canton of Neuchâtel with that in the canton of Geneva, which is perhaps the most advanced in the whole of Switzerland. This problem will be repeated on a larger scale when a national scheme is eventually adopted, as it must be in time.

A serious attempt to set the co-ordination of the twenty-five disparate systems on a constitutional footing was almost successful in 1973 when after several years of preparation a proposed revision of Article 27 of the Constitution, covering the whole range of educational activity from pre-school to post-university, was submitted to the nation under the referendum procedure. The immediate aim of the revision was to transfer a number of educational responsibilities from the cantons to the Confederation, and it was this political aspect of the revision, rather than its purely educational content, that caused its rejection; for although the majority of the people approved the proposal it was narrowly rejected by the majority of the cantons and thus the whole project foundered. It is not difficult to find the reasons underlying the opposition: in the first place, education is the last really major area under cantonal administration alone and the idea of what was looked on as federal interference in such an important matter was unpalatable to certain cantons; second, the conservative and right-wing elements feared that the proposed educational innovations would prove to be based on leftist philosophies; third, some of the more traditional German-speaking cantons wished in effect to preserve what can only be described as their feudal heritage; and fourth, some of the non-German-speaking cantons were apprehensive in case a centralised system administered from Bern might chip away at their cultural and linguistic integrity. Tradition is, of course, an integral part of a nation's culture and identity, but in this particular instance it seems as though the weight of tradition has been detrimental to development.

COMPULSORY EDUCATION

Primary education covers the compulsory schooling period, which, as we saw above, lasts from seven to nine years depending on the canton. Pre-school or infant education is free but not compulsory; nevertheless, three out of every four children in the larger urban communes have already completed two years in infant classes by the time they enter the primary school. These infant classes are concerned almost entirely with the development of a child's sensory and linguistic abilities and with self-expression and creative work; it is only towards the end of the second year in the infant classes, when the child is over 6 years old, that the three Rs are touched upon—a slow start by British standards.

The period of compulsory schooling is complete in itself. Its aim is to educate all children without distinction and, by methods carefully adapted to their development and abilities, to prepare them for the activities which will enable them to earn their living and perform their duties as citizens of Switzerland. In the first year of primary school the pace is brisk, with particular emphasis on learning to read, to spell, to write and to tackle basic mathematics. During this year the child is called upon to make an effort as great as any that will be asked of him during his whole school life. With the introduction of the common educational system in the French-speaking cantons (the first stage of which is planned for 1982), the present rather formal primary curriculum will be broadened to include such notions as the provision of a basic general culture, while at the same time the development of the child's intellectual, artistic and physical capacities will be continued.

The age of transfer to upper primary education, by which is meant the second stage of compulsory education, again varies according to the canton. In Vaud, for instance, it takes place after three years of compulsory schooling (there is a proposal to raise this to four years), in Ticino after five, in Zürich after six. An added complication here derives from the lack of a uniform terminology—in some cantons the upper primary stage is known as the secondary stage, in others as the intermediate or lower general stage and so on. Broadly speaking, most cantons stream their children into two or three types of school for the upper primary stage. The first is designed for those children with no particular intellectual pretensions and lays special stress on practical preparation for life. The second group of pupils enter the lower commercial or technical schools, which give them a good general education completed by appropriate vocational training; in cantons with only two types of upper primary education, these schools also serve as the lower schools for the upper secondary *collèges*, *lycées* or *Gymnasia* which offer academic education leading to the university.

The main exception to this pattern is provided by the canton of Geneva. Before the Genevese pupil starts the second stage of compulsory schooling at the age of 12, he carries out various scholastic and psychological tests before entering the *cycle d'orientation* or 'guidance stage' school for three years. These schools, which resemble the more successful English comprehensive schools, were first established in 1962 and differ considerably from the selective secondary, technical or grammar-type schools of the other cantons. The 'guidance stage' is intended to cope with a wide range of abilities, and the Genevese authorities consider that most pupils have been placed in the right courses (literary, scientific, 'modern' (linguistic), general or practical), due account having been taken of parental wishes, by the time they have reached the second year. The scheme as a whole is now sufficiently advanced for it to be looked upon as being beyond the experimental stage. Other cantons have shown interest in the *cycle d'orientation* and it seems probable that in time the system will be taken up elsewhere.

POST-COMPULSORY EDUCATION

At the close of their period of compulsory schooling, those young people who decide to stay on at school may either choose a course of general secondary education leading to the *Matura* or *maturité* examination and university entrance or an advanced teacher training course, or enter a higher technical school. If, on the other hand, they prefer to take up employment in industry or commerce they may at the same time follow complementary day-release courses at a vocational or technical school. The final decision is determined by the pupil's own inclinations and scholastic achievements, with due consideration being given to parents' wishes. This form of 'upper secondary' education is found, with variations, in all but the smallest cantons.

Throughout Switzerland the schools which prepare their pupils for university studies base their syllabuses on those established by the Federal Matriculation Commission which lead to the *Matura*, the main qualification for university entrance. The purpose of this examination, which pupils sit at the age of 17 or 18, is to make it possible to judge whether a candidate has the maturity of thought and independence of judgement necessary for advanced studies—not only as regards answering questions but also as regards assessing and understanding problems. There are now five types of *Matura* certificate: type A, classical with Latin and Greek; type B, literary with Latin and modern languages; type C, scientific and mathematical; type D, modern languages; type E, business studies. The fact that all these syllabuses were drawn up by a federal body means that notwithstanding the autonomy of the cantons the Confederation has exercised a decided influence on education at this level, particularly with regard to the position of Latin as a required language for university entrance.

Other school-leaving certificates include the diplomas awarded by the cantonal higher technical schools, which in certain cases give access to the universities. The 'international baccalaureat' was introduced in 1962 especially to meet the needs of children whose parents are constantly on the move from country to country and which now satisfies the entrance requirements of over 200 universities in Switzerland, the United Kingdom, the United States and many other countries.

HIGHER EDUCATION

Switzerland has seven universities (Basel, Bern, Fribourg, Geneva, Lausanne, Neuchâtel, Zürich), a School of Economics and Public Administration at St Gallen and two federal institutes of technology at Lausanne and Zürich respectively. The latter is the only higher educational establishment founded and wholly financed by the Confederation (this despite the provision in Article 27 of the Constitution authorising the Confederation to create a federal university); the others are all maintained by the cantons. Each university is headed by a rector, supported by a senate or executive board composed of the deans and vice-deans of the various faculties, and a university assembly composed of all professors. The majority of the universities are organised in four faculties: theology, law and economics, medicine, philosophy (arts and science).

In 1973 just under 49,000 students were enrolled at Swiss universities. Some 10,000 of these were following courses at the University of Zürich, with almost 7,000 studying at the University of Geneva. On average, one out of every five students is a foreigner, the proportion being 15 per cent in universities in the German-speaking cantons and almost 30 per cent in those west of the Sarine—a proportion as high as at any university anywhere in the world.

The future prosperity of Switzerland, as a small country with negligible natural resources, is substantially dependent on scientific research. We saw in Chapter 4, 'How They Work', that research is shared between industry, whose scientists are reliably reported to receive more than 500 million francs a year for their work in applied research, and the universities, where pure research is encouraged by the National Fund for Scientific Research, to which the Confederation plans to make the sum of 660 million francs available over the five years from 1975 to 1979. As in the United Kingdom, the contribution of industry to research is thus considerably greater than that of the central government, unlike the situation in, for example, the United States, where 70 per cent of the expenditure on scientific research is borne by the state, and France, where the government share rises to 80 per cent. Here again we have an example of the dislike of the Swiss citizen for centralised federal responsibility and of his esteem for private enterprise.

VOCATIONAL TRAINING

Except for the training of teachers, which is looked upon as a purely educational matter, vocational training is regulated by the federal Vocational Training Law of 1963 and the Agricultural Training Act of 1955. These stipulate the methods to be used and the curricula to be followed in apprenticeship schemes and there is therefore much more uniformity in this branch of education than in others. They also determine the level of subsidies and grants for vocational training. Under the Constitution, no young person may begin an apprenticeship until he is 15 years of age, and during the whole period of training the apprentice must attend a vocational school. The certificate of proficiency awarded to candidates who are successful in the final examination is a federal certificate valid throughout Switzerland, although it is actually awarded by the canton in which the apprentice did his training. The next step, which the successful candidate may take if he wishes, is the certificate of Master Craftsman.

These vocational schools cover a wide range of agricultural and industrial activity: courses are provided for farmers, vinegrowers, horticulturists, precision engineers, watchmakers, joiners, dressmakers and so on. If in any canton there is no course in a particular occupation the authorities of that canton may make arrangements with a neighbouring canton to accept their apprentices. In 1971 over 130,000 young workers, male and female, were receiving training under one or other of these schemes.

Two groups of vocational training institutions form a special category. The cantonal colleges of technology provide further training for those who have successfully completed a technical apprenticeship course of three to four years' duration; and, except in Baselstadt and Geneva where higher qualifications are required, primary school teacher-training colleges offer a four or five year course for those who have completed their compulsory schooling. The training of teachers at secondary level and above is carried out at universities.

ADULT EDUCATION

Courses for adults are mainly of a social and cultural nature and resemble those offered in evening classes in the United Kingdom. They are rather more expensive, 4 francs an hour, on average, and the choice is by no means as wide. Even in the larger towns the courses available tend to be limited to foreign languages and commercial, artistic and practical subjects. A few of these courses are peculiarly Swiss: peasant furniture decoration, for instance, or Schwyzerdütsch for Beginners. The great majority of the courses are run by private commercial organisations, in particular by the Migros chain of retail stores and by the 'Co-op'. Courses provided by the cantonal authorities are still few in number.

FEE-PAYING AND BOARDING SCHOOLS

Compulsory education in Switzerland, even when given in private schools, remains under the supervision of the public authorities. The cantonal educational laws require that the standard of private education must be at least equal to that of public education, and certain cantons have accordingly retained the right to inspect private schools or to check the results of private-school examinations. In many places the education authorities convene the pupils from these schools to the examinations held in the public schools, thereby verifying the level of attainment.

Besides the numerous private day schools, there is a sizeable number of fee-paying boarding schools, some of which have an international reputation—finishing schools for young ladies, and the like. There are no private universities and in this Switzerland differs from the United States. The private schools lay more emphasis on individual tuition, over-all training in the social graces and cultural pursuits than the public schools.

FINANCE

The total expenditure on education in Switzerland in 1970, including capital expenditure, was 3,726 million francs. This represented 18·4 per cent of total government expenditure and 4·2 per cent of the gross national product.

Under Article 27A of the Constitution, the Confederation grants subventions to the cantons in order to help them to carry out their obligations in respect of primary (ie compulsory) education. The amount of each subvention is calculated according to the number of 7 to 15-year-old children in the canton. An additional grant is made to two cantons which, for linguistic reasons, have to incur special expenditure (Graubünden, Ticino) and to the mountain cantons where the provision of adequate schooling is often beset by considerable difficulties

(Uri, Schwyz, Obwalden, Nidwalden, Appenzell, Graubünden, Ticino, Valais). The total amount granted in subventions reaches some 5 million francs annually, but it is of course the cantons and the communes that pay the lion's share of the cost of education, for they defray the entire cost of school building, teachers' salaries, equipment and so on. Only if a new or additional building is intended for vocational education does the Confederation make a grant towards its construction. In the majority of the cantons textbooks and other school materials are supplied free during the period of compulsory schooling.

Teachers' salaries vary according to the educational level, the cost of living in the various cantons and the financial situation in the canton concerned. The annual salary of a married primary school teacher, after ten years of service in a public school, amounts to approximately 28,000 francs after tax in Zürich and 27,000 francs after tax in Geneva.

The cantons meet the greater part of university expenses too —sometimes up to 98 per cent of the total. Scholarships may be awarded either by the cantons, the universities themselves or private foundations. The value of these scholarships tend to be low and one of the primary aims of those concerned with university education is to increase the funds available for this purpose.

THE FUTURE

Federalism, the political tendency which aims at maintaining the sovereignty and power of the cantons, is a vital element in Swiss life. It has been said, however, that the victory of the federalists in obtaining the rejection, in 1973, of the proposed revision of Article 27 of the Constitution set back the cause of Swiss education by at least ten years. The task of the Federal Council now is to renew its efforts to make large sections of the population aware of the difficulties inherent in maintaining twenty-five school systems in a country with a population of six million souls, and to work with the cantons in drawing up new plans for education with the ultimate aim of uniting the many separate parts into one homogeneous whole.

6

How They Get About

The great highways, passable for carriages, over the high Alps, are, indeed, most surprising monuments of human skill and enterprise in surmounting, what would appear, at first sight, to be intended by nature as insurmountable.

So wrote John Murray III in *A Handbook for Travellers in Switzerland* (published in 1838 and reprinted in 1970 by Leicester University Press).

These proud constructions of art thread the valleys, cross the debris of rivers on long causeways, skirt the edge of the precipice, with walls of rock tottering over them, and torrents thundering below. . . . Every opportunity is seized of gaining, by easy ascents, a higher level for the road; at length comes the main ascent, the central ridge, to be surmounted only by hard climbing. This is overcome by a succession of zigzag terraces . . . connected together by wide curves, to allow carriages to turn easily and rapidly. So skilful is their construction, with such easy bends and so gradual a slope, that in many alpine roads the postilions, with horses accustomed to the road, trot down at a rapid pace.

One may smile at the quaint charm of Murray's words but with very little modification they would be equally valid today, nearly a century and a half later. When Murray was writing, the first of these great carriage-roads, the one over the granite and gneiss barrier of the Simplon, had been open for only thirty years. Its construction had been decided upon by

Napoleon Bonaparte at the end of the eighteenth century, and it had taken six years to build. Other roads followed at regular intervals during the nineteenth century—the St Gotthard, the Splügen, the San Bernardino, the Great St Bernard and so on—and now there are no fewer than twenty-five major roads over the Swiss Alpine passes. Some of these are open from April-June to late autumn, depending on the snow; others (for instance, the Maloja and the Col des Mosses) remain practicable more or less throughout the winter, provided that chains or snow tyres are fitted to vehicle wheels. The inauguration of the Great St Bernard and San Bernardino road tunnels in the 1960s marked the opening of the first north-south highways through the Swiss Alps that can be used regularly all the year round. The St Gotthard road tunnel, which is now being driven through ten miles of mountain between Göschenen and Airolo, is expected to open in the late 1970s. Motor vehicles may also travel from one side of the Alps to the other by rail ferry, through the St Gotthard, Simplon, Lötschberg or Albula tunnels.

The roads of the Swiss Alps, with their stupendous views and spectacular engineering, form one of the main attractions for holiday visitors, but they do not cater exclusively, or even primarily, for tourist traffic. Napoleon built his epoch-making road across the Simplon for strategic purposes and for many years before then the St Gotthard pass had been (as it still remains) the main trade route, albeit narrow and sinuous, between central Switzerland and Italy. A country that is so dependent on imports and exports needs a highly developed communications system, and Switzerland now has a dense network of well surfaced main and subsidiary roads covering some 38,000 miles. Existing and projected motorways account for about 1,150 miles; after a slow start, the motorway system as a whole is expected to be completed by the late 1980s, and the last gap in the trans-European through motorway from Stockholm to Sicily will then, at last, have been filled. The construction of these national roads is being subsidised by the Confederation, partly through a tax on motor fuels. By the end of 1974, 12,880 million francs had been spent on the project, a sum which will inevitably increase considerably before the network is finished, if only because of the enormous increase in the cost of land and labour that Switzerland has experienced since the motorway building programme was approved in 1958. The system is already fairly well developed in the German-speaking region, but considerably less so west of the Sarine, and the lack of a motorway link between the German and French-speaking areas has for years been a source of protest for the French-speaking cantons. The completion of such a link is, in fact, not foreseen until the late 1970s.

Although at the start of the motorway building programme the general public was not unduly troubled by the problem of noise, as the new roads crept nearer and nearer to built-up areas and as the juggernaut lorries began to rumble past there was a notable rise in public concern over this and other problems of environmental pollution. It has therefore been necessary to incur considerable unforeseen expenditure in an attempt to limit the effects of excessive noise by realigning motorways and by erecting anti-noise screenings. This increasing public awareness of the environmental problems connected with motorway construction in particular has had its effect on attitudes towards road traffic as a whole; indeed, in 1974 the citizens of the canton of Neuchâtel rejected a proposal to allocate 32 million francs for the expansion of the cantonal road system—a decision that would have been unthinkable a few years ago.

Despite many discussions about the protection of the environment and road safety in general, the rapid increase in the number of private cars and commercial vehicles has not been curbed. Towards the end of 1974 these numbered 1,723,023 and 176,487 respectively; there were also 111,867 motor-cycles, 657,794 mopeds and other light, powered cycles, as well as some 1,325,000 bicycles on the road. When we note that in 1964 there were fewer than 950,000 private cars in the country we gain some idea of the prodigious increase in their use during the past decade—the point of saturation has by no means been reached. The number of inhabitants per private car in various countries is shown in the first table below; the second table lists the six most popular makes of new car registered in Switzerland in 1974 and their country of origin.

Number of Inhabitants per Private Car

Country	1959	1960	1970	1972
Canada	4·7	4·6	3·4	3·4
France	10·0	9·0	4·3	3·9
Fed. Rep. of Germany	17·0	15·0	4·6	4·0
Greece	176·0	179·0	36·9	33·3
Switzerland	13·0	12·0	4·8	4·3
Turkey	574·0	565·0	222·2	212·8
United Kingdom	11·0	10·0	4·8	4·5
United States	3·1	3·1	2·3	2·3

Make	Country of origin	No.	Share of market (%)
Opel	Fed. Rep. of Germany	23,729	11·7
Volkswagen	Fed. Rep. of Germany	20,704	10·2
Renault	France	17,840	8·8
Fiat	Italy	17,614	8·7
Ford	Fed. Rep. of Germany, United Kingdom, United States	15,075	7·5
Citroën	France	13,610	6·7

The increase in the total number of private cars has been counterbalanced by a steady decline in the number of people using public transport. Two out of every three Swiss public transport systems operated at a loss in 1972, for whereas in 1950 public transport accounted for 60 per cent of the total 'passenger-kilometres' covered, this figure was down to 20 per cent by 1970; and it has been estimated that, unless energetic measures are taken to curb or discourage the use of private cars in favour of public transport, its share will fall to 10 per cent by the end of the century. To date various tentative steps have been taken in this direction (for instance, a small area in central Geneva has been closed to all but buses and trams), but far more vigorous action is called for.

The most remarkable public road transport system in Switzerland is undoubtedly the closely linked, 4,700-mile network of post bus routes. These bright-yellow, modern buses bound up and down the twisty mountain roads (on which they have priority) and provide a social service of inestimable value for the inhabitants of the uplands. Indeed in winter, for those villages that are not ski-ing resorts, the rattle of the post bus's chained wheels on the snowy roads heralds the main event of the day. Each year well over 50 million passengers and nearly 46,000 tons of baggage and freight are transported by post bus to and from the main centres in the valleys.

Road surfaces in Switzerland are generally good, and the driver who enters the country from France, for instance, notices a marked difference when he crosses the frontier. Indeed, what the Swiss denote by the appropriate road sign as a bumpy road would frequently be considered as exceptionally smooth in some other European countries. The standard of driving of the average Swiss driver (in so far as he exists) is reasonably good; as in every country, however, there are unwritten driving conventions which may take the foreigner by surprise.

In 1974 the police were notified of 68,500 road accidents, in which 31,750 people were injured and 1,372 killed. During the decade of the 1960s, 13,910 people were killed on the roads. The sole redeeming feature of these statistics is that the rate of deaths per year has remained quite stable since 1960, fluctuating between 1,300 and 1,700, notwithstanding the tremendous increase in the number of vehicles on Swiss roads.

RAILWAYS

The idea of a Swiss railway network was first mooted in the 1830s, but owing to lack of funds and to the internal political dissension of the time it was not until 1844 that the first track was actually laid on Swiss soil, and even this was a French line, connecting Strasbourg with the Swiss frontier city of Basel. The first railway laid entirely on Swiss soil ran between Zürich and Baden, in Aargau, and was opened in 1847.

The return of peace to the country after the Sonderbund war, the introduction of the new Federal Constitution in 1848 and the simultaneous sweeping away of the hundreds of internal cantonal and communal tariff and customs barriers gave a new impetus to railway construction, and from then onwards the system developed rapidly. Inevitably, because of the nature of the terrain, it was both costly and complicated to build. The original plan was drawn up in 1850 by Robert Stephenson, son of the famous British engineer George Stephenson, and although the number of railway companies ran into dozens his plan was closely adhered to. The network was virtually complete by 1914. It is now 3,207 miles in length, of which 3,111 miles are made up of standard and narrow-gauge main and branch lines and the remaining 96 miles of mountain cog and funicular railways. About three-fifths of the total mileage is operated by the State-owned Swiss Federal Railways, which came into being in 1902 through the nationalisation of five private companies. The remaining companies, some 65 in all, are still privately owned, either by local authorities or by commercial undertakings. The most important of these private lines are the Bern-Lötschberg-Simplon, owned by the canton of Bern, which, with the 9-mile-long Lötschberg tunnel, form the main line linking Bern, Thun, Brig and the Simplon tunnel; and the Rhaetian Railway, the property of the canton of the Graubünden, which runs on metre-gauge tracks in the south-east of the country and, with the Furka-Oberalp Railway, forms part of the important, strategic east-west route linking the Rhine and Rhône valleys across the Alps. Indeed so important is this link that a new railway tunnel, 9·6 miles long, is under construction, with completion expected in 1978–79, through the Furka massif; this will replace the present rack railway section which climbs to 7,086ft in crossing the Furka pass and which is closed by snow for more than six months each year. The new tunnel will allow all-year-round railway operation on this section and will bring important economic and social benefits to the upper Rhône valley east of Brig by making possible quick and dependable communication with the east and north in the winter months.

Swiss railways enjoy an enviable reputation for safety, punctuality and cleanliness, and the feats of engineering realised during their construction are legendary. Anyone who has ever been borne smoothly through a twisting, spiralling tunnel in the heart of the Alpine massif, out on to the slender and graceful structure of a lofty viaduct spanning the precipitous gorge of a mountain torrent, and back again into the solid mountain wall, time after time, is overwhelmed by the sheer grandeur of the Swiss achievement. (He should also spare a thought for the workers who bored and blasted their way through those mountains, yard by yard, fifty and more years ago, or who flung the bridges over those plunging valleys, in order to speed his journey by a few hours.) The first of the really long tunnels to be opened, in 1882, was the St Gotthard, which is 9·3 miles in length and thus slightly longer than the Lötschberg's 9 miles. The longest of all, the Simplon, bores 12·3 miles through the rocky heart of the Monte Leone massif to connect Brig with the Val di Vedro in northern Italy; the most audacious must be the famous tunnel of the narrow-gauge Jungfrau Railway, whose trains burrow into the lower slopes of the Eiger at an altitude of 7,612 feet, wind round inside the Eiger and Mönch for nearly 4½ miles and 50 minutes later reach the Jungfraujoch terminal station, 11,333 feet up and the highest in Europe. The construction of this awesome railway was completed in 1912. Other famous mountain railways are the Viznau-Rigi cog railway, which celebrated its centenary in 1971, and that from Zermatt to Gornergrat, the highest entirely in the open air, which climbs to 10,269 feet.

In mountainous countries like Switzerland, successful railway working can be achieved only if a constant battle is waged against the forces of nature. It is by no means uncommon for falls of snow to cover the exposed lines in the high valleys to a depth of several feet, and to keep the tracks clear the Swiss have developed highly efficient rotary snowploughs, whose spinning blades slice into the deep drifts and spray the snow high in the air and well away from the side of the track. During the periods of heavy snowfall this is a daily operation and, as the snow piles up on either side of the line, the trains may at times be running through cuttings of solid packed snow 20 and more feet high. Avalanches, too, are a source of danger for trains moving along the tracks that cling to the mountain wall high above the valley slopes. In all places where the line crosses a recognised avalanche path massive concrete shelters have been built to ensure that the roaring torrent of boulders and snow passes harmlessly over the rails and on down the mountain side.

H

Since World War II the various railway companies, and the Swiss Federal Railways above all, have embarked on an extensive modernisation programme designed to maintain the high standards to which the travelling public is accustomed and to meet the increased demands of industry while at the same time remaining competitive with road transport. These modernisations include the expansion of the dual-track network, the construction of new passenger and goods stations, the introduction of new signalling and safety equipment, the reconstruction of bridges and tunnels, the use of new transport methods (automation, container transport, etc), the introduction of more powerful locomotives and custom-built rolling stock and so on. The number of passengers conveyed by rail rose steadily over the years to reach a peak of 323 million in 1970, of whom the Federal Railways carried 230 million. Since the start of the 1970s passenger traffic on the state railways has shown a slight decline, falling to 223·9 million by 1973. This decrease is not to be wondered at in view of the startling increase in the number of private cars on the road during the previous decade. On the other hand, the volume of goods traffic on the Federal Railways continues to increase, with a new record of 46·8 million tons being attained in 1973. As long-distance road haulage in Switzerland is seldom so efficient as railway goods traffic, and provided that the railways can maintain their present level of service and keep abreast of modern technological developments in railway practice, their role in the future seems assured. Nonetheless, in recent years the financial situation of the railways, which since World War II has usually been in balance, has shown a disquieting tendency towards an over-all deficit, for while operating revenue is still comfortably above operating expenditure (the figures for 1973 were 2,357·5 million francs and 2,017·1 million francs respectively), the profit is now insufficient to cover loan repayments, essential capital expenditure and other non-operating costs, notwithstanding the inclusion in the profit-and-loss account of some 100 million francs annually in government payments for 'services rendered in the interest of the over-all economy'.

AIR

Switzerland's air transport policy is influenced by two factors: first, both the area of the country and the number of its inhabitants are small; second, Switzerland is situated in the heart of the continent of Europe and thus occupies an important position on the world's air routes. Its policy is therefore resolutely international. The Swiss national airline, Swissair, founded in 1931 through the amalgamation of two smaller airlines, is now 22nd in the list of the 110 airlines which are members of the International Air Transport Association (IATA) and has a network length of some 144,000 miles. Bilateral air transport agreements have been signed with over seventy foreign countries, and some 150 cities all over the world, from Helsinki to Johannesburg, from Tokyo to Santiago de Chile, may be reached by through flights from the main Swiss airports. About half of these flights are operated by Swissair; the remainder are shared between over fifty foreign airlines.

Swissair operates from the two major international airports situated on Swiss soil—Zürich-Kloten, with a total of 90,032 aircraft movements in 1973, and Geneva-Cointrin, with 53,058 —and from Basel-Mulhouse (16,560 movements in 1973), an airport of lesser importance shared with France. There are also forty-three smaller airfields for tourist air traffic and private flying. The capital, Bern, is served by a small airport of no great significance, and the would-be Bernese globetrotter is obliged to board his plane at one or other of the major airports. In 1975, 5·6 million people 'flew Swissair'; the company now has a staff of 13,700 people and operates forty-six aircraft, including two Boeing 747-B 'Jumbos' and eight almost equally huge Douglas DC-10-30s. Ten Douglas DC-9-50 aircraft are due to join the fleet between 1975 and 1977. Charter flights from Switzerland are operated mainly by three private Swiss companies, Balair, Phoenix and SATA, and are responsible for about 7 per cent of air traffic movements from the Swiss airports.

In recent years Swissair has had its share of problems and difficulties. The increasing public hostility to noise pollution in the vicinity of the main airports led, in 1973, to a ban on night flights which is still in force. It remains to be seen whether this ban will be maintained when the new generation of 'silent' aircraft enters into general service a few years hence. Public opposition to the unlimited expansion of airports was demonstrated in striking fashion when a proposal to extend the main runway at Cointrin was so decisively rejected by the voters of Geneva that the project was quickly dropped by the cantonal authorities. Plans to build smaller airports in other parts of Switzerland have met with a similar fate. In matters such as these, which affect so many people to such a degree, the Swiss system of the popular vote has the invaluable merit of enabling the general public to have its say in a decisive and effective manner.

This section would not be complete without a mention of the renowned Swiss Air-Rescue service, founded in 1952 and supported for the most part by its 135,000 members, both Swiss and non-Swiss. Many a mountaineer in difficulties, many an injured skier, many a seriously ill inhabitant of the high villages has had cause to be grateful to the pilots of the brilliant-red Air-Rescue helicopters—the 'lifeboats' of the Alps—which swoop up the valleys on their life-saving missions, pick up the sufferer and whisk him down to safety in a matter of minutes. In 1974 the Air-Rescue, which is affiliated to the Red Cross, flew more than 1,300 such missions and rescued more than 1,600 persons from danger.

WATER TRANSPORT: LAKE, RIVER AND SEA

One of the pleasures of travel in Switzerland is that, if one is not in too much of a hurry, it is often possible to go part of one's way by lake or by river. In summertime more than 130 ships, with total accommodation for over 60,000 passengers, ply on many of the lakes and on certain stretches of the Rhine. On Lake Geneva alone there are almost a score of such boats and the largest, the *Helvetia*, can carry 1,600 passengers. The most attractive of these lake-going vessels are undoubtedly the big, stately paddle-boats of Lakes Lucerne, Geneva and Zürich, their vanes churning the water to a white froth as they come alongside the jetty of some small lakeside town. Evening trips, with music, dancing and dining, are particularly popular with both tourists and the Swiss themselves.

These boats are operated either by private companies or by the railways: the Swiss Federal Railways maintains a fleet of passenger ships on Lake Constance and the Lötschberg Railway operates boats on the Lake of Thun and Lake Brienz. The lakes are not restricted to passenger vessels alone; in 1974 the volume of cargo transported by boat (particularly building materials such as gravel, sand and stone) was in the vicinity of 6–7 million tons, which is not far short of the annual volume handled by the two busy Rhine ports at Basel. For many years a considerable share (now over 20 per cent) of Switzerland's vital imports and, to a lesser degree, exports, have passed through these two ports. More than 500 boats sail under the Swiss flag between Basel and the Dutch port of Rotterdam, and Basel is in fact the third most important port on the river as regards the volume of goods handled. Petroleum products currently account for over 4 million tons of these goods, out of a total of 8·5 million tons. The main hazard to which Rhine shipping traffic is exposed is that of low water levels following a spell of dry weather. However, it is hoped that a series of widening and dredging operations on the Franco-German stretch of the river will help to solve this problem.

Over the years various plans have been put forward for the further expansion of Switzerland's inland waterways system: for instance, making the Upper Rhine navigable from Basel to Lake Constance; linking the river Aare with the Lake of Neuchâtel and thence by canal to Lake Geneva; encouraging the French authorities to make the Rhône navigable as far as Geneva. Inevitably, these plans have met with fierce opposition from a somewhat unholy alliance of environmentalists on the one hand and road and rail haulage interests on the other.

Switzerland, a landlocked country, does not immediately spring to mind as a seafaring nation. Nevertheless, twenty-seven ocean-going ships, all built since 1952, do sail under the Swiss flag, from the diminutive coaster *Dornach* (1,518 deadweight tons) to the new *Général Guisan* (54,085 deadweight tons), launched in 1973 and the largest vessel ever put to sea by Switzerland. It was in fact in 1941, during World War II, that the Swiss authorities realised the need for a purely Swiss fleet that could sail the high seas and ensure the delivery of the vital raw materials and foodstuffs from abroad.

TRAVELLING TO WORK

The report of a federal inquiry into commuting habits, based on a random survey of 30,000 Swiss households and published in 1974, revealed the surprising fact that no fewer than 44 per cent of daily commuters (including schoolchildren and students) go to their place of work or study on foot and 40 per cent live less than 1·25 miles from their destination. The average distance travelled by all commuters is 2·6 miles, for a journey which lasts 15·2 minutes. Those living in the medium-sized towns (of between 30,000 and 125,000 inhabitants) are particularly fortunate in this respect, since their times and distances are below the average. Even in the larger cities 'commuting' is by no means the awful daily grind it has become in London, New York and other sprawling conurbations with their millions of inhabitants. Of those who travel to work 11 per cent go by bicycle or motorcycle, and 18 per cent by private car. Here again, traffic and parking problems are less serious than elsewhere and the rush hour rarely lasts longer than 30–40 minutes. This does not mean, of course, that parking problems are non-existent: the narrow streets of the old quarters were not conceived for twentieth-century traffic and are usually unsuitable for parking, and in other parts of the towns deliberately induced difficulties (pedestrian precincts, parking meters, bus lanes, etc) have been introduced in order to encourage the use of public transport. There are also signs that people are moving away from densely built-up areas, a trend which will inevitably lead to a steady increase in the number of commuters using cars to get to work.

The remaining 37 per cent travel to work or school by public transport (bus, tram, train). As we saw above, two out of every three public transport systems operated at a loss in 1972. If in this affluent country public transport is ever again to offer an effective alternative to the private car, a determined effort is required on the part of the public authorities. The aim of this effort must be as much to prevent Swiss towns from being choked to death by private traffic as to provide an essential social service for the citizen.

How They Amuse Themselves

FOLKLORE AND TRADITION

IN past centuries Swiss leisure-time activities, and Swiss culture generally, were much influenced by the fact that communications between the different regions, particularly in the upland areas, were far from easy. Moreover, in winter most of the mountain villages were virtually cut off for weeks on end by heavy snowfalls which blocked the access roads and made travel a perilous business that was not undertaken lightly. Regular social and cultural contacts with the valley towns and with other mountain villages were therefore unknown, and in these circumstances it is hardly surprising that each community came to devise its own means of entertainment. Inevitably, local folklore traditions grew up which, like the local costumes, local houses and local dialects, showed a marked individuality. To give but one example, there are unmistakable differences between the folk music of Zermatt and of Saas Fee, two Valaisan villages situated about ten miles apart as the crow flies—a brisk afternoon's walk there and back, one might think, and so it would be, if the 12,000ft high Mischabel range did not separate the two townships, so that to go from one to the other involves a detour of over thirty miles.

Even today, despite the levelling influence of radio and television and the opening-up of the high valleys to year-round road or rail traffic and to regular trade and 'consumer benefits', the traditions of the past live on. The Swiss folklore tradition is indeed remarkably rich and alive and not only in the remoter parts of the country. The cities too have their annual centuries-old festivals, ceremonies and processions: for example, the Baslerfest, or Basel carnival, with its parade of drummers and fifers wearing grotesque masks, on the Monday, Tuesday and Wednesday following Ash Wednesday; the Zürich 'Sechseläuten' in mid-April, marking the end of winter; the 'Zibelmärit', or onion market, in Bern on the last Monday in November; the Fête de l'Escalade in Geneva on 11–12 December, when men in seventeenth-century uniforms and armed with pikes parade through the streets to commemorate the repulse of the Savoyard attack on the city in 1602. It is in fact rare to be able to give an exact date to the origin of these festivals, which in most cases are a survival of traditions going back to the Middle Ages and beyond. What immediately strikes the spectator is the important role played by masked revellers, whose fearsome headgear and elaborate costumes seem to reflect a direct link with pagan times; some ethnologists have seen in them a continuation of prehistoric ancestor worship and fertility rites. Their survival to the twentieth century bears witness once again to the Swiss love for its national tradition.

These festivities and processions are usually led by one or more *fanfares*—fife, bugle and drum bands, occasionally augmented by other brass instruments—of which each town or village can usually boast at least one. Another form of traditional musical offering that is particularly common in the German-speaking region is provided by trios of curious instrumentation—clarinet, accordion and bowed double-bass—with the lead instruments endlessly interweaving elaborate strands of melody against the plodding background laid down by the bass. The virtuosity of some of these essentially part-time clarinettists and accordionists is often quite remarkable. A folk music concert, in which all participants will, of course, wear the local costume, would not be complete without a contribution by a choir of yodellers, singing either alone or accompanied by an accordionist, with perhaps, as a special treat, a solo item on the alphorn, that extraordinary instrument seven or more feet long, the sound of which carries for miles across the valleys.

A number of traditional sports and contests have survived down the centuries. *Hornussen*, or 'hornets', a primitive and rather lumbering form of lacrosse, is played with a sort of puck that is hurled through the air; each player is armed with a heavy wooden board, about three feet square and firmly mounted on a pole, with which he attempts to stop the hornet's flight in mid-air. *Schwingen* is the Swiss version of open-air wrestling; the opponents are dressed in a baggy, full-length outfit over which a pair of stout cloth breeches are worn, the idea being to seize hold of one's opponent's breeches in order to throw him to the ground. Flag-throwing is another peculiarly Swiss competition, the aim here being to toss the flag, on its heavy pole, high into the air and to catch it before it falls.

Another traditional form of entertainment, the circus, is well supported in Switzerland. There is in fact a Swiss national circus (the Knie Circus) which for well over half a century has trundled regularly round the country, giving some 350 performances annually.

RADIO AND TELEVISION

The great majority of the Swiss people, of course, do not belong to the accordion-playing, yodelling or flag-throwing set, nor do they wander round the town decked out in traditional costume. Most of them rely on the radio or the television set for their indoor entertainment. In 1974 there were 1,714,336 television (including colour television) and 2,036,431 radio licences in Switzerland which means that, roughly speaking, there is one television set to every four people and one radio to every three people. These proportions are slightly lower than in the United Kingdom and considerably lower than in the United States, where there is one television receiver for every two people and almost two radios per person. Swiss radio and television programmes are controlled by the Swiss Radio and Television Company (SRG/SSR), a public company established in 1931 and operating under a federal concession (and for this reason Swiss radio and television cannot be said to be totally independent of the State), and are broadcast by transmitters and over land-lines provided and maintained by the Post Office. These programmes are run on a shoestring, in comparison with what is spent on broadcasting in the United Kingdom and the United States. In 1973 the sum realised by the issue of radio and television licences amounted to 314 million francs, of which 70 per cent was made available to the SRG/SSR; the company also collected 75·5 million francs in television advertising revenue and 4·5 million francs in federal subsidies for its short-wave transmissions.

Notwithstanding its limited funds, the SRG/SSR is obliged to offer radio and television programmes in the three official languages and also, to a lesser extent, in Romansch, and the stretching of its resources is apparent from the limited range and ambition of the programmes offered: for example, stereophonic radio transmissions are as yet unknown. However, the presence of French, German, Austrian and Italian television relay stations just over the frontier means that in most areas the Swiss viewer has five, six and sometimes more television stations to choose from, although if he wants to receive colour television transmissions from these countries he has to buy a set incorporating both the rival PAL and SECAM colour systems. Mention should be made too of the Swiss wire-broadcasting system, which pipes a choice of six different programmes from various European radio stations into over 400,000 Swiss homes. This facility, which makes use of the telephone network, provides listening of a high technical quality. There are no commercial radio or television stations within the Swiss frontiers: advertising, in a series of three- to four-minute spots, is allowed on television, but there is no advertising on Swiss radio.

THE PRESS

Unlike radio and television, which as we saw above are subject to an indirect form of state influence, the press is independent of any governmental control and indeed the freedom of the press is guaranteed under Article 55 of the Federal Constitution. Because the country is divided into four linguistic regions and because these regions are made up of areas with differing social and cultural backgrounds, there is no 'national' press in the British sense. In its place is an abundance of local

newspapers, well over a hundred in all, with a combined print-
ing run of about 2·7 million copies (an increase of over 70 per
cent on the 1939 figure).

Many of these papers are associated with one or other of the
political parties, although these links are less strong now than
formerly. Some 'quality' papers have an influence much
greater than their circulation figures might lead one to believe.
The *Neue Zürcher Zeitung* (Zürich, 95,000), the *National-Zeitung*
(Basel, 88,000), the *Gazette de Lausanne* (Lausanne, 26,000) and
the *Journal de Genève* (Geneva, 17,000) are among the most important in this category. Nevertheless, some of the minor newspapers find it difficult to survive and since 1965 twenty-one
daily papers have either ceased publication or have been taken
over.

On the whole, the standard of Switzerland's newspapers is
high. There is little pandering to sensational or scabrous tastes
and the fact that there are no large newspaper trusts to swamp
the country with hundreds of thousands of low-quality dailies
has helped to maintain these standards. Most newspapers are
sold to subscribers who take out a monthly or annual subscrip-
tion in advance; others are sold by newsagents or booksellers
or appear on the counters of general stores, breadshops, groceries and so forth. Other sales points are the unattended open
metal boxes that replace newsboys; the purchaser slips his coins
into a slot and takes his paper out of the box.

Illustrated weekly and monthly periodicals and family magazines, of which there are many, adopt a more popular approach
than the dailies and some have large circulations. They include
Der Schweizerische Beobachter (460,000 copies), *Schweizer Illu-
strierte Zeitung* (220,000), *L'Illustré* (150,000) and *Sie und Er*
(130,000). There is also a large number of specialist trade and
semi-technical publications, the most important of which are
the Touring Club Suisse journal *Touring* (three language edi-
tions, 550,000 copies in all) and the German and French radio
and television magazines *Radio und Fernsehen* and *Radio-Télé-Je
Vois Tout*, with a combined circulation of some 350,000 copies.

Swiss newspapers and magazines do not by any means hold
the monopoly of the bookstalls. Journals and periodicals from

France, Italy and the Federal Republic of Germany are widely available and not only in the areas closest to the frontiers. Some of these publications provide the cheesecake and scandal missing from the discreet pages of the Helvetic press.

Almost all the films shown in Swiss cinemas are of American, French, Italian, German or British origin, dubbed or subtitled as necessary. Swiss-produced films are comparatively few and with certain exceptions their appeal is mainly local. The story behind the genesis of the Swiss film industry is an interesting one. Although a number of feature films had been made in the period between the wars, the birth of the Swiss cinema may be said to have occurred just before the outbreak of World War II, at a time when a high proportion of the films projected in Swiss cinemas east of the Sarine came from Nazi Germany. It was in a deliberate attempt to stem the flow of Nazi propaganda that the Federal Council of the time began to encourage the production of Swiss-made films in German. It was unfortunate, however, that for the first few years of its life the infant Swiss cinema drew its inspiration from traditional Switzerland's folksy past and during the war Swiss cinema-goers were subjected to a virtually unrelieved diet of heavy and uninspired films about rustic life, past and present. The one outstanding film of this period was an adaptation by Valerian Schmidely and Hans Trommer of Gottfried Keller's *A Village Romeo and Juliet* (1941). This has lost none of its charm and lyricism over the years.

After the war, when it became possible once again to import foreign films, the local film industry went into decline and it was not until the middle 1960s that this trend was reversed. A law passed in 1963 authorising the granting of financial assistance for Swiss film-makers was in large part responsible for this revival. Now the younger Swiss-German producers and directors came to the fore; they strove to break with the traditions of the past and to establish the Swiss cinema as a genuine art form, first introducing fantasy, imagination and *cinéma-vérité* techniques and subsequently using their cameras as a means of social criticism. Films from this period include F.-M. Murer's *Sad is Fiction*, H. J. Siber's *Arise Like a Fire*, Jürg Hassler's *The Pack* and Kurt Gloor's *The Landscape Gardeners*, all from the end of the 1960s.

One ever-present problem facing Swiss-German film-makers is that, unlike their colleagues in the French-speaking region, for each film they are obliged to choose between scripting their dialogue either in Schwyzerdütsch, and thereby losing all chance of seeing their films projected in other German-speaking countries, or in German, and thereby losing their Swiss authenticity. There seems to be no miracle solution to this problem and the varied attempts to provide an answer have considerably hindered the creation of a homogeneous Swiss-German cinema with a distinctive style.

The French-speaking area was less directly affected by the Nazi propaganda films and by far the greater part of the federal subsidies was therefore channelled into the production of Swiss-German films. Thus a native Swiss-French film tradition was slower to develop. In the 1950s the talents of the Geneva-born Jean-Luc Godard were taken over by the French cinema industry and France's gain was Switzerland's loss; in the 1960s Henry Brandt, from Neuchâtel, created a number of long documentary films, of which *When We Were Children* (1961) is the best known. It was not until the early 1970s, however, that a recognisable Swiss-French style began to emerge. At that time a number of young French-speaking producers, some of whom came to the cinema from the world of television, began to attract interest—men like Alain Tanner, Michel Soutter and Claude Goretta. Their work shows a much greater stylistic unity than that of their Swiss-German counterparts and the award of a prize at the Cannes Film Festival to Goretta's *The Invitation* (1973), a pessimistic study of the behaviour of a group of people placed in unfamiliar surroundings, indicates that the Swiss-French cinema is beginning to attract interest outside Switzerland itself. Tanner, Soutter, Goretta and two others make up what is known as Group Five, a body whose activities are partly financed by the SRG/SSR.

The increasing popularity of television in Switzerland has, as in other countries, brought about a decrease in the number of cinemas. In the first half of the century the number had risen steadily as the world's cinema industries expanded: 325 in 1931, 351 in 1941, 459 in 1951, with a peak being reached in 1961 with a total of 637 cinemas. In the 1960s the decline set in and by 1972 the number was down to 539; the total number of seats fell from 230,921 in 1961 to 199,405 (ie thirty-one seats per 1,000 people) in 1971 and it seems improbable now that this downward trend will be reversed. On average, each person resident in Switzerland now goes to the cinema 4·8 times a year; this compares with 5 times a year in the United States and 2·8 times in the United Kingdom.

THE LITERARY AND DRAMATIC HERITAGE

Of all the arts, literature and drama are, in Switzerland, the most affected by the presence of thriving and vigorous cultural traditions in the neighbouring countries of France, Germany and Italy. There can indeed be no Swiss 'national literature', any more than there can be a Belgian 'national literature', if by this term we mean the whole range of works written, not necessarily in a single country, but certainly in the same language and with a common inspiration. C.-F. Ramuz and Gottfried Keller were both Swiss writers, but one leant towards the French literary tradition and the other towards the German (whether or not the French and Germans accept them as part of their tradition is immaterial). As it is, the only point common to every (or almost every) Swiss writer is a critical disapproval of the narrow-minded and mercenary side of the Swiss character.

In speaking of Swiss writers and dramatists one must constantly bear this diversity in mind. It is of course true that Switzerland's association with the neighbouring French, German and Italian cultural circles has stimulated the development of literature, as indeed of all the arts, in Switzerland. Jean-Jacques Rousseau (1712–78) made a remarkable contribution to French literature. C.-F. Ramuz (1878–1947) is equally well known; his works, with their slow, painstaking development, well reflect the character of the country-dwellers of Vaud and the Valais. Among the leading Swiss-German writers of the past, we may mention Jeremias Gotthelf (1797–1854), who also wrote of Swiss peasants but from a politico-realist viewpoint; Gottfried Keller (1819–90), one of the greatest writers of the nineteenth century; C.-F. Meyer (1825–98), poet and novelist; the poet Carl Spitteler (1845–1924), winner of the Nobel Prize for literature in 1919; and Herman Hesse (1877–1962), who received that prize in 1946. The Germanic tradition is currently being upheld by two important writers and dramatists of the present day: the agnostic humanist Max Frisch (1911–) and the Christian humanist Friedrich Dürrenmatt (1921–). Both these men have received world acclaim and in their very different ways they are without doubt the most influential Swiss writers of the twentieth century. Frisch's *Andorra* (1961) is a satire on xenophobia, the morbid dislike of foreigners, and Dürrenmatt's *Visit of the Old Lady* (1956) is a troubling play which has been accorded varying interpretations. Swiss-Italian writers whose fame has extended beyond the frontiers of Switzerland are fewer in number: Francesco Chiesa (1871–1973), poet, humanist and chronicler of life in Ticino, is the best known. The tiny steam of Romansch literature is, however, virtually unknown outside the Engadine and the Upper Rhine valley.

There is a thriving book trade in Switzerland. In 1972 Swiss publishers brought out 5,318 titles in German, 2,115 in French, 165 in Italian and 28 in Romansch; 544 books were published in other languages and 279 were bi or trilingual, making a grand total of 8,449. In addition, 1,077 books either about Switzerland or by Swiss authors were published in foreign countries; and of course, Swiss bookshops stock a large number of books published by German, French and Italian publishers. The dissemination of books is helped, first, by a number of book clubs, of which the largest (Ex Libris, a member of the Migros family) is said to have several hundred thousand adherents in all parts of the country; and second, by the public library system. In all, there are forty-one cantonal, municipal or university libraries open to the public. In the larger towns the municipal library has several branches; country areas are frequently served by a mobile library or 'Bibliobus'.

As there are not too many theatres in Switzerland, opportunities for seeing live performances are perhaps fewer than in other countries. However, the important part played by the Zürich theatres during World War II must not be overlooked. At that time Zürich was a stronghold of German intellectual freedom, and all that was best in the German theatre found a home in the city's theatres. Amateur dramatics play only a small role in Swiss cultural life; the reason for this is undoubtedly that dramatic play and the 'school concert' do not feature to any large extent in the Swiss educational pattern.

THE VISUAL ARTS

An early civilisation known as 'La Tène' flourished in the regions of Europe occupied by the Celts during the centuries immediately preceding the beginning of the Christian era and was so called after the locality of the same name in the canton of Neuchâtel, where important archaeological finds of that period were made; but excluding this early instance, we may say that the first flowering of Swiss art occurred a thousand and more years ago at the great abbey of St Gallen in eastern Switzerland. Here the monk scribes of the monastery school wrote the priceless St Gallen manuscripts; the clarity, intensity and definition of these Irish-inspired masterworks (of which 2,000 are preserved in the abbey library) places them among the most important testimonies of the Swiss artistic heritage. One of the first secular books of mediaeval times is the Manesse manuscript, a collection of paintings of poets, lovers and troubadours made for Rudger Manesse von Maneck of Zürich round the year 1300, which is a supremely decorative work of art. This manuscript is now kept in the Heidelberg University Library in the Federal Republic of Germany.

At the end of the Middle Ages and during succeeding centuries, artists in most European countries flourished under the patronage and protection of royal courts and ecclesiastical

I

princedoms. Under the Swiss system of 'direct democracy', matters were different. Where the people themselves were the sovereign power they were less inclined to spend money on sheer culture, and so it was that, with one or two exceptions, noteworthy art centres have been non-existent in Switzerland until comparatively recently. One should of course remember that for many centuries the main aim of the Swiss was merely to survive—at first by resisting the attacks of hostile neighbours and subsequently by scratching out their living under unfavourable climatic and topographical conditions.

As we have said, there were exceptions—notably the urban cultures of Geneva and Basel, where Konrad Witz (1400–47), one of the greatest painters of the age, created his masterpieces of religious art. Like his contemporaries, the early Flemish painters, Witz placed his figures against realist backgrounds: the setting of his 'Miraculous Draught of Fishes' (1444), now in the Geneva Art Museum, is unmistakably Lake Geneva. The German portraitist Hans Holbein the Younger (1497–1543) also did most of his work in Basel, as did Urs Graf (1485–1527), an artist best known for his bold, assured line drawings. From the eighteenth century the Geneva-born artist Jean-Etienne Liotard (1702–89) has left a large number of portraits in pastels, and Johann Heinrich Füssli (1741–1825), a precursor of the Romantic movement, became well known in London art circles under the name Henry Fuseli. In the nineteenth century Arnold Böcklin from Basel (1827–1901) specialised in mystical, Romantic subjects drawn from legend and mythology, whereas Alexandre Calame (1810–64) was primarily a painter of landscapes. The Italian-born Giovanni Segantini (1858–99) concentrated on rural scenes depicting the hard life of the Swiss peasant. A less distinguished figure was Charles Gleyre (1806–74), notorious as the academic painter under whom many of the young Impressionists studied in Paris in the 1860s.

In recent years another landscape and portrait painter, Ferdinand Hodler (1853–1918), has been increasingly recognised as Switzerland's main contributor to the development of modern painting. Hodler's vigorous Alpine scenes and rough-hewn character studies are often looked upon as the first genuinely national Swiss paintings and it is true that he was less influenced by the work of other artists than were his predecessors. His early interest in the Impressionists was not maintained, if only because the clear mountain air of the Alps was quite unlike the luminous, shimmering light of the Ile-de-France, to which his own temperament was in any case alien.

The twentieth century has produced a number of internationally known Swiss artists. For the abstract painter Paul Klee (1879–1940), who was born near Bern, the contemporary division between abstract and figurative painting was never an obstacle; in his work, as it wells up from the subconscious, there is always some connection between the imaginary and the real world. Klee's influence has not been superficial for it reaches down to the very source of inspiration, and is still at work. The distinctive, skeleton-like sculptures of Alberto Giacometti (1901–66) are immediately recognisable. Giacometti, from the Graubünden, strove all his life to create his own vision of transient reality. Although his drawings and paintings were as important in his artistic development as were his sculptures, it is through the latter that he came to be considered as one of the greatest artists of the present century.

Of living Swiss artists, Max Bill (1908–) and Jean Tinguely (1925–) have both achieved world renown. Bill's work reveals his fascination with shapes based on mathematical formulae, 'a *forme-esprit* in which the non-sensory beauty of numerical relations can be contemplated', as Werner Haftmann has said. Tinguely is one of the leading representatives of the abstract 'new realism'; his work is diametrically opposed to Bill's. A third contemporary Swiss artist is Jean Roll (1921–), who concentrates on still-life paintings through which he reveals his obsession with the sheer beauty of shapes and forms.

The influence of Le Corbusier (C.-E. Jeanneret, 1887–1965) on twentieth-century architecture has been profound and the work of his disciples and followers can be seen in the four corners of the world. However, buildings that may (or may not) be pleasing to the eye are not always pleasant for their inhabitants and Le Corbusier-inspired high-density housing and high-rise or ribbon apartment blocks have frequently been criticised for the destructive effect they have had on the lives of those who live or work in them.

The Public Art Collection of the Basel Art Museum and the Oskar Reinhart Foundation and Collection in Winterthur are both world-famous and should on no account be overlooked by the art lover. Almost equally famous are the art museums of Zürich, Bern (with its hundreds of examples of Klee's work) and Geneva, together with a number of private collections to which the public have access. Besides these art galleries, numerous local museums contain exhibits related to the history of art and archaeology and to the story of Switzerland in general, from the magnificent collection of the Swiss National Museum in Zürich to the smaller cantonal and municipal collections and the fascinating collections of folklore in some of the larger villages.

MUSIC

Every town of any size has its resident symphony orchestra and although most of these never see the inside of a radio or recording studio the standard of playing is reasonably good. The most famous of Swiss orchestras is undoubtedly the Geneva-based Suisse Romande Orchestra. Founded in 1918 by Ernest Ansermet (1883–1969), it has now regained the lustre it was in danger of losing after Ansermet's death and is once again one of the world's major orchestras. The Lausanne Chamber Orchestra, the Bern Symphony Orchestra and the Zürich Tonhalle Orchestra are other well known Swiss ensembles.

The theatre and concert season begins in September and lasts until the end of May. During the summer and early autumn musicians and music lovers from all over the world come to the numerous music festivals held during these months in various parts of Switzerland—Lucerne, Montreux, Zürich, Geneva, Lausanne, Gstaad, Lugano, Locarno, Ascona, Neuchâtel, Interlaken and so on.

Few Swiss composers have been fortunate enough to have had their works included in the international concert repertoire. Three, however—Bloch, Honegger and Frank Martin—have become known beyond the Confederation's frontiers. Many of the works of Ernest Bloch (1880–1959) make much use of Jewish themes, which give to them the appearance of a skein of endlessly unwinding melodic thread, while others are impressionistic in nature. The Hebrew rhapsody 'Schelomo' (1916) is an example of the former style. One of the best-known of the compositions of Arthur Honegger (1892–1955), and for a time the only one to enjoy any popularity, is 'Pacific 231'; this has now virtually disappeared from the concert hall and today it is on his more serious works—the symphonies and the large-scale choral works—that Honegger's reputation is based. Frank Martin (1890–1974) synthesised both Germanic and Latin influences in his very distinctive work; he experimented with the twelve-note scale but rejected its atonal consequences while accepting the new elements it brought to melody and harmony.

Another Swiss composer, Emile Jaques-Dalcroze (1865–1950), is now known less for his numerous musical compositions than for the system of 'Eurhythmics'—musical training through rhythmic movement—that he devised before World War I and put into practice at his headquarters in Geneva; subsequently the movement spread to many parts of the world.

SPORT AND LEISURE ACTIVITIES

It is understandable that, in a country of lakes and mountains, the most popular outdoor pastimes are swimming, skiing, walking and sailing. An interesting investigation carried out in 1973 into the sporting preferences of a sample of Swiss people between the ages of 15 and 40 showed that, for well over half those interviewed, swimming rather than skiing was the favourite athletic activity. Few of these people actually swim in the lakes, in view of the current high levels of pollution, but rather in public swimming pools, which are scrupulously clean and often set in beautifully landscaped parkland where other sports may be practised—tennis, volleyball, and so forth.

The foreigner's impression of the Swiss as a nation of skiers is nevertheless valid, since some 45 per cent of the sample interviewed ski regularly at weekends, if only to escape from the monochrome landscape beneath the layer of low-level stratus

that frequently covers the plateau towns in winter to the techni-
colour scenery of blue sky, white snow and dark green conifers
above. Downhill, or *piste*, skiing is by far the most popular and
over 1,500 mountain railways or ski lifts have been constructed
to convey skiers effortlessly to the starting point of a host of
downhill runs. Both beginners and advanced skiers can, if they
wish, join a class in one of the 130 and more Swiss ski schools,
which are staffed by over 2,000 ski instructors. There is, however, another side to the coin: each year there are about 30,000
serious skiing accidents, of which 22,000 result in broken bones,
and on average there are ten fatal skiing accidents annually.
The number of less serious accidents varies between 30,000 and
50,000 each year. It has been estimated that skiing accidents
cost the Swiss economy some 500 million francs annually—
hence the regular exhortations from official sources regarding
safety on the ski slopes. Cross-country skiing is a much safer
and less costly (but far less popular) pastime. There are well
prepared and well marked tracks in all the big resorts, but as the
appeal of cross-country skiing lies in the skier's lonely communion with nature he will frequently strike out, alone or with
a few friends, into uncharted territory.

Of all the sports practised in Switzerland, long-distance cross-
country walking is perhaps the most typically Swiss. This is no
leisurely afternoon stroll but a real race against time, when the
entire population of a village may turn out and set off, rucksack
on back, for a brisk 15-mile walk. This sport is particularly
popular in the French-speaking region, where it was practised
by 30 per cent of those interviewed in the 1973 survey. There are
in fact some 30,000 miles of well marked paths leading away
from the roads to the valleys and heights of the Alps and the
Jura. About the same percentage performs some form of
physical training, either at home or in 'fitness' groups. A special
mention must be made here of the 'Parcours Vita' maintained
by the Vita Insurance Company. These are woodland walks
open to all, one to two miles long, with the equipment and
instructions for performing various physical exercises set out at
intervals of 100–200 yards. There are about 250 'Parcours Vita'
in all regions of the country and they provide the opportunity

for health-giving gymnastics in pleasant woodland surroundings.

Opportunities for sailing abound on most of the Swiss lakes,
with yachting schools on the Lakes of Thun, Neuchâtel and
Lugano and on Lakes Maggiore, Geneva and Constance.
Rowing and canoeing are possible on all lakes and many
rivers: the Rotsee, near Lucerne, has no equal for rowing and
every year this stretch of water is the scene of international
rowing championships. Water skiing may be practised on most
of the lakes and there are water-skiing schools in the major
resorts.

The traditional summer sport in Switzerland is, of course,
climbing, although the percentage of Swiss who are mountaineers is rather low. Indeed, a good number of those who climb
in the Alps come from other countries. The art of climbing is
taught in special mountaineering schools, while experienced
guides are available to accompany those who wish to scale the
walls or scramble over the glaciers of Switzerland's lofty
mountains.

Football is the most popular team sport for men, as well as
being the spectator sport that attracts the biggest crowds.
Switzerland's national football team has not yet distinguished
itself in any dramatic fashion on the world's playing fields and
remains essentially one of the 'also-rans' of international soccer.
There is considerable interest in professional cycling, with the
Tour de Suisse as one of the highlights of the season.

HOLIDAYS

The first federal legislation on paid annual holidays, enacted in
1964, prescribed a minimum of two weeks for adults and three
weeks for workers under 19 and apprentices under 20 years of
age. In addition there are eight paid statutory holidays. Of
course, it might be said that, with the mountains and lakes
within such easy reach, every weekend is a holiday too. It is
true that the proximity of comparatively unspoilt natural surroundings, together with the difficulty that most people experience in buying their own house or flat in the place where

they live, has led many families to buy a chalet or apartment somewhere in the mountains in which to spend their weekends. In 1970 there were 131,000 of these 'secondary residences', representing 6 per cent of the total number of dwelling places; various estimates have been made of the likely number of such havens by the end of the century, all of which forecast a greater or lesser increase over the present total. One way of preventing hitherto unspoilt regions from being dotted with weekend villas would be to convert and modernise the numerous empty dwelling places that are to be found in the more remote villages. The depopulation of these villages would thereby be arrested, while at the same time the beauty of the countryside would be preserved.

As the school summer holidays in almost all the cantons fall in July and August, it is inevitable that the great majority of Swiss families take their main holidays during these months. The situation of Switzerland at the heart of the continent makes for easy access to other European countries by both rail and road. The strength of the Swiss franc has meant that for Swiss tourists the cost of accommodation and food abroad is frequently less expensive, in Swiss franc terms, than in Switzerland itself. In summer the majority of Swiss holiday-makers head south: the French and Italian Rivieras are an easy day's drive away; those going by car to Spain or Yugoslavia generally have to make an overnight stop on the way. Perhaps because they live in a landlocked country, the Swiss have a distinct liking for island holidays and the popularity of Majorca, Ibiza, Corfu, the Canary Isles, Corsica and Sardinia has increased steadily in recent years, whereas the number of Swiss visitors to the well known Spanish, French and Italian mainland resorts has remained virtually stable. The introduction of cheap charter flights to Africa, Asia and the Americas has brought a new dimension to international travel, and here again the favourable conversion rate between the Swiss franc and other world currencies has worked to the benefit of the Swiss tourist.

8

Hints for Visitors

THE peak holiday months are mid-May to September and, for winter sports, February and March. At these times hotels can be crowded and advance booking is essential, particularly in the cities which happen to be international conference centres as well as holiday resorts, and in the popular winter sports villages. For those who wish to avoid the peak summer period, the attractions of a spring or autumn holiday should not be overlooked. Although Swiss weather can be as temperamental as English, long spells of fine weather are by no means unusual at these times and the lucky traveller who experiences a golden Swiss autumn will find that, for once, the hues of his colour photographs are not exaggerated. For winter sports enthusiasts a skiing holiday at Christmas, in January, in April or even later can be enjoyable if taken in one of the higher resorts.

Switzerland is not a cheap country for travellers from abroad. The appreciation of the Swiss franc against other currencies has been a recurrent theme of this book, and the strength of the franc does mean that, at the present time, hotel prices, expressed in terms of other European currencies, tend to appear high. You get excellent value for your money, of course, but you do have to pay for what you get. Hotels are unofficially classified into four categories: luxury, first, second and economy. The lists put out by the local tourist offices indicate the maximum and minimum price for each hotel. Note that the cost may be reduced for those who travel as members of an organised group.

A cheaper and equally enjoyable way of taking a family holiday, particularly a winter holiday, is in one of Switzerland's

30,000 or so furnished chalets or chalet apartments. These are invariably clean, well equipped and well maintained and offer a degree of independence that may be missing in hotels. It is interesting to note that in 1974, for the first time, this so-called 'para-hotel' business accounted for more than 50 per cent of overnight stays. Details of such premises are available from tourist offices, usually with a supplementary list giving the dates for which each chalet is free at the time the inquiry is made. Camping and caravanning have their devotees too, and hundreds of fully equipped sites are dotted about in all parts of the country: many are run by the Touring Club Suisse (TCS), 9 rue Pierre-Fatio, 1204 Geneva, or the Federation Suisse de Camping et de Caravanning (FSCC), 35 Habsburgerstrasse, 6003 Lucerne, from where further details may be obtained. Young people holidaying on a shoestring will find simple but clean accommodation in the youth hostels run by the Schweizerbund für Jugendherbergen, Einkaufs-Zentrum 9, 8958 Spreitenbach.

The needs of motorists are met by the Touring Club Suisse and by the Automobile Club de Suisse (ACS), 2 Laupenstrasse, 3008 Bern. One or other of these clubs is affiliated to similar organisations in most other countries, and the wise British motorist, whose car may not be designed for the long and steep gradients of the Alpine passes, will take the precaution of insuring himself under one of the foreign touring rescue services offered by his own club. The speed limit in Switzerland is normally 60km per hour in built-up areas, 100km on the open road and 130km on motorways, and the Swiss police are enthusiastic devotees of the radar-operated speed trap. Reports on road conditions and the state of the mountain passes may be had by dialling 163 on any public or private telephone. In the event of breakdown, dial 140, ask for 'Touring Secours' and you will be put in touch with the garage nearest to you. The TCS and the ACS have placed 'SOS' telephones at regular intervals on the motorways and major mountain roads for use in an emergency.

Although many Swiss people speak English well, a knowledge of German or French is a distinct advantage outside the big cities and the main ski resorts. If your inquiry in halting German elicits an answer in Schwyzerdütsch or Romansch, do not despair—your interviewee will always be able to express himself in High German as well.

The practice of tipping has not yet become the curse it is in other countries. As a service charge of 15 per cent is now included in all bills, both in hotels and in restaurants, there is no need to leave any more unless you wish to reward some special personal attention. Taxi drivers expect a tip of 10 to 15 per cent of the fare. It is not the practice to tip cinema and theatre usherettes although this insidious habit appears to be gaining a foothold in the cities. If you are invited for dinner in a Swiss private house or flat, it is usual to offer your hostess flowers or chocolate.

The advantages that Switzerland has to offer as a holiday country are innumerable and it is indeed a country for *holidays* rather than for travel for its own sake. All parts of the country can be reached within a day; from the snowy Alpine villages to the palms of Lake Lugano, from the hills of the Jura to the Engadine National Park there are no great distances to be overcome. Several excellent series of maps (Kummerly & Frey, Michelin, etc) help the armchair traveller to plan his holiday route and a number of popular guidebooks fill in the details. Switzerland is Switzerland and a Swiss holiday can be restful or vigorous, carefree or culturally rewarding—a unique and unforgettable experience.

Index